T0038642

# STAR WARS

# THRAWN
## ASCENDANCY
### GREATER GOOD

STAR WARS

# THRAWN
## ASCENDANCY
### BOOK II:
### GREATER GOOD

## TIMOTHY ZAHN

DEL
REY

**NEW YORK**

2022 Del Rey Trade Paperback Edition

Copyright © 2021 by Lucasfilm Ltd. & ® or ™ where indicated.
All rights reserved.
Excerpt from *Star Wars: Thrawn Ascendancy: Lesser Evil*
by Timothy Zahn copyright © 2021 by Lucasfilm Ltd. & ® or ™
where indicated. All rights reserved.

Published in the United States by Del Rey,
an imprint of Random House, a division of
Penguin Random House LLC, New York.

DEL REY is a registered trademark and the CIRCLE colophon
is a trademark of Penguin Random House LLC.

Originally published in hardcover in the United States by
Del Rey, an imprint of Random House, a division of
Penguin Random House LLC, in 2021.

ISBN 978-0-593-15831-9
Ebook ISBN 978-0-593-15830-2

Printed in the United States of America on acid-free paper

randomhousebooks.com

6 8 9 7 5

Book design by Elizabeth A. D. Eno

For those who recognize that "the greater good"
is seldom good for all

# THE **STAR WARS** NOVELS TIMELINE

## THE HIGH REPUBLIC

Light of the Jedi
The Rising Storm
Tempest Runner
The Fallen Star

Dooku: Jedi Lost
Master and Apprentice

## I THE PHANTOM MENACE

## II ATTACK OF THE CLONES

Thrawn Ascendancy: Chaos Rising
Thrawn Ascendancy: Greater Good
Thrawn Ascendancy: Lesser Evil
Dark Disciple: A Clone Wars Novel

## III REVENGE OF THE SITH

Catalyst: A Rogue One Novel
Lords of the Sith
Tarkin

## SOLO

Thrawn
A New Dawn: A Rebels Novel
Thrawn: Alliances
Thrawn: Treason

## ROGUE ONE

## IV A NEW HOPE

Battlefront II: Inferno Squad
Heir to the Jedi
Doctor Aphra
Battlefront: Twilight Company

## V THE EMPIRE STRIKES BACK

## VI RETURN OF THE JEDI

The Alphabet Squadron Trilogy
The Aftermath Trilogy
Last Shot

Bloodline
Phasma
Canto Bight

## VII THE FORCE AWAKENS

## VIII THE LAST JEDI

Resistance Reborn
Galaxy's Edge: Black Spire

## IX THE RISE OF SKYWALKER

# DRAMATIS PERSONAE

**SENIOR CAPTAIN THRAWN** | Mitth'raw'nuruodo—Trial-born

**ADMIRAL AR'ALANI**

**THALIAS** | Mitth'ali'astov—Trial-born

**SYNDIC PRIME THURFIAN** | Mitth'urf'ianico—blood

**MID CAPTAIN SAMAKRO** | Ufsa'mak'ro—cousin

**SENIOR CAPTAIN LAKINDA** | Xodlak'in'daro—merit adoptive

**GENERAL BA'KIF**

**CHE'RI**—sky-walker

**THE MAGYS**


**COUNCILOR LAKUVIV** | Xodlak'uvi'vil—ranking distant

**RANCHER LAKPHRO** | Xodlak'phr'ooa

**YOPONEK** | Coduyo'po'nekri


**QILORI OF UANDUALON**—Pathfinder navigator (non-Chiss)

**JIXTUS**

**HAPLIF**—Agbui

# CHISS ASCENDANCY

## Nine Ruling Families

UFSA

IRIZI

DASKLO

CLARR

CHAF

PLIKH

BOADIL

MITTH

OBBIC

## Chiss Family Ranks

BLOOD

COUSIN

RANKING DISTANT

TRIAL-BORN

MERIT ADOPTIVE

## Political Hierarchy

**PATRIARCH**—head of the family

**SPEAKER**—head of the family's delegation to the Syndicure

**SYNDIC PRIME**—head syndic

**SYNDIC**—member of the Syndicure, the main governmental body

**PATRIEL**—handles family affairs on a planetary scale

**COUNCILOR**—handles family affairs at the local level

**ARISTOCRA**—mid-level member of one of the Nine Ruling Families

## Military Ranks

SUPREME ADMIRAL

SUPREME GENERAL

FLEET ADMIRAL

SENIOR GENERAL

ADMIRAL

GENERAL

MID ADMIRAL

MID GENERAL

COMMODORE

SENIOR CAPTAIN

MID CAPTAIN

JUNIOR CAPTAIN

SENIOR COMMANDER

MID COMMANDER

JUNIOR COMMANDER

LIEUTENANT COMMANDER

LIEUTENANT

SENIOR WARRIOR

MID WARRIOR

JUNIOR WARRIOR

A long time ago, *beyond* a galaxy far, far away. . . .

For thousands of years it has been an island of calm within the Chaos. It is a center of power, a model of stability, and a beacon of integrity. The Nine Ruling Families guard it from within; the Expansionary Defense Fleet guards it from without. Its neighbors are left in peace, its enemies are left in ruin. It is light and culture and glory.

It is the Chiss Ascendancy.

STAR WARS™

THRAWN
ASCENDANCY
GREATER GOOD

# CHAPTER ONE

Throughout her years in the Chiss Expansionary Defense Fleet, Admiral Ar'alani had lived through more than fifty battles and smaller armed clashes. The opponents in those encounters, like the battles themselves, had varied widely. Some of them had been clever, others had been cautious, still others—particularly political appointees who had been promoted far beyond their abilities—had been painfully incompetent. The strategies and tactics employed had also varied, ranging from simple to obscure to screamingly violent. The battle results themselves had sometimes been mixed, sometimes inconclusive, often a defeat for the enemy, and—occasionally—a defeat for the Chiss.

But never in all that time had Ar'alani experienced such a mix of determination, viciousness, and utter pointlessness as in the scene now unfolding in front of her.

"Watch it, *Vigilant*—you've got four more coming at you from starboard-nadir." The voice of Senior Captain Xodlak'in'daro came from the *Vigilant*'s bridge speaker, her resonant alto glacially calm as always.

"Acknowledged, *Grayshrike*," Ar'alani called back, looking at the tactical. Four more Nikardun gunboats had indeed appeared from around the small moon, driving at full power toward the *Vigilant*. "Looks like you have a few latecomers to your party, as well," she added.

"We're on it, ma'am," Lakinda said.

"Good," Ar'alani said, studying the six missile boats that had appeared from behind the hulk of the battle cruiser she and the other two Chiss ships had hammered into rubble fifteen minutes ago. Sneaking into cover that way without being spotted had taken some ingenuity, and many commanders with that level of competence would have used their skill to exercise the better part of valor and abandon such a clearly hopeless battle.

But that wasn't what these last pockets of Nikardun resistance were about. They were about complete self-sacrifice, throwing themselves at the Chiss warships that had rooted them from their burrows, apparently with the sole goal of taking some of the hated enemies with them.

That wasn't going to happen. Not today. Not to Ar'alani's force. "Thrawn, the *Grayshrike* has picked up a new nest of nighthunters," she called. "Can you offer them some assistance?"

"Certainly," Senior Captain Mitth'raw'nuruodo replied. "Captain Lakinda, if you'll turn thirty degrees to starboard, I believe we can draw your attackers into a crossfire."

"Thirty degrees, acknowledged," Lakinda said, and Ar'alani saw the *Grayshrike*'s tactical display image angle away from the incoming missile boats and head toward Thrawn's *Springhawk*. "Though with all due respect to the admiral, I'd say they're more whisker cubs than nighthunters."

"Agreed," Thrawn said. "If these are the same ones we thought were caught in the battle cruiser explosion, they should be down to a single missile each."

"Actually, our tally makes two of them completely empty," Lakinda said. "Just along for the glory of martyrdom, I suppose."

"Such as it is," Ar'alani said. "I doubt anyone out there is going to be singing the elegiac praises of Yiv the Benevolent anytime soon. Wutroow?"

"Spheres are ready, Admiral," Senior Captain Kiwu'tro'owmis confirmed from across the *Vigilant*'s bridge. "Ready to rain on their picnic?"

"One moment," Ar'alani said, watching the tactical and gauging the distances. Plasma spheres' ability to deliver electronics-freezing blasts of ionic energy made them capable of disabling attackers without having to plow through the tough nyix-alloy hulls that sheathed most warships in this part of the Chaos. Smaller fighter-class ships, like the Nikardun missile boats currently charging the *Vigilant*, were especially vulnerable to such attacks.

But the missile boats' smaller size also meant they were more nimble than larger warships, and could sometimes dodge out of harm's way if the relatively slow plasma spheres were launched too soon.

There were tables and balance charts to calculate that sort of thing. Ar'alani preferred to do it by eyesight and experienced judgment.

And that judgment told her they had a sudden opportunity here. Another two seconds . . . "Fire spheres," she ordered.

There was a small, muffled thud as the plasma spheres shot from their launchers. Ar'alani kept her eyes on the tactical, watching as the missile boats realized they were under attack and scrambled to evade the spheres. The rearmost of them almost made it, the sphere flickering into its aft port side and paralyzing its thrusters, sending it spinning off into space along its final evasion vector. The other three caught the spheres squarely amidships, killing their major systems as they, too, went gliding helplessly away.

"Three down, one still wiggling," Wutroow reported. "You want us to take them?"

"Hold on that for now," Ar'alani told her. It would be at least another few minutes before the missile boats recovered. In the meantime . . . "Thrawn?" she called. "Over to you."

"Acknowledged, Admiral."

Ar'alani shifted her attention to the *Springhawk*. Normally, she would never do this to the captain of one of her task force ships: giving a vague order on the assumption that the other would pick up on her intent. But she and Thrawn had worked together long enough that she knew he would see what she was seeing and know exactly what she wanted him to do.

And so he did. As the four momentarily stunned missile boats headed off on their individual vectors, a tractor beam shot out from the *Springhawk*'s bow, grabbed one of them, and started to pull it in.

Pulling it directly into the path of the cluster of missile boats charging toward the *Grayshrike*.

The Nikardun, their full attention focused on their suicidal attack on the Chiss cruiser, were caught completely off guard by the vessel angling in on them. At the last second they scattered, all six managing to evade the incoming obstacle.

But the disruption had thrown off their rhythm and their aim. Worse than that, from their point of view, Thrawn had timed that distraction for the precise moment when the Nikardun fighters came into full effective range of the *Grayshrike*'s and *Springhawk*'s spectrum lasers. The missile ships were still trying to reestablish their configuration when the Chiss lasers opened fire.

Twenty seconds later, that section of space was once again clear of enemies.

"Well done, both of you," Ar'alani said, checking the tactical. Aside from the disabled missile boats, only two Nikardun ships out there still showed signs of life. "Wutroow, move us toward target seven. Spectrum lasers should be adequate to finish him off. *Grayshrike*, what's your status?"

"Still working on the thrusters, Admiral," Lakinda said. "But we're sealed again, and the engineers say they should have us back at full power in a quarter hour or less."

"Good," Ar'alani said, doing a quick analysis of the debris and battered ships visible through the *Vigilant*'s bridge viewport. There shouldn't be any places out there where more ships could be lurking.

On the other hand, that was what she'd thought before those six missile boats popped into view from the battle cruiser's hulk. There could be a few more small ships gone to ground in the fog of battle in the hope that they'd be missed until the time was right for their own suicide runs.

And at the moment, with its main thrusters down, the *Grayshrike* was a sitting flashfly. "*Springhawk,* stay with *Grayshrike,*" she ordered. "We'll clean out these last two."

"That's really not necessary, Admiral," Lakinda said, a hint of carefully controlled protest in her voice. "We can still maneuver enough to fight."

"You just concentrate on your repairs," Ar'alani told her. "If you get bored, you can finish off those four missile boats when they wake up."

"We're not going to offer them the chance to surrender?" Thrawn asked.

"You can make that offer if you want," Ar'alani said. "I can't see them accepting it any more than any of their late comrades did. But I'm willing to be surprised." She hesitated. "*Grayshrike,* you can also start a full scan of the area. There could be someone else lurking nearby, and I'm tired of people charging out of nowhere and shooting at us."

"Yes, Admiral," Lakinda said.

Ar'alani smiled to herself. Lakinda hadn't actually said *thank you,* but she could hear it in the senior captain's voice. Of all the officers in Ar'alani's task force, Lakinda was the most focused and driven, and she absolutely hated to be left out of things.

There was a brush of air as Wutroow stepped up beside Ar'alani's command chair. "Hopefully, this is the last of them," the *Vigilant's* first officer commented. "The Vaks should be able to sleep a bit easier now." She considered. "So should the Syndicure."

Ar'alani touched the comm mute key. As far as *she'd* been able to tell, the supreme ruling body of the Chiss Ascendancy had been as unenthusiastic about this cleanup mission as it was possible for politicians to get. "I didn't know the Syndicure was worried about rogue Nikardun threats to the Vak Combine."

"I'm sure they aren't," Wutroow said. "I'm equally sure they *are* worried about why we're way out here engaging in warlike actions."

Ar'alani cocked an eyebrow at her. "You raise that question as if you already knew the answer."

"Not really," Wutroow said, giving Ar'alani one of those significant looks she did so well. "I was hoping *you* knew."

"Sadly, the Aristocra seldom consult with me these days," Ar'alani said.

"Oddly enough, they don't consult with me, either," Wutroow said. "But I'm sure they have their reasons."

Ar'alani nodded. Normally, the Nine Ruling Families—and the full weight of official Ascendancy policy—were dead-set against any military action unless Chiss worlds or holdings had been directly attacked first. She could only assume that the interrogation of General Yiv the Benevolent and a thorough examination of his captured files and records had proved the Nikardun had been such an imminent threat that the Syndicure had been willing to bend the usual rules.

"At least Thrawn must be pleased," Wutroow continued. "It's rare to get vindication *and* retaliation delivered in the same neat package."

"If you're trying to get me to tell you what he and I talked about with Supreme General Ba'kif before we left on this little jaunt, you're in for a disappointment," Ar'alani said. "But yes, I imagine Senior Captain Thrawn is pleased at how things turned out."

"Yes, ma'am," Wutroow said, her voice making a subtle shift from the admiral's friend to the admiral's first officer. "Coming into range of target seven."

"Very good," Ar'alani said. "You may fire at your convenience."

"Yes, ma'am." With a crisp nod, Wutroow headed back across the bridge. "Oeskym, stand by lasers," she called to the weapons officer.

Two minutes later, it was over. Ar'alani ordered the *Vigilant* back around, to find that the last four missile boats had vanished into expanding clouds of debris. Briefly, she thought about asking Thrawn and Lakinda if they'd offered the Nikardun the chance to surrender and decided it would be a waste of breath. The enemy had been annihilated, and that was what mattered.

"Well done, all of you," Ar'alani said as Wutroow returned to her side. "Captain Thrawn, I believe the *Grayshrike* and I can handle the rest of the mission. You're hereby authorized to move on."

"If you're certain, Admiral," Thrawn said.

"I am," Ar'alani said. "May warrior's luck smile on your efforts."

"And yours," Thrawn said. "*Springhawk* out."

Wutroow cleared her throat. "Supreme General Ba'kif's conversation, I presume?"

"You may presume whatever you wish," Ar'alani said.

"Ah," Wutroow said. "Well. If there's nothing else, I'll get started on the post-battle report."

"Thank you," Ar'alani said.

She watched as Wutroow headed across toward the systems monitor console. Her first officer was right about one thing, at least. The Vak Combine *would* be relieved and pleased.

The Nine Ruling Families and the Defense Hierarchy Council would also be relieved. But she doubted very much that anyone in either of those particular groups would be genuinely pleased.

Syndic Prime Mitth'urf'ianico had been waiting in the March of Silence in the Syndicure's prestigious and historical Convocate Hall for nearly half an hour before the man he'd arranged to speak with finally arrived.

But that was all right. The idle time gave Thurfian a chance to observe, and to brood, and to plan.

The observation part was easy. The March of Silence, a favorite spot for Speakers, syndics, and others of the Aristocra to meet on neutral yet private ground, was surprisingly empty today. Most of that, Thurfian suspected, was because the syndics were back in their offices with the Council's latest report on the mop-up efforts against what was left of General Yiv's scattered forces, while the mid-level Ruling Family members that constituted the Aristocra helped them prep for the upcoming Syndicure session or simply worked their usual jobs in the various government agencies. The Speakers, as the top representatives of their families, were probably having long conversations with their homesteads, discussing the situation and getting their Patriarchs' orders on what exactly their families' responses would be once the data sifting was finished.

The brooding part was equally easy. Thurfian had already read the report, or as much of it as he could stomach at one sitting. Woven through all the military data and maps and charts was the understated but clear fact that Senior Captain Thrawn had—*again*—come out looking like a bright star in the Csilla sky. All that despite the fact that he had disobeyed the spirit of standing orders, put an invaluable sky-walker in deadly danger, and risked drawing the Ascendancy into a blatantly illegal and unethical war.

Thurfian was still working on the planning part when Syndic Irizi'stal'mustro finally made his appearance.

As always, Zistalmu waited until he was in earshot of Thurfian—and out of earshot of the other small groups in the hall—before speaking. "Syndic Thurfian," he said, nodding in greeting. "My apologies for the delay."

Despite the seriousness of the situation they were meeting to discuss, Thurfian nevertheless had to suppress a smile. *Syndic Thurfian.* Zistalmu had no idea that his colleague had just been elevated to Syndic Prime, the highest Syndicure position below the Speakership itself.

Zistalmu didn't know the new title, and he probably never would. Such rankings were closely guarded family secrets, for internal Syndicure use only, unless the Speaker or Patriarch decided some extra authority was needed somewhere. But those situations were few and far between. Thurfian would most likely carry the rank in secret until the day of his retirement, and only his memorial pillar at the Mitth homestead would reveal it.

But he didn't need anyone else to know. Secrets were such delicious morsels that they could be enjoyed alone.

"I was getting ready to leave," Zistalmu continued, "when a delegation of Xodlak descended on my office, and I couldn't get rid of them."

"They came to *you*?" Thurfian asked.

"No, they *came* to Speaker Ziemol," Zistalmu said sourly. "He generously foisted them off onto me."

"That sounds like Ziemol." Thurfian huffed out a commiserating breath. "Let me guess. They wanted the Irizi to sponsor their return to Ruling Family status?"

"What else?" Zistalmu growled. "I suppose you have delegates from the Forty come to you on occasion, too?"

"More often than I'd like," Thurfian said. Though now that he was Syndic Prime, that would never happen again. As Speaker Ziemol had handed the Xodlak off to Zistalmu, so Thurfian could now hand such annoyances off to a lower-ranking Mitth syndic. "Usually they just want support or a temporary alliance, but a lot of them want to get into the Nine, too. I sometimes daydream about proposing a law that the number of Ruling Families be permanently set at nine."

"I'd be on board with that," Zistalmu said. "Though one should be wary of unintended consequences. If at some future date the Syndicure decided they wanted the Xodlak or perhaps even the Stybla back in, the Mitth might get booted out to make room for them."

"Never happen," Thurfian said firmly. "Speaking of unintended consequences, I assume you read the Council's latest report?"

"On the Nikardun campaigns?" Zistalmu nodded. "Your boy Thrawn just can't seem to lose, can he?"

"If you ask me, he loses all the time," Thurfian growled. "The problem is that every disaster he breaks over his knee is followed so quickly by a glowing success that everyone forgets or ignores what came before."

"The fact that he has people with brooms sweeping up behind him doesn't hurt, either," Zistalmu said. "I don't know, Thurfian. I'm starting to wonder if we'll ever be able to take him down." He raised his eyebrows. "And to be perfectly honest, I'm also starting to wonder if you still want to."

"If you'll cast your mind back, you may remember I first broached this topic when he was also riding high," Thurfian said stiffly. "You think just because he hasn't yet fallen from his implausible mountaintop means I'm happy to see him continue unimpeded?"

"He *is* bringing honor to the Mitth," Zistalmu countered, just as stiffly.

"Honor that could evaporate tomorrow," Thurfian said. "Along with whatever gains he's brought to the Ascendancy as a whole. No, Zistalmu. Rest assured that I still want him out. The only question is how to do it so that his ultimate self-destruction creates a minimum of collateral damage."

"Agreed," Zistalmu said. To Thurfian's ears, he still didn't sound completely convinced. But at this point, even partial cooperation was enough. "I presume you brought a proposal?"

"The beginnings of one, yes," Thurfian said. "It seems to me that we want him as far away from the Ascendancy as possible when he falls. One possibility would be to persuade the Council to send him against the Paataatus."

"Which they won't do," Zistalmu said. "They're bending the preemptive-strike laws hard enough right now with the Nikardun. They're not going to turn around and send him against someone else. Certainly not without provocation."

"But what if there *was* provocation?" Thurfian asked. "Specifically, what if there were rumors that the Paataatus were allying with a large pirate group to attack us? At the very least, the Syndicure and Council would want someone to go out and investigate such a possibility."

"*Are* there any such rumors?"

"Actually, there are," Thurfian said. "Nothing all that solid at the moment, I admit. But they're there, they're strengthening, and they're definitely provocative. I imagine that with a little effort we could boost their credibility."

"That's fine as far as it goes," Zistalmu said, eyeing him closely. "How do we persuade the Council to send Thrawn?"

"I doubt they'll need much persuasion," Thurfian said, feeling a smug smile crease his lips. "It turns out the alleged pirates are a group he's already faced off against. Specifically, the Vagaari."

Zistalmu opened his mouth. Closed it again without speaking, his presumably reflexive dismissal of the idea morphing into something more contemplative. "I thought he'd already destroyed them."

"He destroyed one group of them," Thurfian corrected. "But who's to say there aren't more lurking in the shadows?"

"That was certainly one of his most mixed-result exploits,"

Zistalmu mused. "He captured that gravity-well generator the researchers are still trying to figure out, but then lost the big alien ship from Lesser Space before anyone could get a look inside."

"*And* lost a respected Mitth syndic along with it," Thurfian growled. All Chiss lives were important, but the fact that Syndic Mitth'ras'safis had been a Mitth automatically meant his disappearance wouldn't mean as much to an Irizi like Zistalmu.

It was supposed to be different when the one who'd been lost was kin, though. It still rankled Thurfian that Thrawn would so casually throw away the life of one of his own family members.

"Yes, of course," Zistalmu said. "A sad day, indeed. You knew Syndic Thrass, didn't you?"

"Mostly just in passing," Thurfian said, feeling slightly mollified. At least Zistalmu had the grace to acknowledge the Mitth loss. "I oversaw the transportation and commerce office back then, while he worked directly under the Speaker."

"I understand he was close to Thrawn?"

"So I've heard," Thurfian said. "I'm not sure I ever saw them together, though. Syndicure and Expansionary Defense Fleet circles don't overlap very much."

"Hardly at all, in fact," Zistalmu conceded.

"But to return to the point, what the Council and Syndicure will remember most is the gravity generator Thrawn brought back," Thurfian said. "We can hint that if they send him out there again, the same lightning might strike twice."

"Hopefully with technology that will be a bit easier to crack," Zistalmu said. "You have a plan for getting this enhanced rumor started?"

"There are some pathways I can use that won't lead back to me," Thurfian said. "That part is key, of course. You'll want to find some similar pathways of your own."

"So that if it explodes in *our* faces instead of Thrawn's, you won't take all the blame?"

"So that we have two different credible sources to present to the Council and Syndicure," Thurfian said. "One story is an unfounded rumor, and we already have a few of those. Two independent stories from Chiss sources are a pattern worth paying attention to."

"I hope so." Zistalmu paused. "I trust you see the possible flaw in your plan?"

"That he'll succeed yet again?" Thurfian scowled. "I know. But once the Nikardun have been destroyed, that will be the end as far as any real danger to the Ascendancy is concerned. A Paataatus-Vagaari alliance may not be much of a threat, but it's all we have to work with. And surely between the two of them they can handle a single Chiss warship."

"*If* the Council sends him alone," Zistalmu said. "All right, I'll see what I can do about getting some rumor pathways set up. Let me know when you're ready so that we can coordinate the revelations. You have any idea when Thrawn is due back from the Vak Combine?"

"Not really," Thurfian said. "Ar'alani is committed to finishing the job, and there's no way of knowing how long that will take. Especially since what she finds may require her task force to make a side trip or two to clean out other Nikardun nests. The point is that we have time to get this moving in the proper direction."

"Let's just make sure we do it right," Zistalmu warned. "If we let people get too comfortable, he'll continue to skate along while they all forget him, after which his next disaster will catch everyone by surprise."

"Don't worry," Thurfian assured him. "We'll do it right. And this time, we'll do it permanently."

Only they probably wouldn't, Thurfian conceded glumly as he left Zistalmu and headed out of the March of Silence. People saw what they wanted to see, and too many of the people in authority chose to remember Thrawn's successes and ignore his failures. Thurfian was certainly willing to give this latest attempt a try, but he suspected it would end the same way as all the others.

What they needed was a new approach. He and Zistalmu were trying to hit Thrawn with a hammer, but Thrawn was too big and the hammer was too small. They needed a new angle with which to hit him.

Or they needed a bigger hammer.

Syndic Thurfian had held a certain degree of power. Syndic Prime Thurfian held a little more. But he realized now that neither of those positions gave him enough.

It was time to try something new. It was time for Syndic Thurfian to become Speaker Thurfian.

By the time he reached his office he had the outlines of a plan. Speaker Mitth'ykl'omi, he knew, was considered to be a vital part of the Mitth political structure.

It was time for Thurfian to make himself equally indispensable.

# MEMORIES I

"There," Haplif of the Agbui said, pointing through the scout ship's viewport at the half-lit planet in front of them. "You can't see the damage from here—"

"I see it quite clearly," the veiled being seated beside him said calmly in that exotic voice of his, that strange mixture of rasping and melodic wrapped up inside an obscure accent. "It extends across the entire planet, I presume?"

"It does," Haplif confirmed. He'd never seen Jixtus without his cloak and hood, his gloves concealing his hands, his black veil covering his face. He had no idea what the creature looked like.

But that voice would stay with him forever.

"Then you can add this to your list of successes," Jixtus said. "Well done."

"Thank you, my lord," Haplif said, squinting a little. Now that Jixtus mentioned it, there were indeed subtle signs of the global destruction down there. The clouds on the sun-lit side, which would be glistening white on an untouched world, were here laced with gray and black from the fire and blast debris thrown up from the vicious civil war he and his team had engineered. On the night side, the clusters of city lights that had once shone cheerfully in the darkness had all but vanished.

Haplif smiled to himself. The near-total destruction of an entire world, and it had all been accomplished in barely six months. *Six months.*

Yes. He was *that* good.

"I understand a single refugee ship escaped."

Haplif scowled. Trust Jixtus to take the shine off a crowning moment. "Only temporarily," he said. "The Nikardun are taking care of it."

"Really," Jixtus said. "You were told not to have any direct contact with them."

"I had no choice," Haplif said. "You told me you didn't want anyone knowing what happened here. The planet never had a communications triad, you were out of range of the standard transmitters, and we didn't have any ships of our own. One of Yiv's ships was poking around, so I contacted them."

For a long moment Jixtus was silent. "You *did* say you didn't want anyone knowing about the war, didn't you?" Haplif prompted.

"Yes, of course," Jixtus said, sounding a bit put out. "I trust you at least kept my name out of it?"

"Your name and mine both," Haplif assured him. "I didn't identify or locate the system for them, either. I just gave the ship's vector and told them it was a group trying to recruit forces against General Yiv. Naturally, they headed after them in hot pursuit, with no doubt righteous fervor in their hearts and minds."

"No doubt," Jixtus said. "You understand Yiv and his people very well."

"I understand *everyone* very well," Haplif said. It wasn't bragging, after all, if it was true.

"I presume you gave the Nikardun their destination?"

"I'm not absolutely sure they had one," Haplif said, keying a line across the navigational display. "All we had was their departure vector, and they mostly took that because it was as far away from the last group of enemy ships as possible. I only know of one advanced civilization along that route, and I'm not sure the refugees were able to get any data on it with the government computers demolished."

"Still, there's a great deal of life in the Chaos," Jixtus said. "Even our records presumably show only a fraction of it."

"That's what they're counting on," Haplif said. "From what the Magys said—that's their title for their leader—from what she said before they took off, I gather the plan was to check each likely system along their path until they found someone they could appeal to for sanctuary. Failing that, they were hoping to find an uninhabited but livable world where they could go to ground. All the Nikardun have to do is follow that same plan, and they'll eventually find whoever takes them in."

"Unless you were lied to," Jixtus said. "Perhaps the refugees know exactly where they're going."

Haplif scowled. Unlikely, but possible. His talent for reading and analyzing cultures was unmatched, but individuals could still surprise him, especially those he hadn't had good opportunities to read. If the Magys had been deliberately vague so as to throw off any possibility of pursuit . . .

He felt his throat briefly palpitate. Jixtus was playing with him, he realized belatedly. Poking at the very set of skills that made him so valuable, teasing the possibility that Haplif wasn't as good as he knew he was. "It doesn't matter," he said. "The Nikardun are following. Whether the refugees reach a sanctuary and are destroyed there or whether they run out of fuel and air and die in space, the end result is the same."

"But you hope the latter?"

Haplif shrugged. "Fewer chances of loose ends," he

said, keeping his voice casual. "But as I said, the end is the same." He smiled. "The end that only *I* could orchestrate."

Jixtus chuckled, a dry, raspy sort of sound. "Never let it be said that Haplif of the Agbui lacks confidence and pride."

"Even when his employer suggests those qualities are unwarranted?"

"Especially then," Jixtus said. "But beware of overconfidence. Eyes held high in pride are less able to see uneven ground ahead."

"Fortunately for your needs, I can see both," Haplif said. "At any rate, we're finished here. We can go home now?"

"You spoke of a Nikardun ship," Jixtus said. "Are there bases in the area?"

"A couple of small ones, yes," Haplif said. "Listening and relay points, with limited defenses. They're not likely to send any warships roaring out to bother anyone."

"Yet you were able to persuade them to do just that," Jixtus pointed out. "Others might be able to, as well. Not to mention, Yiv himself may find a new task for them."

"Well, even if he does, they're not likely to find this place," Haplif said doggedly. "The people here keep mostly to themselves these days. I'm not sure any of them has even been outside the system in decades."

"Except for the refugee ship."

"Which will be gone soon enough."

"I trust you're right," Jixtus said. "As to your question. Since you mention my needs and your unique ability to fulfill them, there's one more job I want you to do."

Haplif looked sideways at the other, a bitter taste in his mouth. He should have guessed this wouldn't be the end of it, despite Jixtus's promise. As Haplif understood most beings, he also understood his employer.

Or did he? With the obscuring cloak, hood, and veil hiding all the usual cues of face and eyes, Jixtus could be nearly anyone, from virtually any bipedal species. For that matter, for all the evidence of Haplif's eyes and ears, he might be sitting next to one of the demons from Agbui myth he'd so often been threatened with as a child.

He shook the thought away. Superstitious nonsense. "You promised we would be done."

"I've changed my mind," Jixtus said calmly. "What do you know about the Chiss?"

Haplif felt his eyes narrow. "I thought Yiv was going to take care of them."

"*Yiv* thinks he's going to take care of them," Jixtus corrected. "Some of my colleagues think that, too. Unfortunately, I know better." Deliberately, the obscured face turned toward Haplif. "Unless you feel the job is beyond you."

Haplif forced himself to hold that unseen gaze. The Chiss were also the stuff of legend, as terrifying in their own way as the mythical demons. But unlike the demons, they were real. "No, of course not. We can handle them."

And he meant it. Whatever else the Chiss might be, they had the same hopes, dreams, fears, and blind spots as everyone else. Anyone with those qualities could be taken down. "But I don't know much about them, so it may take longer than usual."

"Take all the time you need," Jixtus said. "After all, Yiv and the Nikardun still have their part of this drama to work through. Your task won't begin until theirs is ended."

"Yes," Haplif said. "A question. If you're convinced Yiv will fail to destroy the Chiss, why let him continue?"

"Even failures can serve a purpose," Jixtus said. "In this case, Yiv will draw the Ascendancy's attention outward, which will better prepare your path."

"And will presumably also drain Chiss military resources," Haplif said, nodding.

"Yes," Jixtus said thoughtfully. "Though perhaps not as successfully as I'd hoped."

Haplif frowned. "Trouble?"

"I don't know," Jixtus said in that same half-thoughtful, half-uneasy tone. "Twenty years ago, even ten, I would have said the destruction of the Chiss Ascendancy would be a straightforward exercise. No longer. A new generation of military leaders has arisen, warriors who cannot be trusted to walk recklessly down the well-worn paths of manipulation set before them. Supreme General Ba'kif, Admiral Ar'alani, a few others—they think and plan outside the normal patterns. Unpredictable. It may make your task more challenging."

"You give them too much credit," Haplif said contemptuously. "Or perhaps you give *me* too little. Military minds and reactions are of no consequence. I deal in the political realm, and I doubt the Chiss leaders have any less ambition and lust for power than anyone else in the Chaos."

"So I assume," Jixtus agreed. "I'm simply warning you that it won't be as easy as this was." He gestured toward the planet in front of them. "Take whatever resources you need. Others will take over from you here."

"We could do more," Haplif offered. "I still think we should move more of the survivors out of the zone."

"We'll decide whether and how to deal with them," Jixtus said severely. "This task is finished. The next lies ahead."

"Yes, my lord," Haplif growled. He hated leaving any job uncompleted, even when all that remained was mop-up.

"And I'll want the locations of the Nikardun bases you mentioned before we part company," Jixtus added. "We don't want someone stumbling across your success here."

"Definitely not," Haplif agreed. Still, if Jixtus considered the job done, who was he to argue? "So. Once we've destroyed the Chiss for you, *then* we go home?"

"Then you go home, Haplif of the Agbui," Jixtus said. "*And* with double payment."

"Thank you," Haplif said. "Though after everything you said about the Chiss, I'm wondering if the payment perhaps should be tripled."

"Perhaps it should," Jixtus acknowledged. "We shall see. You said there was one known advanced civilization along the refugees' vector. Which one?"

"It's a minor, off-the-path world, barely worth notice," Haplif said. "A place called Rapacc."

# CHAPTER TWO

With one jump left to the Rapacc system, Mid Captain Ufsa'mak'ro had called for the *Springhawk*'s bridge personnel to take a short rest break.

Which was fine with Mitth'ali'astov. As Sky-walker Che'ri's caregiver—her *official* caregiver, now—she'd seen the subtle signs of fatigue in the young girl during the last section of twisting path through the Chaos. If Samakro hadn't called for a break, Thalias would have asked him to do so.

But he had, and all was well. Che'ri sat at her navigation station, sipping fruit juice and looking idly around. That was pretty standard, at least as Thalias remembered her own days as a sky-walker: After spending hours deep in Third Sight, she'd often felt the need to stretch her eyes a little during her breaks.

Unlike Thalias's old routine, though, she saw how Che'ri's eyes kept coming back to the piloting console beside hers. To Thalias, the pilot's realm had always been little more than a slab of mystery with controls attached. To Che'ri, it was almost like a familiar friend.

The girl's juice packet looked to be almost empty. "Would you like some more?" Thalias asked, stepping up beside her. "Or something to eat?"

"No, thank you," Che'ri said. She put the sipper to her lips, her cheeks puckering briefly. "Okay, I'm ready."

Thalias looked around the bridge as she took the empty packet. Samakro, she saw, was over by Senior Commander Chaf'pri'uhme at the weapons station, talking softly with both Afpriuh and one of the plasma sphere specialists—Lieutenant Commander Laknym, if she was remembering his name right. "Doesn't look like we're in a hurry," she told Che'ri. "Besides, Senior Captain Thrawn isn't here yet. I imagine he'll want to be present when we contact the Paccosh."

"Okay." Che'ri hesitated. "What are they like?"

"The Paccosh?" Thalias shrugged. "Alien. Voices that are kind of whinnying, though you can understand them okay. Speak Taarja, which I never liked."

"You mean they whinny like packbulls?"

"A little," Thalias said, trying to remember when she'd heard a packbull in real life. She was pretty sure she had, but she couldn't place where or when that might have been. "The Paccosh we saw in the mining station were about my height, maybe a little taller. Big chest and hip bulges, light-pink skin, and they've got head crests that look like woven feathers. Their arms and legs are thin but they seem strong enough. Oh, and they've got purple splotches around their eyes that sometimes change when they're talking to people."

"Sounds interesting," Che'ri murmured. "I wish I could see them."

"I'm sure we'll bring back vids."

"It's not the same."

"No, it's not," Thalias conceded. "But really, some downtime would be good for you. You can draw, play with your building snaps—"

"And do lessons," Che'ri said with a distinct lack of enthusiasm.

"Oh, right," Thalias said brightly, as if she'd completely forgotten that part of a sky-walker's routine. "Thanks for reminding me."

Che'ri peered up over her shoulder, giving Thalias the kind of strained-patience look that ten-year-olds pulled off so well. "You're welcome."

"Oh, don't be like that," Thalias said, mock-chiding. "There might even be some lessons you'd like." She pointed at the pilot control board. "If you want, I'll help you sweet-talk Lieutenant Commander Azmordi into teaching you how to fly the *Springhawk*."

To Thalias's surprise, Che'ri seemed to shrink into herself. "I don't think so," she said. "I got in enough trouble just learning how to fly a scout ship."

"One: *You* didn't get in trouble," Thalias said firmly. "Maybe Senior Captain Thrawn did, a little, but it all worked out. Two: Learning things should never get you in trouble. Now, if you actually took the *Springhawk* for a ride around some planet without permission, *that* might be a problem. But just learning how to do it shouldn't. Three: You're—"

She broke off with a sudden flicker of embarrassment. "Three: If someone doesn't like it, we'll just refer them to Captain Thrawn, and he'll set them straight."

"That's not what you were going to say," Che'ri said, frowning suspiciously up at her. "What were you going to say?"

Thalias sighed. So embarrassing . . . "I was going to say you're ten now," she said. "And that reminded me that I missed your starday. I'm so sorry. With all that was going on last month, I just totally forgot it."

"It's okay," Che'ri said, hunching her shoulders. Her voice was quiet, and Thalias could hear the distant hurt beneath it. "It's not like I remember being taken to the skylight to see my first star. And, you know. Parties and treasure-puzzle poems are mostly for little kids."

"I still feel terrible for forgetting it," Thalias said. "Maybe we could do something now. A belated starday celebration. I could make something special for dinner, and then we could play whatever games you wanted."

"It's okay," Che'ri said again. "Anyway, there's not much we can do when I'm on duty."

"All right, then," Thalias said, determined not to just let it slide. "We'll wait until we're back on Csilla or someplace and do you a tenth-and-a-half starday. How about that?"

"Okay," Che'ri said. She seemed to straighten in her chair. "Senior Captain Thrawn's here."

Thalias turned around, mentally counting out the time. She was at a second and a half when the hatch opened and Thrawn stepped onto the bridge. His eyes flicked around the room, lingered a moment on Thalias—he could tell that she'd already been turned to face him before he entered, she guessed, and had deduced that the reason for that was Che'ri's Third Sight—then came to rest on Samakro. "Report, Mid Captain Samakro?" he said, stepping toward the first officer.

"Ready for our final jump, sir," Samakro said, turning away from Laknym and taking a step toward his captain. "Weapons and defenses all show green." He flicked a glance at Thalias and Che'ri. "Shall I have the sky-walker and caregiver escorted to their suite?"

Thalias braced herself. She'd been with Thrawn when he first met the Paccosh people, with her life on the block right alongside his. She wanted to be here—she *deserved* to be here—to see what had become of them. If Samakro insisted on shunting her and Che'ri out of the action, he and Thrawn were both going to have an argument on their hands.

Thrawn looked at her again, and she had the eerie feeling that he knew exactly what was going on behind her eyes. "I think not," he told Samakro. "Given the inherent difficulties of travel in and out of the Rapacc system, I'd like our sky-walker to be ready in case we need her for a quick exit."

Samakro took a breath, and Thalias could see him lining up his own argument—

"But you're right, they shouldn't be on the bridge," Thrawn continued, looking around. His gaze stopped at the weapons station, where Laknym was still consulting with Afpriuh. "Lieutenant Commander Laknym, do you feel qualified to handle secondary command weapons control?"

Laknym spun around to face him, his eyes widening. "*Me,* sir? I—ah—" His eyes flicked nervously to Samakro. "Sir, I'm just a plasma sphere specialist."

"None of us was born into the command structure, Commander," Thrawn said, a little drily. "Opinion, Senior Commander Afpriuh?"

"Yes, he's qualified," Afpriuh said, looking up at Laknym.

"Good," Thrawn said. "Don't be overly concerned, Commander.

I'm not expecting serious trouble, and this would be useful experience for you. Please escort Sky-walker Che'ri and Caregiver Thalias to secondary command and take the weapons control station there."

Laknym swallowed visibly but gave Thrawn a crisp nod. "Yes, sir. Sky-walker; Caregiver . . . ?"

Thalias had been in the *Springhawk*'s secondary command room only once, back when she first came aboard and was given a tour of the ship. It was smaller than the bridge and located in the heart of the ship, the last stronghold of control should a battle go horribly wrong.

Between its size and its lack of viewports, it was also seriously claustrophobic, and she felt her skin itching as Laknym pointed her to the navigation station. With Che'ri in tow, she wove her way through the other warriors already on station. By the time she got the girl strapped into her seat, all of the displays had come to life, showing not only the status boards and the view outside the ship but also a view of the bridge itself.

The outside views helped the claustrophobia a little. But not much.

The *Springhawk* was already on its way, with Azmordi guiding them in a short jump-by-jump toward the Rapacc system. There wasn't a spare seat for Thalias, so she stood behind Che'ri, pressed against the girl's chair. Somehow, having her head closer to the ceiling made the claustrophobia worse. She kept her eyes moving to try to distract herself, shifting among the hyperspace swirl outside, the status monitors, Che'ri sitting in front of her, Thrawn standing motionless behind the bridge comm station. Azmordi called a warning—

The swirl vanished into star-flares, and they had arrived.

"Full sensor scan," Thrawn ordered. "Focus especially on ships or battle debris—"

"Contact," Samakro cut in. "Ship directly ahead, Captain. Looks like a Nikardun frigate."

Thalias winced. She'd hoped that the Nikardun who'd been blockading Rapacc had run away and left the Paccosh in peace after Yiv's defeat and capture. Clearly, they hadn't.

On the bridge monitor, Thrawn leaned over the comm officer's shoulder and touched a key. "Unidentified ship, this is Senior Captain Thrawn of the Chiss Expansionary Defense Fleet warship *Spring-hawk*," he announced in the Taarja trade language. "We come in friendship and peace."

"We have no friends," a voice came back, the harsh Taarja words sounding even harsher coming from him. "We will have peace when you are gone. Leave immediately or be destroyed."

"Big talk coming from a half-sized ship," someone behind Thalias muttered.

"Maybe he's got friends nearby," someone else warned.

"I would urge you to reconsider," Thrawn said calmly. "The offer of friendship is not given lightly."

"If you come in peace, prove it," the voice said. On the main display, something broke away from the frigate—

"Missile incoming," Samakro snapped.

"Not a missile, sir," Mid Commander Dalvu corrected him from the sensor station. "It's a single-passenger shuttle, heading . . ." On the display Thalias saw Dalvu lean closer to her board. "Heading thirty degrees off target," she continued, sounding confused.

"A test," the voice continued. "If you are truly Chiss, disable without destruction."

"As you wish," Thrawn said. "Senior Commander Afpriuh? At your convenience."

"Yes, sir," Afpriuh said. "Sphere launcher aligning . . . firing sphere."

Thalias looked at the tactical display, watching as the mark indicating a plasma sphere raced away from the *Springhawk* toward the shuttle. The two marks intersected—

"Shuttle has been flickered," Afpriuh reported. "All systems down."

Thrawn nodded acknowledgment. "Have we proven our identity?" he called.

"What is your purpose here?"

"To assure ourselves that the Paccosh have regained the peace that was stolen from them by the Nikardun," Thrawn said. "To eliminate the last of that enemy, if that goal has not yet been achieved." He lifted up something and held it toward the comm station cam. "And to return this to its rightful owner."

"What's he holding?" Laknym muttered.

"It's a ring," Thalias told him. "One of the Paccosh we met on the mining station gave it to him for safekeeping."

"And the name of that owner?" the Taarja words came.

"Uingali foar Marocsaa," Thrawn said. "I trust you are well?"

There was a strange, almost chuckling sound from the speaker. "I am indeed well," the voice said. The same voice, but with a subtle difference.

And now with the harshness gone, Thalias, too, could hear the voice of the Pacc from the mining station.

"You might have led with the ring," Uingali continued, sounding much calmer now. "Others have come with false claims and statements, and we have necessarily grown wary. Showing the ring from the beginning would have saved us the task of retrieving the shuttle you disabled. But no matter. Follow us, Chiss Senior Captain Thrawn. My people are eager to meet you." On the display the frigate's bow angled up as it began a pitch turn.

Thalias felt her mouth drop open. Emblazoned on the underside of the Nikardun frigate was a familiar image: a nest of small stylized snakes with two larger ones curving up from among them. The same image as the ring Thrawn was still holding to the cam.

She huffed out a breath. "And *you*," she muttered in the direction of the display, "might have led with *that*."


The Rapacc capital city was named Boropacc, and from what Samakro had seen as the *Springhawk*'s shuttle flew over it the place had definitely been through the grinder. Apparently, whatever Nikardun forces had been on the ground at the time hadn't been very tidy when they pulled out.

"Yes, they destroyed what they could as we drove them back to the void," Uingali conceded, nodding out the window at the damaged city as he gestured his visitors to the meeting room's comfortable-looking lounge chairs. The four charric-armed warriors who had accompanied Thrawn, Samakro, and Thalias from the *Springhawk* remained on guard at the door, as per Thrawn's orders, where they'd be out of earshot of the conversation but close at hand should they be needed. "Most of the ships had already left, though why they left so quickly I could not say."

Samakro felt a grim smile tug at the corners of his mouth. *That* one, at least, he could answer. The minute Yiv disappeared, his chief captains had scrambled themselves into a power struggle, each one vying for what was left of the Nikardun forces. Some had used those forces to try to take new star systems, apparently attempting to show they were ready and able to step into the Benevolent's footsteps. Others had simply used their power to try to claim a bigger chunk of the existing territory, cannibalizing other captains' worlds and ships. Whoever had been in charge of the forces blockading Rapacc had apparently decided they had better use for them elsewhere and had withdrawn the majority of them.

"Of course, to be fair," Uingali conceded, "we also caused some of the damage as we killed all of them that we could."

"We're just glad it didn't go worse for you," Thalias said.

Samakro looked over at her, his smile disappearing. The Paccosh had framed this meeting as a high-level discussion between some of their leaders and *those who could speak for the Chiss*, as Uingali had put it. Since the *Springhawk* had no diplomats aboard, Thrawn had decided that he and Samakro would represent the Ascendancy, making sure the Paccosh knew from the start that the two officers had no official standing.

But Uingali had also specifically requested that Thalias join them, and Thrawn had agreed. So now a mere caregiver—and an only recently confirmed one, at that—was to have equal voice with senior Expansionary Defense Fleet officers?

Samakro could see no reason for it. And things with no clear purpose always made him nervous.

"We are also relieved," Uingali told her. He cocked his head, his eyes shifting back and forth among the three of them. "So you are indeed Chiss. We thought you might be after the first meeting between us, but the records of your physical appearance were second- and thirdhand and badly incomplete. But those same records spoke of your ability to neutralize enemies without their complete destruction. Hence, our test. I apologize if it offended you."

"Not at all," Thrawn assured him. "The Ascendancy has always encouraged stories that describe and emphasize our military strength. The easiest battles to win are those that are never fought. But I'm curious. The Nikardun came to Rapacc, yet never in sufficient numbers to totally subjugate you. How did General Yiv make such a miscalculation?"

"Indeed," Uingali said, his voice going deeper. "There is a saying among our people: *Grief is the child of mercy*. And so it was here. A ship carrying two hundred refugees arrived from an unknown system three months before you and I first met. They told us their world was being ravaged by civil war."

"Which world is this?" Thrawn asked.

"We don't know," Uingali said. "They wouldn't give its name, nor the name they call themselves. They spoke of massive destruction and pleaded with us to give them shelter lest their entire culture die with no trace."

He gave a whinnying sort of sound. "You can imagine our thoughts when you later spoke of collecting the art of peoples who could not preserve it themselves. It seemed you spoke pointedly of the situation faced both by our guests and by the Paccosh themselves."

Samakro's eyes flicked to Thrawn's impassive face, and to the play of emotions on Thalias's less guarded one. Thrawn's report hadn't mentioned anything about desperate people or offering to collect their art for safekeeping. Had that been a deliberate omission, or was it simply something Thrawn had thought was irrelevant to the military situation? "How soon after the refugees arrived did the Nikardun show up?" he asked Uingali.

"All too quickly," the Pacc said ruefully. "Even as the refugees spoke of their fears, the invaders appeared. The refugees pleaded with us to allow them to leave, and urged us to send a remnant of our own peo-

ple lest our world and culture, too, cease to exist. They told us—
rather, reminded us—of the mysterious Chiss, whom they hoped
would come to their aid."

"Why didn't you let them leave with your own refugee ships?"
Thrawn asked.

"We could not," Uingali said with a sigh. "We had already informed
the Nikardun that no such refugees had arrived. If their ship had appeared from concealment, the invaders would know we had lied. But
our subclan leaders saw reason in the twin ideas of protecting a remnant of the Paccosh and pleading for assistance. We prepared and
populated two vessels and attempted to slip them out past the Nikardun warships."

He looked hopefully at Thrawn. "Did they reach you? You have
not spoken of them, neither now nor earlier aboard the mining station. And yet, here you are."

"One ship reached Chiss space," Thrawn said. "Sadly, they were
attacked and destroyed before they could deliver your message. The
other ship's hyperdrive failed at their chosen rendezvous point, leaving them doomed."

"So all are dead," Uingali said, lowering his gaze to the floor. "The
hope was indeed for nothing."

"Not at all," Thalias said, and Samakro could hear both sadness
and compassion in her voice. "Because you sent them, we were able
to find you, and through you we found and defeated General Yiv."
She waved a hand out at the ruined city. "And despite the cost, you
were then able to drive them from your world."

"And to capture one of their ships along the way," Samakro added.
"May I ask how you pulled that one off?"

Uingali looked up again, his feathered crest flowing briefly as if
from an invisible wind. "You will forgive me if that remains a Paccian
secret. Now that the entire Chaos is aware of our presence and vul-
nerability, we may again have need of those techniques."

"Understood," Thrawn said. "However, I don't believe that awareness of Rapacc is as widespread as you fear. The Nikardun are dead or
scattered, and the refugees you sheltered seem unlikely to be a threat."

"Yet threats come in many forms," Uingali said, his crest flowing again. "Indeed, I must now reveal that my invitation was not solely to offer the thanks of the Paccosh people. There is a problem with the refugees that I hoped you could help us solve."

His eyes shifted to Thalias. "Or perhaps that *you* could help us solve."

Thalias straightened in her chair, her eyes darting to Thrawn. "*Me?*"

"Indeed," Uingali said. "The refugees appear to be a matriarchal society, led by a female called the Magys. It is hoped she will be more open to advice and counsel from you than from us."

"Why not use one of your own females?" Thrawn asked.

"It is . . . complicated," Uingali said reluctantly. "There were some incidents early on that unfortunately eroded the relationship between the Magys and the Paccosh. Indeed, there were times I despaired of ever regaining their trust."

"What sort of incidents?" Samakro asked.

"Misunderstandings," Uingali said. "Cultural conflicts. Matters we cannot reveal deeply to others."

He looked at Thalias. "But when I spoke to them of aliens who had expressed interest in preserving our art, and to whom I had entrusted a treasured subclan ring, the Magys was clearly intrigued. My hope is that she is intrigued enough to speak with you."

"I don't know," Thalias said, again looking uncertainly at Thrawn. "I'm not a diplomat or counselor. And these are aliens. I wouldn't know the first thing about talking to them." She looked again at Thrawn. "Or even if I *could* talk to them?"

"You have good instincts for such things," Thrawn assured her.

*And you've been dealing with a ten-year-old girl for the past few months,* Samakro added silently to himself. *Children that age are as alien as anything you'll find in the Chaos.*

He couldn't say the words aloud, of course, not even if he switched from Taarja to Cheunh. Not with an alien sitting there. Anyway, Thalias was bound to have thought of that on her own.

Or maybe she hadn't. Her face was still pinched with uncertainty.

"I don't know," she said again. "What kind of counsel are you talking about?"

"As I stated, the refugees came to Rapacc under the leadership of the Magys. Many of them wish to return to their home, but the Magys is the only one who can make that decision. She is also the only one who can provide navigational data to their world."

"And she doesn't want to go?" Thalias asked.

"She does not wish to leave," Uingali said. "Nor does she wish to stay." He paused. "She wishes only to die."

Thalias's eyes widened. "She wants to *die*?"

"Yes," Uingali said. "To give up all hope and die."

"Can she not appoint another Magys?" Thrawn asked.

"Wait a minute," Thalias said, frowning at him. "Are you saying that we should just let her kill herself?"

"If she chooses to die, she is effectively giving up her leadership," Thrawn said. "In such a case, she should recognize an obligation to transfer her authority. Given your statement that some of her people wish to return, they should allow her to die and choose a new leader to take her place."

"What they *should* do is try to change her mind," Thalias countered.

"I believe that is indeed the opportunity Uingali is offering you," Thrawn reminded her.

"Great," Thalias said with a sigh. "So now it's not just me offering advice. I have to try to keep someone alive."

"It's more complicated even than that," Uingali said. "She does not wish death only for herself. She wishes it for *all* of her people."

"She *what*?" Thalias breathed, staring at him. "*All* of them?"

"What do the others say about that?" Thrawn asked.

"Many wish to live and return home, as I stated," Uingali said. "But they also have an unbreakable obligation to obey their leaders. If the Magys chooses death and orders them to do the same, they have indicated they will do so."

"Like we haven't seen *that* one before," Samakro muttered.

"What do you mean?" Uingali asked. "Do you know these people?"

"Not the people, but the attitude," Samakro said. "You remember, Senior Captain, that the Nikardun from the frigate we captured opted to kill themselves rather than be taken prisoner."

"This is hardly the same situation," Thalias insisted, a small tremor in her voice.

"I didn't say it was," Samakro said. "I simply said it was the same attitude that chooses mass death over all the alternatives."

"Actually, you and Thalias together bring up an interesting point, Mid Captain," Thrawn said thoughtfully. "If the Magys prefers death to a return to her world, does that mean that her situation is indeed similar to that of the captured Nikardun? Could she fear that return will mean capture or interrogation?"

"That would make sense, sir," Samakro agreed. "They left a planetary civil war. We don't know what they would be going back into." He looked at Thalias. "I suppose we'll never know unless someone talks to her."

Thalias held his eyes a moment, then dropped her gaze to the floor. She wanted to help, he could see, wanted it desperately. The thought of someone deliberately choosing death for herself and her people was horrifying.

But Uingali had thrown the idea at her too hard and too fast. This wasn't what Thalias was used to, and her mind and emotions had frozen up.

Not that Samakro could really blame her. As a military officer he'd had to make his fair share of hard decisions, some of them with as little warning as Thalias had been given with this one. But he'd grown into that level of responsibility gradually, with time and experience and the example of others to guide him.

"Yes, someone will talk to her," Thrawn said. "You say, Uingali, that she expressed interest when you spoke of art. Perhaps she and I can find common ground."

"They are a *matriarchal* society," Uingali reminded him. "She may not wish to speak to you."

"Hopefully, I can persuade her to do so," Thrawn said. "I assume they speak one of the trade languages?"

"The Magys speaks Taarja," Uingali confirmed.

"Very good," Thrawn said. "Where are they located?"

"They're at some small distance," Uingali hedged. "Your arrival, and the opportunity that it presented, were unexpected. But I can have them brought here."

"You said they arrived three months before we first met," Thrawn said. "That means they've now been here for seven and a half months?"

"Yes, approximately."

"Have they been in this same place that entire time?"

"Yes, except for the first three days," Uingali said. "During that time we were questioning them. When the Nikardun ships first appeared, they were removed from Boropacc so they would be harder to find."

"Then we shall go to them," Thrawn said. "How they have adapted and arranged themselves may be instructive in learning how to deal with them."

"Very well," Uingali said, standing up. "Shall I travel with you in your shuttle, or shall I take my own?"

# CHAPTER THREE

The refugees had been housed in a city about four hours' flight from Boropacc. Thalias, Thrawn, Samakro, Uingali, and the *Springhawk* guard detail rode in the Chiss shuttle while a group of other Paccosh officials paralleled them in their own vehicle. Uingali spent the entire trip talking about Rapacc, both history and culture. Thrawn listened intently, sometimes asking questions, while Samakro sat working at his questis, wrapped in his own bubble of silence.

Thalias, for her part, spent the entire trip listening to the conversation and feeling miserable and guilty.

She had no reason to feel guilty, she insisted to herself. Dealing with this sort of thing was far out of any of her training or experience. Neither Uingali nor Thrawn nor anyone else could expect her to simply step calmly into this situation.

But Uingali knew the Magys far better than she did. What if he was right, and she refused to talk to Thrawn or Samakro? Would the Chiss just turn around and leave the refugees to whatever the future held for them?

In that case, shouldn't Thalias at least try?

Logic and reason told her she should. But there was a huge emotional difference between standing idly by and letting a crisis happen and stepping in, trying to solve the problem, and failing.

It would be all right, she told herself over and over. Thrawn was good at everything. He would find a way to fix it.

She was still telling herself that when they finally arrived.

The refugees had been housed in what appeared to be a school or office building, with many midsized rooms opening off identical tiled hallways. At the moment they were all gathered together in what would have been a convocation hall in one of Thalias's old schools, seated cross-legged in concentric circles.

She eyed them as Uingali led the way toward the group. They were wizened creatures, smaller and thinner than Chiss, with brown skins and flowing white hair cut in asymmetric but clearly deliberate patterns. Their clothing consisted of loose shirts and trousers of various colors and styles with wraparound shoes on their wide feet. Their facial skin was tight, looking almost like it had been stretched over their cheeks and split jawbones.

She frowned, taking another look at the way the circles were laid out. It was hard to tell age or gender, but—

"You can see that they present themselves in a specific pattern," Uingali said softly as their group approached the outer circle. "Inward from the outer edge are the younger males, then the older males, then the older females, followed by the younger females and children. The Magys sits in the center."

"The tactics of desperation," Thrawn said thoughtfully. "Interesting."

"What do you mean?" Thalias asked.

"The outer rim consists of those who can fight and best defend the others," Thrawn explained. "They're followed by the next best at defense, the older males, should the first line fall. Then the females, with those most expendable protecting those of child-bearing capability. Then the children, and finally the Magys."

"Who will be killed only when there's no one left for her to lead," Samakro muttered.

"As I said: the tactics of desperation," Thrawn said. "I assume the Magys expects us?"

Before Uingali could answer, the two young males closest to the Chiss on the outer circle stood up and stepped close to the ones on either side, opening up a narrow space between them. One by one, the pairs farther inward also stood and moved aside until they had formed an open path to the center.

"I believe the Magys is inviting me in," Thrawn said. He started forward—

"Another moment," Uingali said, holding a cautioning hand in front of him. Two of the children from the center were on the move, standing and walking out through the path the others had created. They passed through to the outer rim and moved to the sides, again clearing the way.

"They have made space for you in front of the Magys," Uingali continued. "Now you may go in."

Thrawn nodded and continued forward. Thalias watched him go, feeling the weight easing from her shoulders. Certainly Thrawn would do a much better job than she would. Briefly, she wondered if she would be able to hear the conversation from where she and the others stood. Not that it really mattered—

"No!" a crackly voice bit out the Taarja word.

Thrawn stopped. "I am Senior Captain Thrawn of the Chiss Asce—"

"No," the voice said again. This time, Thalias could see that it was the Magys who had spoken. "Not you." The alien lifted a hand.

And to Thalias's surprise and horror she pointed straight at her. "That one," the Magys said. "That one only."

Thrawn glanced over his shoulder to see who the Magys was pointing at, then turned back. "She is not prepared to speak with you," he said. "Her language skills are inadequate to the task."

"That one only," the Magys repeated.

Thrawn hesitated, then turned around. "Thalias?" he asked.

Thalias took a deep breath, the full weight of the responsibility she'd hoped to avoid crashing down again on her shoulders. She wasn't ready for this.

And yet . . .

Back in Boropacc, when Uingali first proposed she talk to the aliens, the suddenness of the request had all but frozen her brain. But somehow, in the intervening four hours, her mind had worked through much of that shock and all of the crippling fear.

She still felt wholly inadequate. But now she was at least willing to try.

She took a deep breath. "All right," she said, starting forward. "I'll do it."

Thrawn stayed where he was, watching as she approached. "You don't have to do this," he said quietly as she reached him. "This isn't your responsibility. This isn't *our* responsibility."

"I know," Thalias said. She tried to smile reassuringly but was pretty sure she just managed to look scared. "But I have to try."

"I understand," he said, and she thought she saw a hint of approval in his eyes. "I'll be here if you need me."

"Thank you," she said, and started toward the aliens. It was a comforting offer, and she had no doubt it was sincere.

But Thrawn would be out here, and Thalias would be in there, and there would really be no chance for him to help or even offer advice. For the moment, at least, it was all on her. She would have to do the talking, the listening, and the observing.

She reached the gap in the circles. Bracing herself, she headed in.

The path was narrow, and Thalias's shoulders brushed each of the flanking aliens as she passed. She winced at each touch, wishing they would take the hint and move farther apart, wondering if she should turn sideways and try to edge her way through.

But none of the aliens were moving, and she had a strong feeling that turning to avoid them would be seen as weakness or insult or both. Forcing herself to continue, still cringing at each small bump, she reached the center. The Magys had meanwhile lowered her gaze to the open spot in front of her where the two children had been sitting.

Thalias reached the spot and lowered herself to the floor. "Good day to you," she said in Taarja, trying to cross her legs in the same way as the alien female. It wasn't easy—Chiss knees didn't bend quite as far as the aliens' did—but she managed it. "My name is Thalias. What's yours?"

"I am the Magys," the woman said, looking up. Her Taarja was heavily accented and with a lot of the same pronunciation and grammar problems Thalias remembered working through during her own first months of instruction in that language. Did that mean these aliens didn't have cause to use trade languages very much?

"I see," Thalias said. So the woman didn't have a name, but only a title? Or did they simply not give their names to strangers? "My people are the Chiss. May I ask what you call yourselves?"

"I am the Magys. We are the people."

So they didn't give out even their species name. So much for Thalias's vague hope of connecting with them on a more personal level. "I'm told your world has suffered a great deal of devastation. We came here hoping we can help."

"How?" the Magys demanded. "Do you bring back our cities? Do you bring back our people? Do you bring back our children?"

Thalias winced. "Some things are beyond anyone's power to change," she admitted.

"Then do not speak of help." The Magys opened her mouth wide, and Thalias saw now that the two jutting sections of jaw each came with its own tongue. "The cities are fallen. The people are lost. Our time is ended." She closed her mouth and again lowered her head. "All that remains is the final hope, and for me and my remnant to join our fathers, mothers, and children."

Thalias looked down at her hands, noticing to her surprise that they'd clenched into fists. She hadn't realized her reaction to the Magys's outburst had been so intense. "I understand you're angry and fearful," she said, forcing her hands to relax. "But you must not give up hope for your people."

"Are *your* children dead?" the Magys shot back. "Are *your* father and *your* mother dead? Then do not lecture on hope for the people."

"I have no children," Thalias murmured, her mind flicking back to Syndic Thurfian's efforts a few months back to make her betray

Thrawn, and his mocking references to her blood family before her adoption into the Mitth. "And I never knew my father and mother. What I *do* know is that our world, too, was once destroyed."

The Magys spat something, both tongues flicking out with the word. "You lie," she said. "Destroyed is destroyed. If it was truly gone, no one would be left to speak of it. *You* would not be left to speak of it."

"I never said the *people* were all destroyed," Thalias said, feeling a touch of annoyance creeping into the sense of helplessness. People who fell back on pedantic nitpicking always irritated her. "I said the *world* was destroyed. Our sun's output suddenly changed, and the temperature dropped until the entire surface was frozen beyond anyone's ability to survive."

Almost unwillingly, Thalias thought, the Magys raised her eyes again. "What did you do?"

"What we had to," Thalias told her. "A few of the bigger cities were left in place, with heavy insulation added to the buildings and transport structures to protect the inhabitants. Many live there still. The rest were moved deep underground, where heat from the planet's core could balance the cold from the surface."

"Are you mole creatures, that you could thus burrow into the ground?"

"You can see that our hands are not built for such digging," Thalias said, holding out her hands with the palms upward. "A few were housed in existing caverns, modified to create homes for them. But most were moved to places created especially for the crisis, vast chambers torn from the rock and fitted with homes, power supplies, and systems for growing food and creating clean air."

"A massive undertaking for such small return," the Magys said, flicking her tongues out again. "How many can possibly live in such squalor? A thousand? Ten thousand?"

Thalias felt her back straighten with pride. "It's not squalor. And it's not just a thousand, or ten thousand. It's eight billion."

Until that point in the conversation, the rest of the nearby aliens had made no sound and showed no reaction. But now a soft ripple of surprise or disbelief ran through them. "You lie," the Magys said accusingly. "Or you speak the wrong word."

"I speak the correct word," Thalias said firmly. "And for what reason would I lie? Whether eight billion survived or eight thousand, that is still a victory when measured against the death of all. If we can bring our world back from the brink, you can do the same with yours."

"That is indeed the hope," the Magys said. "That is why we must die."

Thalias frowned. Had she mistranslated something in her mind? Or had the Magys completely missed the whole point she'd been making? "The hope for your world is why you must live," she said.

The Magys's tongues flicked out again. "You do not understand," she said. "Tell me, how long has it been since you touched the Beyond?"

Another mistranslation? "I don't know what that means," she said. "I don't know what the Beyond is."

"Certainly you have touched it," the Magys insisted. "I can see it in you. That was why I wished to speak only to you. Only you would truly understand. I ask again: How long since you touched it?"

And then, suddenly, Thalias understood. "You're talking about my time as a sky-walker," she said. "Many years ago, when I used Third Sight."

"Third Sight," the Magys said thoughtfully, as if listening to the sound of the words. "You speak strangely of the Beyond. But that is correct. You have touched the Beyond, as we, too, will soon rest in it. Do you now understand?"

"No," Thalias said. "Will you please explain?"

The Magys did a sort of double twitch of her tongues. Impatience? Resignation? "Our time is ended," she said. "The people are gone. But we may perhaps still bring healing to our world."

"You said that before, that your time is ended," Thalias said. "What does that mean?"

"That there is no reason to go back," the Magys said. "No hope that others of the people still live. So we will therefore die and rest in the Beyond, and through the Beyond bring healing to our world."

"How can you bring healing when the people are gone?"

Another double tongue flick. "Do you not even listen to your own words?" the Magys said scornfully. "You said it yourself: The world is not the people. Our world has been torn and scarred, but perhaps it can be healed. We will join the Beyond and make the attempt."

Thalias frowned, trying to make sense of it all. So the Magys believed that by dying she and the rest of her group could join with some greater cosmic system and through it work to heal the damage caused by their civil war? "But what's the point of healing the world if there's no one left to live there?" she asked.

"There are others in the universe," the Magys said. "Many others. Some of them may one day come to live on the world we leave to them. Why should we not strive to properly prepare it?"

"Because those others may or may not come," Thalias said. "You and your people, on the other hand, are already here. Shouldn't you be trying instead to return and rebuild your world and culture for yourselves? *We* did. Why not you?"

"No," the Magys said. "We are not you. It cannot be done." She lowered her eyes again. "All that can be done is death, and the Beyond."

Thalias took a deep breath. So much for trying optimism and real-life positive examples. Arguing wasn't going to get her anywhere, either. What she needed was an idea, something positive to present.

Or maybe just something that could delay the Magys's decision until she could come up with that better idea. "You say redemption of your people can't be done," she said. "You say they are lost. Here's what *I* say: Prove it."

The Magys looked up again, both tongues sticking out of her slightly opened jaw. "What do you say?"

"Let us travel to your world and see what has become of it," Thalias said, feeling her stomach tighten as she belatedly realized that she had no authority whatsoever to make this offer. If Thrawn decided a long side trip wasn't within their mission parameters, he could simply say no, and that would be the end of it. In that case, the Magys would almost certainly proclaim death, and the rest of the aliens would meekly go along with it.

But then that was the end that had faced them before the *Springhawk* arrived anyway. She might as well give this a try and see if she could talk Thrawn into it. "By your own statements to the Paccosh, you admit the battles hadn't yet ended when you left. The situation there may not be as bad as you think."

"The time is close at hand," the Magys said quietly. "The situation is without hope."

"Then let us prove it," Thalias said. "If it is—if your people truly can't be saved—then we'll bring you back here and you can do as you wish."

"And if you are right?"

For the first time since the conversation started, Thalias felt a stirring of hope. Was that actually a crack in the Magys's steadfast belief that her people were gone? "Then we'll figure out together what needs to be done," she said. "Will you come with me to your world?"

For a long moment, the Magys stared at her. Then her tongues flicked out again. "I will," she said. "One other will join us as witness to all that occurs."

"Of course," Thalias said, her newfound hope fading a little. Getting Thrawn to let a single alien aboard his ship was already problematic. Adding a second to the mix was going to strain her persuasive abilities to the limit.

But she could hardly tell the Magys that she couldn't bring along someone else, whether as witness or protector. At least she hadn't asked to bring all two hundred of them.

"I'll make the arrangements," she said, uncrossing her legs and standing up. A small jolt of pain shot through her knees as the joints complained about their mistreatment. Nodding to the Magys, she turned and made her way back between the pairs of silent aliens.

Thrawn and Samakro were still where she'd left them, though Uingali had moved to the side of the chamber and was conversing with two of the Paccosh who'd been here when their group arrived. "What have you concluded?" Thrawn asked.

"First of all, it's not as simple as her killing herself out of hopelessness," Thalias said. "She believes that the people of her world are dead, but that if she and the others here . . . die . . . they'll join something called the Beyond and be able to heal their world. And by *world,* I mean the physical planet."

"How do they expect to do *that*?" Samakro asked.

"I don't know," Thalias said. "But she seems to think this Beyond is connected somehow to how I used to navigate as a sky-walker."

"The Force," Thrawn murmured, his voice thoughtful.

Thalias frowned at him. "The what?"

"A concept from Lesser Space that General Anakin Skywalker told me about when we were working together," Thrawn said. "He defined it as an energy field created by all living things from which he and others could draw power and guidance."

"So that's what sky-walkers do?" Thalias asked.

"Perhaps," Thrawn said. "The concept seemed somewhat vague. But if living things create the Force, perhaps it can work in reverse, with the Force creating or nurturing living things."

"In order to heal the planet," Thalias said, nodding. So that was what the Magys was getting at.

"Doesn't make sense," Samakro said firmly. "If these alien deaths are what's necessary to fix their planet, and if all the millions or billions who died in the war weren't enough, what makes her think an additional two hundred will make the difference?"

"Another good question, Mid Captain," Thrawn agreed. "Unfortunately, we may not have a chance to inquire further."

"Or we might," Thalias said. "I've persuaded her to hold off for now. But to do that, I had to promise we'd take her back to their world and see whether the situation there can be fixed." She stopped, mentally bracing herself for the verbal explosion.

To her surprise, it didn't come. "Excellent," Thrawn said calmly. "Did you specify a time frame?"

"I—no, I didn't," Thalias said, feeling a bit sandbagged. Thrawn didn't seem the least bit angry that she'd overstepped her authority. Even more surprising, neither did Samakro. "I'm sorry—I thought you'd be angry."

"Not at all." Thrawn gestured to Samakro. "Mid Captain Samakro has been doing some research."

"Senior Captain Thrawn asked me to take a look at the region the refugees most likely came from," Samakro said, making a notation on his questis. "There are a couple of small Nikardun listening and comm relay posts in that area, but nothing on Yiv's list of conquered worlds. As far as we can tell, he never really focused much attention there."

"But then why did the Nikardun chase the refugees here and put Rapacc under siege?" Thalias asked.

"An interesting question," Thrawn agreed. "If he wanted their world, why didn't he move to take it? Conversely, if it was of no use to him, why spend the effort to foment a civil war there?"

"*If* he did start or at least encourage it," Samakro cautioned. "That still hasn't been established. It's possible the war was just coincidence and had nothing to do with Yiv."

"Except—" Thalias began.

"Except that, as you just pointed out," Samakro continued, talking over her, "the Nikardun *did* spend some effort chasing down the refugees. Even if Yiv wasn't the primary instigator of the war, something about the system or its people seems to have caught the Benevolent's interest."

"Or it caught *some* Nikardun's interest," Thrawn added. "We've already seen how the general's disappearance caused a splintering of his empire as his top captains rushed to claim parts of it for themselves. It could be the refugees' situation was interesting to one of those captains but not Yiv himself. Regardless, Mid Captain Samakro and I have already agreed we need more information, which fits very well with your agreement."

"Yes, I see," Thalias said, wilting a little with relief. So not only had she avoided a rebuke from her commander, she also didn't have to tell the Magys that the deal was off. "I wish you'd told me that was what you wanted before I went in there."

"The lack of direction wasn't intentional," Thrawn said. "You'd already begun your conversation by the time the mid captain finished his analysis and we agreed on the optimal course of action. All is well."

"For the moment," Thalias said, wincing. "But if the damage to their people is as bad as she expects . . ."

"If it is, we'll deal with it then," Thrawn said.

"If she's even willing to wait that long," Thalias said. "She told me the time was close at hand. Any idea what she meant by that?"

"We think so, yes." Thrawn beckoned to Uingali. "Please tell Thalias what you told us."

"They must be out of contact from anyone with higher authority than the Magys for nine of their months before she can make this decision," Uingali said, walking over to them again. "The Magys has been waiting for a follow-up ship from their world with a message, but none has arrived. If our calculations are correct . . ." He looked expectantly at Thrawn.

"We have approximately two weeks," Thrawn finished for him. "More than enough time to make the journey and learn the status of their world and people."

Thalias felt a shiver run through her. If the *Springhawk* had waited with Ar'alani until all the Nikardun bases had been dealt with, they would almost certainly have been too late. "Then we'd better get moving," she said.

A small smile tweaked Thrawn's lips; an equally small grimace tweaked Samakro's. "I mean—" Thalias said, cringing to herself as she belatedly realized she'd just given orders to her commander and his first officer.

"Your enthusiasm is noted," Thrawn said, sounding more amused than offended. "Mid Captain Samakro, alert Senior Commander Kharill to prepare the *Springhawk* to depart. We'll lift directly from here with the Magys; Uingali can return to the capital aboard the

Paccian transport. Let the senior commander know we're bringing a guest, and have him prepare quarters for her."

"Yes, sir," Samakro said.

Thalias braced herself. "We'll need quarters for her companion, too," she said. "She wanted to bring a witness."

"I see," Thrawn said, again taking it in stride. "And a companion, Mid Captain."

"Yes, sir," Samakro said, giving Thalias one last look as he pulled out his comm.

"One other thing," Thrawn continued. "Make sure all officers are aware that, when in either alien's presence, they're to treat Caregiver Thalias as if she's a senior officer."

Samakro froze with the comm halfway to his lips. *"Sir?"*

"Thalias will be the Magys's primary contact aboard the *Springhawk*," Thrawn said. "By diverting the *Springhawk* to their world, she's demonstrated that she has both the authority to make agreements and the power to carry them out. The Magys may have further requests, and we need her to believe that Thalias continues to have the ability to fulfill them."

"Are we then going to do everything she demands?" Samakro asked stiffly.

"Of course not," Thrawn assured him. "But sometimes the request alone gives information that would otherwise not come to light. The Magys clearly assumes Thalias is one of the *Springhawk*'s leaders, and we need to continue playing to that impression. More important, identifying Thalias as a senior officer will explain why she's often unavailable to meet or speak with her."

Samakro looked at Thalias. "Those being the times when she's carrying out her caregiver duties?"

"Precisely."

To Thalias, Samakro looked very much like he wanted to argue the point further. But he simply gave a small, stiff nod. "Yes, sir." Half turning away, he brought the comm the rest of the way to his lips and began talking softly into it.

"With all respect, Senior Captain, I'm not sure that's a good idea," Thalias said quietly. "Asking other officers to obey my orders—or even pretend to do so—could cause discord and confusion aboard the ship. Not to mention what the Magys's reaction might be if she finds out we misled her."

"She won't be aboard the *Springhawk* long enough for that," Thrawn said.

"But—"

"This situation is a mystery, Caregiver," Thrawn said. "It needs to be followed until it can be resolved."

"Yes, sir, I understand," Thalias said, trying one last time. "But Mid Captain Samakro—"

"Mid Captain Samakro will accept the reasoning in time," Thrawn said, his tone making it clear the discussion was over. "Inform the Magys that she needs to gather whatever she and her companion wish to take with them. I'll also need her navigational data before we leave here."

"Yes, sir," Thalias said with a sigh, flicking a quick look at Samakro's profile as the *Springhawk*'s first officer continued his conversation with the ship. He was a good officer, she knew, and would follow Thrawn's order. And he probably *would* accept the reasoning in time.

But that time wasn't right now. Not even close.

*Mid Captain Samakro will accept the reasoning in time,* Thrawn had told Thalias at the edge of Samakro's hearing. Maybe he would.

But then again, Samakro glowered to himself, maybe he wouldn't.

What the hell was happening to his life? What the hell was happening to the fleet?

First he was summarily removed as captain of the *Springhawk* and Thrawn put in charge. Then there was the business of identifying and tracking down General Yiv and the Nikardun who were quietly chewing up territory on their way to the Ascendancy. That had ultimately turned out all right, but along the way Thrawn had taken the

*Springhawk* right to the edge of insubordination and violation of standing orders.

Sometimes, in the opinion of many, Thrawn hadn't just gone to the edge but had stepped across it. Along the way he'd thrown the ship into battle after battle, skirmish after skirmish, beating it and battering it and risking the lives of every officer and warrior aboard.

And now this. There was an order to things aboard a warship of the Chiss Expansionary Defense Fleet, regulations and protocols that needed to be followed. And while a caregiver could give orders even to the captain when a situation involved the welfare of the sky-walker, she was otherwise completely outside the chain of command. Ordering the *Springhawk*'s officers even to *pretend* that she had additional authority held the potential for confusion and hesitation and risked the smooth operation of the ship.

And the fact that it was Thalias made it even worse.

Samakro didn't trust her. Not a single binary bit. She'd first come aboard without qualifications, and under suspicious circumstances. She professed loyalty to Thrawn and to the *Springhawk,* and to her credit Samakro had never caught her in anything that belied that allegiance.

But the personnel officer who'd first alerted Samakro to the irregularities in Thalias's arrival had also told him that Syndic Thurfian had essentially forced through her request. And Samakro trusted Thurfian—or any other member of the Aristocra—even less than he trusted Thalias.

He'd met Thurfian only once, at one of the hearings the Syndicure had called after the climactic battle over the Vak homeworld of Primea, the battle that had defeated General Yiv and shattered the Nikardun Destiny as a threat. By that time the Syndicure had received the Council's preliminary report on Yiv's future plans against the Ascendancy, and most of the syndics had asked questions that were placid and perfunctory.

Not Thurfian. He'd pushed relentlessly against Samakro and the other *Springhawk* officers, leaning especially hard on questions regarding Thrawn's role during the battle, his orders to them, and the subsequent damage to the ship. Even the other syndics had seemed surprised by Thurfian's single-mindedness, one of them going so far as to offer a bit of mild and heavily veiled criticism.

Thurfian hadn't even blinked. His goal seemed to be to discredit Thrawn, and if he needed to take down Samakro and the entire *Springhawk* in the process he seemed more than willing to do so.

What made it that much more astonishing was the fact that he and Thrawn were both from the same family. Intrafamily disputes were certainly common enough, but Samakro had never seen one bleed out into public view this way.

Which brought him straight back to Thalias. Before she'd ever come aboard the *Springhawk* she'd had some nebulous association with Thurfian. If Thurfian was violently opposed to Thrawn, could Thalias's loyalty to her captain really be as solid as she professed?

He clenched his teeth. *Politics.* Every single time the thrice-damned Ascendancy politics came aboard his ship—every time internal squabbles or interfamily rivalries oozed their way into the precise and well-honed fleet machinery—he lived to regret it.

Not this time. Whether Thrawn was playing family games with Thalias, or whether Thalias was playing them with Thurfian, or whether all of them were playing games with, against, or sideways to one another, Samakro wasn't going to let any of it make a mess. Not on his ship.

He finished his conversation with Kharill and closed down the comm. "All set, sir," he said, turning back to Thrawn. Thalias, he noted, had in the meantime returned to the alien leader and was talking softly with her. "Your ship will be ready by the time we return."

"Thank you, Mid Captain," Thrawn said, nodding in acknowledgment. "You don't approve."

Samakro braced himself. "No, sir, I don't," he said. "I don't like aliens aboard an Ascendancy warship. I especially don't like heading out to an unknown system and an unknown situation without informing Csilla of our intentions."

"Understood," Thrawn said. "To be honest, I don't like it, either.

But the Paccosh don't have a triad, and the *Springhawk*'s comm system won't reach to any Ascendancy world from here."

"We could head back into range and give our report," Samakro suggested. "There should be enough time to do that, return here and pick up the Magys, and head to her world before we run into Uingali's time limit."

"And if that limit was miscalculated?"

Samakro scowled. There was always that possibility when dealing with three different time scales. Thrawn would certainly have checked Uingali's numbers, but if the raw data was wrong, doing the math would only yield the same wrong answer.

And even if the numbers were right, the *Springhawk* could be delayed or, worse, summarily ordered to report back to Csilla. If Syndic Thurfian was still looking for something to use against Thrawn, an alien's death aboard the *Springhawk* would be an entire salvo's worth of ammunition on a platter. "Understood, sir," he said. "I just hope this place will turn out to be worth it."

"I think it will, Mid Captain," Thrawn said, his voice grim. "Unfortunately."

# CHAPTER FOUR

It had been a bad morning, Councilor Xodlak'uvi'vil groused silently to himself as he trudged up the three steps to the White Judgment Seat of Redhill Hall. It was an impressive title, he had to admit, for what was basically just a big chair in a big room. The chair lived up to the title, what with all the white marble and gold filigree and inset glitterstones.

But the seat and the title were just a fancy-dream way of saying this was where the local family head listened to the requests, demands, and teary-eyed slobberings of the people of Redhill province, here on the economically valuable but politically insignificant Ascendancy world of Celwis.

Lakuviv had no idea which of his predecessors had dreamed up this affront to any sense of proportion. Certainly Patriel Lakooni, who looked after Xodlak family interests for all of Celwis from a quarter of the way across the planet in Brickwalk, didn't have anything nearly this pretentious from which to hear her cases.

But then, Lakooni could afford to be casual. She was blood, with no need to prove herself to the Patriarch or anyone else in the family. She would move to a more prestigious post whenever the family saw fit, perhaps becoming Patriel of one of the more important worlds, perhaps becoming a syndic or even Speaker in the Syndicure. If she was very talented, or made enough friends and allies, she might even rise someday to the Patriarchy itself.

Her life and future were secure. It was local Councilors like Lakuviv who needed to scramble for every bit of notice and contact and good impression they could get, in the hope of catching someone's eye and being lifted from ranking distants to cousins. If and when that happened to Lakuviv his future, too, would be assured.

But that was a far-distant hope. For now, he would do his job: listening to complaints, dealing out justice, and working with the other families' Councilors toward the common goal of making Celwis a shining example of what a Chiss world should be.

After all, what was good for the Ascendancy was also good for the families. And, Lakuviv hoped, for him personally.

The first five cases on the day's roster were a typical mix: family squabbles that fell outside criminal court jurisdiction but were too high-end for local arbiters to deal with. Three of them were fairly straightforward, though the other two were a bit knotty. But Lakuviv had had plenty of experience at this sort of thing and sorted them out without too much trouble.

Not that everyone was happy with his decisions. But that was the nature of negotiation. Still, he was the Xodlak Councilor, with the family firmly behind him, and they all left the Judgment Seat quietly and in good order. If any of them truly felt they'd been unfairly treated, they could always appeal to the Patriel.

And then came the sixth case.

It was instantly apparent that this wasn't going to be like any of those that had gone before, or really like anything Lakuviv had ever dealt with.

Four people entered the chamber, passing between the two ceremonial guards flanking the door. Three of them were aliens of a sort Lakuviv had never seen before: two of them about Chiss height with one slightly shorter than the other, the third about two-thirds the others' height. An adult male, an adult female, and a child or midager, he tentatively identified them. Probably from the alien ship that had put down yesterday at the Brickwalk landing field, he guessed, though the Patriel's preliminary report hadn't given any details aside from the simple fact of their arrival.

More important, the report hadn't said anything about them leaving Brickwalk and coming to Redhill. Perhaps the fourth member of the group was about to expound on that.

Lakuviv focused on him. He was a young Chiss, possibly a late midager, certainly no more than twenty years old. The cut and patterns of his clothing weren't familiar—they weren't any Xodlak style he'd seen—but the outfit had the air of stateliness and expense. He was talking softly to the aliens as they all approached the Judgment Seat. A guide or escort, maybe?

A third guard stepped into the chamber behind them and took up a watchful position beside the other two guards. Lakuviv sent him a questioning look, was answered with a small nod. So the standard weapons check had come up empty. They wouldn't have been allowed in with anything like that, of course, but the simple fact that they hadn't had any weapons for the guards to take away said something about them.

Lakuviv took another look at the aliens. Their facial skin was a mess of dark red and off-white folds, the mix of the two colors seemingly at random. The pattern was also slightly different on all three, perhaps how the species distinguished among themselves. Their mouths were lipless slits tucked away amid all the folds. Their eyes were black and yet, somehow, bright and clear. All three wore wraparound robes: dark red for the tallest alien, dark blue for the other two, all three robes with patterns of silver woven into the cloth.

Three paces from the Judgment Seat, the young Chiss motioned the aliens to stop. He himself took one more pace forward and bowed to Lakuviv. "Greetings and honor to you, Councilor Xodlak'uvi'vil," he said. "I am Coduyo'po'nekri, here as a visitor to your world and province."

"Welcome, Yoponek," Lakuviv said, eyeing the youth with new interest. The Coduyo, like the Xodlak, were one of the Forty Great Families, the second tier of Ascendancy power, poised just behind the Nine Ruling Families. Whoever these aliens were, getting Yoponek to speak for them had at least guaranteed themselves Lakuviv's full attention. "May I ask why you've come to Redhill instead of one of the Coduyo family lands on Celwis?"

"I'm currently on a wandering year, Councilor Lakuviv," Yoponek said. "I'm traveling the Ascendancy, seeking knowledge and experience outside the classroom walls."

"Ah," Lakuviv said, nodding. Wandering years were a staple of some families: a gap year after basic schooling when a young person could travel and learn, meditate and self-examine, before returning to advanced schooling or other job training.

Proponents of the program claimed it helped young people better decide their goals and talents in order to avoid false starts in future studies. Critics saw it as a waste of parental money, with little evidence that it did anything but allow the midager to wallow in an extended period of self-indulgent laziness. Cynics said its true purpose was to get them out from underfoot during what was traditionally the most pompous and condescending time in their lives.

"During my travels I was fortunate enough to meet Haplif, his wife Shimkif, and their daughter Frosif," Yoponek continued, gesturing to the three aliens in turn. "I've learned a great deal while traveling with them. We arrived on Celwis yesterday, and they've come here today to ask a favor of you and the Xodlak family."

"Have they, now," Lakuviv said, shifting his attention to the taller alien.

"They have," Yoponek said. "They themselves are—"

"Do you do all their speaking for them?" Lakuviv interrupted.

"—cultural nomads who—" Yoponek broke off. "What?"

"If they want a favor, they must ask for it themselves," Lakuviv said. "You—Haplif—do you speak Cheunh?"

"He wants you to talk to him," Yoponek said to the aliens, switching to the Minnisiat trade language.

Haplif bowed his head low to Yoponek. He took a step forward to stand beside the midager and bowed again, this time to Lakuviv. "I greet you, Councilor Xodlak'uvi'vil of the family Xodlak," he said, his voice surprisingly melodious, the trade language words coming out with more clarity than Lakuviv had expected from such an undeveloped mouth slit. "As our honored companion said, our group of

Agbui are cultural nomads. For thirty years and more we have traveled the Chaos—"

"Just a moment," Lakuviv said, his eyes narrowing in suspicion.
"How did you know what Yoponek called you? He implied you didn't
speak Cheunh."

"They don't speak it, but they understand a little," Yoponek spoke
up, sounding puzzled. "There are a number of other aliens who are
the same way. The Paataatus, some of the Pathfinder navigators—
there are many historical anecdotes of travelers outside the Ascendancy—"

"Of course, of course," Lakuviv again cut him off, feeling a bit embarrassed. The boy was right—not speaking Cheunh didn't necessarily mean a person couldn't understand it. One of the occupational
hazards of his position: Once he got into judge mode, searching for
discrepancies and inconsistencies, it was sometimes hard to get back
out. "Please continue."

Haplif looked at Yoponek, got an affirmative nod in return, and
again faced Lakuviv. "Our group of Agbui are cultural nomads," he
repeated. "For thirty years the fifty of us have traveled throughout the
Chaos, seeking knowledge, making new friends, and expanding the
width and breadth of our lives. Our new friend Yoponek suggested
Celwis might be a place where we could borrow a small tract of land
for a short time to grow the spices we sell in order to fund our journeys."

"I see," Lakuviv said. The Ascendancy had seen occasional refugee
groups come through its territory over the centuries. Some of those
groups had petitioned the local Patriels for new homes, and nearly all
of them had been turned down and sent on their way. Cultural nomads who weren't looking to settle on Chiss soil but merely wished
to borrow some was something new. "How much land would you
need, and how long would you need it?"

"Not much, and not long." Haplif held his long-fingered hands
about a meter apart. "A tract twenty of these on a side would be sufficient." He lowered the hands again to his sides. "A place nearby to

ground our ship would also be helpful, though that land need not be useful for other purposes. As to time, five or six months is all we would need."

Lakuviv tapped his chin thoughtfully. It could be done, he knew. Four hundred square meters was hardly anything. Moreover, Redhill province included several rocky hills, most of them with an encirclement of barely arable land that was good for little except animal grazing. If that was good enough for Haplif's spices, there should be a plot that could be pulled out of service for a few months.

At least now he knew why Yoponek had come to him instead of any of his own family's Councilors. The Coduyo's Celwis territory was exclusively city and homestead, with no farmland to speak of. "What kind of spices are they?" he asked.

"I bring a sampling." Haplif reached into his robe and pulled out a small plastic envelope with four smaller envelopes inside it. "They have been tested many times, on many worlds, and none has posed a threat or malice to local plants, animals, or sentients."

"We'll have them tested," Lakuviv said. Senior Aide Xodlak'ji'iprip was standing at her customary place a respectful meter from his right elbow. Beckoning her forward, Lakuviv handed her the envelope. "Have these sent to Vlidan Labs. Tell them I want an analysis as soon as possible."

"Yes, sir," Lakjiip said. With a brief but penetrating look at the aliens, she turned and left the chamber.

"They also make jewelry and art objects," Yoponek spoke up helpfully. He dug into his hip pouch. "I have one here I can show you—"

"Nay, my young friend," Haplif said, putting a restraining hand gently on Yoponek's wrist. "That was a gift. Permit me to offer our host his own."

He dug into his robe again, this time coming up with two thumb-sized objects. "For you," he said, stepping forward and holding them out.

Cautiously, Lakuviv took them. They were a pair of brooches, he saw, one a mirror image of the other, shaped rather like stylized leaves made of intertwined strands of silver, blue, red, and gold metal. They were also considerably lighter than he'd expected, suggesting the metals weren't real silver or gold but something cheaper.

Still, intrinsically valuable or not, they *were* genuinely pretty. More important, they were the sort of design that would probably appeal to a fair number of Chiss buyers. If the spice thing didn't work out, Haplif and his nomads ought to be able to raise enough with jewelry sales to refuel and be on their way within their six-month timetable.

But there were other possibilities here, as well. Possibilities that might make it work even better for the Xodlak and for Lakuviv himself. "Thank you," he said to Haplif, putting the brooches on the armrest table alongside his questis. "You—Yoponek."

"Yes, Councilor?" the young Chiss said.

"Are you willing to make this an official request from the Coduyo to the Xodlak?" Lakuviv asked.

Some of Yoponek's youthful exuberance faltered. "I'm not sure I can do that. Can I? I mean, I'm not anyone official."

"You're a member of the Coduyo family in good standing," Xodlak reminded him.

"Yes, but . . ." Yoponek paused, still clearly puzzled.

"Let's make it simpler," Lakuviv offered. "Are you willing to make it an official request from *you*?"

"Oh," Yoponek said, brightening. "Yes, I can do that. Will that be good enough?"

"Absolutely," Lakuviv said, smiling reassuringly. A lot of family business on Celwis ran on favors and owings, and if he couldn't get an official Coduyo stamp on this one, at least the family name would be on it. Good enough to be useful somewhere down the line. "Haplif, where is your ship currently parked?"

"In the southern landing field," Haplif said.

"Berthing Strip Twenty-Nine," Yoponek added.

"Excellent," Lakuviv said. Close at hand in case he needed to talk to them again, but not tying up Redhill's main cargo or passenger landing facilities. "Return there and wait. I'll be in contact soon."

"Yes, Councilor," Yoponek said, bowing again. "Thank you for your attention to this matter."

"And the Agbui thank you as well for your kindness," Haplif added, also bowing. "I trust you will find gladness and value in our humble artwork."

"I'm sure I will," Lakuviv said. "And welcome to Celwis."

He watched until the group had left the chamber. As the door closed behind them, Senior Aide Lakjiip returned through the side door. Once again Lakuviv beckoned her over. "You sent the spice packet?" he asked.

She nodded. "I also talked directly to the Vlidan supervisor. He said they'll start an analysis immediately."

"Good." Lakuviv handed her the brooches. "Add these to their list."

Lakjiip peered closely at the jewelry. "Also from Haplif?"

"Yes," Lakuviv said. "I have the feeling this is their fallback funding plan in case we don't grant them a temporary land use."

"Interesting metal," Lakjiip said, hefting it experimentally. "Are they four different types, or just different colors of the same one?"

"That's one of the things I want Vlidan to find out," Lakuviv said. "It's too light to be gold or platinum or anything else valuable. I want to know what the things are worth, so that I can make sure the Agbui don't gouge their customers when they start selling them."

"And if they do, you'll put an extra tax on their profits to compensate?" Lakjiip suggested.

"Perhaps," Lakuviv said. "Or I could go ahead and let them overcharge in order to get them off our planet a little sooner."

"A little hard on the citizens."

"Some people don't learn valuable life lessons unless they lose money in the process," Lakuviv said with a shrug. "And since our young friend Yoponek will be on record as asking for this favor, we might find a way to bring the Coduyo in on any fallout, as well."

"Or earn a favor by *not* bringing them into it?"

"Possibilities abound," Lakuviv agreed. He pointed to the brooches. "But the first step is to see what exactly we're working with."

"Yes, sir," Lakjiip said. "Anything else?"

"We need to find a place for them to grow their spices," he said. "Someplace not too far away—but also not too close—with the kind of marginal land where they can borrow a couple of plots without cutting some farmer or rancher out of any prime property. A small operation would be best, probably family-run. Oh, and the whole family has to speak Minnisiat so they'll be able to communicate. I presume you can cross-reference all of that?"

"No problem," Lakjiip said.

"Good," Lakuviv said. "Then I'll leave you to it."

"Yes, sir." Giving him a brisk nod, Lakjiip turned and once again headed to the side door.

Lakuviv watched her a moment, then turned forward again. With that, the excitement of the day was over. "All right," he said, nodding to the appointments secretary near the main door. "Bring in the next one."

Xodlak'phr'ooa's first hint that his afternoon was going to be drastically different from his morning was when he saw the brightly marked official family skycar fly over his ranch, low and slow, clearly looking for a place to land.

Lakphro scowled, shielding his eyes from the sun as he watched the skycar turn toward the rocky hill that jutted up from the middle of his grazing land. If this was another bureaucrat come to count his yubals for tax purposes, he was going to throw the son of a growzer right off his land, then throw the skycar after him. Three different number-squinters had been here in the past month, all three of them coming up with different livestock counts before finally settling on the number Lakphro had filed in the first place. An immense time sink, as well as a pain in the neck.

The skycar had stopped now and was sinking toward the edge of the landing area where Lakphro's own skytruck was usually parked. That particular spot was also right at the edge of his wife Lakansu's swirl garden. If the pilot was careless enough to damage her vegetables, Lakphro knew, his own annoyance would be the least of the bureaucrat's problems.

The skycar was down, and Lakphro was striding toward it and rehearsing his angry speech when a new shadow suddenly fell over him.

He looked up, feeling his eyes widen. The vehicle passing over him wasn't just a skycar, but a full-blown freighter-sized starship.

And it, too, was heading toward the rocky hill and the parked skycar.

"Dad?" the anxious voice of Lakphro's twelve-year-old daughter Lakris came from the comm on his shoulder band.

"It's okay, hun-bun," Lakphro soothed, watching the ship closely. It looked like it was going to land near the crest, up where there wasn't anything but rock and scrub. "I think they're going for the hill. Are the calves skittering?"

"I don't think so," Lakris said. "But they *are* a little nervous. I don't think they've ever seen anything that big up close. But I'm holding them together."

"Good girl," Lakphro said. "As soon as you can do it safely, head them back to the barn. We'll keep them there until this nonsense is over."

"Okay," Lakris said. "Mom?"

"I'm here," Lakansu came back promptly. "And yes, they're putting down on the northern edge."

Lakphro nodded. Up where the hill was flattest. At least the pilot had sense enough not to put down on any of the grazing land. "I'm heading up there now," he said, picking up his pace. "A family skycar came with them. I'll find out what's going on."

"I just hope it's not a confiscation," Lakansu said, a hint of nervousness in her voice. "If this is another blight epidemic, the whole district could be in trouble."

"Yeah," Lakphro said, wincing. And a ship that size could hold a *lot* of confiscated yubals.

But if this was another disease scare, why bring in a ship designed for space? Quarantining or slaughtering infected animals could be done right here on Celwis.

For that matter, where had a ship like that come from in the first place? The design and markings weren't like anything Lakphro had ever seen. Certainly it wasn't from the family or any of the local merchants.

"Well, if it is, they damn well better be ready to prove that our herd has it," Lakphro continued firmly. A woman had emerged from the skycar now and was walking toward him. "Okay, there she is. Looks like a Councilor's Office shoulder band. I'll let you know what happens."

"All right," Lakansu said. "Just watch your temper."

"Who, me?" Lakphro said as innocently as he could manage. "I'll be back on in a minute."

He keyed off the comm, knowing whoever that woman was would probably tell him to do so anyway. Official types never liked their conversations with private citizens to be overheard by other private citizens.

And as the two of them closed the gap, he was finally able to make out her face.

It was Senior Aide Lakjiip, head flunky for Councilor Lakuviv.

Great.

"Good day," Lakjiip called as they reached conversation distance. "Are you Rancher Lakphro?"

Lakphro's first impulse was to ask who else she thought would be walking around his ranch with a yubal lurestick sheathed at his hip. But he resisted the temptation. "I am he," he said instead.

"Excellent," she said. "My name is—"

"You're Lakjiip," Lakphro said. "Senior aide to Councilor Lakuviv. Everyone in the district knows about you."

"Ah," Lakjiip said, giving him a pleased and slightly embarrassed smile. "Thank you."

"Of course, everyone in the district also knows about hoof fungus," Lakphro continued. "And if you're serving another random confiscation notice, you'd better have solid evidence that my livestock are diseased."

Lakjiip's smile, which had gone frosty at the hoof-fungus comment, disappeared completely. "You misunderstand, Rancher," she said coldly. "I'm not picking up. I'm delivering."

Lakphro flicked a glance over her shoulder at the big ship. Two beings had appeared through the front hatch: one a young Chiss, the other an alien of a type he'd never seen before. "What do you mean, delivering? Delivering what?"

"Not *what*," Lakjiip corrected, a layer of refined malice in her tone. She *really* hadn't liked that hoof-fungus comment. "*Who*. That alien on his way over here is Haplif. He and his people are going to take up residence on your ranch for a few months."

Lakphro felt his mouth drop open. "They're *what*? No—you can't do that. You can't just take land from family ownership without compensation—"

"Oh, stop it," Lakjiip said scornfully. "We're not taking it, just borrowing it for a few months. Besides, that scrub land up on the hill? Worthless."

Lakphro took a deep breath, working hard to hold on to his temper like Lakansu had told him. "That's extra grazing land for my yubals," he said. "Just because it won't grow crops doesn't mean it's worthless."

"Maybe not crops, but it *will* grow spices," Lakjiip said. "Or so our Agbui guests claim. I'm sorry; *your* Agbui guests."

Lakphro looked past her again at the approaching alien and the Chiss trotting along beside him. The Chiss was young, Lakphro could see now, maybe nineteen or twenty years old, though he still had the bright-eyed, chirpy look of a midager. "What kind of spices?"

"I'll let Haplif tell you all about it," Lakjiip said. "As for compensation for the land rental, the Agbui will be handling that."

Lakphro gave a little snort. "Thanks, but we don't need any foreign spices."

"No, I suppose the kind of cooking you do out here wouldn't lend itself to anything exotic," Lakjiip said coolly. "But they also have some handmade jewelry they'll be offering at local markets. Even if *you* don't appreciate *foreign* items"—she leaned on the word way harder than necessary—"I'm sure your wife could use a new pendant for those times when you go out on the town. Or whatever you do for excitement out here."

"Out here, we don't *get* excited," Lakphro countered. "We live longer that way."

"Whatever you say," Lakjiip said. "Good day, Rancher."

With a perfunctory nod, she turned and headed back toward her skycar. She nodded to the alien and young Chiss as she passed them, said something inaudible while gesturing back over her shoulder, then continued on. The alien and Chiss, the latter still smiling cheerfully, walked toward Lakphro.

With a sigh, he keyed his comm back on. "Looks like we're going to have company for a while," he told his wife and daughter. "The family has generously offered some of our land for some aliens to park their ship on and grow some hardscrabble spices or weeds or something."

"At least no one's taking our yubals," Lakansu said. That was his wife: always looking on the bright side of things. "You'll be sure to ask them in, won't you?"

"Sure," Lakphro said with a sigh. *Some days you're the growzer,* he quoted the old saying to himself, *and some days you're the growzer's son.* Today, clearly, he was the latter.

All he could say was that it had better be some *really* nice jewelry.

# MEMORIES II

Haplif had taken the first two months to organize and prep his people and to learn as much of the Chiss language Cheunh as he could manage in so brief a time. Since then, the group had spent three months in the Chiss Ascendancy, visiting eleven different regions on five different planets, talking with everyone from mid-range family officials to regular working citizens. The supply of spices they'd brought to fund the operation was slowly but steadily decreasing, roughly in proportion with the steady increase in Haplif's frustration.

Three months. Three completely wasted months.

Seated at an outdoor table in a town whose name he'd forgotten, feeling the mocking sunshine on his face, he listened to the even more mocking music of the street festival going on all around him and glowered to himself. Three months and five worlds, and he still was no closer to getting a handle on these people.

That there *were* such handles wasn't in doubt. There was no way an ordered society could function without them. But the way the family structure and hierarchy operated internally, combined with how all the families interacted with one another, offered no obvious entry point that a non-Chiss could find and exploit.

The festival music was swelling to yet another climax. If it followed the pattern he'd already heard three times this afternoon, that peak would be followed by about a quarter hour of silence. At least he would have that much peace before the raucous sound resumed.

He took a sip of his drink—it didn't taste very much like his favorite ale, but it was the closest he'd found so far in this worthless collection of planets—and pulled out his datarec. He'd already decided it was time to move on to another Chiss world and try again. The question was, which one?

He had no idea which would be the most promising. There was a fair chance that none of them would. But Jixtus had given him a task, and the promised payment and the hope of finally being done with this wearying work for a while would keep him going.

That, plus his own pride. No alien species had yet been able to resist him, and the Chiss were *not* going to be the exception.

But if it was going to happen, it had to happen soon. Two days ago he'd received news from Jixtus that the Chiss had defeated the Nikardun forces over Primea and General Yiv the Benevolent had vanished from sight. Haplif's plan had been to get his operation here fully under way while Yiv's threat pulled official attention outward, but now that hope was gone. There would be a short period before life in the Ascendancy returned to normal, at which point the people in charge of order and security would be once again paying full attention to their own backyards.

That wouldn't be an insurmountable barrier. But it *would* make things harder.

The music ended. Finally. Hunching over the table, Haplif punched up the Ascendancy star charts and began tapping up the data sheets on the nearest planets. He'd read those summaries a dozen times already, but maybe this time around something would catch his eye with a hint on how he should proceed.

He frowned. With the music silenced, he was now able to hear the conversation going on two tables over. A pair of young Chiss, one male, one female, were chattering away to each other, and despite Haplif's language limitations it was quickly clear that they, too, were discussing finances and trying to decide where to go next. Not where to go in the local festival, but which planet they would travel to.

It was worth a shot. "Excuse me," he said in Minnisiat as he turned to face them. "Do you speak this language?"

The two Chiss seemed startled to see an alien face peering out from beneath the hooded cloak Haplif had taken to wearing after one too many patroller stops on various streets. A close look would immediately reveal his features, of course, but there were enough Chiss who also wore such garments that he now blended better into the crowds. At least the hood limited the number of stops that had been due solely to worried passerby call-ins.

The boy recovered first. "Yes, we speak it," he said, though his halting cadence suggested he had more book learning than actual experience. "Forgive my surprise, but we haven't seen any other beings of your type in our travels. Who are you?"

"I am Haplif of the Agbui," Haplif said, giving him a little head bow. "I and my people are cultural nomads, who travel the stars seeking knowledge and enrichment for our lives."

The boy's face lit up. "Really? That's just what *we're* doing." He got up from his seat, picked up his drink, and crossed to Haplif's table. After a second's hesitation, the girl followed suit. "I'm Yoponek, and this is Yomie, my betrothed," the boy said as they sat down across from him.

"Honored to meet you both," Haplif said, trying to read their voices and faces. Young and enthusiastic, which often came pre-packaged with idealism. That should make them easy to manipulate.

Still, he needed to step carefully. He couldn't afford to bungle this chance. "That is indeed a blessing of luck," he continued. "I was puzzling on where my people should travel next. As you are engaged in the same quest for wisdom, perhaps you could offer advice."

"Certainly," Yoponek said. "What exactly are you looking for?"

"We have tasted some of the breadth of what the Chiss people have to offer," Haplif said. "But I feel we are missing the true depth and grandeur of your worlds. Where, would you say, is the full richness of the Chiss Ascendancy to be found?"

"A stroke of luck indeed," Yoponek said. "Again, that's also our quest. We're in our wandering year, the period of time between primary and final education. We've chosen to spend it traveling the Ascendancy."

"An amazing and unique concept," Haplif said, skipping over the fact that he could name at least five other cultures that did the same thing. "Do you have a specific field of study?"

"Well, I'm a student of history and Chiss culture," Yoponek said. "So pretty much anything we see and experience is in my area. Yomie—" he sent her an appraising look "—is much more a student of everything."

"So even more intrigued by everything in the Ascendancy," Haplif concluded, nodding. "An exciting time for you, indeed. So for a year you are free to move about as you wish?"

"For another five months," Yomie corrected, her nose wrinkling a bit. "And it's hardly free."

"We're doing all right," Yoponek said, giving her a slightly annoyed look. "We just have to be careful with our money from now on."

Haplif suppressed a smile. Perfect. "I understand the challenges of limited funds," he said, switching his attention to the girl. Clearly, she was the practical one of the pair. If he could convince her, the boy would follow. "But there's an obvious solution for both our problems. I suggest we combine our efforts."

"What do you mean?" the girl asked, frowning.

"I offer you passage aboard our ship," Haplif said. "That will save a great deal of your funding. In exchange, you would offer your services as guides and mentors, saving us missteps and wasted efforts."

The two Chiss exchanged looks. "What if we want to go someplace you don't?" Yoponek asked.

"Not a problem," Haplif said. "We have no fixed itinerary, nor have we anywhere in particular we wish to go. Cultural nomads go where the wind of fate takes them. We would happily allow you to be that wind, following wherever you lead."

Again, the two looked at each other. "What do you think?" Yoponek asked, switching back to Cheunh.

"It would make the finances work better," the girl said, sounding a little hesitant. "Not exactly what we'd planned, though."

"We would also of course provide sustenance throughout our journey," Haplif put in. "Our experience has shown that our two species can eat the same food and require the same nutrients. And of course, we'll also be buying other exotic foods, which will offer you more variety."

"We *did* talk about sampling the various cuisines along the way," Yoponek pointed out.

"I know," Yomie said.

But Haplif could still hear the doubt in her voice . . . and if she didn't come around in the next few seconds, he'd have lost them both.

He gave a silent inner growl. He'd wanted to continue using only the spices for their income and hold off on bringing out the jewelry until the time and place where they would do the most strategic good. But Yomie was teetering on the line, and the two rings and woven necklace she was wearing suggested that she appreciated fine jewelry. No choice but to switch plans.

"You seem uncertain," he said. "If I may, allow me to offer one more inducement." Reaching into his pocket, he pulled out a brooch, one of several he carried. "I would be honored if you would accept a small gift," he continued, placing it on the table in front of her. "There's no commitment suggested or required. I gift it to you simply in gratitude for listening to my offer."

The girl tried to play it casual, pausing for a full two seconds before picking it up. But Haplif could see the gleam in those glowing red eyes as she gazed at the delicate swirl and interweaving of the metal threads. "It's nice," she allowed, again trying to hide the true depth of her interest. Haplif watched her closely, noting that the boy was doing the same. Definitely the decision maker of the pair.

She took a deep, deciding breath. "All right," she said. "If Yoponek's happy to go with you, so am I. At least, for a time."

"Then it's settled," Haplif said, beaming his best cheerful smile. "Whenever you're ready, I'd be honored to show you to our ship. Once we're there, you can discuss and then decide what our next destination should be."

"We'll also need separate sleeping compartments," Yoponek said. "Not just separate beds, but separate compartments."

"Yes, of course," Haplif said, hiding his surprise. Most

species' betrothal customs and restrictions, at least those he'd seen on his various jobs, seemed to be held more in theory than in actual practice. This couple was apparently more serious about following them. "Whatever you need, we can supply."

From across the festival grounds came the sounds of musicians warming up their instruments. "Can we listen to one more set first?" Yomie asked, looking at the boy. "I really like their style."

"Of course." Yoponek looked at Haplif. "If that's all right?"

"Absolutely," Haplif said, being careful not to let his cheerful façade slip. "As I said, I and the Agbui are completely at your disposal."

He hesitated, recognizing that this next step might be a little too early in their still-tenuous relationship. But he needed to be sure. Reaching across the table, he brushed his fingertips across Yoponek's temple, pushing back a few strands of hair as he did so.

The boy twitched, but didn't pull away. "What was that for?" he asked.

"It's an Agbui gesture of greeting and friendship," Haplif said, reaching next toward Yomie. The girl tried to duck away from the approaching fingers, but Haplif managed a brief touch. "I'm sorry—is it offensive to you?"

"It's all right," Yoponek said. "Yomie?"

"It's fine," Yomie said stiffly, her glowing red eyes narrowed and glaring.

"My apologies," Haplif said, ducking his head toward her. "With like-minded souls, I sometimes forget I'm not among fellow Agbui."

"It's all right," Yomie said, relaxing a little.

"But I intruded," Haplif said humbly. "I will try to remember my proper place in the future. In the meantime, let us enjoy the performance together."

The music started up. Yoponek turned his chair around in the direction of the musicians; with a lingering look at Haplif, Yomie did likewise. They settled back to listen, their hands entwined in each other's.

With their faces turned away, Haplif finally permitted himself a small, triumphant smile. Yoponek was already enthusiastic about the free travel and cultural opportunities, he'd seen in that quick pass-by. Yomie, while more cautious, was at least warming up to the idea. As long as Haplif and the others didn't make any blatant missteps, their new guests should settle in comfortably.

And with a pair of Chiss aboard from whom he could study and glean information, the handle he was looking for was bound to show itself.

And once he had the handle, he would have the whole ax.

He settled back in his seat to wait on the convenience of his new unwitting allies. And really, the music wasn't *that* bad.

# CHAPTER FIVE

"**B**reakout in thirty seconds," Wutroow called from her position behind the *Vigilant*'s helm.

Ar'alani looked around the bridge, confirming one final time that her ship was prepared for battle. Sky-walker Ab'begh and her caregiver were safely tucked away in their suite, the weapons and defense status boards all showed green, and all stations were cleared for action.

Two more Nikardun bases in this region, if Yiv's records were accurate. Two more battles, and then they could go home. She took a steady breath, setting her mind into combat mode.

And then the view outside changed, and they had arrived.

"Contact," Senior Commander Obbic'lia'nuf called from the sensor station. "Three ships, bearing . . ." His voice trailed off.

Ar'alani frowned, shifting her attention from the tactical display to the sensor readouts. If those energy profiles were correct . . .

"Make that three derelicts," Wutroow corrected, a grim edge to her voice. "Don't really qualify as ships anymore."

"Confirmed," Biclian said. "Reading severe battle damage on all three."

Ar'alani nodded. "*Grayshrike*?" she called. "Anything over there?"

"Six more ships, Admiral," Senior Captain Lakinda's voice came over the bridge speaker. "Badly mauled, all of them. Looks like someone beat us to them."

"So it would seem," Ar'alani agreed.

Only who in the region had both the reason and the massive firepower necessary to take on this many Nikardun ships? *And* to win?

"Start a full sensor scan, Captain," she ordered Lakinda. "Full range, full depth. Get us on that, too, Biclian. Let's see if we can figure out what weapons were used on them."

"Spectrum lasers were definitely involved," Biclian said, manipulating his sensor controls. "But of course, everyone uses those. Looks like a fair number of missile strikes, too. We'll need a closer look if you want a blast profile."

"I do," Ar'alani said, nodding toward the helm. "Mid Commander Octrimo, take us in. Be ready to go to evasive if they're playing cute."

"Yes, ma'am," the pilot acknowledged.

Wutroow crossed to Ar'alani's command chair. "You really think the Nikardun have picked up some tactical sense at this late stage?" she asked.

"You mean, as in setting the derelicts out as bait for us?"

"Or for anyone else who might wander along," Wutroow said. "Or someone could be quietly hunkered down inside the listening post, hoping whoever comes along will see the wrecked ships, assume everyone's gone, and not take a closer look."

"If that's the plan, they're going to be disappointed," Ar'alani said. "We're definitely taking a closer look. I don't like the idea of someone with this much military power working this neighborhood without us knowing about them."

"As long as we don't spend too much time at it," Wutroow warned, pulling out her questis. "The Aristocra already think we're cleaning house way farther down the walkway than we ought to be."

Ar'alani felt her lips compress. Wutroow was right, of course. The *Vigilant*'s sole purpose out here was to eliminate any lingering Nikardun and Nikardun influence. If they did anything beyond that, she'd better be able to justify it to the Council and Syndicure. "Consider it a threat assessment," she said. "Until we know who did this, we won't have any idea what their motives are or what they might intend for the Ascendancy."

"No argument here, ma'am," Wutroow assured her, giving her questis a couple of taps and peering at the results. "But that kind of ignorance is considered fashionable in certain circles. Well, whoever was involved, they don't seem to be local. There aren't any planets nearby on Yiv's list of conquests and tributaries. No one who would have known about the Nikardun and had a reason to come after what was left of them."

"No one that we know of," Ar'alani corrected. "Lots of small one- and two-system nations out here that we've never made direct contact with. Though I'll grant that if Yiv hadn't already been threatening them, they would hardly be likely to go out of their way to take on one of his bases."

"My point exactly," Wutroow said, putting the questis away. "And Yiv *really* liked to talk about his conquests. Hard to believe he'd leave any of them off his brag list."

"Admiral?" Junior Commander Stybla'rsi'omli called from the *Vigilant*'s comm station. "Message coming through from Schesa; relay from Csilla and Supreme Admiral Ja'fosk."

"Thank you," Ar'alani said. Schesa was the closest Ascendancy world with a long-range triad transmitter, but even with that kind of power behind the signal the *Vigilant* was far enough that it was pushing the limit. "Send it here as soon as it's decrypted."

"Yes, ma'am."

"There've always been rumors that Ja'fosk could hear his officers' conversations through solid walls," Wutroow commented. "First I've heard that he could also hear us over multiple light-years of space."

"You'd be amazed at what they issue flag officers along with these," Ar'alani said drily, tapping the collar insignia pins on her white uniform.

"I'm sure I would," Wutroow said. "Ah," she added as the message appeared on the command chair personal display.

From: Supreme Admiral Ja'fosk, Csilla
To: *Springhawk, Vigilant, Grayshrike*

Senior Captain Mitth'raw'nuruodo and the *Springhawk* are to return to Csilla with all due speed for a new assignment.

"Interesting," Wutroow said as she read over Ar'alani's shoulder. "I wonder what the Syndicure wants with him now."

"The Syndicure?" Ar'alani asked, wincing a little. The fact that she and the *Grayshrike* had been copied on the message implied that Ja'fosk thought the *Springhawk* was still with the *Vigilant*'s task force.

Only, of course, he wasn't. Had Ba'kif forgotten to clue Ja'fosk in on Thrawn's unofficial side trip?

"Has to be," Wutroow said. "Ja'fosk or Ba'kif or anyone else on the Council would have added *once mission has been completed* or some such language. It's only the Aristocra who expect people to drop everything at the twitch of their collective finger. So *now* do I get to know where Ba'kif sent the *Springhawk*?"

"It's not a huge mystery," Ar'alani said. Though it *was*, of course, supposed to have been kept quiet. So much for that plan. "You'll remember that one of the Paccosh who met Thrawn and Caregiver Thalias on the Rapacc mining station gave him a ring for safekeeping. Thrawn's gone there to return it to him."

"Oh," Wutroow said.

Ar'alani raised her eyebrows. "You sound disappointed."

"Not *disappointed*, exactly," Wutroow said. "But the last time Thrawn went off-mission we got the Republic shield generator, and the time before *that* we identified Yiv and the Nikardun. I was hoping he was somewhere kicking up that level of excitement."

"Don't underestimate him," Ar'alani warned. "You'd be amazed what Thrawn can do with what looks like a straightforward assignment."

"I probably would," Wutroow agreed, half turning toward the navigation display. "Speaking of straightforward . . . ?"

"I know," Ar'alani said, scowling. If Thrawn was on his planned schedule, he was almost certainly out of range of the Schesa triad right now. He was also out of range of the *Vigilant*'s own ship-to-ship comm transmitter. If he lingered long enough at Rapacc to make the unofficial assessment of the Paccosh that Ba'kif had privately requested, it could be another week or more before he even knew he'd been summoned home.

And if it was indeed the Syndicure who'd put through the order, they would *not* be amused at being kept waiting.

Unfortunately, that left Ar'alani only one real option. Knowing exactly how this order would be perceived, she keyed for ship-to-ship comm. "*Grayshrike,* this is Admiral Ar'alani for Senior Captain Lakinda."

"I'm here, Admiral," Lakinda's voice came back.

"I assume you picked up Schesa's transmission?"

"Yes, ma'am," Lakinda said, the sudden caution in her tone showing she'd already guessed where this was going. "Do I assume Senior Captain Thrawn is out of comm range?"

"He is," Ar'alani confirmed. "And while there weren't any specific imperatives in the message, I have the feeling that Csilla wants the *Springhawk* back as soon as possible."

"Yes, ma'am." Lakinda's voice was steady, but Ar'alani could hear the unhappiness she'd expected floating beneath the surface. "May I offer the *Grayshrike*'s services to travel to his current location and deliver the message?"

"Yes, Senior Captain, thank you," Ar'alani said. "That would be most helpful."

"My one concern would be whether or not you and the *Vigilant* can carry out our assigned mission alone," Lakinda continued. "Notwithstanding this latest example, our previous encounters with Nikardun remnants would suggest that a single-ship incursion may be ill advised. It might be better if the *Grayshrike* first accompanied you to the final target."

"I appreciate the analysis and suggestion," Ar'alani said. "But Yiv's list indicates that the previous bases were far larger than these final two listening posts. I think the *Vigilant* can handle the last one alone."

"Understood," Lakinda said. Which didn't necessarily mean she agreed, of course. "I'll need the *Springhawk*'s current location."

Wutroow already had her questis in hand. "Senior Captain Wutroow is sending the coordinates now," Ar'alani said. "It's the Rapacc system, which should already be in your nav package for confirmation."

"Yes, ma'am." There was a short pause. "Coordinates acknowledged and confirmed. I'll get our sky-walker to the bridge, and we'll be off."

"Just make sure you've first pulled all the data you can on those derelict ships," Ar'alani said. "I want us to take back as complete a picture as possible."

"Yes, ma'am," Lakinda said again. "We already have most of it. I'll make sure we get the rest."

"Good," Ar'alani said. "Let me know before you leave."

"You realize," Wutroow said softly as Ar'alani keyed off the comm, "that there *is* one other possibility for the carnage out there we haven't considered. The rest of the Nikardun may have left all their unflyable ships here, riddled with lasers and missiles, in the hope that we would assume these last two posts had both been destroyed and wouldn't bother checking out the other one."

"While whatever forces they have left assemble there with the goal of making one last glorious assault somewhere?" Ar'alani suggested.

"Okay; so you *did* consider it," Wutroow said drily. "Apologies for my impudence."

"No apology needed," Ar'alani said. "Part of your job is to watch for anything I might have missed."

"I do my best, ma'am," Wutroow said. "I assume you have a strategy in mind should that turn out to be the situation?"

"Of course," Ar'alani said. "Inflict as much damage as we can, then run like a whisker cub and get help."

"Sounds good to me," Wutroow said. "And then, of course, *not* tell Lakinda that she was right about us going into the packbull's field alone?"

"On the contrary," Ar'alani said. "She and Thrawn will be the first ones I call in to help finish them off."

"Of course," Wutroow said, maintaining a straight face. "Ah. The confidence and absence of false pride that comes of already having achieved flag rank. Would that all officers saw things so clearly."

"Would that they did," Ar'alani agreed, giving Wutroow's straight face right back at her.

Which would never happen, of course. Family pressures and ambitions would forever be an entanglement to the officers and warriors of the fleet, despite the Council's best efforts to eliminate such influences.

Most of Ar'alani's colleagues condemned the politics. Ar'alani had found it more effective to simply accept the fact and factor it into her assessments and plans.

"Admiral?" Larsiom called from the comm station. "Senior Captain Lakinda reports the *Grayshrike* is ready to leave."

Ar'alani tapped the mike switch. "Safe travels, Captain Lakinda," she said. "We'll plan to rendezvous back here once we've returned from our individual tasks."

"Understood," Lakinda said. "Safe travels to you as well, Admiral, and successful combat." The comm keyed off. Ar'alani turned to look out the bridge viewport just as the *Grayshrike* disappeared into hyperspace.

"Orders, Admiral?" Wutroow asked.

"Finish scanning the derelict ships," Ar'alani said. "Then do a cursory sweep of the base itself."

"Just a cursory one, ma'am?"

"We'll save the full survey until after we've dealt with the final listening post," Ar'alani explained. "Hopefully, Lakinda and Thrawn will be back in time to join in the fun."

"Because cataloging is such fun," Wutroow said. "And after our cursory sweep?"

Ar'alani straightened her shoulders. "We end the Nikardun threat. Forever."

It was nearly the end of Samakro's watch when the *Springhawk*'s bridge hatch opened and Thalias came in.

Though really, in Samakro's critical opinion, it wasn't so much *came in* as it was *staggered in*. The young woman's eyes were half closed, her shoulders were sagging, and her general air was of someone who was dead on her feet.

"Good evening, Mid Captain Samakro," Thalias said as she made her way toward him. "I'm here to pick up Che'ri."

"I hope you don't mean that literally," Samakro said, looking her up and down. "You look barely able to pick up yourself."

"I'm okay," Thalias said, peering past his shoulder at the girl seated at the navigator's station. "It's been an hour since her last break?"

Samakro checked the log. "Just under," he said. "I was going to have Lieutenant Commander Azmordi bring her out in about five minutes."

"I'd like to wait a bit, if you don't mind," Thalias said, stopping beside him and consulting her chrono. "About fifteen more minutes."

"Why fifteen?"

"Because that's when she'll be at a lighter stage of Third Sight," Thalias said. "It'll be easier to bring her out then. It'll also leave her with less physical and mental stress."

Samakro frowned. He'd never heard about Third Sight stages before. Or any of the rest of it, for that matter. "So you're saying an hour and ten minutes is the optimal time?"

"Well, it is for Che'ri," Thalias said, closing her eyes and rubbing at her temples. "Not necessarily for anyone else. Third Sight stages roughly mirror a sky-walker's normal sleep cycle, and for Che'ri that's an hour ten."

"How do you know what her sleep cycle is?" Samakro asked. An unpleasant image flashed through his mind: Thalias sitting silently in the girl's room, watching her eyelids and taking notes on her questis.

Thalias gave him a wan smile. "Don't worry, I'm not staring at her while she sleeps. I had her wear a diagnostic patch for a few days, that's all. Her cycles are actually pretty consistent, which makes them easy to work with. I remember mine being all over the map when I was her age. Still are, really."

"Interesting," Samakro said, looking over at Che'ri. "Why haven't I ever heard of this before?"

"Probably because most caregivers and sky-walkers don't know about it, either," Thalias said. "I only figured it out after I lost Third Sight and left the program."

"And it really works?"

Thalias gestured toward Che'ri. "It's worked the last two times I tried the coordination. We'll find out in a few minutes if third time's the charm."

"So we will." Samakro eyed her. "You sure you want her to see you like this?"

Thalias gave him a patient look through her half-lidded eyes. "I'm not drunk, if that's what you're worried about. The Magys wanted to perform a religious ceremony to the Beyond before we arrive, and it requires at least two observers."

"Those observers being her companion and you?"

Thalias nodded. "I tried reminding her that I'm not of her people or their religion, but apparently all that matters in this one are the numbers." She considered. "The fact that she sees former sky-walkers as having touched the Beyond—whatever she means by that—may also have been a factor."

"Possibly the biggest." And since Thrawn had put her in charge of the aliens, she probably hadn't felt like she could refuse. "Do you understand this Beyond she talks about?"

"Not really," Thalias admitted. "But I suppose there are people who don't understand how sky-walkers can navigate the Chaos, either."

Samakro shrugged. "I know they can do it. Do I also have to understand *how*?"

Thalias smiled faintly. "I never understood how hyperdrives work, either. If that answers your question."

"More or less," Samakro said. "I rather like religions that have a visitors-welcome policy. You *did* run a bioclear scan first on whatever you drank, right?"

"Actually, there was no drinking involved," Thalias said. "Or incense, or vapor, or skin rubs. This"—she pointed at her eyes—"is from a sort of audiovisual kaleidoscope she used in the ceremony. Fascinating to watch, but it leaves you feeling like you were run over by a skytruck."

"It's usually a little hard to get run over by something that's flying."

"Agreed," Thalias said. "My statement stands."

"Interesting," Samakro said. "You should probably see about buying one of the gadgets. There are people in the Ascendancy who pay good money to feel that rotten."

"Yes, I knew a few of those back in school," Thalias said. "I'll see if I can work a deal with the Magys."

"Good luck," Samakro said. "I'm still trying to figure out why syncing Third Sight to the sleep cycle isn't part of standard procedure. We've been using sky-walkers for hundreds of years. Even if the caregivers missed the connection, *someone* must have noticed it. We Chiss are nothing if not good record keepers."

"I don't know," Thalias said, and Samakro saw her throat tighten briefly. "I suppose because it's easier to specify a standard ten-minutes-per-hour break, which for most sky-walkers is probably close enough, than to order the caregiver to take the time to calculate a more personal cycle."

"Because it's *easier*?" Samakro growled. "This is the Expansionary Defense Fleet, Caregiver. We don't do things just because they're *easier*. We do things because they *work*. The sky-walkers are the key to our entire mission statement. We need to protect that resource as much as we can."

Thalias gave a little snort. "You make it sound like she's just another plasma sphere launcher."

"So?" Samakro countered. "We're all resources here—you, me, the whole damn *Springhawk*. That's how you have to think in the military."

"Sorry," Thalias said with thinly veiled sarcasm. "I always assumed we were real, live, socially valuable people."

"I didn't say we weren't," Samakro said. "But captains who start to think of their officers and warriors that way will never be able to send anyone into danger. We have to numb that kind of compassion if we're going to do our jobs."

"Because otherwise you'll hurt every time one of them dies?"

Samakro looked away from her, all the ghosts from his past flickering across his memory. "We hurt anyway," he said quietly. "That's why we do our damnedest to make sure those lost lives are minimal, and that none of them are wasted."

Thalias shivered. "Just as well I'm not in your position. I don't think I could handle it."

"You're running close enough to it as it is," Samakro said. "No. I don't buy that the caregivers just don't want to put extra effort into their jobs. There has to be another reason."

"Like I said, they probably haven't noticed," Thalias said. "I don't know if you knew this, but I'm the first sky-walker in at least a hundred years who's gone on to become a caregiver. And as I said, it took me years to figure all this out. Someone who'd never been through the program wouldn't even think to look."

"Yes, I'd heard about that," Samakro said, feeling his eyes narrowing in thought. "Seems strange. I'd think you'd be the perfect candidates for the job."

"I've heard most sky-walkers don't really want to come back," Thalias said. "They leave the program exhausted, and don't want anything more to do with it."

"Maybe," Samakro said. "But remember what I said about *easier* a minute ago?"

"You can't force someone to do this job," Thalias said. "If they resent it, or don't want to do it, the sky-walker suffers. There are already enough caregivers in the program who just seem to be going through the motions."

"I suppose," Samakro said reluctantly. "It strikes me as something that ought to be looked into."

"I agree," Thalias said. "Good luck getting anyone to listen to you." She cocked her head a little. "May I ask you a question, Mid Captain?"

"Go ahead."

"What do you think of this mission?" she asked. "Because at the beginning I had the feeling you didn't approve."

"Whether or not I approve of a given decision is irrelevant," Samakro said. "Senior Captain Thrawn has given an order. It's my job to obey it."

"I know," Thalias said. "I'm just saying you seem to be . . . I don't know. Calmer right now, or at least less stiff." She offered a small smile. "This conversation, for one thing. I don't think you and I have ever had anything like it before. I was just wondering if that calmer attitude toward me means you're also calmer about the mission."

"Interesting leap of logic," Samakro said, thinking quickly, a small part of his mind noting the unusual combination of irony and opportunity that had just presented itself. "Fine. Since you ask . . . Senior Captain Thrawn and I did some checking on the location of the refugees' planet, and it turns out it's not all that far from the final group of Nikardun bases we've been clearing out. We're now wondering if what the Magys called a *civil war* was actually a massive attack by General Yiv."

"I thought he liked to conquer planets, not destroy them."

"Usually he did," Samakro said. "We're guessing his plan here was to wipe out the whole population, or reduce it far enough that he could move in his forces without leaving any possible resistance. We think that when we arrive we'll find the rest of the Nikardun survivors there, probably under the command of one or more of Yiv's warlords, gathering their forces for a renewed military campaign."

He stopped. Thalias's mouth, he noted, was hanging slightly open. "That's a . . . terrifying thought," she said.

"Isn't it?" Samakro agreed soberly. "Anyway, if our analysis is true, this will be our chance to finally make an end to the whole Nikardun threat."

"Which is what we're supposed to be doing out here anyway," Thalias said, her eyes narrowed in thought.

"Exactly," Samakro said. "One of those serendipitous things that always seem to fall across Thrawn's path." He gestured toward the nav station. "About time for Che'ri to come out of Third Sight, isn't it?"

Thalias seemed to shake herself. "Oh. Yes. Thank you." Nodding to him, she crossed to the nav station and leaned over Che'ri's shoulder. Samakro couldn't hear what she said to the girl, but there was a sudden half-seen movement. A moment later, Thalias stepped back, holding the girl's hand and helping her out of the chair.

"Welcome back," Samakro said as the two of them reached him. "How are you feeling?"

"I'm okay," Che'ri said, frowning a little. "I didn't really go any-where."

"It's a figure of speech," Samakro said. "I believe you and your caregiver are on for some food and rest now."

"Unless you need me," Che'ri offered. "Lieutenant Commander Azmordi told me we're only a few hours from where we're going."

Samakro flicked a glance at Thalias. She wasn't saying anything, but the look in her eye told him clearly that the correct answer was an emphatic *no*. "That's true," he said to Che'ri. "But you've already put in a full day's work, and you need rest as much as anybody else. We'll go jump-by-jump for a bit, and then you can bring us the rest of the way in. Okay?"

"Okay." Che'ri looked up at Thalias. "What are we going to eat?"

"That's a surprise," Thalias said, smiling at her. "But you'll like it—I promise. Good evening, Mid Captain."

"Good evening, Caregiver; Sky-walker."

They walked past him, Che'ri making some comment about how she'd know what was cooking before they even got through the hatch to their suite. Then they were gone, the bridge hatch closing behind them.

Samakro turned back. "Let's get back to hyperspace, Commander Azmordi," he ordered. "Best jump-by-jump you can do without wrapping us around a star or asteroid."

"Yes, sir," Azmordi said, flashing Samakro a smile before turning back to his board.

Samakro settled back in his chair, feeling a grim satisfaction. The story he'd spun for Thalias was a complete soap bubble, of course—there was no way Yiv would have set up in the middle of nowhere that way, especially not if he had to spend the resources to burn it to bedrock first.

But Thalias had originally come aboard the *Springhawk* as a spy. She'd never fully admitted it, and would probably deny it vehemently if she was asked. But Samakro had never had any doubts.

And now he'd given her a plausible-sounding story, with Thrawn's name attached. A story that, when it was proved false, would probably be used by Thrawn's enemies to chastise him for ridiculous knee-jerk thinking.

A story that could *only* have come from her.

The trap was laid. Thalias was a spy . . . and when the story surfaced in the Syndicure, he would finally be able to prove it.


Thurfian had just put the finishing touches on the latest agreement when, with perfect timing, Speaker Thyklo summoned him to her office.

"Syndic Prime," Thyklo greeted him gravely. "I wanted to know the status of your discussions with the Krovi."

"They're finished, Speaker," Thurfian said.

Thyklo's eyebrows went up. "Already?"

"Already," Thurfian confirmed. "We're going to supply them with enough transports for their projected harvest overage in return for one percent of that overage."

"Only one?" Thyklo asked, the eyebrows going back down. "I assumed you'd be able to do a bit better than that."

"I decided to accept current losses in return for future gains," Thurfian said. "This way we'll have their gratitude to tap into when it'll be most useful to us."

"Perhaps," Thyklo said. "Still, I've often found gratitude to be a currency that may or may not hold its value."

"In this case, I think it will," Thurfian said. "But that's really just the surface stratagem, the one everybody's supposed to see. More important to me is the fact that the Stybla are also helping the Krovi, and having our people there should give us some insights into the Stybla transport system. If we can learn how to match their efficiency, it will pay off immensely for us in the future."

"Interesting approach," Thyklo said thoughtfully. "Nicely layered, and definitely a valuable goal if you can pull it off." Her expression hardened. "Just make sure your spies aren't caught."

"They never are," Thurfian assured her.

"And make sure they don't push or prod or do anything else that could be seen as aggressive," the Speaker continued. "The Stybla may be mostly shippers and merchants now, but in the old days . . . well, you know."

"Yes, ma'am," Thurfian said, keeping the flicker of contempt out of his voice. Like everyone else in the Ascendancy, he knew the legends of the Stybla and their ancient fame and glory. In his opinion, a family that cared so little about power that they simply gave it away deserved every bit of the obscurity they got. "It will just be passive observation and information gathering. Nothing more blatant."

"Good," Thyklo said. "What about the Irizi? Weren't they also trying to work a deal with the Krovi?"

"They were," Thurfian said. "But I spoke with Syndic Zistalmu, and he's agreed to step aside and let us take this one."

"In return for . . . ?"

"In return, we're giving them free rein to work with the Boadil on their new Rentor defense platform."

"Which we didn't want to be bothered with anyway," Thyklo said nodding. "Very good, Syndic Prime. Adroitly done."

"Thank you, ma'am." Briefly, Thurfian wondered if the Speaker would be so complimentary if she knew Zistalmu's cooperation was largely a result of the fact that he and Thurfian were working together to take down Thrawn. Probably not. "Now that the Krovi discussions are out of the way, I'll be meeting with two of the Csap syndics this afternoon to discuss their proposed Dioya building project."

"Excellent," Thyklo said. She cocked her head slightly. "I have to say, Thurfian, that the Patriarch had some reservations about my elevating you to Syndic Prime. But you're well on the way to proving even to him that I made the right decision."

"You honor me, Speaker," Thurfian said. "I hope you'll never be disappointed in my work. I assume you'll have something else ready for me when I'm finished with the Csap?"

"Actually, I have one now, if you want to take it with you," Thyklo said, her voice sober as she tapped her questis and sent him a file.

"This one's an internal matter. Two of your fellow syndics are engaged in some kind of feud, and while it's still at a low level I want it stopped before it spills out into the Syndicure."

Thurfian nodded as he glanced at the first page. Unfortunately, internal squabbles were all too common among the Aristocra, and they could be more detrimental to a family than any of the more visible interfamily rivalries. "I'll deal with it, Speaker," he said.

"Privately, of course," Thyklo reminded him. "And now I'll let you get back to your work. Good day, Syndic Prime. Be sure to offer my greetings to the Csap."

A minute later, Thurfian was heading back down the corridor, his mind busy sorting out the rest of the day's tasks and priorities.

The Csap meeting would be first, easiest, and potentially the most valuable. A discussion of Dioya, where the presence of that Paccian refugee ship had first started the Ascendancy on its path to General Yiv, would be the perfect opportunity to remind them of Thrawn's risky adventurism. Whether or not the Csap agreed with Thurfian's subtle warnings, they would still leave the meeting with those thoughts lurking in the backs of their minds. After that he would call the two warring Mitth syndics to his office, find out what was going on, and hopefully find a way to smooth things over. When that was finished, he and Zistalmu were scheduled to hold another of their meetings in the March of Silence.

And after *that,* once he was finally back in the privacy of his own quarters, he would continue his study of Caregiver Thalias. She was to have been the key in his private duel with Thrawn, an asset who would remain totally invisible until he was ready to use her. The fact that she'd defied him once, and in fact had found a way to wriggle out from under his thumb, still rankled.

But she was still in place, she was still invisible, and there would still be opportunities to use her. And Thurfian had long since learned the value of patience.

His first attempt to use her had failed. His next attempt would not.

# CHAPTER SIX

The shifting patterns of hyperspace swirled outside the *Grayshrike*'s bridge, a hypnotic spectacle that never failed to amaze or intimidate first-time viewers.

Lakinda hardly noticed. With no shipboard duties currently vying for her attention, her full focus was on how Ar'alani's almost off-handed order was going to affect her life.

On the surface, of course, there would be no effect. Her admiral had detached one of her ship captains from the attack force in order to contact her other ship captain. All perfectly proper, reasonable, and necessary. No one on Csilla would blink twice over the order or Lakinda's obedience to it.

But that was on Csilla. On Cioral, stronghold of the Xodlak family, it would be a different story.

*Honor and glory to the family.* That was the Xodlak watchword these days. Not just a slogan, but the single most important goal for all who called themselves by the Xodlak name.

And Lakinda had now failed—twice in a row—to earn that glory.

She felt a knot in her stomach. The first blow had been at their last skirmish with the Nikardun, where untimely battle damage to the *Grayshrike*'s thrusters had robbed her of her part in the final cleanup operation. That had left the *Vigilant* and *Springhawk* to gather those last bits of glory. Now she'd been taken out of the final, climactic battle against the remnants of General Yiv's forces in order to play messenger.

To play *messenger*.

"Senior Captain?"

Lakinda shifted her eyes away from the hypnotic swirl. Her first officer, Mid Captain Csap'ro'strob, was standing beside her command chair, an uncertain expression on his face. "What is it?"

"I have the follow-up report on the thruster repairs, ma'am," Apros said, offering his questis. "Did you want to look at it now or wait until later?"

"Now is good," she said, taking the questis and skimming the report. The thrusters were still not up to full strength, but they were solidly functional. "They've made good progress," she continued. "Relay my compliments and have them keep at it."

"Yes, ma'am." Apros hesitated. "Ma'am?"

"Something else, Mid Captain?"

"I was wondering if you could enlighten me as to what the *Springhawk* is doing way over in the Rapacc system."

"I assume it's because of the Nikardun presence Thrawn reported after his first incursion there," Lakinda said. "Apparently, Rapacc is included in the region our force was tasked to clear out."

"That would be reasonable," Apros agreed, a slight frown creasing his forehead. "I'm mostly wondering why Ar'alani would send the *Springhawk* out there alone."

"Thrawn went toe-to-toe with them once before," Lakinda reminded him. "Even brought back one of their smaller warships for us to study."

"Which we all appreciated when we tangled with them over Primea," Apros said. "My point is that the *Vigilant*'s now about to go in alone against that final Nikardun listening post. This just seems . . . unwise."

"Perhaps," Lakinda said. "Or perhaps the admiral's decided that a single Chiss warship is enough to take on a group of desperate and badly organized Nikardun."

"That wasn't the case at that last base," Apros pointed out darkly. "It took all three of us there to finish them off."

"I suppose we'll just have to see," Lakinda said, keeping her voice neutral as she handed back the questis. "The *Springhawk* and *Vigilant* are excellent ships, with superb officers and warriors. Whatever Ar'alani and Thrawn run into, I'm sure they'll be able to handle it."

"I hope so." Apros offered a small smile. "It would be embarrassing to have beaten Yiv's main force at Primea only to get kicked in the teeth by his dregs."

"Never happen," Lakinda said firmly. "Carry on, Mid Captain."

Apros nodded and headed back to his station. Lakinda watched him go, the knot in her stomach tightening. *That wasn't the case at that last base,* he'd said. *It took all three of us there to finish them off.* That was how most of the officers and warriors in the task force probably saw it. It was almost certainly how Ar'alani's report would paint it.

Only it wasn't true.

Lakinda had run through the battle over and over again in her mind. She'd examined it from every angle, looked at every possibility, and had come to the unshakable conclusion that her heavy cruiser, all by itself, could have and would have defeated the enemy. It had been faster and easier with the *Vigilant* and *Springhawk,* true, but the fact remained that she and the *Grayshrike* could have done it alone.

But Ar'alani had never even considered that approach. Instead she'd taken in all three ships, and as a result the glory of the victory had been diffused and diminished. Worse, that single unlucky hit on the *Grayshrike*'s main thrusters had left her and the Xodlak family with even less than their proper third of the honor.

It wasn't due to any ulterior motives on Ar'alani's part. Of that Lakinda had no doubt. It was inconceivable that a flag officer would have deliberately skewed the battle results that way. Ar'alani had no family honor to satisfy, no family alliances to defend, no family ambitions to promote. She had nothing to gain by siphoning off Xodlak honor to herself.

Thrawn, though, was a different story.

Often, connections among Chiss families were obscure and tangled. Not here. In this case, the lines of influence and motive were painfully clear. Fifty years ago, when the Xodlak had been one of the Ten Ruling Families, their closest ally had been the Irizi family. After the Xodlak were demoted to merely one of the Forty, the Irizi had still stood by them, though of course not as closely as they did with the allies who were still among the Ruling Families.

But they were still on the side of the Xodlak . . . and the Irizi and Thrawn's Mitth family were bitter rivals. Anything Thrawn could do to keep the Xodlak down would also indirectly hurt the Irizi.

What made it more disturbing was the fact that Ar'alani and Thrawn had a long history together, going all the way back to the Taharim Academy.

It was unthinkable that a flag officer would show favoritism toward any one family or group of families. That was the whole idea behind stripping the higher ranks of their family connections. But the undeniable fact remained that Thrawn seemed to get all the assignments that were heavy with potential honor.

Unfortunately, there was no way to prove anything improper was going on. At least, not yet.

She checked the chrono. The *Grayshrike* wouldn't need to go all the way to Rapacc, of course, but only within range of the ship-to-ship comm. At their current speed, that would be another twenty to twenty-six hours.

She looked across at the navigational station, where the small hands and delicate fingers of their sky-walker, Bet'nih, were visible around the edge of the chair. A few years ago, on one of Lakinda's previous ships, the captain had been able to nudge a little more speed out of their sky-walker by giving her extra helpings of the treats that particular girl had loved. Maybe, at Bet'nih's next break, Lakinda would see if she was similarly open to such bribery.


Bet'nih, it turned out, was extremely partial to a particular type of dark cheese, a blend that Lakinda herself rather enjoyed. Unfortunately, Lakinda's promises of an extra bar from her private stockpile, while enthusiastically accepted, made no difference in the seven-year-old's navigational proficiency. Twenty-nine hours after leaving the *Vigilant*, twenty-three after the idea of a bribe had first occurred to Lakinda, the *Grayshrike* came out of hyperspace into the center of a magnificent array of cold-edged stars.

Like the hyperspace spectacle itself, Lakinda had long since ceased to notice any of that splendor.

"Signaling the *Springhawk* now, Captain," Apros called, peering over the comm officer's shoulder. "Strength at full; directionals two degrees off optimum."

"Acknowledged," Lakinda said, resisting the impulse to order them to clear those last two degrees. The comm's primary focal cone covered a solid 20 percent of the sky in that direction, putting Rapacc well within the tolerances.

Behind her, the hatch opened, and she turned to see Bet'nih's caregiver step onto the bridge. "Caregiver Soomret," she greeted the other woman. "I was about to call you. I believe Bet'nih's due for a meal and a sleep period."

"Yes, I was just coming to tell you that," Soomret said. "I do hate it when you military types forget about the needs of our sky-walkers."

"We appreciate that you're here to remind us," Lakinda said, making sure to filter the sarcasm out of her voice.

Which wasn't easy, given that Bet'nih's official schedule actually marked her break time as having started nearly half an hour ago. Granted, the girl had still been navigating the ship in Third Sight at that time; but if Soomret was really on top of things she should have arrived on the bridge then. That close to the end of a cycle she couldn't have ordered Lakinda to stop the ship, but she could at least have stood there giving everyone on the bridge the stink eye until they released Bet'nih into her care.

To Lakinda, that delay strongly suggested that Soomret was being just as casual about her duties as some previous caregivers aboard the *Grayshrike* had been over the years, and that her current vocal indignation was largely for Bet'nih's benefit. Probably designed to give the girl the comfortable impression that her caregiver was looking out for her more than Soomret's behavior actually indicated.

Which was also, unfortunately, the way Lakinda herself now had to play it. She'd been on ships where the sky-walker was anxious or overstressed or could see conflict between her caregiver and the ship's officers, and that never ended well. "Bet'nih?" she called, turning back toward the nav station.

The girl peeked anxiously around the back of the chair. Her eyes flicked to Soomret, then back to Lakinda. "Yes, Senior Captain?"

"Your caregiver's here," Lakinda told her. "Time for a meal and some rest."

"Okay," Bet'nih said. She unfastened her restraints and climbed out of the chair. For a moment she staggered, but the pilot, Wikivv, was ready and caught her arm in a steadying grip. "Sorry," the girl murmured, sounding embarrassed.

"It's all right," Wikivv soothed. Still holding the girl's arm, she popped her own restraints and stood up, and together they made their way over to Lakinda and Soomret. "Caregiver," Wikivv said. Her voice was steady, Lakinda noted, and as carefully nonjudgmental as Lakinda had herself tried to sound a moment ago.

"Thank you," Soomret said perfunctorily. Gesturing Wikivv back, she stepped forward and took Bet'nih's arm in her own grip. "Come along, Bet'nih."

"Are we going any farther today, Senior Captain?" Bet'nih asked as Soomret steered her toward the hatchway.

"No, we're done for now," Lakinda said. "Go get some food and relax."

"Yes, ma'am," Bet'nih said. She gave Lakinda a tentative smile, and then she and Soomret walked off the bridge together.

"I really don't think she cares much for her," Wikivv said, gazing back at the closed hatch.

"Soomret doesn't care for Bet'nih?" Lakinda asked. "Or the other way around?"

Wikivv gave a little snort. "In my experience, if it goes one way it usually goes both."

"So I've noticed," Lakinda conceded. "Nice catch, by the way. Does that happen often?"

"Temporary loss of balance?" Wikivv shrugged. "It's not uncommon. Particularly with the younger sky-walkers, those under the age of ten or eleven. They tend to get woozy if they spend more than five or six hours in a row in Third Sight." Her lip twitched. "That's not a criticism of you, Senior Captain," she added quickly. "That was also the case on my last two ships. I've often felt there's a serious disconnect between reality and the Council's manual."

"Wouldn't be the first time that's happened," Lakinda said. So five or six hours, a number that presumably included all the mandated breaks, left younger sky-walkers unsteady . . . yet official regulations permitted a sky-walker to run a full nine hours at a stretch under normal circumstances, and up to twelve in emergencies.

Six hours versus nine. A serious disconnect, indeed. Something Lakinda should take up with someone in Supreme Admiral Ja'fosk's office the next time she was on Csilla. "Keep an eye on her," she told Wikivv. "Make sure she doesn't get overloaded."

"Yes, ma'am." With a nod, Wikivv headed back to her seat.

Lakinda shifted her attention to the comm station. "Commander Shrent?" she prompted.

"No response, Captain," Shrent reported. "Multiple attempts, all standard frequencies and encryptions."

Lakinda gazed out at the stars, weighing the options. She'd assumed that Thrawn would still be at Rapacc when the *Grayshrike* got within comm range, but maybe that wasn't the case. If he'd finished up his errand faster than Ar'alani had assumed, he might already be on his way back to the Ascendancy or possibly heading to regroup with the *Vigilant*.

If he was going either place, then Lakinda's job was basically over. While the *Springhawk* was in hyperspace all communications were cut off, but once it was back in space-normal he would presumably get the Syndicure's message, either directly or from Ar'alani.

But that assumed he'd had clear directives for what to do after Rapacc and, more critically, that he'd actually followed those directives. If he'd gone off on some tangent instead, he could be anywhere. Without knowing when he'd left or where he was going, aiming a transmission and coordinating it with the *Springhawk*'s sky-walker's break schedule would be tricky.

"The *Springhawk* could just be in the comm shadow on the far side of the planet," Apros reminded her. "Unless Thrawn's in an unusually high orbit, it shouldn't be more than an hour before he's back in range."

Lakinda tapped gently at her lips. True enough. But she wasn't ready to just sit here doing nothing but sending transmissions into the Chaos for the next hour. "New signal, non-encrypted," she ordered, keying her mike. Thrawn's report on the Paccosh, she remembered, listed Taarja as one of their preferred trade languages. "Rapacc government, this is Senior Captain Lakinda aboard the Chiss Expansionary Defense Fleet warship *Grayshrike*," she said in Taarja. "I have a message for Senior Captain Thrawn. Is he currently with you and your people?"

She keyed off the mike. "Continuous transmission, both that message and the encrypted one to Thrawn," she ordered Shrent.

"Yes, ma'am."

"We don't know if the Paccosh even have long-distance communication," Apros pointed out as he stepped away from Shrent and rejoined her at her command chair. "We may have to go all the way to Rapacc if we want to talk to them."

"I know," Lakinda said. The only problem with that was the fact that for the next few hours their sky-walker was on break. Rapacc wasn't too far away, but if they had to get there via jump-by-jump it was going to take more hours than she wanted to spend.

Not to mention the problem that if she picked the wrong moment to enter hyperspace, she and Thrawn could easily run communications tag against each other.

But unless she got an answer from someone in the next half hour, she would just have to try it. "Commander Wikivv, run a course plot to Rapacc," she ordered. "Jump-by-jump, best time."

"Yes, ma'am," Wikivv said, busying herself with her board.

"For the record," Apros said quietly, "and given that the message for Thrawn likely came from the Syndicure, you could legitimately invoke emergency regulations to get Bet'nih back before her sleep time is over."

"I'll take that under advisement," Lakinda said. "We'll give Thrawn half an hour to respond, then head for Rapacc."

"Captain, we've got a signal from Rapacc," Shrent called. He keyed his board—

"Greetings, Senior Captain Lakinda." The accented voice came from the bridge speaker, the alien's Taarja noticeably better than Lakinda's. "I am Uingali foar Marocsaa, with the honor of speaking for the Paccian Governance. How may the Paccosh serve you?"

Lakinda exhaled a silent breath as she keyed her mike. Finally. "Greetings, Uingali foar Marocsaa," she replied. "As my message stated, I'm trying to communicate with Senior Captain Thrawn. Is he still with you?"

"Not at the current time," Uingali said. "He and his ship are returning the leader of a refugee group to her world, there to discover whether their civil war has left any of their species still alive."

"He's doing *what*?" Apros muttered under his breath.

Lakinda threw him a glance. "Uingali foar Marocsaa, I don't understand. Senior Captain Thrawn had no orders to travel anywhere except the Rapacc system."

"It is a humanitarian gesture," Uingali said. "If their world is lost, the Magys is determined that she and all the refugees under her authority shall give up their lives."

"Why?" Lakinda asked.

"I am not certain," Uingali said. "The reasons are largely unclear to me. Senior Captain Thrawn hopes to ease their minds and thus spare their lives."

"I see," Lakinda said, frowning. She hadn't heard of any civil wars out this way, at least among the various nations the Ascendancy got sporadic information from. Something new? "Who are these people? What do they call themselves?"

"We do not know."

"What do they name their world?"

"We do not know."

Lakinda keyed off her mike and looked up at Apros. "Comments?"

"Awfully convenient, not giving us anything we can look up," he said, his eyes narrowed in suspicion. "You suppose they caught the *Springhawk* unprepared and captured or destroyed it?"

"With Thrawn in command?" Lakinda shook her head. "Not likely. If they'd tried, I doubt there'd be much left of their authority structure still able to talk to us." She keyed her mike back on. "Do you have the coordinates for the refugees' system? And when exactly did Senior Captain Thrawn depart?"

"He left approximately seven hours ago," Uingali said. "I'm sending you the coordinates the Magys gave us, plus recordings of the interactions between Senior Captain Thrawn and the refugees, as well as some of the interactions between the senior captain's people and mine."

Lakinda looked over at Shrent, got a nodded confirmation that a transmission was coming through. She pointed at Wikivv's helm board, got another nod. "Did he say how long he'd be staying there?" she asked Uingali.

"If he made such a decision, it was not shared with me," Uingali said. "But I believe he was motivated by a desire to prove the planet inhabitable, and the refugees thus worthy of continued life. I do not know how long such proofs would require."

Unfortunately, neither did Lakinda. A cursory flyby could be done in hours; a more detailed ground examination could take weeks. "Understood," she said. "One moment." She keyed off again. "Commander Wikivv?"

"Got it, ma'am," Wikivv said, peering closely at her displays. "There's definitely a star at those coordinates. We don't have a data list for it, so I don't know if it has any habitable planets. But the star's spectrum is compatible with standard life-form parameters."

"How far away is it?"

"For Thrawn, coming from Rapacc, approximately sixty-three hours via jump-by-jump," Wikivv said. "Fifteen by sky-walker." She made another adjustment. "Actually, we're currently quite a bit closer than he is—the system's back toward the Nikardun bases we've been clearing out."

Lakinda checked the nav display, where Wikivv had now marked the target system. She was right; it was back toward the area where they'd left the *Vigilant*, though north and a little bit zenith of that position.

"For us, approximately forty-two hours via jump-by-jump," Wikivv continued. She half turned toward Lakinda, her expression wooden. "Ten hours via sky-walker."

"Understood," Lakinda said. In other words, if she hauled Bet'nih out of her rest time, the *Grayshrike* could get to the target system barely two hours behind the *Springhawk*. That would all but guarantee she could rendezvous with Thrawn and deliver her message without the two ships playing blindman's tag all over the Chaos.

But in her mind's eye she could see how tired and stressed Bet'nih had looked as she left the bridge.

She keyed the mike. "What password did Senior Captain Thrawn give you to confirm you were speaking for him?"

"A *password*?" Uingali echoed, his smooth speech pattern faltering. "I was given no password. Unless he spoke one and I did not recognize its true meaning. I have sent you the recordings—perhaps you will find it in there."

"Perhaps," Lakinda said. "Very well. We'll seek him at the refugees' location. If he returns prematurely, please inform him we're looking for him. Even better, give him the recording you're certainly making of this conversation."

"I will do both," Uingali promised. "A safe and profitable voyage to you, Senior Captain Lakinda."

"Thank you. *Grayshrike* out."

Lakinda keyed off the mike. "Helm, get us moving. Jump-by-jump, best speed."

"Yes, ma'am," Wikivv said, and busied herself with her board.

"Depending on how thorough Thrawn decides to be," Apros said, "a jump-by-jump may well get us there after he's already left. Again, I remind the captain that emergency regulations likely apply here."

"One: Thrawn's not going to run his sky-walker all sixteen of those hours," Lakinda said. "Not for something like this. He'll give her time to rest, which means he won't be getting there ahead of Wikivv's projected schedule."

"Even if it means he arrives very late back at the *Vigilant* to complete the Council's mandated task?"

"Thrawn's extremely good at arguing from points of weakness and even marginal insubordination," Lakinda said sourly. Especially when it resulted in better standing for his family and worse standing for everyone else. "Two: You saw how tired Bet'nih is. We'll start jump-by-jump and bring her in after she's had her full rest period."

"Understood," Apros said. He was still unhappy with the decision, Lakinda could tell, especially since there were members of the Aristocra who would have no qualms at all about slapping the *Grayshrike*'s own delays onto its captain's and senior officers' shoulders.

But he knew better than to keep pushing once Lakinda's mind was made up. "May I ask what that bit was about a password?" he asked. "I didn't know we *had* passwords for situations like this."

"As far as I know, we don't," Lakinda agreed. "I threw that in mostly to see how he would react to the question."

"Did he pass the test?"

"I'm not sure I know," Lakinda admitted. "He's alien, and I don't know any of his verbal parameters."

She checked her chrono. Her bridge watch had been over for half an hour. "I'll be in my quarters if you need me," she said, standing up. "Make sure Junior Captain Ovinon is fully apprised of the situation when you turn the watch over to him. I'll want him to switch over from jump-by-jump as soon as Bet'nih's ready to return to duty."

"Yes, ma'am," Apros said. "Sleep well, Captain."

She would sleep, all right, Lakinda thought as she left the bridge and headed down the corridor. But how fast she got there, and how deep that sleep turned out to be, would depend largely on whether or not she could figure out how exactly Thrawn intended to use all this to his advantage.

And just where and how badly his family's success would hurt her own.

The wind whistled across Thurfian's face and hair, rustling the knee-high grass he and his Evroes guide were standing in and sending a mist of loose soil off the edge of the cliff two meters in front of them. "There," Evroes'pu'titor said, staying well back from the edge as he pointed past the winding river below toward the section of young forest to their right. "That's the area of dispute."

"Yes, I see it," Thurfian said, feeling a very unstatesmanlike amusement at Oesputi's obvious discomfort. The other had mentioned at least twice that the disputed region could be seen more efficiently from the air than from the edge of the low mountain they were currently standing on. But Thurfian had wanted to see things from the Xodlak side of the issue, so here they were.

And now, with the breeze and the subtle odors of the farm, forest, and river swirling around him, one conclusion rose uppermost in his mind.

He *really* needed to get out of his underground Csilla office more often.

"You can see the problem," Oesputi continued. "The seeds from the forest below us were blown across the river to our farmland, where they started a new forest."

"All of which began, what, twenty years ago?" Thurfian asked.

"Closer to thirty," Oesputi conceded. "At first, you see, the trees were sparse and not a concern to the farmers. Then, as they grew, they provided homes for the blinkbirds that controlled the fields' vermin population. But now you can see what it's like."

"Yes," Thurfian said, his earlier amusement fading back into the underlying seriousness of the situation. The forest canopy had grown too thick for ground crops to thrive beneath it, and as the forest slowly spread outward, more and more arable ground was being lost. "And you can't just cut down the trees?"

"The Xodlak forbid it," Oesputi said with a sigh. "They claim the trees are a specific hybrid they own title to, and that no one can harvest them without permission."

And of course, the license the local Xodlak Patriel was offering the farmers was expensive enough to suck all the profit out of any logging they might do. Typical Xodlak self-centered worldview. "What exactly do you want me to do?" he asked.

"To be honest, I'm not sure there's anything you *can* do," Oesputi admitted. "The Xodlak are of the Forty Great Families. The Evroes are . . ." He sighed again. "Of nothing."

"You're a family and a people of the Chiss Ascendancy," Thurfian said firmly. "As such, you're owed justice."

Justice that should have come via the Irizi, Thurfian added sourly to himself. The Xodlak were *their* allies, and they should have been the ones to step in and handle this negotiation.

But the Irizi were apparently too preoccupied with yet another attempt to court the Chaf family into a full alliance to be bothered with anything this small and petty.

He frowned, leaning a little closer to the edge. Were those purple flowers he was glimpsing through the trees of the main forest?

"Careful," Oesputi said nervously. "These cliffs can be treacherous."

"I'm all right," Thurfian said, shifting his gaze back across the river to the Evroes farmland. Those fields were dotted with the same purple, all right. "Tell me, Oesputi, do the winds here shift direction during the year?"

"Yes, quite dramatically, in fact," Oesputi said. "In winter they come from the south, while in summer they come from the north."

"So winter is when the Xodlak seeds ride the winds across the river to your land." Thurfian pointed downward. "And summer, then, is when your seeds go the other direction."

Carefully, Oesputi eased a few centimeters forward. "Why, yes," he said, sounding puzzled. "I never noticed that before." He took a long step back. "But as I've already said, the grain down there will be of poor quality."

"I'm not concerned about the quality," Thurfian said. "I'm pointing out that your crops are on Xodlak land." He smiled tightly. "And if you can't harvest or damage their trees without permission, neither can they harvest or damage your crops."

"But they aren't harvesting any of—"

"*Or damage them*," Thurfian interrupted, leaning on the words.

For a long minute Oesputi stared at the forest. Thurfian waited, again savoring the feel of the wind in his hair. "But our crops aren't a protected hybrid," the other said at last.

"Doesn't matter," Thurfian said. "The point is that both families have a claim against the other. More to the point is that the Xodlak have a lot more to lose from any cross-compensation decision that might be rendered. That threat alone should be enough to bring them to negotiation."

"Oh, my," Oesputi breathed, looking at Thurfian with an expression that was disturbingly close to adulation. "Syndic Thurfian, if you could give us even that much hope, the Evroes will forever be in your debt."

"I think I can give you more than just hope," Thurfian said, taking his arm and leading him away from the cliff edge and back toward their skycar. "Let's head back to your hearing chamber and give the Xodlak Patriel a call. I think there's a good chance we can get this resolved by dinnertime."

For once, Thurfian was wrong. It actually took them until nearly midnight.

# CHAPTER SEVEN

It was the final Nikardun base, the last one listed in General Yiv's records in this part of space. As such, Ar'alani had anticipated a major battle against whatever desperate, hopeless enemy forces might have hitherto escaped the overall sweep of Chiss vengeance. Nothing a Nightdragon man-of-war couldn't handle.

That was what she expected. What she got was silence, emptiness, and more debris.

A *lot* more debris.

"Looks like our mysterious friends with the sledgehammers got here first," Wutroow commented as she and Ar'alani stood gazing out at the twisted shards of metal and ceramic floating across the starscape. Most of the wreckage was dark or dulled, but there were occasional small glints as something turned enough to catch the light from the distant sun.

"So it would seem," Ar'alani agreed, frowning at the rubble. Something about the whole scene seemed odd. Odd, and wrong.

"That base," Wutroow said, pointing toward the twisted and broken metal shell drifting in the midst of the field. "Does it look too big to you?"

"Too big for a listening post, you mean?" Ar'alani eyed the shell. "Probably. But Yiv's records didn't specifically identify this base as such. We just assumed that because that's what all the rest of his group were."

"I know," Wutroow said. "And that bothers me, too. All the rest of the bases were marked as to size and purpose: listening post, scout re-fueling depot, sector coordination base—whatever. Why not this one?"

"Good point," Ar'alani said. Wutroow was right. But there was something else out there . . .

Abruptly, she had it. "Biclian: that clump about thirty degrees star-board, ten nadir," she called toward the sensor station. "The one that looks almost spherical. Scan that and tell me what it is."

"Yes, ma'am," Biclian said, his hands moving across his control board.

"Looks like ordinary battle debris to me," Wutroow said, craning her neck to check the main sensor display.

"Probably," Ar'alani said. "But it seems to be clumped too close together."

"Good point," Wutroow said, her voice suddenly thoughtful. "A normal explosion should have sent the pieces way farther apart. And you're right about the array being too spherical. Not a missile, then. A spectrum laser barrage?"

"I don't think so," Ar'alani said. "It's too clean, somehow."

"It's also too rocky," Biclian put in. "It's not refined metal, ceramic, or plastic, Admiral, but solid rock. Spectral analysis suggests it's the remnants of an asteroid."

Ar'alani and Wutroow looked at each other. "So our mysterious attackers are taking potshots at *asteroids* now?" Wutroow asked.

"Or something else is going on," Ar'alani said grimly, a strange thought starting to form in the back of her mind . . . "Octrimo, take us over there," she instructed the pilot. "Slow and easy—I don't want to disrupt the debris field any more than we have to. Biclian, does our asteroid clump have any overall vector?"

"Yes, Admiral, it does," Biclian said. "Backtracking it now."

"Good." The asteroid's path would likely have been distorted by the battle that had taken place around it, Ar'alani knew, but a back-track might still be useful. "Specifically—no," she interrupted herself.

"Admiral?" Biclian asked, frowning at her.

"I was going to offer a thought, but I don't want to influence your analysis," Ar'alani said. "Carry on."

"Yes, ma'am." Biclian turned back to his board.

"If you can't tell him, can you at least tell *me*?" Wutroow asked.

"I *especially* can't tell you," Ar'alani said, giving her a wry smile. "Your brain is the one I rely on to make sure mine is functioning properly."

"Ah." Wutroow gave Ar'alani a sideways look. "Always something of a disappointment when you open up a compliment and find a *no* wrapped inside."

"Patience is a virtue," Ar'alani reminded her.

"So I've heard. Not a big fan of it, myself."

For a few minutes the bridge was silent as Octrimo delicately maneuvered the massive warship through the debris toward the odd cluster of rock. Ar'alani found herself gazing at the remains of the Nikardun base, studying the damage with particular focus on the large gaps where heavy missiles had gotten through the defenses. That big one had probably been the first impact, she decided, shifting her attention back and forth between the wreckage and the analysis data scrolling across the secondary sensor display. The edges of the jagged hole had some odd coloration to them, the scan had noted, which the analysts were still working to identify.

"Got it, Admiral," Biclian spoke up. "Asteroid backtrack on the tactical."

Ar'alani looked at the display. The plot was fuzzy, reflecting the inherent uncertainties of tracking something that had been drifting through multiple volleys of missiles and laserfire.

"And here," the sensor officer added, his voice going darker as the new data overlaid the plot, "is where I estimate it was when the pieces first came apart."

Wutroow muttered something under her breath. "I will be—" She shot a look at Ar'alani. "How did you know?"

"I didn't," Ar'alani said, her stomach tightening. If Biclian's track was accurate, the asteroid had broken apart directly in front of the gap in the station she'd identified as the point of first impact. "I just wondered why anyone would waste a missile on an asteroid."

"Because no one did," Wutroow said darkly.

Ar'alani nodded, mentally re-creating the scenario. A harmless-looking asteroid, drifting through the Nikardun station's defense perimeter . . . reaching its closest approach to the base . . . the outer shell shattering to reveal the missile launcher concealed inside it . . . a single massive missile, blasting through the base's hull before the Nikardun had any hope of reacting . . . the rest of the attackers then blazing in through the confusion to wreak havoc on the stunned and disorganized defenders.

"They would have had to set that up well in advance," Wutroow continued, clearly thinking aloud. "Start the asteroid from far enough out that the Nikardun didn't spot it."

"And have it moving leisurely enough that it didn't look out of place," Ar'alani agreed. "We're talking months of prep time to make it work."

"Before Yiv's little empire even collapsed?" Wutroow asked doubtfully. "Who knew back then what was going to happen to him?"

"I don't know," Ar'alani said. "Maybe it wasn't anything to do with Yiv. Maybe someone just didn't want anyone else setting up shop in this part of space."

Wutroow made a sound in her throat. "That sounds ominous."

"I know."

"Admiral?" Biclian said. "We have an analysis of the blast hole edge discoloration now. It's a chemical reaction to unusually high amounts of flash-burned missile fuel."

"Consistent with a missile fired at point-blank range," Wutroow said, nodding. "Most of the time they get to burn off more of their fuel before they reach their target. This one's tanks burst open and were fried the same time the warhead went off."

"Yes." Ar'alani took a deep breath. "I want full sensor and tactical readings on everything here," she ordered, raising her voice to carry across the entire bridge. "Deploy a squad to check out the base, see if there's anything useful in there, and send a shuttle to examine the asteroid fragments. Full sensor scan there, too, and collect a few pieces to take back to Csilla."

She looked at Wutroow. "After that, we'll head back to that last

Nikardun base, the one our friends here also got to first, and do a full analysis of that one. If we're lucky, between the two of them we'll find a clue as to who exactly is trying to move into this neighborhood."

Thalias hadn't thought very much of her first time down in the secondary command room. She'd hoped her second time would be better.

Unfortunately, that wasn't looking likely.

But there was no choice. Thrawn wanted the Magys on the bridge in case he had any questions about what they found, or needed to talk to someone on the ground. He also needed Che'ri and her Third Sight to bring the ship in across the last few light-years and to be ready to get them out quickly if the need arose, which meant the girl needed to be at a control console.

Technically, of course, *only* Che'ri had to be down here. But there was no way Thalias was going to abandon the girl at such a critical moment, especially among a group of officers neither of them knew very well.

As Thalias had noted the first time she was here, the room's designers had apparently never thought a caregiver might join the skywalker and therefore hadn't included a dedicated chair for her near the nav station. At that first visit, Thalias had simply stood behind Che'ri, squeezing herself into the narrow space behind the girl. This time, though, Senior Commander Kharill was in charge, and he insisted that everyone be properly seated and strapped in.

Thalias was fully prepared to fight that ruling if she had to. Fortunately, it didn't come to that. Kharill didn't argue against her presence, but instead found a way to shuffle the sensor officer elsewhere so that Thalias could have the seat next to Che'ri.

Though from the scowl on Kharill's face, she guessed that the repositioning and accommodation hadn't been his idea.

Almost there. Thalias looked closely at Che'ri's face, expressionless while at the same time with an underlying concentration as her Third Sight guided the *Springhawk* through the final minutes of the flight. The space between Rapacc and the Magys's world was more tangled than usual, even for the Chaos, which had put an additional strain on Che'ri. Thalias could only watch the girl struggling with her task and hope that this side trip would be worth it.

"Your strap's twisted."

She looked up. Laknym, the plasma sphere specialist she'd met the last time she and Che'ri were down here, had unstrapped and was maneuvering into the narrow space between the helm and his own seat at the weapons station. "What?" she asked.

"I said your strap's twisted," he repeated as he sidled behind Che'ri to Thalias's side. "Pop the catch and I'll fix it."

Thalias craned her neck, trying to look over her shoulder. Sure enough, there was an extra half turn in the strap. "Thanks," she said, releasing the tension on the restraints.

"It's easy to do," Laknym said, giving the strap a half turn and handing the end back to her. "Not as much room for the anchors down here, so the restraints are done a little differently than those on the bridge."

"Hopefully we won't need them," Thalias said. "You're on official duty here now? I thought the last time was just a one-shot."

"So did I," Laknym said, giving Che'ri's restraints a quick look and nodding in satisfaction. "As you may have noticed, sometimes Senior Captain Thrawn throws people into new positions or situations just to see how they react. For whatever reason, I guess he or Mid Captain Samakro liked what they saw the last time he put me down here."

"Unless this is another one-time thing."

"It could be that, too," Laknym conceded. "Either way, it's a promising sign. Especially for someone of my rank."

Thalias winced. Officially, *lieutenant commander* was a sort of probationary rank, sandwiched between lieutenant and junior commander and given to officers who showed promise of someday being deemed capable of moving up the higher command structure.

But unofficially, at least from what Thalias had been able to piece together from bits of overheard conversation, it had also become a convenient place to dump officers from the Nine Ruling Families or the Forty Great Families whom the Council had already concluded would never rise any higher. It was supposed to be a sop to those individuals, a grand-sounding label to keep the more powerful Chiss families from taking offense that their beloved blood and cousins and ranking distants hadn't been as good as they'd all hoped.

Of course, since the whole thing had become pretty much an open secret, it hardly qualified as a subterfuge anymore. But the continued willingness of all parties to play along kept the game going.

Laknym, as a member of one of the Forty, was already poised to be in the second category. Whether he broke out of that and joined the first was something only time would tell.

"Prepare for breakout," Thrawn's voice came over the speaker from the bridge.

"That's you," Laknym said as he again squeezed past Che'ri and took his own seat. "Is she ready?"

"Yes," Thalias said, studying the bridge monitor display. The Magys, she noted, was standing beside Thrawn's command chair, with her companion a half step farther back. On Thrawn's other side stood Mid Captain Samakro, his hands clasped behind him. To the rear of the whole group were two watchful guards, holstered charrics at their sides. "It's really no different for her being down here than it would be on the bridge," she added to Laknym.

"Civilians will be quiet," Kharill growled from his seat behind the helm station. "And officers will not engage in idle conversation. Everyone stay sharp—we don't know what we're heading into."

Thalias hunched her shoulders once, working out a bit of her tension. Whatever they found, she reminded herself firmly, Thrawn could handle it. The hyperspace swirl became star-flares became stars—

A *lot* of stars, she saw, emblazoned all across the exterior displays. Stars, and absolutely nothing else.

Flying blind into an unknown system, Thalias knew, was likely to put a ship into the middle of nowhere. Apparently, that was exactly where they'd landed.

"Scan for planetary bodies and space vehicles," Thrawn ordered. "We are in your system, Magys," he continued, switching to Taarja. "As soon as we locate your world, we will learn its condition. What is its name, if I may ask?"

"We do not share that with outsiders," the Magys said stiffly.

"Ah," Thrawn said. "Well, then, for our convenience, we'll name it Sunrise."

The Magys's tongues darted out. "You mock our destruction?"

"Not at all," Thrawn said. "I choose to nurture hope."

"There is no hope."

"We will know soon enough," Thrawn said. "Until then, I will hold to hope."

Belatedly, Thalias noticed that Che'ri was breathing a little heavily. "You okay?" she whispered, reaching over and touching the girl's arm.

"Yes," Che'ri said. "That was a little . . . weird."

"In what way?" Thalias asked.

"Just . . . I don't know," Che'ri said, flexing her fingers. "It seemed harder than the charts showed."

"Well, that's the Chaos for you," Thalias said. Thrawn had suspected this region would be trickier than the projections had suggested, she knew, which was why he'd wanted Che'ri to do the last leg instead of going jump-by-jump. "It'll be easier on the way out—no time pressure," she added. "Are you thirsty?"

"A little," Che'ri said, looking uncertainly around the room. "Are you allowed to leave?"

"Don't need to," Thalias said, producing a grillig-juice packet from her pocket.

"Thank you," Che'ri said, some of the tension fading into a tentative smile as she took the packet.

"You're welcome," Thalias said. "I have two more if you want them."

"Just don't spill it on the control board," Laknym warned.

Che'ri rolled her eyes. Turning toward Laknym, she flipped out the packet's sipper with exaggerated care. Laknym gave her an exaggerated pretend glower in return, changed it into a smile, then turned back to his board.

"Got it, sir," Dalvu announced from the bridge sensor station. "Planetary coordinates sent."

"Very good," Thrawn said. "Lieutenant Commander Azmordi: In-system jump. Bring us in over the equator and forty thousand kilometers out."

"Yes, sir."

"Those in-system jumps always seem tricky," Thalias said to Che'ri. "Did Senior Captain Thrawn show you how to do those when you were out in Lesser Space?"

"I did a couple," Che'ri said. "They're really hard to get right. On one of them I overshot and got us way too far from the planet he wanted to look at. The other one was okay. But we mostly just did long-range scans." She scrunched up her nose. "Most of the places we went didn't have much to look at, anyway."

The forward visual display made an odd sort of twitch, and suddenly there was a planet centered in it. "Wow," Che'ri said under her breath. "He's good."

"Years of practice, I imagine," Thalias said, eyeing the distant image. Most of the habitable planets she'd seen presented a similar mixture of white clouds and mountain peaks, blue waters, brown or gray or red deserts, and mixtures of vegetation that usually ranged from dark red to vivid violet.

The planet in front of them was different. There were still decent-sized areas of white and blue, and a few ribbons with blended shades of blue-green.

But there were also patches of black. *Big* patches. Patches that dotted the entire sunlit side.

The Magys had been right. Her world had suffered a devastating, horrendous war.

The sensor officer a couple of stations down from Laknym muttered something shocked sounding. "What did she say?" Thalias asked him softly.

"Pattern bombing," Laknym said, his voice grim. "You can see a lot of the black spots are along the larger rivers. Rivers are where most people build their cities."

Thalias nodded, the taste of stomach acid in her mouth. So the damage hadn't just been a warning, or a single reprisal against a single attack. The two sides of the civil war had each been hell-bent on wiping out the other.

"We've prepared a remote drone shuttle, Magys, with sensing and recording gear," Thrawn said. "We'll move closer, then launch it toward the surface for low-altitude studies."

"There is no need," the Magys said, her voice dull. "It is as I said. You can see the evidence. Our world is no more. Our people are no more."

"There is still a great deal of vegetation," Thrawn pointed out. "Where plant life remains, there is hope for the entire ecosystem."

"All the more reason for us to touch the Beyond and strive for that healing," the Magys said.

"But is not your first allegiance to your own people?" Thrawn countered. "If there are others alive, struggling and trying to rebuild, should you not add your group's strength and numbers to aid them?"

"Our people are no more."

"We have not yet proven that."

"Our people are no more." The Magys waved a hand at the viewport. "All can see that clearly."

"We can see nothing clearly from this distance," Thrawn insisted. "You must give us time to investigate. Thalias would want you to do that."

"Yet she who has touched the Beyond is not here."

"She has duties elsewhere," Thrawn said.

Thalias winced. The proverbial unstoppable and immovable objects.

"Do you need to go talk to her?" Che'ri asked hesitantly. "I'll be okay here."

Thalias hesitated. Would her presence or her words really make a difference?

They might, she conceded. She should at least try. "I'll be right back," she whispered to Che'ri. Wondering what Kharill was going to say if she left, she got a grip on her restraints' release—

"Captain, we have incoming," Dalvu cut in. "Five ships, gunboat size, coming around portside planetary disk."

"Never mind," Thalias said, letting go of the release and reaching over for a quick reassuring squeeze of Che'ri's arm. "I'm staying here."

"Secondary command status?" Samakro called, looking at the bridge cam.

"Sensors?" Kharill prompted.

"Sensor repeaters confirm ready," the secondary command room sensor officer a few stations down from Thalias said. "Pulling in both bridge and secondary feeds."

"Weapons systems confirm ready," Laknym added. "Repeater controls online."

"Bridge: Secondary command is ready," Kharill reported.

"Very good," Samakro said. "Stand by."

"Barriers," Thrawn ordered. Thalias looked over at Laknym's board, saw the indicators for the *Springhawk*'s electrostatic barriers go active.

"What are these ships?" the Magys asked.

"That is what we intend to learn," Thrawn said. "Enhance image. Are these ships from your people?"

"I do not recognize them," the Magys said. The words sounded mechanical, Thalias noted, as if neither the ships nor anything else mattered anymore. "Perhaps these are the people who have now come to take our lost world to themselves."

"Perhaps," Thrawn said. "Let us find out." On the monitor, Thalias saw him key the mike control on his command chair. "Unidentified ships, this is Senior Captain Thrawn aboard the Chiss Expansionary Defense Fleet warship *Springhawk*," he called in Taarja. "Please identify yourselves."

There was no response. The five ships angled toward the *Springhawk*, shifting into a circular formation. "Well, well," Laknym muttered.

"What?" Thalias asked.

"Civilians will be *quiet*," Kharill bit out before Laknym could answer.

"What?" Thalias asked again, lowering her voice this time.

"That's a rosette pattern," Laknym murmured back. "Usually an attack formation."

Thalias felt her stomach tighten. "Is that going to be a problem?"

"Not really," he said. "Five gunboats are a decent enough battle force, but not against a heavy cruiser like the *Springhawk*."

"More incoming," Dalvu spoke up. "Two more groups of five, from portside planetary disk."

Thalias felt her throat tighten. "Lieutenant Commander Laknym?" she whispered.

Laknym took a deep breath. "Yes," he said quietly. "Fifteen gunboats is definitely a problem."

# CHAPTER EIGHT

Thalias looked at the tactical display, her throat tightening even more. All fifteen gunboats had come from the same direction, she noted. Had they all been having a meeting somewhere on the other side of the planet?

Or could there be something else lurking back there, hidden from the *Springhawk*'s view? An orbital defense platform, maybe, or even a bigger warship?

On the bridge display, Samakro stepped to Thrawn's side. "They don't look very friendly," he commented.

"Perhaps they're just being cautious," Thrawn said. "Is the drone shuttle ready?"

"Ready, sir," Kharill called back.

Thalias nodded to herself as she got the answer to a small puzzle. She'd noticed on her way in that the secondary control helm console seemed more active than most of the rest of them; as if the officer there had been planning to take over from Azmordi's bridge station. Now she realized that this was where the drone shuttle would be flown from.

"Adjust vector toward starboard planetary rim and launch," Thrawn ordered.

"Yes, sir."

Thalias frowned. One puzzle solved; another manifesting. She'd assumed he was trying to draw out the alien ships' intentions by sending a clearly unarmed shuttle to rendezvous with them. But he was instead sending the shuttle in the *opposite* direction?

On one of the outside displays the drone appeared, accelerating away from the *Springhawk* en route to the far edge of the planet. "Let's see what they do," Samakro commented.

The words were barely out of his mouth when all five of the closer gunboat group opened fire with spectrum lasers, sending a withering barrage at the drone.

Beside Thalias, Che'ri inhaled sharply. "It's okay," Thalias said softly, putting a soothing hand on the girl's arm. Normally, she and Che'ri were nestled safely away in their suite when all the shooting started.

"Evasive," Thrawn ordered calmly.

Thalias held her breath as the drone went into a convulsion of jerky movements, matching the smaller but no less intense movements of the helm officer on Laknym's far side. The drone ducked in and out of the laser blasts as the operator tried to confuse the gunboats' targeting.

And it was working, Thalias saw. If the drone could keep it up a little longer, maybe a minute or two, it might make it out of the gunboats' effective range. At that point, if they still wanted to destroy it they would have to chase it down.

Which would mean crossing right in front of the *Springhawk*.

Thalias smiled tightly. Of course. Thrawn was trying to lure them in where he could use his lasers and breacher missiles to destroy them with a flanking attack right when their main forward-aiming lasers would be useless against him.

She was still working out the details in her mind, congratulating herself on how Thrawn's informal teaching methods had sharpened her analytical skills, when a final laser barrage shattered the drone into shards.

Thalias sighed. So much for that plan.

"Too bad," Samakro said. "I thought that at that range they'd have to use their missiles."

"It's not too late," Thrawn said. "Perhaps we can convince them to launch if we offer a more suitable target."

"I don't know," Samakro said doubtfully. "With fifteen fighters already on station, they may think they can get away with just their lasers."

Thalias felt her eyes narrow. Were he and Thrawn suggesting they *wanted* the gunboats to launch missiles at the *Springhawk*? She looked sideways at Laknym, wondering if he knew the plan or whether he was also in the dark. But his face was expressionless, his full attention on his board.

"We should at least give them the opportunity," Thrawn said, his voice as calm as Samakro's. "Azmordi: Take us toward the leading group. Low speed."

"Yes, sir."

"Thalias?" Che'ri whispered tensely.

"It's okay," Thalias soothed. The *Springhawk* was moving toward the nearest gunboats at what looked to her like a far faster pace than Thrawn's low-speed order should have generated. Behind them, the other two enemy groups were hurrying to close the distance and join in the confrontation.

Thalias craned her neck to look at Laknym's status boards, trying to find the electrostatic barrier readouts. But she didn't know the boards' layout, and her angle wasn't good enough to make out the descriptions beneath the displays. She looked back at the main display, to see the gunboats of the first rosette splitting farther apart to allow a better field of fire from the groups moving up behind them.

"Senior Captain?" Samakro asked.

"Hold course," Thrawn said. "Target the first rosette with spectrum lasers, but hold fire until ordered. Let's see how much they know about the Chiss."

Thalias frowned. The Syndicure prohibition against preemptive strikes, even against a clearly defined enemy, had never made much sense to her. It didn't make sense to Thrawn, either, she knew, having watched him time and again find ways around the ban.

But this situation seemed far more straightforward. In destroying the shuttle, even with no Chiss having been put in danger, hadn't the attackers handed the *Springhawk* all the excuse it needed to return fire?

Maybe that was the point. Maybe Thrawn and Samakro wanted to see if their attackers knew precisely where the invisible line was that Chiss warships weren't supposed to cross.

"Apparently, they know *something* about our rules of engagement," Samakro commented. "We're well past the point where they fired at the drone. Probably think we can't engage until the ship itself is attacked, so they're trying to close to a better kill range."

"Perhaps," Thrawn said. "Alternatively, they could be waiting for us to move deeper into the planet's gravity well."

"There's that," Samakro conceded. "Orders?"

"Let's continue to behave as they clearly expect us to," Thrawn said. "Prepare a breacher missile, targeted down the center of the lead rosette pattern."

"Down the *center,* sir?"

"The center," Thrawn confirmed.

"But—ah." Samakro nodded in understanding. "If there's no actual threat, there's no official attack."

"Exactly," Thrawn said. "It can be tactically advantageous for an enemy to believe in limits that don't actually exist."

Surreptitiously Thalias looked over her shoulder at Kharill in his command chair, noting his stony expression. Maybe he wasn't as certain that the attack on the shuttle was a sufficient reason to engage the gunboats. Maybe he just wasn't certain that the Syndicure would see things that way.

Still, Thrawn's plan of firing first into the center of the enemy formation should mollify even the fleet's harshest critics.

Or maybe Kharill simply didn't like the idea of wasting time playing games when there were ten more gunboats coming up behind the first group.

"Yes, sir," Samakro said briskly. "Breacher ready."

"Fire."

On the display the missile leapt from its launch tube, burning through space toward the cluster of incoming gunboats. The closest rosette spread a little wider as the missile arrowed toward them . . .

And in perfect unison five lasers lanced out, one from each gunboat, converging on the missile. The breacher's armor held out for a second or two, and then the missile disintegrated, its acid payload gushing into space.

"There," Thrawn said, nodding toward the expanding cloud. "You saw it, Mid Captain?"

"Yes, sir," Samakro said. "Our reputation does indeed precede us."

"That it does," Thrawn agreed.

"What did he mean?" Che'ri whispered.

Thalias shook her head. "I don't know."

Laknym leaned closer to them. "Letting a normal explosive missile get that close before destroying it would have endangered the gunboats," he explained softly. "But destroying a breacher farther out would have risked the acid spreading far enough outward to splash them. That means they know how our missiles work."

"I wonder if they know about plasma spheres, too," Samakro commented.

Laknym nodded. "They do," he said.

"You have something to say, Laknym?" Kharill spoke up.

Laknym winced. "I was just commenting on Mid Captain Samakro's question about the spheres," he said, looking back at Kharill. "From their formation—"

"Don't tell *me*, Laknym," Kharill interrupted. "Tell *them*." He keyed his mike. "Sir, Laknym has a comment."

Thrawn looked at the monitor. "Laknym?" he invited.

Thalias saw Laknym's throat tighten at being suddenly pushed into the spotlight. "I believe they know about plasma spheres, sir," he said. "Their formation is wide enough to avoid breachers, but compact enough to allow any one of them to move back to the center position in time to intercept a sphere if they wanted to protect a larger target behind them."

"Sounds a bit heavy on the speculation," Samakro said.

"Well . . ." Laknym floundered.

"But essentially correct," Thrawn said, coming to his rescue. "Particularly because the rosette is slowly closing as we approach and the time they would need to execute that sort of blocking maneuver decreases."

"Doesn't that tactic assume they actually *have* a larger target behind them that requires protection?" Samakro asked, a little stiffly.

"Not necessarily," Thrawn said. "Battle tactics are often so deeply entrenched that they're followed even when a given situation doesn't require them. But you raise another interesting point."

"That there may in fact *be* a larger ship out there?" Samakro asked.

"Exactly," Thrawn said, his voice gone darker. "In which case, now that we're sufficiently deep to prevent a quick escape it should make its appearance."

Thalias winced. She'd seen enough of Thrawn's logic and deductions to know there was a good chance he was right on this one, too.

And if the hidden ship was something nasty, the *Springhawk* could be in serious trouble.

"Perhaps we should reconsider our own strategy, sir," Samakro said, just loudly enough for the bridge mike to pick up. "Getting a blast profile on their missiles doesn't do much good if we're not around to take that data back to the Ascendancy."

"I think we can proceed a bit longer," Thrawn said. "Any warship that comes around the planet will offer us plenty of warning."

The words were barely out of his mouth when a ship suddenly appeared. Not from behind the planetary disk, as Thrawn had predicted, but jumping in from hyperspace in the distance behind the rearmost of the gunboat formations.

Thalias frowned, focusing on its design. Hadn't she seen that configuration before somewhere?

Abruptly, she caught her breath in stunned disbelief. She'd seen it before, all right. It was—

"Oh, great," Kharill bit out from behind her.

"What is it?" Che'ri asked, her voice cracking. "Is that a Nikardun?"

"Not a Nikardun," Kharill said grimly. "Just a problem. A *big* problem."

"Breakout in thirty seconds," Wikivv called from the *Grayshrike*'s helm.

"Acknowledged," Lakinda said. She sent her gaze slowly around the bridge, checking each station in turn, making particularly sure Senior Commander Erighal'ok'sumf was at his weapons console and that all the indicators there showed green.

Some of the warriors had grumbled a bit about that—mostly out of her hearing, of course—wondering if their captain was erring way too far on the side of caution, especially for a non-combat incursion into a presumably dripwater system in the middle of nowhere. Even Mid Captain Apros had tactfully pointed out that it was extremely unlikely that a blind jump would put the ship so close to a combat situation that they wouldn't have plenty of time for a leisurely ramp-up to full alert status.

Lakinda didn't care about any of that. Standing regs recommended it, she was pretty sure Thrawn would do it, and whatever was at the end of this trip she was *not* going to let him and the Mitth show her up again.

At least Ghaloksu was enthusiastically on her side on this one. Not really surprising—Lakinda had never yet seen her weapons officer pass up the chance to give his crews a little exercise.

The hyperspace swirl faded into star-flares into stars. "Full sensor sweep," Lakinda ordered, looking through the bridge viewport and then checking the tactical display as the sensors began filling it in. There was a cluster of asteroids nearby, but no planets or ships. "Double-check those asteroids," she added. "Make sure nothing is lurking in there."

"Combat range clear," Vimsk reported from the sensors, her large hands and stubby fingers displaying an unlikely deftness as she worked the sensor station controls. "Mid-range clear. Far range continuing. Asteroids show negative for ships or platforms."

"Acknowledged," Lakinda said. Though the more she looked at the asteroids, the more they seemed like an excellent place to stage an ambush, should one be required. Something to keep in mind if the Ascendancy ever needed to mount a military operation here.

"Laserfire!" Ghaloksu snapped. "Bearing thirty degrees level."

Lakinda bit back a curse as the image came up on the tactical. In the far distance, she could see the tiny flashes of laserfire glinting against the half disk of a planetary body. "Full mag," she ordered.

The scene wavered a moment, then came back with the slight fuzziness inherent in a high-magnification image. A large ship was silhouetted against the light side of the planet, she saw, its bow facing partially toward the sun. The ships currently firing lasers were too small for even the sensor's best magnification to resolve, but the number of shots indicated there were at least five of them. "Ship ID?" she called.

"Full ID impossible at this range," Ghaloksu said. "But profile and emissions are compatible with a Chiss heavy cruiser."

"The *Springhawk*?" Apros suggested.

"Who else would be here?" Lakinda said, feeling her eyes narrowing. What was Thrawn up to now?

Abruptly, a small explosion burst over the dark side of the planet, and the attackers' lasers went dark. "Something went boom," Lakinda said. "Any idea what it was?"

"Sorry, I wasn't on it," Ghaloksu said.

"I was," Vimsk said, peering closely at the sensor station's displays. "It was small. Shuttle or missile boat size."

Lakinda looked at Apros. "Could have been one of the *Springhawk*'s shuttles."

"Possible," Apros said. "Or Thrawn may have gotten himself in the middle of the civil war the Paccosh mentioned, and he's watching the two sides shoot at each other."

And no doubt trying to get them to stop their war. Thrawn's exaggerated concern for aliens and alien worlds that the Ascendancy had no business caring about was both a joke and a curse.

"Cruiser's on the move," Ghaloksu reported. "Heading toward origin of laserfire."

Apros muttered a curse. "He's going to attack them, isn't he?"

"Could be," Lakinda said. "Vimsk, read me his altitude. Is he inside the gravity well?"

"Yes, ma'am."

Lakinda hissed out a breath. Which meant that whatever Thrawn was doing—whether he was on the edge of violating Ascendancy standing orders or merely preparing to defend himself—a quick escape wasn't an option.

And with that, she no longer had a choice. "Wikivv, get me an in-system jump," she ordered. "Take the position of the attackers, extrapolate a reasonable backstop depth behind them, add fifty percent more for safety, and put us there."

"Yes, ma'am," Wikivv said, turning toward her board.

Apros took half a step closer to Lakinda. "So we're going in?" he asked, his voice low.

"The *Springhawk*'s in danger," Lakinda said. "With luck, we'll come out behind whatever Thrawn's facing and get them in a pincer."

Apros's lip twitched. "You realize, ma'am, that we're dangerously close to joining in a preemptive strike."

"No, we're coming to the aid of a fellow Ascendancy warship," Lakinda corrected. "*Thrawn's* the one walking that particular line."

Apros looked out the viewport. "I hope you're right."

*As do we all,* Lakinda thought. "Wikivv?"

"Ready, Senior Captain."

"All warriors: Stand ready for combat," Lakinda called, feeling a trickle of satisfaction. She'd been right to have the *Grayshrike* on full battle alert. She'd been right, and all the rest of them had been wrong. Score one for the Xodlak. "Wikivv, as soon as we arrive, spin us around toward the *Springhawk* where we can target whoever's facing it."

"Yes, ma'am."

"Stand ready," Lakinda said, squaring her shoulders. There was no way the Mitth were going to spin *this* one into Thrawn being the hero. "Three, two, *one*." There was a brief flicker from the starscape, almost more imagined than seen, and the *Grayshrike* had arrived.

And in a single frozen instant, everything went straight to hell.

Even as Wikivv began the yaw rotation that would bring them to Lakinda's planned pincer position, the proximity alarm sounded, warning of a large vessel within combat range. Lakinda twisted her head to look that direction—

She felt her breath catch in her throat. The ship was coming up fast around the curve of the planet, where up to now it had been out of sight of both her and Thrawn. "Ghaloksu?"

"Warship, *Battle Dreadnought* class, unknown configuration," the weapons officer snapped. "Coming up fast on portside."

Lakinda felt her throat tighten. Battle Dreadnoughts were a class of alien warships, ranging from a little smaller than a Chiss Night-dragon man-of-war to half again as large. This particular version was about midway in that range, slightly larger than a Nightdragon and probably comparably armed.

Which made it considerably larger than the *Grayshrike* and *Springhawk* combined.

"Wikivv, belay the yaw turn," Lakinda ordered, checking the tactical as the sensor sweep began filling it in. Moving away from her, heading toward the *Springhawk,* were three groups of five small ships, gunboat or missile boat size. The lead group, presumably, were the ships that had been pumping out all the laserfire she'd seen when the *Grayshrike* first arrived in the system.

She clenched her teeth. Now that she knew about the Battle Dreadnought, the smart move would be to jump before the *Grayshrike* drifted inward across the invisible marker that would also put them too deep in the planet's gravity well to escape into hyperspace.

But that would leave the *Springhawk* to face this new threat alone. And extricating Thrawn from the mess he'd gotten himself into had been the whole idea behind this sortie in the first place.

Still, her first duty was to her own ship and the Ascendancy. If this was a new and hitherto unrecognized threat, the *Grayshrike* needed to survive long enough to bring a warning to Csilla. If that meant she had to abandon the *Springhawk*—

"Incoming!" Ghaloksu called. "Three missiles from the Battle Dreadnought."

"Lasers: Target and destroy," Lakinda ordered.

And with that, the decision had effectively been made for her. The *Grayshrike* had been attacked without warning or challenge . . . and if whoever was master of that ship thought a Chiss commander of her reputation and family was going to cut and run from such a provocation, they were about to receive a *very* rude awakening.

"Shrent, signal the *Springhawk*," she said, the sudden surge of pride and determination washing away the uncertainty and caution. "Tell Thrawn we're going in."

# CHAPTER NINE

"**S**tand by all weapons," Thrawn said, his head bowed as he worked at his questis, his voice icily calm.

Calmer than Samakro's own voice probably would have been under the same conditions. Certainly calmer than the first officer was feeling right now.

Thrawn's analysis had anticipated the possibility that a warship was concealed around the edge of the planet. He'd also foreseen that such a threat couldn't appear without giving the *Springhawk* ample time to drive up out of the gravity well and make its escape. Moreover, with Sky-walker Che'ri already on station in secondary control, the Chiss could maneuver out of the tangled hyperspace pathways filling this region faster and farther than any pursuer could manage.

The analysis *hadn't* figured on the *Grayshrike* suddenly showing up practically in the warship's lap.

And with that, Thrawn's whole plan had cracked like an overripe egg. From the images and quick-scan stats the *Grayshrike* had transmitted, it was clear there was no way Lakinda could take on that Battle Dreadnought by herself, especially not with those fifteen gunboats on station ready to back it up. The *Grayshrike* needed to get turned around and back into hyperspace, and fast.

Too late. Even as Samakro peered across the distance he saw a sudden volley of laserfire erupt between the *Grayshrike* and the still-unseen ship. The Battle Dreadnought had begun its attack, and the *Grayshrike* had responded.

And Samakro had seen enough of Lakinda to know she would never back down from a fight, even one where she was hopelessly outmatched. Xodlak family honor alone would dictate that.

Which now gave the *Springhawk* no choice but to go to her aid.

Unfortunately, the only way for the *Springhawk* to get to the *Grayshrike* in time was to drive straight through those same fifteen gunboats.

"Guards, escort the Magys and her companion back to their suite and see they remain there," Thrawn ordered.

Samakro watched as the two aliens and their escort walked to the hatchway and left the bridge. The hatch closed, and he turned back to Thrawn. "What's the plan, sir?"

Thrawn pointed out the viewport. "We go straight through the gunboats."

"Understood," Samakro said. He'd called it, all right. "If I may suggest, sir, it might be safer to angle out of the gravity well and try an in-system jump to the *Grayshrike*'s side."

Thrawn shook his head. "An accurate jump that short would be virtually impossible."

"So would surviving a head-on battle against fifteen gunboats," Samakro said tersely, his patience finally starting to fray. Did Thrawn truly believe he was invincible? Did he think his logic and tactical sense were never wrong?

"Not *fifteen*, Mid Captain," Thrawn corrected mildly. He pointed to the tactical. "Five."

Samakro looked at the display, anger churning his stomach. And Thrawn's damn verbal deflection techniques—

The boiling emotion inside him abruptly cooled into ice. The ten gunboats that had been approaching in backup position had turned and were now heading back toward the distant *Grayshrike*.

"Apparently the Battle Dreadnought isn't nearly as confident of victory as the size differential between him and the *Grayshrike* would suggest," Thrawn continued. "Lakinda's telemetry showed a smaller escort ship close to its side, possibly a tender or supply ship, possibly indicating unreadiness for full combat."

"So they're calling back the gunboats," Samakro said.

"Indeed," Thrawn said. "I believe we can handle five gunboats without serious problems."

"Yes, sir, we can," Samakro said, feeling like an idiot. Intent on watching the two aliens leave the bridge, he'd allowed a fluid battle situation to get ahead of him. He knew better than that. "Spheres and lasers?"

"Just lasers, I think," Thrawn said. "I have something else in mind for the spheres. Afpriuh?"

"All systems ready, sir," the weapons officer said, his voice crisp and confident.

"Lasers on all five gunboats," Thrawn ordered, tapping his questis one final time. "Fire at optimal range. Azmordi, on my order take us at full speed along the indicated course. Continue data feed to the *Grayshrike*."

Samakro looked at the tactical, where Thrawn's course had now appeared. The *Springhawk* would be accelerating along a vector straight toward the *Grayshrike*, dipping deeper into the planet's gravity well until it passed the midpoint of that line segment and started climbing out again.

The plot also marked the point where he expected Afpriuh to open fire. Samakro eyed the distances involved, mentally pulling up the laser profile they'd recorded when gunboats attacked the drone shuttle . . . "We're going to take some damage, sir," he warned.

"Yes," Thrawn said. "But it should be minimal."

"Understood," Samakro said reluctantly. Going against five gunboats with only lasers was still a gamble. But it was one they had to take. The *Springhawk*'s electrostatic barriers and thick nyix-alloy hull could take a fair amount of damage without danger to the ship, and their remaining plasma spheres and breacher missiles had to be saved for the Battle Dreadnought.

"Course ready, sir," Azmordi called from the helm.

"Lasers ready, sir," Afpriuh added from the weapons station.

Thrawn keyed for general intercom. "*Springhawk*, prepare for battle," he called, his voice echoing across the bridge and through every part of the ship. "Azmordi: Three, two, *one*."

The *Springhawk* leapt forward, charging toward the five remaining gunboats. Their response was to open their rosette formation a little. Samakro checked the monitors, confirming the *Springhawk*'s electrostatic barriers were at full power and the spectrum lasers ready—

A second later five lasers slashed out from the gunboats, stabbing at the *Springhawk*'s hull. The barriers were diffusing a good 84 percent of the laser energy, but that left 16 percent that was still getting through. If the beams stayed focused on the same hull plates too long, it could mean trouble.

"Azmordi, evasive rotation and jinking," Thrawn ordered. "Coordinate pattern with laser control. Afpriuh?"

"Almost to range, sir," Afpriuh said. "Targeting pattern?"

"Simultaneous followed by sequential," Thrawn said.

"Simultaneous, then sequential," Afpriuh repeated, nodding. "Pattern locked."

"Stand by simultaneous," Thrawn said. "Three, two, *one*."

Through the viewport Samakro saw the multiple blazes of fire as the *Springhawk*'s forward spectrum lasers lanced out, one shot targeting each of the five gunboats, the flash-ionized interplanetary medium marking the beams' passage.

Samakro checked the readouts. The gunboats' power levels were unchanged, their own lasers still intact and firing. Not surprising—at this range a single laser would have only a minor effect against even the limited electrostatic barriers warships that size could deploy.

But then, damage wasn't the purpose of a simultaneous laser attack. Samakro shifted his attention back to the tactical—

"Sequential: Three, two, *one*."

And with the gunboats' sensors temporarily overloaded and their pilots dazzled by the earlier blasts, the full force of the *Springhawk*'s forward laser array blasted into each in turn, breaking the barriers and shattering one, then the next, then the next, all the way around the circular formation.

"Secure from evasive," Thrawn ordered. There was a brief clatter against the hull as the *Springhawk* drove through the debris from the destroyed gunboats. "Sensor sweep."

"Ten gunboats ahead, closing on the *Grayshrike*," Dalvu said. "Battle Dreadnought still hidden behind planetary rim."

"Good," Thrawn said. "Increase speed thirty percent."

"Thirty percent, acknowledged," Azmordi confirmed.

"Just thirty percent, sir?" Samakro asked softly. "At that speed we'll barely be gaining on them."

"Understood," Thrawn said. "Plasma spheres ready?"

"Ready, sir," Afpriuh said.

"Good," Thrawn said. "Open a secure channel to *Grayshrike*." He looked up at Samakro. "We need to talk with Senior Captain Lakinda."

"We're holding our own," Lakinda assured Thrawn. "I get the feeling they weren't really prepared for a fight."

Which wasn't to say the Battle Dreadnought hadn't fully risen to the occasion, she privately conceded. Its electrostatic barriers, which the sensor record showed had been at minimal power when the *Grayshrike* first appeared, had now reached full strength. More critically, the number of lasers firing at the Chiss cruiser had increased, and the launchers seemed to be firing as fast as new missiles could be loaded into them.

So far the *Grayshrike*'s own barriers and point defenses were keeping pace with the barrage. But as the Battle Dreadnought continued forward, and the reaction time between missile launch and laser lock-fire-destroy decreased, the situation was edging toward critical.

"Which raises the question of why it attacked in the first place instead of simply running," Thrawn said. "But that's a topic for later. Is it still driving toward you?"

"Yes, and increasing speed," Lakinda said, risking a quick look at the tactical. The ten gunboats sweeping toward her starboard flank were coming up fast, too.

The *Springhawk*, in contrast, seemed almost to be dawdling. "And those gunboats who were trying to ruin your day are now hoping to ruin mine," she added. "I don't suppose you can pick up a little speed, maybe get in range of them before they're in range of me?"

"In a moment," Thrawn promised. "I'm sending an attack plan. Can you play your part?"

Lakinda felt her eyes narrow. Play your *part*? The *Grayshrike* was in the hot seat here, not the *Springhawk*. Since when was Thrawn in charge of their joint battle plan, and Lakinda merely playing a *part*?

The plan came up on the tactical, and she felt her eyes narrow even further. Of all the *insane*—

"Whoa," Apros muttered. "Does he *ever* come up with a battle plan that's not borderline insane?"

"Not that I've noticed," Lakinda growled.

Still, facing an enemy warship that could theoretically take out both Chiss cruisers, and with the *Springhawk* still unable to escape to hyperspace, any plan that *did* sound sane would probably fail. Much as she hated to admit it, even to herself, Thrawn's craziness might be just what they needed here. "Wikivv?" she called toward the helm. "Can you do it?"

"I agree about the overall sanity level," Wikivv said, her voice strained as she peered at the tactical diagram Thrawn had sent. "That aside . . . yes, I can do it."

"Apros?" Lakinda asked, looking at him.

He gave a little shrug. "It's risky," he said. "But most of the risk is Thrawn's." He gave her a tight smile. "Your ship, ma'am. Your decision."

Lakinda nodded. He was right, on all counts. "All right, Thrawn. We're ready."

"Thank you," Thrawn said. "Keep feeding us telemetry—the timing is going to be critical."

A warning alarm sounded: The electrostatic barriers were down to 50 percent. "Our timing's getting pretty damn critical, too," she warned.

"Understood," Thrawn said. "Afpriuh, Azmordi: On my mark. Three, two, *one*."

———

And with a shudder of multiple launch tubes, all twenty of the *Spring-hawk*'s remaining plasma spheres blasted into space.

Samakro watched the tactical, his throat tight. Twenty spheres, two targeting each of the fleeing gunboats. If Thrawn's gamble didn't work, one of their best weapons against the still-hidden Battle Dreadnought would be gone, and with nothing to show for it.

Which could still happen. The gunboats were far enough away that if they noticed the spheres, there was still time for them to veer out of their path.

But the fighters were maintaining their original vectors. With the pilots' full attention on the *Grayshrike,* and with the plasma plumes from their own thrusters obscuring their aft sensors, they were apparently oblivious to the subtle threat rapidly overtaking them. Samakro held his breath . . .

And watched as all twenty spheres slammed squarely into their targets, the ion bursts knocking out the gunboats' controls, sensors, life-support systems, and drives. And most important of all, their comms.

"Emergency acceleration," Thrawn ordered, and Samakro could hear a little of his own relief half hidden beneath the confidence and determination in his captain's voice. This whole thing was still a gamble, but the first part had just paid off.

An instant later he had to grab at the back of Thrawn's command chair for balance as Azmordi threw full emergency power to the drive, the sudden acceleration leaving the compensators lagging just slightly behind. "Afpriuh, my compliments to the sphere gunners," Thrawn continued. "Time to see if your breacher specialists are up to the same challenge."

"They are, sir," Afpriuh said confidently. "Gunners and launchers standing by."

"Captain Lakinda?" Thrawn called.

"We're ready here," Lakinda said over the speaker.

"Excellent," Thrawn said. "Stand by."

For a dozen heartbeats, the bridge was silent. Samakro gazed at the tactical, wincing once as the *Springhawk* drove through the drifting gunboats they'd just disabled, scattering the smaller craft and probably breaking at least a couple of them open to space and death. The images marking the capital ships continued to move across the tactical: the *Grayshrike* holding position, fending off the missiles and lasers of the Battle Dreadnought; the Battle Dreadnought itself moving inexorably toward the embattled Chiss warship; the *Springhawk* sprinting at full speed toward both. If the *Grayshrike*'s telemetry was correct, the Battle Dreadnought was nearly to the edge of the planetary disk . . .

"*Grayshrike*, execute on my mark," Thrawn said calmly. "Three, two, *one*."

On the tactical, a dozen new images flashed onto the display: plasma spheres, launched from the *Grayshrike*, targeting the Battle Dreadnought.

All of them impacting the hull along its port side. "*That* should confuse them," Samakro said under his breath.

"Indeed," Thrawn agreed. "Hopefully, that confusion won't lead to caution."

But so far a sudden surge of caution didn't look likely. Even with its port side largely incapacitated by the plasma spheres, the Battle Dreadnought was still driving toward the *Grayshrike*, throwing missiles and laserfire at its target from its unaffected bow and starboard weapons clusters. Through the viewport Samakro saw the big warship come into sight from behind the planetary disk.

He hissed out a breath. The *Grayshrike*'s telemetry had mostly shown the Battle Dreadnought from the front, with only brief and foreshortened views of its sides as the flank and shoulder launchers fired their missiles and lasers. Only now that he was finally getting a full side view did he realize just how big the damn thing was.

He looked down at Thrawn. If his commander was surprised or daunted, it didn't show in his expression. "Afpriuh, ready breachers," Thrawn ordered. "Captain Lakinda, at your convenience."

"Good luck," Lakinda's voice came from the speakers. Samakro looked back out the viewport, to see the *Grayshrike* turn partially away from the Battle Dreadnought and disappear into hyperspace. The Battle Dreadnought continued toward the spot where the Chiss ship had been, probably preparing for its own jump as soon as it was out of the gravity well—

"Breachers: Fire," Thrawn ordered.

The deck vibrated beneath Samakro's feet as all their remaining breacher missiles blasted away toward the Battle Dreadnought, leaping forward as their own acceleration was enhanced by the speed the *Springhawk* itself had built up.

Even with that extra speed advantage, Samakro knew, the range here was longer than optimal for breachers. But with the Battle Dreadnought's portside sensors and point defenses paralyzed by the *Grayshrike*'s plasma spheres, its commander had no inkling of the destructive force arrowing toward them. The only warning could have come from the gunboats, and Thrawn's own plasma sphere strike had rendered them silent.

And with the Battle Dreadnought still oblivious, the entire spread of breachers slammed into its hull.

At that range, and with such a large target looming in front of them, most commanders and weapons officers would have been content to deliver whatever random destruction the missiles could cause. But not Thrawn. At his order, Afpriuh had sifted through the *Grayshrike*'s telemetry data to locate the Battle Dreadnought's sensor and weapons clusters and target his breachers accordingly. The breachers exploded, flooding their acid across the hull to eat away metal and ceramic and burrow into hardened electronics and optical crystals. Thirty seconds later, the systems that the *Grayshrike*'s plasma sphere attack had only temporarily paralyzed were permanently destroyed.

Leaving the enemy's entire portside flank open to attack.

"Spectrum lasers: Fire," Thrawn ordered. "Follow-up spread." He looked up at Samakro. "Let's see just how well they know us."

Samakro nodded. A follow-up spread was the basic one–two punch of Chiss battle tactics: breachers to eat gouges into the hull, followed by lasers whose energy would now be more readily absorbed by the pitted and blackened metal, digging even deeper into the armor. If the Battle Dreadnought's commander knew about that strategy, they should be ready to counter it.

Sure enough, even as the lasers dug into its hull, the enemy warship began a yaw turn, rotating ponderously toward the *Springhawk,* preparing to bring its bow and starboard weapons to bear on its attacker and put its damaged port side out of the lasers' reach.

"Looks like they're ready for another round," Samakro commented.

"A decision they may regret," Thrawn said. "Azmordi, secure from emergency acceleration. Afpriuh, I see barriers are at eighty-two percent?"

"Yes, sir," the weapons officer confirmed. "Still recovering from the gunboat attacks. We're working to get them to full power."

"Understood," Thrawn said. "Stand by lasers. I anticipate they'll turn far enough to bring their starboard weapons to bear, but no farther."

"We're ready, sir," Afpriuh said. "Weapons cluster locations on that flank already keyed into targeting systems."

"Good," Thrawn said, checking his chrono. "Just make certain your shots are *very* precise."

"Yes, sir," Afpriuh said. "Starboard systems almost in sight."

"Prepare to fire on my mark," Thrawn said. "Single laser volleys on my marks. First volley: Three, two, *one.*"

Once again, the sky outside the viewport lit up as the *Springhawk*'s spectrum lasers blazed toward the distant warship.

But the range was still on the long side, and the Battle Dreadnought was well armored, and without the softening-up that had been provided by the breachers on the port side the starboard hull and shoulder weapons clusters shrugged off the attack. The warship continued its turn, its own lasers now opening up toward the *Springhawk.*

"Second and third volleys: Three, two, *one,*" Thrawn called. Once again he checked his chrono as the lasers spat out two more attacks—

"Cease fire."

Samakro swallowed hard, his eyes flicking between the viewport and the tactical display . . .

Then suddenly there it was, appearing in the near distance behind the Battle Dreadnought.

The *Grayshrike* had returned.

Not only returned, but in the precise tactical position Thrawn had specified: within close-combat range, and with a perfect view of the Battle Dreadnought's damaged port side.

And as the Battle Dreadnought continued to pour laserfire at the *Springhawk*, Lakinda opened up her own attack.

"Afpriuh: Fire at will," Thrawn ordered.

Samakro looked at the sensor display, shifted to the tactical, then back to the sensor. At this distance, it was hard to get a good read on how much damage the Chiss crossfire was doing to the Battle Dreadnought. Or for that matter, whether it was doing any at all.

But that was only the case on the *Springhawk*'s side of the battle. The telemetry from the *Grayshrike* showed their lasers digging deep into the mutilated part of the enemy's hull. If the *Grayshrike* could keep that up, and if the *Springhawk* could at least hold its own—

"Afpriuh, stand by to cease fire," Thrawn called.

Samakro frowned at the sensor display. What was Thrawn seeing that made him think the enemy was about to give up?

He was still trying to figure it out when the Battle Dreadnought abruptly lunged forward, driving hard out of the planetary gravity well. The *Springhawk*'s lasers shifted aim to follow, the *Grayshrike*'s doing likewise. The Battle Dreadnought blasted away one final laser volley that missed the *Springhawk* completely—

And then, with a flicker, it escaped to hyperspace.

"Cease fire," Thrawn ordered. "Assess and report damage."

Samakro took a deep breath, feeling the subtle sounds and stirrings across the bridge as the other officers also mentally disengaged from combat. "Well," he said. "*That* was different."

"Indeed," Thrawn said, keying his comm. "Captain Lakinda, report."

"We're still assessing damage, Captain," Lakinda's voice came. "But so far it doesn't look too bad. You?"

"The same," Thrawn said. "My compliments to your pilot, by the way. I've never seen so precise a pair of in-system jumps. Please add my appreciation to your log entry."

"I'll do so," Lakinda said. "Did you notice our playmate's parting shot?"

"I did," Thrawn said, his voice going grim. "A shame, too. I was looking forward to seeing what those gunboats and pilots could offer us."

Samakro looked back at the tactical, scowling as he saw that all ten of the paralyzed gunboats had been turned into expanding clouds of dust. He'd assumed the Battle Dreadnought had simply missed its intended target—the *Springhawk*—with that final volley. Clearly, it hadn't.

"Will Admiral Ar'alani be joining us?" Thrawn continued.

"No," Lakinda said. "And I'm only here because the admiral sent me to deliver a message."

"Interesting," Thrawn said. "A moment while I set up a secure channel."

"Actually, I'd prefer to deliver it to you directly," Lakinda said. "Since we also ought to talk about what just happened here."

"Very well," Thrawn said. "I suggest we both continue our damage assessments. There are also one or two things I need to check into. Once those have been completed, we'll arrange a meeting."

"Agreed," Lakinda said. "*Grayshrike* out."

"*Springhawk* out." Thrawn keyed off his mike.

"She's a good commander," Samakro commented. "If a little brash sometimes."

"You mean taking on a major warship with a single heavy cruiser?" Thrawn asked.

"Yes, sir." Samakro dared a small smile. "I thought you were the only one who could take on impossible odds and get away with it."

"The odds are never impossible," Thrawn said calmly. "Merely unfavorable."

"I'll remember that," Samakro said. "What are these one or two things we need to check into?"

"Did you notice what happened just before the Battle Dreadnought escaped?"

"You mean aside from destroying the gunboats?" Samakro asked, eyeing him closely. "Not really. I assumed they just got tired of taking damage."

"I'm sure that was part of it," Thrawn said. "And make no mistake— they *were* being seriously hurt. But I believe the reason they stayed as long as they did was to occupy our attention so their companions could make their own escape."

Samakro frowned. "Their companion? You mean the tender we saw on Lakinda's telemetry?"

"We *assumed* it was a tender," Thrawn said. "But I believe that when we examine the *Grayshrike*'s records more thoroughly, we'll find it was either a passenger ship or a freighter."

Samakro looked at the devastated planet below them. "Someone wanted someone or something from this place," he said slowly. "Something worth wrecking the whole planet for."

"And something worth sending a Battle Dreadnought to guard its transfer."

"Yes," Samakro murmured. "What now?"

"First, we bring the Magys and her companion back to the bridge," Thrawn said. "The Battle Dreadnought and transport were in geo-synchronous positions, presumably over a significant location. Perhaps she can tell us what occupies that area."

"We *could* go down and take a look for ourselves," Samakro pointed out.

Thrawn shook his head. "Perhaps later, but not yet. The *Spring-hawk* and *Grayshrike* are both damaged and effectively disarmed, offering only limited support for such an incursion."

"I realize that," Samakro said. "I'll just point out that if we wait too long, whoever might still be down there could finish whatever they were doing and disappear."

"Unlikely," Thrawn said thoughtfully. "Whatever their purpose, it isn't simply a grab-and-run. Not when they invested the time and effort to foment a civil war in order to keep the locals from interfering. No, I believe it's a long-term investment and will keep until we can bring back a proper force."

"Yes, sir," Samakro said.

Which didn't mean that the Battle Dreadnought's masters might not summarily shut down their operation, taking whatever losses were necessary, rather than face a full Chiss battle force. Still, Thrawn's instincts on this whole mission had been pretty much on the mark, while Samakro's had been mostly off it. Not really a good position to argue from. "And after we've talked to the Magys?"

"We meet with Senior Captain Lakinda," Thrawn said, gazing out the viewport. "And try to solve the mystery of what's going on here."

# MEMORIES III

For Yoponek and his betrothed, the next five weeks were undoubtedly a dream come true. Thanks to the Agbui, the two Chiss—who had once worried about limited finances and resources during their wandering year—now had free passage, mostly free food, and final decisions on where their cultural nomad hosts traveled next.

For Haplif, those same five weeks were filled with careful observation, equally careful cultivation, and putting up with a lot of enthusiastic and nonsensical drivel from his guests.

It also brought his first real comprehension as to why he'd had such trouble penetrating the Ascendancy's social and political structures.

Nine Ruling Families. Forty Great Families. Neither of those numbers was fixed, either—as recently as fifty years ago there had been ten ruling families, and at times throughout the historical record there had been as many as twelve and as few as three. Once, if Yoponek's stories about the Stybla and the dawn of the Ascendancy were accurate, there had been only one.

The good news, at least for Haplif's purposes, was that both Yoponek and Yomie were members of the Coduyo family, one of the Forty. The bad news was that neither of them had much knowledge of the current state of family politics. Haplif heard a great deal of gossip from them, plus a lot of history and historical anecdotes from Yoponek, and between them he was able to pull out a few important names. But there was never any hint that either of the travelers had the connections he needed to get a face-to-face with any of those names.

And connections were definitely needed. The Mitth and Obbic were allies, for example, with the Irizi and Ufsa aligned against them. The Chaf had a mild degree of opposition going with the Mitth, but weren't particularly enthusiastic about the Irizi, either. The Dasklo and Clarr had their own rivalry going on in parallel with the others, while the Plikh and Boadil seemed to shift alliances as the need, the mood, or possibly just the current solar cycle required. And that didn't even count the snarled social and political networks inside the Forty and between them and the Nine.

Plus there were the thousands of other families across the Ascendancy, some of which aspired to join the Forty, others of which were content to jockey for local power with other local families. Without contacts and an up-to-date mapping of the political landscape, there was no chance of getting anywhere.

It wasn't just annoying, though it was certainly also that. The looming problem was that Jixtus's timetable marked certain must-make tether points, and at the moment Haplif was on the edge of falling dangerously behind those goals. Shimkif, whose job was mainly to manage the ship and crew and who didn't have to concern herself with all these cultural nuances, had already been on his case about it, and her reminders were getting more and more pointed.

And she was right. If Yoponek and Yomie didn't come through soon with something useful, Haplif would have no choice but to cut the two Chiss loose and start over. That approach carried its own risks, not the least being that he might fall so far behind schedule he would never catch up. But at least then the Agbui could fly free again without having to cater to the travel whims of a couple of spoiled brats.

He had privately decided to give them two more days when the deadlock suddenly and unexpectedly broke.

"—and then old Yokado allegedly told Lakuviv to take a hyperspace leap straight back to Celwis," Yoponek said, finishing yet another story with his usual flourish, nearly choking on his cromas nectar as he tried to drink, talk, and laugh at the same time. Yomie, sitting beside him, merely drained her own cup in silence. Clearly, she'd heard this one before. "It wasn't the first time a Xodlak Councilor tried to get a Coduyo Patriarch to do what he wanted in front of witnesses," Yoponek continued. "There are at least two other recorded instances in the past hundred fifty years. But even if it wasn't the first, it was definitely the loudest."

"I'm sure it was," Haplif said, smiling perfunctorily, his mind racing across the tangle of names and connections Yoponek had just spread out in front of him. Celwis, a minor world in the grand scheme of things, but notable as a stronghold of the Xodlak family. Xodlak and Coduyo, two of the Forty who usually got along quite well together, both of whom had once been among the Ruling Families. Councilor Lakuviv, a local Xodlak official on Celwis who clearly had ambitions and frustrations and sounded like he might be open to someone offering relief on both counts.

It was the best entry point Haplif had seen yet. It might also be the best he was going to get. "Sounds like an interesting person," he commented, taking the flask of nectar from the salon's side table and topping off Yoponek's cup.

"Yokado? I don't think so." Yoponek took a sip. "I mean, yes, he's our Patriarch, but aside from that I don't think I've ever heard anyone call him *interesting*."

"Not Yokado," Haplif corrected, offering Yomie a refill. She shook her head, as he'd expected her to. "This Councilor Lakuviv. I don't suppose you know him personally?"

"Me? Oh, no. Not at all." Yoponek shook his head, as if his words hadn't made it clear enough. "I've barely even heard his name. What makes you think he's interesting?"

"A fiery spirit who directly and confidently pursues what he wants?" Haplif waved a hand in an all-encompassing gesture he'd picked up from his guests. "Such people are rare and priceless. Even without his position in the Xodlak family, that spirit alone would make him interesting."

"Mm," Yoponek said, taking a sip. "I suppose we can only guess about that."

"Why can we only guess?" Haplif asked. "Why can't we go meet him?"

Yoponek's eyes widened. "What, you mean go to *Celwis*?"

"Why not?" Haplif countered. "We've already agreed he would be worth meeting and talking to. Our purpose in traveling the Chaos, after all, is to learn all we can about the cultures we meet. This Councilor Lakuviv would be well worth the journey."

"I suppose," Yoponek said, still sounding hesitant.

"Look at it this way," Haplif urged. "You're a student of history and historical figures. This Lakuviv—well, I have a strong sense he's going to be one of the key figures to historians yet to come." He lifted a finger. "Only you would get to see him *now*. You would get to see history as it's being made."

"I never thought of it like that," Yoponek said, his eyes glowing a bit brighter. "History has always been something in the . . . well, of course it's in the past. Basic definition. You never think about how you might actually be experiencing it."

"But you'd be experiencing it *after* the Grand Migration on Shihon, right?" Yomie put in.

"That was the plan, certainly," Haplif acknowledged. "However—"

"*Was*?" Yomie pounced on the word. "We talked about this. You agreed we would go to Shihon."

"Of course we're going," Haplif hastened to assure her. "I was merely going to point out that we're already at the eastern edge of the Ascendancy, and that Shihon is in the other direction and a good way past Csilla. If we went to Celwis first, perhaps spending a day or two with Councilor Lakuviv—if he permits it, of course—we could still get to Shihon in time for the migration."

"For *part* of the migration," Yomie corrected frostily. "We'd miss the first week. Maybe even more."

"Yes, I suppose we would," Haplif admitted. "But we weren't intending to be there for all of it anyway."

"We weren't?" Yomie countered. "*I* was."

"Yomie, the migration covers a whole month," Yoponek soothed. "We can't expect the Agbui to spend that much time watching us watch birds."

"Why not?" Yomie shot back. "Haplif said they'd go anywhere we wanted. Besides, I thought they wanted to see everything in the Ascendancy, and birds are as interesting as anything else. Certainly as interesting as some Xodlak Councilor on a backward world."

Yoponek gave Haplif a hooded look. "We don't need to discuss this right now," he said, setting down his cup. "It's late. We should get ready for bed."

Yomie looked at Haplif, a mix of challenge and stubbornness in her eyes. "Fine," she said, her voice a little calmer. "We'll talk about it tomorrow. Good night, Haplif."

"Good night to you both," Haplif said, stretching out his hand and brushing his fingertips across Yoponek's temple and cheek as the boy stood up. "Sleep well, my friends."

"You, too," Yoponek said. He returned Haplif's cheek-brushing gesture, then took Yomie's hand and headed for the salon hatch.

They were nearly there when the hatch opened and Shimkif appeared. "Ah—there you are," she said brightly, smiling at them. "I was hoping to wish you pleasant sleep before you retired to your rooms for the night."

"We're just heading there now," Yoponek said.

"Well, good night, then," Shimkif said. She held her hand up in farewell, her fingers drifting toward the side of Yomie's head.

"Good night," Yoponek said. Yomie just nodded, casually moving her head to the side just far enough to avoid Shimkif's fingers as the two passed each other.

The two Chiss disappeared through the opening. Shimkif closed the hatch behind them and turned back toward Haplif, scowling. "She's getting a little too good at that."

"What, avoiding your touch?" Haplif asked, picking up the nectar bottle and a fresh cup. "I don't think she's doing it on purpose."

"Of course she's doing it on purpose," Shimkif growled. "She doesn't like being touched by strangers."

"I know," Haplif said, pouring her a drink. "I'd hoped that attitude might soften once she got to know us better. Apparently, it hasn't. Maybe I should be offended that she still considers us strangers."

"Joke all you like," Shimkif said as she sat down in Yoponek's vacated chair and took a long swallow of nectar. "If I were you, I'd worry more about the detrimental velvethold she has over Yoponek."

"Well, they *are* betrothed to each other," Haplif pointed out. "He probably likes it."

"I meant detrimental to *us.*"

Haplif gave a little snort. "No argument there. You were listening, I assume?"

"*And* looking up whatever I could find on this Councilor Lakuviv. Unfortunately, the public access listings don't have much beyond his name, family, and current position."

"He's a very small darter in a very big tide pool," Haplif reminded her. "And his part of the pool is a long way away. Not surprised there isn't much on him here."

"I don't disagree," Shimkif said. "I'm just saying we don't have much to go on." She crinkled her forehead skin. "Unless you got something just then from Yoponek?"

"A little," Haplif said. Sustained contact was always more effective for his readings, but even though Yoponek had accepted the supposed Agbui friendship touch Haplif knew better than to push that too far. "He wants to go to Celwis, and I think especially likes the idea of getting his name and face before an official of one of the Forty."

"I thought he was already one of the Forty."

"He is, but spreading out contacts to other families is important to these people," Haplif said. "He's also intrigued by the idea of being part of history."

"Oh, he's going to be part of history, all right," Shimkif said darkly.

"Indeed he is," Haplif agreed. "At the same time, he's worried about Yomie. He doesn't want to stand in her way, but I can't tell whether he's worried it'll make her angry or simply doesn't want to disappoint her."

"Or both?"

"Could be," Haplif agreed. "Emotional nuances are never easy to get in a pass-by. But his life-craving hasn't changed."

"Social position and recognition?"

"Yes," Haplif said. "Which is perfect for getting us in to meet this Councilor Lakuviv."

"Fine," Shimkif said. "So how do we deal with the female?"

"You think she needs dealing with?"

"You *don't*?"

"I'm just saying it could be dangerous."

"No," Shimkif said. "What's dangerous is keeping her around."

"Why, because she won't let you touch her?"

"Because she's playing games with us," Shimkif said flatly. "She's not just the smiling, innocent schoolgirl she pretends to be."

"Of course not," Haplif said sourly. "She's an entitled, whiny brat. The problem is that Yoponek truly cares for her. If we push him too hard we could alienate both of them and end up starting over."

"So let's start over," Shimkif said. "We could still go see Lakuviv."

"Not without Yoponek to introduce us." Haplif considered. "An *enthusiastic* Yoponek."

"Making him enthusiastic is *your* job."

"I know that," Haplif said impatiently. Why was she giving him so much grief over this? Didn't she think he knew what he was doing? "I'm just saying that as long as his loyalties are split between us and his betrothed, that's going to be difficult."

"I've already suggested getting rid of her."

"Still not a good idea," Haplif said. "Come on—you've had at least a little contact with her. What else can you suggest?"

Shimkif huffed out an annoyed breath. "Her life-cravings are wide-ranging travel followed by a long and balanced family. If you really think we need to keep her around, we might be able to do something with the latter."

"Their full marriage is still down the road," Haplif said. "I doubt we can get them to advance that timetable."

"So we give her something sympathetic to relate to," Shimkif said. "Specifically, you and I should be married."

Haplif stared at her. "You're not serious."

"Not *really* married, of course," Shimkif said quickly. "But think about it. With my daughter Frosif also being *your* daughter Frosif, we have the exact kind of balanced family Yomie wants."

"Maybe," Haplif said, thinking it through. "That would be fine for Yomie, but would it also work for Yoponek?"

"You already said he wants social position," Shimkif reminded him. "Surely a family is also included in that craving. In fact, given how Chiss culture works, I'd say it was practically a given."

"Good point," Haplif said. "I'm constrained to remind you that we've been traveling for weeks now without giving them any hint that we were a family. How exactly do we cover that?"

"We don't," Shimkif said, smiling slyly. "We're going to have a marriage ceremony right here aboard ship."

Haplif felt his forehead skin crinkle. "*What?*"

"Think about it," Shimkif urged. "A marriage ceremony puts us in the same position they plan to be in sometime in the next few months. That makes us emotionally sympathetic to them, and presumably vice versa."

"Maybe," Haplif said. To be honest, he wasn't all that convinced it would do any good. Yomie's life-cravings didn't necessarily translate into empathy for a pair of aliens.

But Jixtus's deadlines were looming, and it certainly couldn't hurt. At the very least it might distract Yomie from her damn bird migration. "You can write something properly elaborate and bombastic?" he asked.

"Trust me," Shimkif said. "There won't be an untouched heart in the house. And really, how could our Chiss lovebirds resist the humble requests of two newly happily marrieds?"

# CHAPTER TEN

"I apologize for the quality of the recordings," Lakinda said, tapping her questis to send the *Grayshrike*'s sensor data across the conference room table to Thrawn and his first officer. "But the Battle Dreadnought stayed between us and the smaller ship throughout most of the battle, and on the rare occasions when it moved there was usually missile debris blocking the view."

"All by design, of course," Thrawn commented, looking closely at the images on his questis. "Were you able to make any determination as to the type of craft?"

"No," Lakinda said, feeling unreasonably like she was back at the academy being interviewed under the harsh glare of a senior officer.

Unreasonably, because on a purely intellectual level she recognized that neither Thrawn nor Samakro was leaning on her or even showing any disapproval over how she and her ship had handled their part of the battle. But the very fact that she'd traveled to the *Springhawk* instead of having this meeting on her own ship added an extra and unwanted emotional layer to the whole thing.

Not that the choice of conference site had been anyone's decision. Thrawn was Mitth, one of the Nine, and Lakinda was Xodlak, one of the Forty, and while military regulations expressly forbade any preferential treatment on the basis of family association, everyone knew decisions of etiquette nearly always fell in line with the rest of Ascendancy society.

It might have been easier if Lakinda had brought one or more of her own officers along instead of coming alone. But the *Grayshrike* had taken damage, and she had no intention of pulling any of her people off repair work just to relieve some of her unwarranted anxiety.

Of course, the fact that the day had once again been saved by Thrawn's tactical plan wasn't helping her mood any.

"Interesting that they worked so hard to prevent us from getting a closer look," Thrawn said. "From the size and configuration I'd guess it's either a personnel transport or freighter, but there's no way to tell which."

"If it even matters," Samakro pointed out. "Either ship type can carry cargo or passengers or both."

"Exactly," Thrawn said. "A more solid identification might give us a clue as to the intent, but as you say, that hardly matters."

"So why obscure it?" Samakro asked.

"The likely possibility is that we would recognize the design and therefore learn who the Battle Dreadnought's masters are working with," Thrawn said.

"From which it follows that we may already know these allies," Lakinda said.

"Or may encounter them in the future," Thrawn said. He gazed at the questis another moment, then set it down on the table. "We'll continue to analyze the data, Senior Captain, as I presume you will as well."

"Of course," Lakinda said. "What about the terrain they were flying over? Was the Magistrate, or whatever her title is, able to identify it?"

"The Magys," Thrawn corrected. He pulled up a page on his questis and sent it across to her. "Here's the data and our first-pass analysis of the region. Unfortunately, she was of only limited help. That general region was once largely farmland, with some small rivers and lakes, several medium-sized cities, and two ranges of upthrust mountains."

"Doesn't look like there's much farmland left," Lakinda said, wincing as she peered at the images. Whether it had been deliberate or merely collateral damage, the civil war had made a serious mess of the area.

"True, though it's difficult to tell for certain with all the smoke and dust clouds," Thrawn pointed out. "Still, unless the plants that were grown there thrived on radioactivity and toxic chemicals, I think we can rule out farming as the Battle Dreadnought's objective."

"Maybe they wanted the area cleared so they could put in something new," Samakro suggested. "I don't know offhand of any plants that like damaged soil, but I'm sure there's *something* out there that does."

"And of course, we're only assuming this was the area they were interested in," Lakinda added. "Those gunboats were on the move before we arrived, which means the alarm had already been given. The Battle Dreadnought and transport might have started elsewhere and were simply heading over that spot when we got our first look at them."

"A valid point," Thrawn agreed. "At any rate, there seems to be nothing more we can do right now except alert the Ascendancy and see if the analysts on Csilla can do anything more with our data."

"Unless we want to send down a team for a quick look," Samakro suggested. "If there's something blatantly obvious down there, they might be able to spot it."

"If we can't detect it with the *Springhawk*'s and *Grayshrike*'s sensors, I doubt a cursory flyby would find anything," Thrawn said. "And given Senior Captain Lakinda's news, a flyby would be all we would have time for. Is there anything more you can tell me about the message?"

"Nothing beyond what I've already given you," Lakinda said. "Admiral Ar'alani thought Supreme Admiral Ja'fosk may have sent it at the behest of the Syndicure, but that was just speculation."

"Based on the briefness of the order?"

"And the lack of any *when convenient* modifiers that usually come to a commander who's already on a designated mission," Lakinda said. "If it *did* come from the Syndicure, they're probably going to be annoyed that it's taken this long for you to respond."

"Is that a hint we should get moving?" Samakro asked.

"I'm not saying or hinting anything," Lakinda said, feeling some annoyance. Whatever was going on, and whether it was coming from the Syndicure or even just Ja'fosk himself, there was no reason to put her in the middle of it. "I'm here to deliver a message. I've delivered it. Your assignment is to return to the Ascendancy; mine is to rendezvous with Admiral Ar'alani at the last Nikardun base we cleared out together after you left. I'd suggest due haste for both of us."

"Unfortunately, we still have one more leg to our mission," Samakro said. "Before we can head back to Csilla, we need to return the Magys and her companion to Rapacc."

Lakinda felt her eyes narrow. "If you're suggesting *I* do that instead of you—"

"Actually, Mid Captain," Thrawn said, "none of us are going to Rapacc."

Samakro frowned. "Excuse me, sir?"

"Caregiver Thalias has already spoken to the Magys," Thrawn said. "Having seen the devastation below, she's now even more fully convinced that her people are all dead and that only the physical planet itself can be saved."

"With due respect to you and the Magys, sir, that's a completely unwarranted conclusion," Samakro said. "We were barely able to take a cursory look. A thorough evaluation would take days or weeks."

"Nevertheless, that's the conclusion she has reached," Thrawn said. "She's therefore decided that upon her return to Rapacc she'll order her refugees to join the rest of their people in death."

Lakinda stared at him. "You mean she'll just flat-out *kill* them?"

"Not kill them, but simply order them to die," Thrawn said. "They believe that in death they'll touch something they call the Beyond that will then allow them to join together and begin healing their planet."

"To what end?" Lakinda asked. "If the people are already dead, what does the planet matter?"

"The Magys believes they should prepare a home for those who may someday adopt their former world as their own."

Lakinda felt her throat tighten. "Let me guess. She assumed those alien warships were proof that the real estate has already changed hands?"

"If not proof, certainly a strong indication," Thrawn said. "Caretaker Thalias and I have spoken to her at length and have been unable to change her mind."

"So that's it?" Lakinda asked. "She'll go back to Rapacc and order her people to die, and she expects them to do that?"

Thrawn locked eyes with her. "She's already ordered her companion to die," he said, his voice low and dark. "He's already complied."

"*What?*" Samakro demanded, his eyes going wide. "When?"

"Approximately an hour ago," Thrawn said. "Shortly before the three of us convened this meeting." He paused, and Lakinda saw a shadow of pain cross his face. "Uingali's calculations seem to have been off by a few days."

"So it would seem," Samakro said. His tone was cold, but Lakinda could tell the anger wasn't directed at his commander. "What about their guards? Where were they?"

"On duty as ordered," Thrawn said. "But they knew the presumed time line and weren't anticipating such an action yet."

"And you didn't say anything about it to us until *now*?"

"We had more pressing matters to discuss," Thrawn said. "Speaking out earlier wouldn't have benefited the deceased."

Samakro took a deep breath, and Lakinda could see him forcing his mind and emotions back under control. For herself, she felt like she'd just been kicked in the stomach. "What about the Magys?"

"She's in no danger," Thrawn said.

"You just said she considers her situation hopeless."

"She has a duty to order her people to die," Thrawn said. "She can't do that if she herself is dead."

"You think she'll buy that line of reasoning?"

"Not really," Thrawn conceded. "Caregiver Thalias already made that suggestion, in fact. The Magys argued in return that news of her death would raise a new person to her title, who would then be responsible for making that decision."

"In that case, I don't see how you can say she's out of danger," Samakro persisted. "Sooner or later she'll figure out we're not going back to Rapacc and take the obvious next step."

"She's out of danger," Thrawn said evenly, "because she's currently asleep in a hibernation chamber."

Samakro's mouth dropped open. "She's *what*?"

"Consider our options," Thrawn said. "We could return her to Rapacc, but there's no guarantee the Paccosh could or would keep her incommunicado. Unless we're prepared to let two hundred people die at her command, we can't do that. Furthermore, if I'm to obey Senior Captain Lakinda's message, we don't have time for a side trip of that length. Our options are therefore to let the Magys die or to keep her aboard the *Springhawk*. I've chosen the latter."

"On what grounds?" Samakro asked. "There's no standing order that permits you to carry an alien indefinitely aboard an Ascendancy warship."

"It's not indefinite, but only until we can return her to Rapacc," Thrawn said. "Preferably after finding some hope for her and her people. As to justification, she's the direct cause of death of another passenger aboard my ship. Under those circumstances, I have the authority to put her in confinement until she can be delivered to a place of judgment."

"Her world is spinning its way right below us," Samakro said. "We can send her there."

"We don't have time to find a proper location for her," Thrawn said. "Putting her down in a random spot would likely be sending her to her death."

"Maybe that's what we have to do," Samakro said, starting to sound angry. "Her life is her business. It's certainly none of ours."

"I believe it is," Thrawn said. "All lives are important, and I resist the thought of standing by and watching two hundred possibly needless deaths. Moreover, we know this world was important to the Nikardun. Otherwise, why move to blockade Rapacc when the refugees arrived there? There was—or is—something of interest down there, and the Magys may be the key to that mystery. For the security of the Ascendancy, we need to solve it."

"I doubt the Council or Syndicure would agree," Samakro pointed out. "What do you think they will say to all this?"

Thrawn turned from him to look at Lakinda. "Actually," he said, "I wasn't going to tell them."

Reflexively, Lakinda pressed back against her chair. Up until this point, she'd been feeling like an outsider unwillingly dragged into eavesdropping distance of a family argument. Now, with that look, she was suddenly part of it.

"You can't be serious," Samakro said.

"Why not?" Thrawn countered. "As you yourself said, neither group would agree with this course of action. Yet you must also recognize that the presence of an alien Battle Dreadnought means there is potential danger here that must be uncovered."

"Even if I conceded that, there are practical considerations," Samakro said. "How could you even hide her presence? Too many officers and warriors know she and her companion were aboard."

"Her companion has already ended his life," Thrawn said. "The log will show that she, too, made that decision."

"She—? Oh," Samakro said sourly. "Right. Of course. She made the decision, but wasn't allowed to carry it out."

"The log will leave that point open for interpretation," Thrawn said, his eyes still on Lakinda. "Senior Captain? Comments?"

Lakinda took a deep breath. Not just in the middle of a family argument, but now invited to join in the battle. *Now* what was she supposed to do?

"The *Springhawk* is your ship, Senior Captain Thrawn," she said, a part of her mind noting that her voice had reflexively pitched itself into military-formal. Verbal or not, this was definitely for the record. "These decisions are yours, to stand or fall by. If you order me to remain silent, I will do so." She braced herself. "Provided I'm not required to directly lie to a superior."

"Thank you," Thrawn said gravely. "I ask only that you refer any questions and questioners to me. As you say, I will stand or fall. I don't require or wish for you to stand or fall at my side." He turned back to Samakro. "Nor do I wish that for you, Mid Captain."

"Thank you, sir," Samakro said, his voice as formal as Lakinda's. "But you're my commanding officer. If those are your orders, I of course will obey them."

Thrawn nodded. "Thank you both." He paused, seeming to shift mental gears. "We'll leave for Csilla as soon as both ships are ready to fly. I don't wish either of us to still be here if the Battle Dreadnought sends reinforcements. If there are further repairs that can't be performed in hyperspace, we can stop along the way."

He looked at Lakinda. "If you'll signal me when you're ready, we can jump together."

"Agreed," Lakinda said.

"I'll alert the docking bay to prepare your shuttle," Thrawn continued. He stood up, the other two following suit. "Make sure Admiral Ar'alani gets a copy of the data. The Battle Dreadnought's missile attacks on the *Grayshrike* weren't as definitive as I'd hoped, but we may still be able to determine whether or not they were the same weapons that destroyed the Nikardun base."

"And if they were?" Lakinda said.

Again, Thrawn locked eyes with her. "Then the life and knowledge of the Magys and her people become even more important," he said. "We need to determine if this is a new enemy standing on the Ascendancy's threshold."

"And then she told me we could probably teach the yubals some tricks," Lakris said, stuffing the last bit of breakfast fritter into her mouth and helping herself to another one from the platter. "She said she could teach me how to do it," she added around the bite.

"Not with your mouth full," Lakansu admonished her daughter.

Admonished her for about the tenth time in the past week, Lakphro noted to himself as he took another bite of his own fritter. He'd had a problem with youthful exuberance overwhelming social politeness when he was a midager, and his daughter had clearly inherited those genes from him. Lakansu, on the other hand, had grown up in a much larger family with highly disciplined parents who had imposed that same self-restraint on her and the rest of their children.

Lakphro tried to be more strict. Lakansu tried to be more casual. Their parenting approaches *were* getting closer together, but Lakphro was pretty sure the differences still sometimes drove Lakris crazy.

Still, the midager dutifully finished chewing before continuing her part of the conversation. "I've never heard of anyone training yubals," she said. "Have you?"

"*I* haven't," Lakansu said, looking across the table at her husband. "Lakphro?"

"They can certainly be trained," Lakphro said. "Getting them to follow the lead growzer sort of qualifies, though maybe that's just domestication. But to do *tricks*?" He shook his head. "I'm not sure they're even physically capable of doing anything except walking, eating, and creating crop fertilizer."

"And tasting delicious when roasted," Lakansu added.

"No argument there," Lakphro agreed.

"Well, I'm going to see if she can do it," Lakris said, taking another bite. "Can I—?" She broke off, apparently remembering her mother's warning, and chewed furiously for a couple of seconds until her mouth was clear again. "Can I take her to the yubal pen when I'm letting them out?"

Lakphro hesitated. The Agbui visitors hadn't been nearly as much of a problem as he'd feared they might be when Councilor Lakuviv dropped them onto his land a couple of weeks ago. But while he and the other ranchers in the area were working hard to be good hosts, he also didn't want the aliens getting too comfortable with his land, his animals, and especially his family.

Still, Lakris and Haplif's daughter Frosif seemed to have struck up a tentative friendship, and for a loner like Lakris that was no mean accomplishment. And really, the strangers were only going to be here for a few months. "I suppose so," he told Lakris. "Just make sure you warn her not to get in their way, or between them and the growzers. You know how Slobber gets when someone messes with his herd."

"I'll be careful," Lakris promised. "I'm going to show Frosif some of *his* tricks, too."

"Including the telepathic call?" Lakansu asked with a sly smile.

"*Especially* the telepathic call," Lakris said, smiling back. "Everybody likes that one."

Actually, Lakphro could remember a couple of the other ranchers being rather annoyed when they found out how Lakris's "telepathy" worked. But they'd never had a sense of humor to begin with, so they didn't count. "Just remember the Agbui still don't know a lot about the Chiss," he said. "Make sure you tell her the truth before she leaves today so she doesn't go back to her parents with wild stories about Chiss telepathy."

Lakris made a face, but nodded. "Okay." She finished her fritter and stood up. She hesitated, eyeing the platter, then scooped up two more and wrapped them in her napkin. "See you later," she said, and headed for the door.

"And before you offer Frosif one of those, make sure Agbui can digest everything that's in it," Lakansu called after her.

"I will," Lakris called back over her shoulder. She started to grab her usual jacket, paused, and pulled out the heavy checkered brown one with the brass sealer instead. "I'm going to need this one, okay?" she said, holding it up.

"Go ahead," Lakphro said. "Just remember that if you get kumeg mash in the sealer teeth, *you're* the one who'll be cleaning it."

"I won't," Lakris said. "I mean I will. Clean it. Bye." With a last wave, she bounced out of the house, only the soft-latch keeping the door from slamming behind her.

"She seems to have found a friend," Lakansu commented as she sliced a bite off her own fritter with a knife and fork.

"Yeah," Lakphro said. "*Seems* to."

Lakansu eyed him. "You still don't like having them here, do you?"

"They're not exactly brightening up the neighborhood," Lakphro growled as he took another fritter from the platter.

"Well, they haven't crushed the seedlings," Lakansu said, ticking off fingers. "They haven't frightened the yubals or spread plague through the herd. They haven't poisoned the groundwater with their spice plots."

All of which Lakphro had loudly predicted when the Agbui first arrived. He hated it when people quoted his own words back at him. "They've got crowds of gawkers pressed up against our fences staring at them," he said, ticking off fingers of his own. "They've got number-squinters from Redhill flying in twice a day—"

"Once a day," Lakansu corrected.

"It was twice a day at the beginning," Lakphro said doggedly. "And they're so damn *touchy.*"

Lakansu frowned. "What do you mean, touchy?"

"I mean they want to touch you all the time," Lakphro said, an unpleasant shiver running through him. "That Haplif, mostly. I'm trying to explain our contour bunding on our hillside plots, and he's trying to touch my hair or the back of my neck or someplace. It's creepy."

"I think that's just part of their culture," Lakansu soothed. "I don't think they mean anything by it."

"I know it's part of their culture," Lakphro growled. "You and Lakris may not mind it, but I do."

"Have you told him that?"

"I've been hoping that me dodging away from him every time he tries it would give him a clue," Lakphro said sourly. "So far, not so much."

"Some people have to be told directly," Lakansu said with a shrug. "Especially when it's so much a part of them that they probably don't even notice it."

"Well, if he does it today, maybe I'll try that," Lakphro said, looking at his chrono. "Speaking of *today,* I've already lost way too much of it. See you later."

He took his plate to the sink, gave Lakansu a quick kiss, and headed out. First step would be checking the kumeg seedlings to see if the traps had caught any of the insects that had been sneaking bites. After that he would check on Lakris and see how she was doing with the yubals.

He shaded his eyes from the rising sun. Lakris was over by the yubal pens now, the Agbui girl Frosif beside her.

On second thought, the kumeg seedlings could wait.

The two midagers were chattering away as he walked toward them, and as he got close enough he could hear Lakris insisting that yubals were among the dumbest things on four legs while the Agbui girl insisted she'd seen dumber animals trained to do actual tricks. "I suppose it's possible we could do something with them," Lakris conceded as Lakphro came up behind them. "I mean, if we can telepathically call growzers, we can probably get through a yubal's thick skull, too."

"Are the Chiss telepathic?" Frosif asked. "I didn't know that."

"Of course we are," Lakris said airily, pretending to look around. "Let's see. That growzer over there—see, the big black-and-brown one? Watch—I'm going to mentally call him to me." She pointed to the growzer with one hand, surreptitiously getting a grip on the tab of her jacket's brass-tooth sealer with the other. She pulled the tab down, and Lakphro heard the faint zipping sound—

And with a muffled screech, Frosif threw herself flat on her face on the ground.

Lakphro broke into a sprint, his pulse suddenly pounding in his ears as panic bubbled in his throat. "Are you all right?" he called, images of death and tears and angry Xodlak officials spinning through his mind. "Frosif? Are you hurt? What happened? Are you all right?"

"I'm all right," the alien girl called, already picking herself up off the ground. She was shaking, Lakphro could see, her hands twitching as Lakris helped her brush the dirt off her clothes.

"What happened?" he asked, coming to a halt beside the girls.

"That sound," Frosif said, sounding embarrassed now. "It scared me."

Lakphro looked at Lakris, saw his same confusion in her face. "How?" he asked.

"It just . . . never mind," Frosif said, sounding even more embarrassed. "It was stupid."

"It's not stupid," Lakphro insisted. "Come on, Frosif. You could have been hurt, and it would have been our fault. The least you can do is tell us why it scared you."

Frosif's shoulders seemed to sag. "It reminded me of a bad time," she said, her long fingers stretching out and idly running through Lakris's hair. "It was the sound of something falling out of the sky." Her other hand reached toward Lakphro's head—

Reflexively, he twitched away. "What kind of thing was falling?" he asked.

"Something scary." Abruptly, Frosif dropped her hands to her sides. "I have to go," she said, backing away from them. "I'm sorry. I'll see you tomorrow, Lakris."

"Wait," Lakris said, starting after her. "It was just my coat's sealer. Here—see?" She ran the tab up and then down, the sealer making the faint sound as the metal teeth locked together. "I trained Slobber to come when I did that."

"I have to go," Frosif said. She turned, nearly tripping over Slobber as the growzer obediently trotted up in response to Lakris's call. The alien girl dodged around him and headed toward the Agbui ship, breaking into a run.

"Dad?" Lakris asked, her voice confused and miserable.

"It's okay, hun-bun," he said, wrapping his arm reassuringly around her shoulders. "You didn't do anything wrong. There was no way you could know that sound would set her off."

"I know. But . . ." Lakris trailed off.

"I don't get it, either." Lakphro gestured toward the sealer. "Let me hear it again."

She ran the tab up and down. It sounded just like it always did: small metallic teeth locking together and sealing the garment. "No idea what she thought she heard," he said, shaking his head.

"Do you think I should go apologize?"

Lakphro peered across the grazing land. Frosif was halfway to her ship, and a couple of the aliens who'd been working their hillside spice plantings had paused to watch her. "No, let her be," he said. "I don't know what you could say that we haven't already said. Go ahead and get the yubals out and grazing. Maybe she'll come back on her own."

"Maybe," Lakris said, still sounding unhappy.

"I'll go check the kumeg, then come back and help you," he continued, giving her a quick hug. "It'll be okay, Lakris. Just give her time."

"Okay," Lakris said. "Come on, Slobber."

Lakphro watched her open the pen gate and start the livestock moving toward the north grazing ground, Slobber and his fellow growzers moving in on both sides to keep the herd together. Then he turned and headed toward the kumeg, running the sound of the sealer over and over in his mind, wondering what in there could have scared the alien girl so badly.

By the time he and Lakris headed home for lunch he still didn't have a clue. But an ominous suspicion about these alien visitors was starting to form in the back of his mind.

Someone from Councilor Lakuviv's office should be dropping by soon for their daily Agbui check. Maybe, for once, he'd have something new to ask them.


"I'm sorry," Frosif said petulantly, wincing as her mother dabbed the slowly oozing blood off her cheek from the scratchy grass she'd landed on.

"Sure, sure," Haplif said with some grumpiness of his own. Apologies weren't going to do anything but waste time. Especially since the girl didn't sound particularly sorry anyway. "All these months, and *now* is when you decide to go all trauma victim on us?"

"Enough," Shimkif said. Her voice was quiet, but there was an ominous warning beneath it. "Recriminations are a waste of time and breath."

"I know," Haplif growled. "But *now*?"

"I didn't *mean* to do it," Frosif snapped.

"If you're looking to spread blame, remember that *you're* the one who pushed those flat-blast artillery shells onto both sides," Shimkif said. "Those are probably the ones the Chiss girl's sealer mimicked."

"Yes, fine," Haplif said impatiently. "Speaking of the girl, how did she react to the whole thing?"

Frosif shrugged. "Worried and embarrassed, mostly. I didn't get any suspicion from her."

"What would there have been to be suspicious of?" Shimkif asked.

"Since when does suspicion need anything solid to drive it?" Haplif countered. "What about her father?"

"Lakphro?" Frosif shook her head. "I don't know. He didn't let me touch him."

Haplif muttered a curse. No, of course Lakphro wouldn't have. The damn rancher was absolutely and resolutely paranoid about being touched.

And that could be a problem. Haplif and the other Agbui had everyone else in the area pretty well under control, from Councilor Lakuviv right down to Lakphro's sparky-eyed daughter. They'd done quiet but thorough probes, and everyone's weaknesses and life-cravings were mapped out and already being manipulated.

But not Lakphro. Haplif had managed enough pass-bys to have a vague idea of the rancher's goals, but only the general and ill-defined ones of contented family and successful ranch. In the meantime, Haplif had none of the precise triggers he would need to nudge Lakphro into doing what the Agbui wanted.

"What about Yoponek?" Shimkif asked. "He's one of them, and he hasn't got much to do right now. Maybe he could go talk to them and smooth it out."

"It doesn't *need* smoothing out," Frosif said. "I already told you she's all right."

"Besides, Yoponek's living out his dream of mixing socially with the high and mighty," Haplif said. "We don't want to interrupt that by throwing him at some random rancher."

"A random rancher you can't control," Shimkif reminded him.

"Maybe *I* can't control him, but his wife can," Haplif said. "What would she think of some genuine Agbui jewelry? Especially jewelry that so far has only been given to her family's local leader?"

"She'd be suitably impressed," Shimkif said, her forehead skin crinkling in thought. "Yes, she'd probably be inclined to gloss over anything about us that might bother her."

"And if *she* gives us a pass, Lakphro's not likely to stand in her way," Haplif said. "*That* much I know about the man. Maybe a brooch for the daughter, too, as an apology for frightening her?"

"We could, I suppose," Shimkif said, a little doubtfully. "But that means two more brooches out in public and not in the hands of the elite."

"We have enough to spare," Haplif assured her. "More to the point, I don't want to have to watch my back while I'm focusing on Councilor Lakuviv."

"All right," Shimkif said, still sounding reluctant. "But it'll be on you to keep track of them. We don't want any news leaking out until we're ready."

"It won't," Haplif said. "Everything's on track." He gave a little snort. "Besides, there's nobody around here but other yokels. Who are Lakphro's women going to show off their new baubles to?"

# CHAPTER ELEVEN

It had been a day for the books, Samakro reflected as Supreme General Ba'kif ushered him and Thrawn into the general's private office. First had been a meeting with the entire Defense Hierarchy Council and a debriefing of the skirmish with the unidentified Battle Dreadnought over the Magys's war-torn planet Sunrise. After that had come a combination grilling and exhortation by a select Syndicure committee, with some of the most esteemed names of the Nine Ruling Families on the panel. Now here they were in one of Ba'kif's legendary off-the-record meetings.

And in the midst of those meetings, for possibly the first time since Samakro had welcomed Thrawn back aboard the *Springhawk*, his commander had shown actual surprise.

*Definitely* a day for the books.

"No," Thrawn said firmly even as he and Samakro walked to the chairs in front of Ba'kif's desk. "I don't believe it."

"It's just a rumor, and an unfounded one at that," Ba'kif reminded him as he circled the desk and lowered himself into his own chair. "Evaluating rumors is part of the Expansionary Defense Fleet's job, after all."

"Though this one may not qualify as unfounded," Samakro pointed out. "The Aristocra said their sources on this are usually reliable."

"I don't care how reliable they usually are," Thrawn said. "It's simply not possible. The Paataatus would never ally themselves with the Vagaari pirates, certainly not against the Ascendancy."

"From a strategic point of view—" Samakro began.

He broke off at a small gesture from Ba'kif. "Why not?" the general asked, his eyes on Thrawn.

"The Paataatus aren't going to attack us," Thrawn said flatly. "Not for at least a generation."

"Which for them is what, twenty years?"

"The range is usually given as seventeen to twenty-five," Thrawn said. "My point is that the decisive defeat Admiral Ar'alani delivered last year will keep them from any actions against the Ascendancy for at least that long."

"Maybe the Vagaari have something else in mind," Samakro suggested. "Something to their mutual benefit that doesn't involve the Ascendancy."

"Such as?" Thrawn asked.

"That's what you're being sent out to investigate," Ba'kif said. "Mid Captain Samakro is right, Senior Captain, and there's no use kicking against the wall. The Council has made up its mind, the Syndicure supports their decision—a rare enough occurrence all by itself—and that is that."

For a moment Thrawn was silent, his eyes lowered to his questis. Presumably looking over their orders. Possibly looking for a loophole. "If I may, General?" Samakro asked.

Ba'kif inclined his head. "Of course."

"I've looked over the accounts of Senior Captain Thrawn's last confrontation with the Vagaari," Samakro said. "I noticed those records are, shall we say, incomplete."

"Incomplete in what way, Mid Captain?" Ba'kif said, his eyes now holding steady on Samakro's.

"That's the question, sir," Samakro said, choosing his words carefully. Pressing a senior officer on documents that had obviously been deliberately edited was a risky thing to do, and the more sensitive the excised material, the riskier it got. But if the *Springhawk* was going up against these people, he needed to know the full story. "Specifically, does the Syndicure perhaps have other, more personal reasons for us to take another crack at the Vagaari?"

"You mean is some family's reputation on the line?"

"I'm thinking more that some family's profits may be on the line."

Ba'kif glanced at Thrawn. Samakro followed the look, but there was no reaction there that he could see. "I take it you've been listening to rumors," the general said. "May I ask which ones?"

"Mostly the one about an artificial gravity-well generator," Samakro said. "A device Senior Captain Thrawn took from the Vagaari that can pull a ship out of hyperspace as if it had run close to a stellar or planetary mass."

"Interesting rumor," Ba'kif said, his voice not giving anything away. "You'll recall what I said a moment ago about testing such things?"

"Yes, sir." In other words, the general wasn't going to confirm anything. Samakro hadn't really expected him to. But Ba'kif's reaction— or, rather, complete lack of one—spoke all too clearly. "Because if a rumor like that was true, the Syndicure and Council might be sending us out there hoping we'll be twice lucky."

"Again, an interesting supposition," Ba'kif said. "Just bear in mind that your primary task is to learn whether or not the Vagaari are returning to this area, and if so whether or not they've allied with the Paataatus. Anything else you might happen upon—" He gave a sort of half smile. "Well, you'll be the ones on the scene. Use your own judgment."

"Yes, sir," Thrawn said for both of them. "What about Sunrise?"

"Sunrise?"

"Our name for the Magys's world," Thrawn said. "Are you going to send the *Grayshrike* back to investigate?"

Ba'kif huffed out a breath. "The Council isn't exactly thrilled by the thought of sending a major warship that far from the Ascendancy," he said. "Neither is the Syndicure."

"I was under the impression that exploring distant regions and searching for potential threats was the centerpiece of the Expansionary Defense Fleet's charter."

"It is," Ba'kif said. "But your, shall we say, enthusiasm in identifying and confronting General Yiv has made certain of the Aristocra nervous about sending too many forces outside the Ascendancy and leaving its own worlds less than thoroughly defended. Even bolstered by the Ruling Families' private fleets, the Defense Force is thought by many to be stretched too thin."

"I don't find that assessment valid," Thrawn said.

"Nor do I," Ba'kif said. "But valid or not, the opinions of the Syndicure carry a certain amount of weight."

"I understand," Thrawn said. "Hence the blackdock?"

"Come now, Senior Captain," Ba'kif said with an odd mix of innocence and reproach. "You imagine dots and connecting lines where none exist."

Samakro frowned. What in the world were they talking about?

"My apologies," Thrawn said, inclining his head to the general. "I understand the *Vigilant* is scheduled to return to those last Nikardun bases for more data."

"It is," Ba'kif said. "The Syndicure has also made it clear they don't want Admiral Ar'alani going any farther out than that." He gestured. "As for you and Mid Captain Samakro, you have a mission of your own to prepare for. Dismissed, and good luck."

A minute later Samakro and Thrawn were back in the corridor, heading toward the shuttle docking area. "What was all that about the blackdock?" Samakro asked as they walked.

"The *Grayshrike* is undergoing repairs in Csilla Blackdock Two instead of one of the bluedocks," Thrawn said.

"Yes, I know that," Samakro said. "The facilities there were available and the bluedocks were backed up with other work. What does that have to do with the Syndicure?"

Thrawn glanced casually around. "Only that with the *Grayshrike* that much farther out from Csilla, it won't be nearly as noticeable when it heads away on its next mission."

Samakro stared at him. "You're not serious. They're going to—?"

"The Syndicure doesn't control the Expansionary Defense Fleet," Thrawn reminded him. "All they can do is advise, encourage, and make trouble."

"Especially the latter," Samakro said, his stomach tightening. If and when they found out the Council and Ba'kif had effectively ignored them and sent Lakinda back to Sunrise, they would undoubtedly drop several layers of that trouble on all of them.

And if Samakro was to connect dots and lines that weren't there, he might suspect the *Vigilant* would be joining the *Grayshrike* once they'd cleared the Ascendancy's borders. Something else for the Aristocra to scream about down the line.

Theoretically, Ba'kif at least was immune from Syndicure wrath. But that didn't mean some group of syndics might not set themselves the personal goal of making his life so miserable that he would be forced to resign.

Worse, there was the possibility that one or more families could be persuaded to fully join in that pressure. If that happened, Ba'kif's days as supreme general would be short indeed.

"We need to know who that Battle Dreadnought was, Mid Captain," Thrawn said, his voice going grim. "*And* who in this region they've allied with."

"I'm not arguing, sir," Samakro said. "Just worrying about Lakinda. She and the whole Xodlak family have a *lot* of politics going on at the moment."

"Lakinda will do fine," Thrawn said. "Politics aren't supposed to be part of Expansionary Fleet missions."

"Of course not," Samakro said. "Speaking of alliances and missions, I don't suppose you can confirm that rumor about the Vagaari gravity-well trap? I'd like to have a better feel for what we might be getting into."

"You know I can't do that," Thrawn said. "That said, you may be right about the Syndicure looking to profit from our investigation."

"Profit's always a good motive, sir, yes," Samakro agreed.

But money wasn't the only thing that brought covetous gleams to Aristocra eyes. The fact that both the Mitth and their Irizi rivals supported the *Springhawk*'s expedition had already raised warning flags in his mind.

Did those two families know more than the rest of the Syndicure about what was going on out past the Paataatus, something that perhaps made it worth a temporary alliance? Were they hoping for new technology they could use directly or fashion into a bargaining chip?

Or were the Irizi simply jumping at the chance to get Thrawn out of the Ascendancy for a while, and had somehow talked the Mitth into going along? *That* was also a motive he could understand.

"But I wouldn't worry about it," Thrawn said. "The Vagaari were severely beaten down the last time we met. Whatever's going on out there, I don't anticipate any major surprises."

Councilor Lakuviv gazed at the Agbui brooch nestled in his palm, a chill running through him. "You're sure?" he asked Lakjiip, cursing the quaver in his voice. "*They're* sure?"

"They are," the senior aide said, and Lakuviv cursed the calmness in her voice. A mere functionary shouldn't be calmer than the official she served. "The silver-colored wires are pure nyix."

"Pure nyix," Lakuviv murmured, rubbing his thumb distractedly across the cold metal strands. "How is this even possible?"

Lakjiip shrugged. "The metallurgist at Vlidan who ran it couldn't tell me."

"He couldn't *tell* you?"

"Oh, he made noises about alloys and temperings and annealings," Lakjiip said. "But the bottom line is that he can't figure out how the Agbui pulled it off—"

"I don't mean how they physically did it," Lakuviv cut her off irritably. "I mean who in the Chaos has such an abundance of nyix that they can waste it on jewelry?" He shook the brooch for emphasis. "*And* then offer it for such an absurdly low price?"

"I don't know," Lakjiip said, her own calmness starting to fray a little at the edges. "You're right about the price, though. I was told that the nyix in this one piece is worth at least a thousand times what Haplif told me they would be selling them for."

Lakuviv clenched his teeth. A thousand times. In what version of reality could the Agbui sell these things so cheaply? "Have they started selling them yet?" he asked.

"I don't think so," Lakjiip said. "When I last talked to Haplif a few days ago, he said they wanted to stick to their spice sales first while they decided whether or not the local market could handle their jewelry." She gave Lakuviv a twisted smile. "He was concerned that their prices might be too high."

"Too *high*?"

"I'm just telling you what he said."

"Yes, of course," Lakuviv said, looking at the brooch again. "You found out about this just today, I assume?"

"Actually, it was two days ago," Lakjiip said. "You were—"

"Two *days*?" Lakuviv cut her off. "And you're just telling me *now*?"

"You were working on that petition to the Patriarch of the Irizi family," Lakjiip said evenly. "As I recall, you said you didn't want to be disturbed for anything less than a declaration of war."

Lakuviv ground his teeth. Fine; so he *had* said that. She should still have gone past the words of the order and focused on the intent. "Next time a thunder-maker like this comes to hand, feel free to ignore my orders," he said. "Never mind. Three things we have to do. First: For now you and I are the only ones who know about this. Plus the metallurgist," he added. "We need to talk to him."

"I already have," Lakjiip said. "Fortunately, he's Xodlak, so I could invoke the family secrets protocols. He won't say anything."

"Good," Lakuviv said. "Second: We keep an eye on the Agbui. If they even *look* like they're going to put these things on the market, I want to know about it. And third, I want you to go to Haplif and invite him here for a little get-together." He glanced at his chrono. "Probably too late to do so today without arousing suspicion, so make it tomorrow."

"Yes, sir." Lakjiip hesitated. "There's one other thing, Councilor. I don't know if it qualifies as a thunder-maker—"

"Get on with it," Lakuviv growled.

"Do you think it's possible that the Agbui are refugees?" Lakjiip asked.

Lakuviv blinked. "What on Celwis are you talking about? They're not refugees, they're cultural nomads. Now get moving—we have to get on this right away."

"I know that's what they said," Lakjiip said, making no attempt to move. "I ask because when I went to check on them yesterday afternoon, Rancher Lakphro told me about an incident that was bothering him. It seems his daughter scared one of the Agbui midagers with a brass-tooth sealer."

"Scared her how? And what does this have to do with anything?"

"Scared her into dropping on her face on the ground," Lakjiip said. "The reason it's important is that I made a copy of the sealer sound and spent most of yesterday evening running it through a waveform comparison. It turns out that the sound is a softer version of a flat-blast artillery shell."

"That's absurd," Lakuviv said, frowning as he tried to revive an old memory. Like most unofficial conversations, the details of his first meeting with Haplif had blown away like smoke. But hadn't he said . . . ? "They told us they'd been traveling for the past thirty years."

"Exactly," Lakjiip said. "So how could one of their midagers even know what an artillery shell sounded like? Let alone demonstrate such a violent response to it?"

Lakuviv tapped his chin, trying to think. "Could they have stopped near a war zone? Or even landed in the middle of one?"

"And didn't instantly pack up and get out?"

"Yes, yes, good point," Lakuviv conceded. "An interesting mystery, but a mystery for another day. Right now"—he held up the brooch—"*this* is what's important. We need to find out how the Agbui are working this metal, and why it's so cheap they can make jewelry out of it."

He squeezed the brooch tightly. *Nyix.* The rarest known metal in the Chaos, a vital component of the alloy used to create the incredible toughness of a warship's hull. Only three mines of pure nyix existed in the whole of the Ascendancy, with a handful of other areas offering diffuse seams or single threads. With nyix, a species could conquer and defend; without it, they could only cower and appease. With it, a family could rise to status and power with a speed and sureness nearly unrivaled in Chiss history. Without it, they might stay in the background forever.

But even that lucky family would need to be led. Led and guided by a single individual.

"And most important," he added to Lakjiip, "we need to find out exactly where they got it."

The first thing Thalias saw when she opened her eyes was the coffin lying against the wall beside her bed.

It wasn't actually a coffin, of course, but merely the compact hibernation chamber where the Magys was being held in dreamless sleep until Thrawn could figure out what to do with her. The display lights on the monitor panel confirmed the alien was alive and well in there, and with no immediate danger to her life.

But the chamber was the same cylindrical shape as a coffin, and its occupant really only barely qualified as alive, and Thalias's mental image of a coffin remained.

She tried not to look at it as she gathered her clothes and started dressing. Sometime this morning, if the *Springhawk* was still on Thrawn's schedule, they would leave the relatively smooth volume of hyperspace in which the Chiss Ascendancy nestled and head out into the Chaos. When that happened, she and Che'ri would be summoned to the bridge to begin the journey to the Paataatus hive-home of Nettehi.

Thalias wasn't exactly sure what Thrawn intended to do there, all alone with a single warship. But it wasn't her job to know. Her job was to work with Che'ri to get him there as quickly and safely as possible.

She looked furtively at the hibernation chamber as she got her shoes on. Heading into danger . . . but at least once she had Che'ri on the bridge she wouldn't have to worry about the girl finding out about this monstrosity hidden in their suite. She straightened her tunic, walked to the hatch, and tapped the release.

And as the hatch slid open she saw, too late, that Che'ri had taken up position right at the edge of the hatchway and was looking straight into Thalias's sleeping room at the hibernation chamber.

"No!" Thalias bit out, trying to grab the girl's shoulders, hoping to turn her around before she saw too much.

Too late. Even as Thalias stepped out into the dayroom, she saw Che'ri's eyes go wide and her mouth drop open. "What's *that*?" the girl asked, ducking away from Thalias's hands and pointing into the sleeping room.

"Something you aren't supposed to know about," Thalias said tartly, ushering Che'ri back with one hand as she closed the hatch behind her with the other. "Back. Come on, shoo."

"I *knew* there was something in there," Che'ri said, obediently backing away. "What *is* that?"

"A storage compartment," Thalias improvised. Which was true enough, if somewhat misleading. "What were you doing hanging around my—? Oh," she said as it suddenly hit her. "You used Third Sight, didn't you?"

"Well, you wouldn't let me see it," Che'ri said, a little defensively. "I knew you and Senior Captain Thrawn had put something in there. So when I knew you'd be coming out in a couple of seconds . . ." She gave a little shrug.

"You got into position to see inside as soon as I opened up," Thalias said with a sigh.

"Well, you shouldn't try to keep secrets from people," Che'ri said, her tone going from defensive to accusing. "That's not nice."

"It's not my secret to tell," Thalias said. "If I could have told you . . ." She let the sentence trail off.

"You would have?" Che'ri asked. "Or you wouldn't have?"

Thalias sighed. It really *wasn't* her secret to tell. And yet, in an odd sort of way, it was.

But either way, now that Che'ri had a handle on it, she wasn't going to let go until she had the full story. And it wasn't like they could lock her away in the suite or something. "Come on, let's sit down," Thalias said, gesturing toward the couch. "We'll talk, unless you want breakfast first."

"I can wait," Che'ri said, bounding over and plopping down on the couch, all eagerness now that she was going to get her way and hear a secret. "What's in it?"

Thalias sat down at the other end and braced herself. How did you explain something like this to a ten-year-old? "It's not a *what*," she said. "It's a *who*. It's the Magys."

Again, Che'ri's eyes went wide. "The Magys? *The* Magys?"

"Yes," Thalias said. "She's the alien who came aboard—"

"I know who she is," Che'ri interrupted. "We saw her on the bridge when we were down in secondary command."

"That's right, we did," Thalias said, nodding. "You remember we went to her world, and it was pretty badly wrecked."

"By a war," Che'ri said, her exuberance fading a little.

"Right," Thalias said. "Well. The way the Magys's people do things is that if they think there's no hope for them—no hope at all— they . . . they make a decision to do something called touching the Beyond. It's supposed to let them join with something—people in Lesser Space call it the *Force*—that will let them start healing their planet."

"Okay," Che'ri said, frowning. "So that's why she's in there?"

"Not exactly." Thalias braced herself. "You see, what they have to do to touch the Beyond is . . . die."

Che'ri drew back. "You mean they *kill* themselves?"

Thalias nodded. "Yes."

"But . . ." The girl waved a hand helplessly.

"No, that's not how the Chiss do things," Thalias said. "But different peoples and different cultures . . . people sometimes do things in different ways."

"But what if they make a mistake?" Che'ri asked. "Or change their minds?"

Thalias felt her throat tighten. "They can't change their minds," she said. "Once it's done, it's done."

Che'ri inhaled sharply. "Is that why Thrawn locked her up? Because she was going to . . . do that?"

"Yes," Thalias said. "We put her in my sleeping room because it would be out of the way, and no one but me would see it." She felt her lip twitch. "No one but *us*. So you need to keep this a secret from everyone except—"

"Wait a second," Che'ri interrupted, frowning. "You said the Magys is in there? *Just* the Magys? But there were *two* of them—" She broke off, her expression going rigid. "Did he . . . ?"

For a moment Thalias was tempted to lie. It would be so much easier, and Che'ri didn't need to carry the additional burden.

But as she gazed into the girl's stricken eyes, she knew it would be useless. Truth always came out in the end, and hiding it now would only make it worse later. "Yes," she said gently, reaching over and taking Che'ri's hand. "I'm sorry."

"Why didn't you stop him?" Che'ri asked, her eyes going wet with tears.

"It happened too fast," Thalias said. "There was no way anyone could stop it."

"Not even Senior Captain Thrawn?"

"He was given incorrect information," Thalias said. "On top of that, he probably assumed they would need weapons or tools to do it. I know I would have thought that. But the Magys's companion didn't. He didn't need anything."

"How did he do it?"

Thalias shook her head. "We still don't know. Anyway, like I was saying, the only ones aboard who know about this are Senior Captain Thrawn, Mid Captain Samakro, you, and me. You need to promise you won't say anything to anyone else. All right?"

"All right." Che'ri looked down at the deck. "Can I have breakfast now?"

"Of course," Thalias said, squeezing her hand once and letting go. "Meat-striped fruit squares all right?"

"Sure," Che'ri said, still staring at the deck.

Silently, Thalias stood up and headed to the food prep area. The girl had her answers now, or at least she had the facts. Hopefully, she wouldn't think to ask any of the deeper questions.

The Magys had ordered her companion to die. She'd taken that decision from him—that last, final decision anyone could make. The aliens clearly considered that an acceptable thing to do. Thalias, coming from Chiss culture, didn't.

But wasn't that exactly what she and Thrawn had done to the Magys herself? Hadn't they taken the right of decision away from her by forcibly sedating her and locking her into hibernation? From her point of view, hadn't they violated her rights? It was a troubling question.

Especially since it was Thalias who'd first come up with the idea.

She felt her stomach tighten around the emptiness there. What if the Magys was right, that her people were gone and that the two hundred still on Rapacc faced nothing but loneliness, solitude, and lingering death? If the Beyond truly was an alternative, didn't she have a right to make the decision that her Chiss captors had now taken from her?

Still . . .

*What if they change their minds?* Che'ri had asked. It was a question Thalias had wrestled with, and presumably Thrawn had as well. Because, really, all they'd done was postpone the Magys's decision until they could gather more evidence, one way or another, as to her world's fate.

And if it turned out to be as the Magys herself already believed, Thalias and Thrawn would have to stand by and watch her make the decision to die.

Thalias wasn't ready for that. She could only hope that, somehow, they could find a reason for the Magys and her people to live.

# MEMORIES IV

*Really*, Shimkif had said with all of her boundless self-confidence. *How could our Chiss lovebirds resist the humble requests of two newly happily marrieds?*

They could resist, all right. They could resist just fine.

Not that Shimkif hadn't come through on the wedding ceremony. On the contrary, it was probably the finest make-believe, cobbled-together fruit basket of a fraudulent ritual Haplif had ever seen. All fifty Agbui aboard had played a part, from the pilot all the way down to the engine room mechanics, and all of them had joined in with willing enthusiasm.

Even better, no one had snickered or joked or even smiled at the wrong moment, any of which might have broken the spell of reality they were trying to weave around their naïve Chiss guests. When it was over, everyone crowded around to congratulate the happy couple, and Haplif thought he even saw Yomie get a little misty-eyed.

All of which counted for exactly nothing . . . because when Shimkif talked longingly about the glorious multiple waterfalls on Celwis, and how she'd always wanted to honeymoon amid that kind of awesome spectacle, the implied plea fell on indifferent ears.

Come hell or high winds—come friends, foes, famine, or

frostbite—Yomie was going to that monthlong Grand Migration on Shihon. Every single thrice-damned minute of it.

Which must have put her right on the edge of tearing her face off when, as they passed through the Avidich system, the ship's hyperdrive failed.

Haplif had to knock four times before he finally got a response from inside Yomie's room. "Who is it?"

"It's Haplif, Yomie," Haplif called through the door. "May I speak with you?"

There was another pause. Then the door slid open, to reveal Yomie standing squarely in the opening. "Yes?" she said, her voice and expression almost painfully neutral.

"I have an update on the repairs." He gestured over her shoulder. "May I come in?"

She studied him a moment. Then, silently, she stepped aside.

"Thank you," Haplif said. Gingerly, he eased past her, mindful of her resistance to being touched. "The mechanics have finished the repairs and are putting the hyperdrive back together," he said, giving the room a quick scan. She'd pulled down the foldout table, he saw, and there were several pages of drawings scattered across it. "We should be ready to resume our journey within the next hour or so."

"Thank you," Yomie said, her tone still giving no hint as to the current state of her emotions.

"I also wanted to tell you," Haplif went on, drifting toward the table for a closer look, "that I've spoken to the pilot, and she assures me we can make up some of this time. At worst, you'll only miss the first day of the migration."

"Again, thank you," Yomie said, still facing the door.

Not looking at him. Pointedly ignoring him, in fact, insofar as she could with him standing barely a meter away.

"Thank you in turn for your understanding," Haplif said,

grinding his teeth. She could spread politeness over her words all she wanted, but it was pretty clear she believed he'd deliberately engineered this delay in order to spite her.

Which was not only frustrating but also completely unfair, given that that was the *last* thing he wanted to do. There were pluses and minuses to keeping the two Chiss aboard, as there were pluses and minuses to abandoning them. But simply antagonizing them would be completely counterproductive. "You never told me you were an artist," he commented.

"What?" Out of the corner of his eye he saw her finally turn to face him. "Oh. Those?"

"Yes," Haplif said. He reached out a hand toward the drawings, decided at the last second that touching them might be seen as an intrusion. "They're most impressive."

"They keep me busy," Yomie said, her voice still neutral.

But Haplif could hear a hint of something else beneath it. These drawings were important to her. Maybe important enough to give him the handle that he needed? "May I look closer?" he asked.

She gestured to the table. "Help yourself."

Carefully, Haplif picked up the half-finished picture she must have been working on when he interrupted her. It was a landscape, with a plain on the left, mountains rising up from the right, the glittering edge of an ocean in the distance, and three different types of clouds hovering over everything. The main work seemed to be finished, but he could see where she'd left off detailing the edges of the trees and the left edge of the ocean and clouds. "Very professional," he said. It wasn't laying the praise on too thick; the pictures really *were* quite good. "Especially all the detail around the trees and clouds."

"You like it?" she asked, a bit more animation creeping into her voice. "Look closer."

Frowning, Haplif held the picture up to his eyes, angling it to fully catch the room's light. The squiggles that made up the detailing . . .

He looked sharply at Yomie. "Is that *writing*?"

"Yes, it is," she said, an intense look in her eyes, an odd half smile on her lips. "Very good. It's called a *cloud diary*."

"Art and chronicle combined," Haplif said, feeling a sudden sense of hope. Not just a handle on this girl, but maybe even the window into her soul he and Shimkif had been denied for so long. The writing was necessarily small, but a small lens should make it legible enough—

He twitched as the picture was plucked from his hand. "It's also personal," Yomie said. She gathered the scattered pictures together in a neat pile, then placed the unfinished one facedown on top of the stack. "Don't you need to help get the ship ready to fly?"

"Yes, I do," Haplif said. "Again, my apologies for the delay. Hopefully, the Grand Migration will be all you hope for."

"Yes," Yomie said, her voice back to fully neutral. "I'm sure it will be."

Shimkif was waiting when Haplif arrived in the main control room. "I have news," she said.

"So do I," Haplif said. "Turns out our young snit keeps a journal."

"How wonderful," Shimkif said sourly. "I'm sure it'll be fascinating reading on long winter nights. Jixtus wants to meet."

Haplif felt his forehead skin crinkle, the journal and its possibilities abruptly forgotten. "Where and when?"

"*Where* is one of the outer parking areas for the Grand Migration bird-watchers," Shimkif said. "I've got the landing slot number. *When* is—"

"You told him we were going to the migration?" Haplif demanded, his throat palpitating.

"Of course I told him," Shimkif said. "He has a lot riding on this operation. Did you think he would just let us wander around without keeping track of us?"

"I'd *hoped* he would trust us enough to get the job done without constantly looking over our shoulders."

"You're welcome to tell him that yourself," Shimkif offered. "The *when* is as soon as we arrive." She gave him a significant look. "It sounded like he was already there."

Haplif gave a silent inner growl. Jixtus hated waiting on people. "Did you tell him why we're running late?"

"Oh, relax," Shimkif chided. "He's not angry. He knows things like this happen." She paused, considering. "At least, he's not angry with *me*."

"Thank you so much," Haplif said sarcastically. "I trust you gave orders to get the hyperdrive ready with all possible speed?"

"Of course," she said. "Don't look at me like that. I'm sure he just wants to hear how the operation is going. Oh, and he also wants you to bring along everything you've learned about the Chiss. You'd better get started pulling your notes together."

"Good idea," Haplif said. Most of that information was already codified, but there were some details and speculations that still needed to be put into written form. "You can handle things here?"

"Certainly," she said. "Go. And make it fast and good." Her own throat palpitated briefly. "A delay due to mechanical failure he can understand. A delay because you didn't have your report ready to present to him . . . not so much."

# CHAPTER TWELVE

"**N**o," Lakansu said shyly, her eyes glowing even brighter than usual as she gazed at the delicate brooch Shimkif had just placed in the palm of her hand. "No, really, you mustn't. This is too much."

"Not at all, and I insist," Shimkif said firmly, her lipless slit of a mouth curving up at the corners in a pleased smile. "Your family has been so kind to us. It's the least we can do by way of thanks."

"And for frightening you last week," Frosif added, pulling her hand triumphantly from behind her back and revealing a smaller brooch of a different design, "we want *you* to have *this* one." Stepping up to Lakris, she took the midager's hand, turned it palm up, and placed the brooch in it.

"Oh!" Lakris breathed. She shot a look at Lakphro, looked back at the brooch, then up again at Frosif. "No, that's silly. *You* were the one who was frightened, not me. I should be the one giving *you* something."

"Not at all," Haplif said, draping his arms around his wife's and daughter's shoulders in a show of solidarity. "We're happy to be able to give back at least a little for your generous hospitality. That is, if it's all right with you?" he added, looking questioningly at Lakphro.

Finally, Lakphro thought sourly, someone was asking *him*.

No, it wasn't all right. Not a bit. The gifts were way more extravagant than anyone in his family deserved, way out of line with what little they'd actually done for the visitors. It left him with the sense of being beholden to Haplif and all the rest of the Agbui, and he hated that feeling.

Maybe that was the point of the gifts. Ever since the brass-tooth sealer incident, when Lakjiip had swooped in from Councilor Lakuviv's office and Lakphro had pulled her aside with the question of whether the Agbui might be war refugees, he'd had the creepy feeling that Haplif was keeping a particularly close eye on him.

It might be his imagination. But then again, it might not.

Was he right about the Agbui? Were they more than they claimed? Or less, or maybe just different?

Lakphro had since then looked into the Ascendancy's official policy on accepting war refugees, and it wasn't very encouraging. If the Agbui were trying to find somewhere permanent to live, they had a lot of hurdles to jump, and even then the end result was far from assured. They would most definitely not want questions about them being bandied around at this early stage of the process.

So was this sudden generosity Haplif's way of encouraging Lakphro and his family to keep their mouths shut?

Which, of course, would make it more than just a social obligation. That would make it a bribe.

Lakphro hated bribes. He'd never taken one in his life, and in fact had quit a perfectly good job in his youth when he'd found that a supervisor was taking them. His gut instinct was to bluntly ask the question right here and now, to make Haplif tell him exactly what was going on with him and his so-called cultural nomads.

But he couldn't. Not while his wife and daughter were gazing at their new prizes with such excitement and happiness. Lakansu had always loved exotic-looking jewelry, and Lakris was clearly following in her mother's footsteps. Lakphro couldn't ruin their moment.

Maybe that, too, was the point of the gifts.

"My wife is right," he said instead. "These are far more than we deserve for anything we've done. But if one wants the joy of giving, one must in turn accept the humbleness of receiving, so as to allow others their own joy. You honor us, and we humbly accept your gifts."

"Thank you," Haplif said. "I like those words about the joy of giving. Is that a Chiss proverb?"

"I don't know if it's anything official," Lakphro said. "It was something my parents used to say when I didn't want to accept some gift or favor."

"I think Chiss in general tend to have a problem with false pride," Lakansu added, taking her husband's arm.

"False pride," Haplif said as if trying out the sound. "What does that mean?"

"There are several shades of meaning," Lakansu said. "In this case—"

"Hold it," Lakphro interrupted as the comm on his shoulder band vibrated. "I've got a call." He keyed it on. "Lakphro."

"Rancher, this is Senior Aide Lakjiip," the woman's familiar voice came back. "Do you happen to know where Haplif is?"

"As a matter of fact, he's right here," Lakphro said, frowning as he took a step toward the alien. "Haplif, it's Councilor Lakuviv's senior aide. She wants to talk to you."

"Really?" Haplif said, sounding surprised as he took his own step toward Lakphro. "I thought the official visits for this week had ended."

"Don't ask me, ask her," Lakphro said. He started to pull the comm from the shoulder band, remembered just in time Lakuviv's strict orders that no Chiss technology was to be given to or even handled by any of the aliens. "Speak here—right here—into the comm."

"Yes, I know." Haplif leaned toward his shoulder. "This is Haplif of the Agbui."

"This is Senior Aide Lakjiip," Lakjiip again identified herself. "A freighter claiming to be from another group of Agbui has entered Celwis space. Do you know anything about it?"

"Nothing specific, Senior Aide," Haplif said. "It may be here to see if we need assistance, or to gather a share of our spices if we were sufficiently blessed with land and climate to have a surplus."

"Do you?" Lakjiip asked.

"I believe we can spare some for our brethren," Haplif said. "They may also be bringing more metal filaments for jewelry production."

There was just the slightest of pauses. "Which ones?"

Lakphro frowned. Lakjiip's voice had suddenly gone odd.

"Presumably, all four of those we use," Haplif said. "Though sometimes we use only two or three. Where are they landing? Perhaps I should first ask if they will be permitted to land."

"Councilor Lakuviv's talking with Patriel Lakooni," Lakjiip said. "But I'm sure she'll permit it. We'll have them put down at the main Redhill field. I'll send a skycar for you."

"A moment, Senior Aide?" Lakphro put in as a sudden idea occurred to him. "Sending a skycar will take extra time, and freighters are often on a tight schedule. If you'd like, I'd be more than happy to bring Haplif to you and the Agbui ship and then bring him back here."

"There's really no need for that," Haplif said, his voice now also subtly changed. "I'm sure you have work to do."

"My wife and daughter can easily handle things for a few hours," Lakphro said. "Besides, you've been so generous and kind to us that it's the least I can do."

"I have no objection," Lakjiip said. "Our patrol ships are in contact with them, and as soon as the Patriel gives her authorization Councilor Lakuviv will have them escort the ship to Redhill. Can you be here in an hour or so?"

"No problem, ma'am," Lakphro said. "I'll let Haplif go get whatever he needs while I fire up our skytruck."

"Thank you, Rancher," Lakjiip said. "We'll see you soon." She keyed off.

"Nice day for a flight, anyway," Lakphro commented, taking a step away from Haplif as he keyed off the comm. "I'll get the truck and meet you at your ship."

"Yes, of course," Haplif said. To Lakphro's ear he didn't sound nearly as happy as he had a minute ago when he and Shimkif were handing out jewelry. Maybe he didn't like accepting favors any more than Lakphro did. "Shimkif and I will collect all the spices we can spare to offer our brethren."

"Right," Lakphro said. "I'll be ready."

The aliens turned and headed toward the Agbui ship. "You're really going to go all the way to Redhill?" Lakansu asked, sounding more surprised than annoyed.

"It seemed a reasonable offer," Lakphro said, trying to sound casual. "There's something I wanted to talk to the Councilor or senior aide about anyway. Can I see that brooch?"

"It's not about our yubal assessment again, is it?" Lakansu asked as she handed it over.

"No, no, nothing like that," Lakphro assured her, peering closely at the jewelry. The thing was quite beautiful, he had to admit, with four different metallic threads weaving in and out of one another like a cross between a hair braid and an ancient wedge harp. "Oh, and would you go pack a travel bag for me? I don't know any reason why I'd get stuck in Redhill overnight, but it's always good to be prepared."

"All right," his wife said, giving him a slightly suspicious look.

Not without reason, Lakphro had to admit. He'd had his fair share of headbutts with the Councilor's number-squinters in the past. But today wasn't going to be one of those. "Thank you," he called after her as she headed for the house. "Lakris, would you go check on the herd for me, make sure that water spigot didn't get jammed again?"

"Sure, Dad," Lakris said, stepping forward and wrapping her arms around him in a hug.

"And make sure your lurestick is set on LURE this time," he added into her shoulder. "The last time you zapped Briscol it took him fifteen minutes to unknot, and he walked funny for two days."

"Yeah, but none of the others gave me any trouble after that," she reminded him cheerfully as she pulled back from the hug. "Drive safe."

"I always drive safe."

"Except when you drive like a maniac."

"Which I never do," Lakphro insisted with mock reproof. "Unless I need to."

"Well, don't need to," she admonished him. "We don't want our guest screaming out of the truck the minute you hit ground again. Bad for the Ascendancy's image."

"Trust me," Lakphro promised. "I'll be the most boring driver in the sky."

"Good," she said. "See you tonight. Be boring on the way home, too." She scampered off, tucking her own new brooch safely away in her chest pocket.

Lakphro took a deep breath, sliding his wife's jewelry into his own pocket as he turned toward the skytruck. Hopefully, he and Haplif could get out of here before Lakansu remembered to ask for it back.

Fortunately, Lakansu either forgot about the brooch or just decided her husband had enough other things on his mind. She tossed his overnight bag in the backseat and waved as he got the skytruck a couple of meters off the ground and headed over to the Agbui ship. Haplif was waiting with a bag of his own, not much bigger than Lakphro's, and three minutes later they were in the eastbound air lane burning through the sky toward Redhill.

The ride was mostly quiet. Haplif tried a couple of times to start a conversation, but Lakphro wasn't much interested in talking. After he'd answered a few questions with single words or short comments the alien took the hint and shut up. Halfway to Redhill he got another call from Lakjiip, who confirmed the Agbui freighter was on its way down and directed him to the official family landing area on the far side of the city from the main commercial site. Well within the hour Lakjiip had specified, Lakphro set the skytruck on the ground a hundred meters from the newly arrived freighter.

A small but impressive group was already assembled near the alien ship. Councilor Lakuviv was standing on one side, talking earnestly with one of the newcomers. From the elaborate pendant the alien was wearing Lakphro guessed he was someone important, possibly the ship's captain or maybe even some official. Off to the other side were Senior Aide Lakjiip and a few other Xodlak family officials holding some kind of discussion with three more of the aliens. Lakjiip looked over as Lakphro's skytruck settled to the ground, and by the time he and Haplif had climbed out she was there to greet them.

"Haplif of the Agbui," she said, nodding to Haplif. "Rancher Lak-phro," she added with another nod. "Thank you for your assistance, Rancher. Are those the spices they wanted, Haplif?"

"Yes," Haplif said, hefting his bag. "I offer you the chance to examine them if you wish."

"That won't be necessary." Lakjiip gestured back at the group she'd just left, and Lakphro now saw there were two satchels half again the size of his overnight bag sitting on the ground beside two of the Chiss. "As you anticipated, they've brought more metal for your jewelry."

"Excellent," Haplif said. "I would feel better if you would be kind enough to examine the bags before I take possession. I wouldn't want any question to arise in the future as to whether your Agbui servants brought evil or contraband to your world."

"Oh, we've already searched them," Lakjiip said. She cocked her head slightly. "You didn't tell me they would also be bringing in finished jewelry."

"Did they?" Haplif chuckled, shaking his head. "The combination of long space travel and the firm belief that everyone is an artist. This sometimes happens with long voyages, when the crew becomes bored and resources are readily available."

"So the crew did these?" Lakjiip said. "Interesting. The pieces look as good as the one you gave Councilor Lakuviv."

"I'm sure they do," Haplif said. "But surface quality and long-term durability are not necessarily synonymous. Still, no harm. We'll examine them and make alterations if needed."

"Well, good luck with that," Lakjiip said. "You can take them whenever you wish."

"I thank you." Haplif took a step toward the group, then paused, frowning at the ship. "I'm sorry. I just noticed . . . is that *battle* damage?"

"So it would appear," Lakjiip said, turning her head to look. "Not from the patrol ships that brought it in, of course," she added.

"No, no, that was not at all my thought," Haplif assured her hastily.

"I merely wondered if there were pirates or other dangers they passed through before coming here."

Lakphro's mind flashed back to Haplif's daughter and her reaction to Lakris's brass-tooth sealer. "Or maybe there are dangers right there at your home," he muttered.

Lakjiip sent him a puzzled look. Haplif ignored the comment. "Well, I can ask the captain," the alien said. He bowed to Lakjiip and headed off toward the group with the bags.

"They'll probably want to talk some, maybe compare notes," Lakjiip said to Lakphro. "But I don't expect it to take too long. If you want, you can wait in the receiving lounge over there. There are some refreshments laid out if you're hungry."

"Thank you," Lakphro said. "I have a question," he added quickly as she turned away.

Reluctantly, she turned back. "Yes?"

"I have this thing." Lakphro pulled out the brooch Shimkif had given his wife. "I was wondering how valuable it was, like maybe enough to constitute a bribe—"

"Where did you get that?" Lakjiip demanded, snatching it from his hand.

"Haplif gave it to me," Lakphro said, twitching back from the unexpected intensity of her reaction. "Actually, to my wife—"

"You're not supposed to have this," Lakjiip said, cutting him off. "*No* one is supposed to have these."

"Yes, but—"

"I'm confiscating it, under the authority of Councilor Lakuviv and the Xodlak family." She slid the brooch into her pocket. "And you're not to mention this to anyone. You hear me?"

"No, I *don't* hear you," Lakphro growled, breaking free of the momentary mental paralysis. "You can't just take my property. What gives you the right?"

"The authority of Councilor—"

"Yes, I know what you said," Lakphro interrupted. "But there are laws that govern property confiscation, and there are rationales to be delineated and protocols to be followed. You can't just take some-thing from a Xodlak family member and stuff it away in a pocket and not expect to hear about it."

"I'm not going to hear about it," Lakjiip said, her voice abruptly low and dark, "because you're not going to talk about it. Not to me; not to Councilor Lakuviv; not to anyone. Do you understand, Rancher Xodlak'phr'ooa? *Anyone.*"

Lakphro stared at her, feeling like he'd been punched in the stom-ach. No one on Celwis used anyone's full name after they'd first been introduced. Not unless the circumstances were official, legal, or ex-traordinary.

"Do your wife and daughter know about this?" Lakjiip continued.

"Yes," Lakphro said, his heart pounding. Her next likely question would be—

"Did Haplif give you any more of them?"

Fortunately, that half second of anticipation had already set up his mind and mouth with the proper answer. "No," he said.

For a long moment Lakjiip stared at him, her eyes hard, wonder-ing perhaps if that was a lie. Then her lip twitched, and she gave a reluctant nod. "Warn them not to say anything about this," she said. "If Haplif offers you another one . . ." She hesitated. "You can accept it if you want. But then you're to call me immediately."

"All right," Lakphro said. "But—"

"*Immediately,*" she said. "I know you don't understand, Lakphro, but trust me when I say this is a matter of deepest security. The rip-ples from this day will stretch all the way to the Patriarch, possibly even beyond that to the Syndicure itself. No one—*no one*—is to know about these." She patted the pocket holding the brooch. "Do you understand?"

"You just said I didn't," Lakphro said sourly.

Her face hardened. "Fine—be that way. Just keep it to yourself." She took a deep breath, some of the stress lines in her face smoothing out. "Go wait in the lounge. I'll come get you when Haplif's ready to leave."

"Yes, ma'am."

He trudged across the field toward the reception building, his heart thudding, his mind a strange combination of spinning and numb.

What the *hell*?

Was the brooch poison? Was it dangerous in some other way? Was it evidence of some horrific crime?

Or was it even worse? Was it something so insanely outrageous that he would never in a million years think of it? Could the brooch be a treasure map—or even better, *half* a treasure map—to some fortune in wealth or technology that had been lost in the millennia since the Ascendancy retreated to its worlds from its ill-advised ventures in Lesser Space? There were rumors of such pieces of alien technology, supposedly buried in secret tombs and research labs only the Patriarchs knew about. Even worse, could the metal strands somehow encode a detailed plan for an alien invasion?

He shook his head in disgust. Right. And with that, it was time to haul himself back from the edge of reality before he fell off.

But if the brooch was gone, the memory of Lakjiip's intensity remained. Whether this was as important as she'd said, there was no denying that she at least *believed* it was.

It was a puzzle, but not one he was going to solve today. It would take some thought and some discussion, first with Lakansu, and after that perhaps with trusted friends.

Probably not with Lakris, though, he decided regretfully. His daughter was smart enough, but telling a midager a secret was always a tricky proposition, especially when it was one that would get them all in serious trouble if she slipped up. It was going to be awkward enough explaining to his wife how he'd lost her new jewelry; he didn't need to set himself up for an equally unpleasant future conversation with Councilor Lakuviv.

Hopefully, he and Lakansu could solve it themselves. If they couldn't, the critical question would be who they could turn to for advice.

Picking up his pace, wondering what refreshments the Councilor's people had set out, he began making a mental list of people he trusted.

"So I was right," Haplif said, nodding sagely as he and Lakuviv gazed up at the side of the Agbui freighter. "I saw this—all the way from over there—and I was right. Battle damage."

"It is indeed," Lakuviv confirmed. "A run-in with pirates, the captain said."

Though from the way the captain had described the incident, Lakuviv had the sense it was less battle damage and more running-like-a-whisker-cub damage. The story had been related with a certain vagueness, but given that Lakuviv couldn't see a single hull emplacement that looked like a laser, particle beam, or missile tube he wasn't surprised the captain had chosen to grab for hyperspace at the first hint of trouble.

"Alas," Haplif said ruefully. "We so often are plagued with such dreadful beings."

"Yes, there are way too many of them out there," Lakuviv said. "Have you ever considered arming your ships?"

"A futile effort," Haplif said, shaking his head. "We are cultural nomads, not warriors. We have no knowledge of weapons or tactics or battle."

"It still wouldn't hurt to have a couple of big fat laser turrets visible," Lakuviv persisted. "Even if you're not very good at using them, they'd at least warn potential aggressors that you're not completely helpless."

"And then what of our voyages of knowledge and learning?" Haplif asked, a hint of sadness in his voice. "Tell me: Would *you* have permitted an armed vessel of unknown origin to make a temporary home among your people?"

Lakuviv felt his lip twitch. No, he probably wouldn't, he had to admit. Even if he'd been willing to host them, the Patriel almost certainly wouldn't have let them land.

And even if she had, she'd have wanted to keep them in Brickwalk, under heightened security, instead of sending them out to the more open Redhill province.

Which would have been disastrous. Lakuviv knew the Patriel, and was pretty sure she would have simply tossed Haplif's brooch gift into a drawer somewhere instead of having it analyzed. If that had happened, the Xodlak family would never have recognized the incredible wealth and power the Agbui were sitting on.

"The price of wisdom can be high," Haplif continued in a philosophical tone. "But we have made our choices, as all beings must." He gestured at the scorched hull. "We can only hope their next journey will end more safely."

"We can hope," Lakuviv agreed. "Where are they going next?"

"Our mining world," Haplif said. "Well, not *our* world, really. As far as we can tell, no one owns it. We call it ours because it's where our mines are."

Lakuviv felt his chest suddenly tighten. "These are the mines where you get the metals for your jewelry?"

"Yes," Haplif said. "Ironically, we first sought out the world in the hope there would be a location or two with the right climate and soil for our spices. But that dream proved false." He made a sort of dry chuckling sound. "Imagine our surprise and delight when we accidentally happened on these rich veins of metal, all but exposed on the surface, that would be perfect for jewelry. We knew then that we'd been guided to that world for a purpose."

"It would certainly seem so," Lakuviv said, trying to keep his voice even and only politely interested. "Tell me, do all your metals come from there?"

"Most of them," Haplif said. "The mines are particularly rich in the blue spinpria, but there's some of all the others in the same area."

"Sounds very convenient," Lakuviv said, hearing his heart rate pick up. *Blue spinpria:* the metal the Chiss called *nyix.*

A whole mine of it. A mine, moreover, that was rich enough that the Agbui could afford to make the stuff into trinkets.

A mine that was just sitting on an uninhabited and unclaimed world.

"But of course, the more important issue is the safety of your people," he said. "I sympathize with them, and certainly the Chiss Ascendancy hates pirates."

"I thank you for your compassion," Haplif said. "But what can be done?"

"Well . . ." Lakuviv paused, as if he was working out a brand-new thought that had just occurred to him. "What if I sent along an escort with your freighter? Obviously, it couldn't go everywhere with them, but at least it could get them safely to their next destination."

Haplif turned to him, the dark red and white forehead folds going even more wrinkled. "You would do that for us?" he asked. "You would send one of your mighty Chiss warships to protect us?"

Lakuviv suppressed a scowl. A mighty warship. Once, as one of the Ruling Families, the Xodlak had indeed had its own small fleet of genuine warships.

But that fleet, and the right to fly it, had ended fifty years ago. Now all the Xodlak on Celwis had available were a handful of system patrol ships, little more than oversized gunboats, plus the two decommissioned light cruisers with skeleton crews that acted as planetary defense platforms.

None of which Haplif could possibly know, of course. He and his people would have been escorted to the surface past the watchful lasers of one of the cruisers, and the alien would naturally jump to the conclusion that they were fully functioning warships. He'd no doubt have been even more impressed if he'd gotten a glimpse of the abandoned frigate resting beneath the protection of a cliff wall on Celwis's largest moon, a half-forgotten relic of the old days of glory.

But Lakuviv remembered the warship, just as he remembered the days of glory. That glory would return, he told himself firmly, and when it did that frigate and those cruisers would once again ply the Ascendancy space lanes bearing the crest of a Ruling Family.

"I don't know as I'd call them *mighty*," he told Haplif. "All I could offer you is a system patrol ship, like the ones that escorted your own ship in from orbit."

"You speak far too modestly," Haplif said, his earlier astonishment now turned to eagerness. "Compared with our poor freighters, they are mighty indeed." His mouth slit curved up at the corners. "I daresay it would seem mighty to the cowardly pirate attackers, too."

Lakuviv shrugged. But the alien was right. Even a simple Xodlak patrol ship could easily go head-to-head against most of the small pirate groups that lurked outside the Ascendancy's borders. Certainly it would have no trouble against a gang that was so pathetic it couldn't even chase down a running Agbui freighter. "Let me talk to the Patriel," he said. "The patrol ships are under her ultimate authority, but it's not uncommon for a Councilor to requisition one or two for special purposes. Do you know how far it is to the mining world?"

"Not too far," Haplif said. "Three or four days' journey."

"That's traveling jump-by-jump, I presume?"

"Excuse me?"

"Jump-by-jump," Lakuviv said. "That's where you go only a couple of systems at a time to avoid the problem of unstable hyperspace pathways."

"No, no, our ships have navigators," Haplif said brightly. "We hire them on, usually for several months or a year at a time."

"*You* have a navigator?" Lakuviv asked, frowning.

"Oh, yes," Haplif said. "Have I not mentioned him to you?"

"No, I'm quite sure you haven't," Lakuviv said, eyeing the alien with new eyes. Navigators with the rare ability to guide ships through the Chaos didn't come cheap, and most people who hired them only did so for a single trip at a time. Yet Haplif had one who'd been sitting idly at Lakphro's ranch for almost three weeks now? "So he stays with you through all your trips?"

"Of course," Haplif said, as if it was obvious. "We never know when we might need to go somewhere new, and traveling to a navigator concourse to hire someone would cost valuable time."

"And you pay him the whole time he's with you?"

"Fortunately, he doesn't charge very much," Haplif said. "Like us, he also seeks adventure and cultural enlightenment."

"Fortunately," Lakuviv agreed. Yet so far as he'd heard—and he'd made sure to hear *everything* about their alien visitors—this mysterious pilot hadn't so much as set foot outside Haplif's ship. What kind of culture could he possibly be absorbing in there?

And then, of course, the obvious answer came to him. "He must really like your spices and jewelry," he said.

"Indeed," Haplif said, giving Lakuviv another of those bizarre smiles. "Not so much the spices, for his tastes lie in a different direction from yours or ours. But he likes our modest creations very much. So much so that he's willing to be paid in them."

"Ah," Lakuviv said, hiding a cynical smile. If *he* was being paid in nyix, he'd have no problem sitting idly around for a few months, either. "Well, we unfortunately don't have anyone like that on call. If we're going to keep up with your freighter we'll have to travel jump-by-jump to one of the navigator concourses and hire someone. Unfortunately, that will also take time."

"Oh—I know," Haplif said eagerly. "I have the answer. There's no need for you to hire a navigator. I would be honored if you would accept the loan of ours."

"You'd really do that?" Lakuviv asked, trying to sound surprised.

"Of course," Haplif said. "You are our friends. We also have no reason to leave here, certainly not until our next harvest of spices, and so we can do without him for several weeks at the least."

"That's very generous of you," Lakuviv said. Perfect. He'd been trying to figure out how to talk Haplif into that very solution, and here the alien had come up with the idea on his own. "I'm not sure I should accept, though."

"It's no more than the hospitality you yourselves have offered us," Haplif said. "At any rate, I will hear no objection. Your hospitality aside, your warship will be taking a risk in protecting our freighter. It is the least we can do to add our assistance to their venture."

"Very well," Lakuviv said, his mind racing. He'd need a personal representative aboard the ship, of course—he couldn't risk the officers or crew knowing what he was looking for. Lakjiip was the obvious choice: smart, observant, and loyal. Especially loyal. "I'll give Patriel Lakooni a call and set it up."

"Thank you," Haplif said. "If you'll allow me to return with

Rancher Lakphro, I'll prepare the navigator." He frowned. "Perhaps it would be best if you could send another vehicle behind us," he went on. "I would hate to insist Rancher Lakphro make this same journey twice in the same day."

"I'll get Senior Aide Lakjiip on it right away," Lakuviv promised. "May I ask which guild the navigator belongs to?"

"Of course," Haplif said. "I understand the hesitation of working with the unfamiliar. But I'm told the Chiss have worked with the Pathfinders before."

Lakuviv nodded. "Yes, we have. That should work out well."

"Good," Haplif said. "We do so want this to work to your satisfaction and convenience."

"I'm sure it will," Lakuviv soothed. "Well. Let's go find Lakphro and get the two of you back to his ranch."

He smiled, the most genuine smile he'd ever given this alien. "And let's get this plan off the ground."

# CHAPTER THIRTEEN

There were times, Samakro mused, where something in his life felt vaguely like a bit of personal history repeating itself. There were also times there was no vagueness about it whatsoever.

Today was one of the latter.

Flying the *Springhawk* into the Paataatus hive-home system of Nettehi. Flying along the same approach vector they'd used during the punitive raid with Admiral Ar'alani. Flying in with no idea of what was waiting for them.

Only this time they didn't have the *Vigilant* and the other ships of Ar'alani's task force along. This time, they were going in alone.

"Prepare for breakout," Thrawn called calmly from his command chair.

Samakro glanced around the bridge, long experience enabling him to gauge the officers' moods merely by looking at them. They were tense, he could tell, for all the same reasons he was. But he could see no panic or serious doubt. They'd been with Thrawn long enough to trust him to get them through whatever mess he was leading them into.

Distantly, Samakro wondered if they'd had that same confidence back when *he'd* been the *Springhawk*'s commander.

"Three, two, *one*."

The star-flares flashed and settled into stars framing the planet Nettehi. "Dalvu?" Thrawn asked.

"Combat range: We've got fighters," the sensor officer announced. "Approximately twenty gunboats within combat and mid-range."

"Check planetary orbit," Thrawn said. "I think I see some larger ships there."

"Checking . . . confirmed, sir," Dalvu said. "I make seven ships: six enhanced cruisers, one heavy frigate."

Samakro eyed the display. The seven ships were flying in a Paataatus guard configuration: the frigate in the center with a cruiser on either flank and two cruisers each in a line in front and astern of it.

"Full magnification and status readouts," Thrawn ordered. "Frigate first, then the cruisers."

The image of a medium-sized ship appeared on the sensor display, blurred somewhat by distance and the tenuous planetary atmosphere it was currently orbiting through.

But it was clear enough to see the standard Paataatus heavy warship design: wide and flat, heavy armor with minimal point defenses on top, main lasers arrayed along the leading edge, missile tubes positioned underneath the bow. It was an unusual design among the various aliens the Ascendancy dealt with, but it fit well with the Paataatus tactic of approaching an opponent with lasers blazing, then pitching up to fire missiles as the attacking ship veered up and away to open a path for the next attacker moving in behind it.

"Mid Captain?" Thrawn invited.

"Looks Paataatus to me, sir," Samakro said. "Certainly doesn't match any of the Vagaari ship configurations in our records."

"Agreed," Thrawn said. "Which doesn't conclusively prove anything, of course, given the Vagaari habit of conquering other aliens and adapting their technology. But it's a strong indicator, particularly since I don't see any major ship modifications."

Samakro shifted his attention to the planetary data now streaming across the secondary sensor display. "I also see no evidence of large-scale damage on the planet's surface," he pointed out.

"Excellent observation," Thrawn said approvingly. "The rumors spoke of an alliance, but they could as easily have been a distorted report of a Vagaari invasion. But the Paataatus would hardly have given up without a fight, which would likely have led to visible planetary destruction."

Samakro nodded. Their joint conclusion didn't address the original rumors, he knew. But Thrawn liked to trim the weeds from the edges of an operation, clearing out the unlikely options before focusing on the main thrust. In this case, they were going to find the Paataatus either alone or in full alliance with the pirates.

Either scenario could be trouble, but both left the *Springhawk* free to respond as soon as they were fired on without fear of tearing into victims or—unlikely with the Paataatus—innocent bystanders.

"Captain, we're receiving a transmission," Brisch called from the comm station. He touched a key—

"This is the Prince Militaire," a Paataatus voice came over the bridge speaker.

Samakro frowned. *Prince Militaire*? He'd never heard of that rank before.

If it even *was* a rank. It could just as easily be a title or name or something unique to these aliens. Chiss diplomats had dealt with Paataatus negotiators a few times, but the inner workings of their government remained a complete mystery. Certainly the Expansionary Defense Fleet had had no interaction with them that didn't involve shooting or being shot at.

"You are trespassing within holy Paataatus space," the prince continued.

"Unusually talky today, aren't they?" Afpriuh commented from the weapons station. "Sir, all enemy ships are holding station."

"Talky *and* standing their ground," Samakro said. "Not like them at all."

"No," Thrawn said. "It's not."

Samakro looked sideways at him. Thrawn's eyes were narrowed, his attention shifting back and forth between the sensor and tactical displays. "You said we were going to ask them about the Vagaari?" Samakro reminded his commander quietly.

"Yes," Thrawn said thoughtfully. He hesitated another moment, then touched the comm key on his chair. "Prince Militaire, this is Senior Captain Thrawn aboard the Chiss Expansionary Defense Fleet warship *Springhawk,*" he called. "We come in peace, with a question for you." He keyed the mute.

Samakro frowned. "You're not going to ask the question, sir?" he asked.

"Not yet," Thrawn said. "Call this an experiment."

"Paataatus ships on the move, sir," Dalvu said. "Ten fighters moving toward us; orbiting ships reconfiguring. Remaining fighters holding station."

"Watch closely, Mid Captain," Thrawn said. "Let's see what they do."

"Yes, sir," Samakro said, suppressing a snort. Actually, if the Paataatus followed their standard battle doctrine, what they would do was swarm their target and try to blow it out of the sky. And with the *Springhawk* out here all alone . . .

"There," Thrawn said, pointing at one of the displays. "The orbiting ships. You see it?"

Samakro focused on them. The seven ships were on the move, shifting from sentry to defense configuration. One of the lead cruisers moved up to a position above the frigate, while one of the trailing cruisers moved beneath it. "Defense configuration," he said. "Which suggests our Prince Militaire is aboard the frigate."

"Correct," Thrawn said. "But did you notice *how* the cruisers took up their new positions?"

Samakro frowned. "One of the leading ships moved up, one of the trailing ships moved down."

"The first leading cruiser went up to dorsal guard position, while the one behind it stayed in vanguard position," Thrawn said. "But the trailing cruisers did things in the opposite way, with the one directly behind the frigate dropping beneath it in ventral guard position while the one farthest aft moved forward to take its place."

Samakro played the memory back. Thrawn was right. "Yes, sir," he said. "I'm not sure I see the significance."

"Fighters gathering, sir," Afpriuh called.

"I see them." Thrawn keyed off the mute. "Prince Militaire, this is Senior Captain Thrawn. As I've said already, we come in peace. However, if your current situation remains unchanged, I assure you that you'll witness the full might of the Chiss Ascendancy."

"Do you make threats against the Paataatus Hiveborn, Senior Captain Thrawn?" the prince demanded.

"I stand by the precise words of my statement, Prince Militaire," Thrawn said.

"Do you intend harm to the Paataatus?"

"I stand by the precise words of my statement."

"The consequences are yours."

"I am prepared to accept them."

"Then all is in your hands."

"I am prepared."

A tone sounded from the speaker. "He's cut off transmission, sir," Brisch reported.

"Understood," Thrawn said. "Stand ready, all weapons."

Samakro took a careful breath. What was Thrawn doing? "Sir, we have no authorization to initiate hostilities against the Paataatus."

"Nor do I intend to," Thrawn assured him. "Do you see anything odd about those fighters' attack formation?"

Samakro shifted his attention to the tactical, trying to force back the sudden doubts, his own earlier thoughts whispering back to him. *To trust him to get them through whatever mess he was leading them into . . .*

He frowned. Paataatus fighters typically used a swarm strategy, driving in at full speed from all directions in a horizontally layered attack. But these ships had instead gathered in groups of two and three and were moving warily toward the *Springhawk*. "That's not the usual Paataatus structure," he said.

"Indeed it's not," Thrawn said, a hint of grim amusement in his voice. "But it *is* one we've seen before."

An instant later the two nearest groups of fighters opened fire, their lasers blazing at the *Springhawk*.

"Incoming fire!" Afpriuh snapped. "Response, sir?"

"Hold your fire," Thrawn said calmly.

"Sir, we're being attacked!"

"No, we're not," Thrawn said. "Dalvu? Damage report?"

"Damage—" Dalvu broke off. "None, sir," she said, clearly confused. "Enemy lasers running at . . . one-*tenth* power?"

"That can't be," Samakro insisted, looking at the sensor readout. Those lasers had been fully as bright as anything he'd ever seen from a Paataatus attack.

But Dalvu was right. The energy blasts had barely even gotten the attention of the *Springhawk*'s electrostatic shields, let alone strained them. "I don't understand."

"Dalvu: Analysis on laser spectrum," Thrawn ordered. "What are they keyed to?"

Samakro felt his eyes narrow. A ridiculous question. Spectrum lasers by definition were designed to quickly shift their energy frequencies to whatever would be best absorbed by the material they were focused on.

"They're not keyed to our hull, sir," Dalvu said, still sounding confused. "They're—" Again she stopped . . . but this time, she half turned in her seat to give Thrawn a wry smile. "They're keyed to the interplanetary dust profile."

For a couple of heartbeats, Samakro still didn't get it. Keyed to the *dust profile*?

Then suddenly he understood.

Lasers were only visible because the passing energy ionized the tenuous dust and solar wind medium drifting through the otherwise empty space. By keying to the ionization profile of that mix, the fighters' low-energy lasers were making themselves maximally visible. As visible, in fact, as full-power lasers that were instead keyed to a warship's hull.

"You're right, sir," he said, his words and conclusion sounding incredulous in his ears. "It's not an attack."

He looked at Thrawn. "It's a light show."

"It is indeed," Thrawn said. "Afpriuh, adjust three of our spectrum lasers to that same frequency and power level and begin returning fire. Make your shots misses or glancing blows so that the onlookers don't wonder about the lack of damage."

"Onlookers, sir?" Afpriuh asked, throwing a quick frown back at Thrawn. "You mean the Paataatus?"

"Hardly," Thrawn said. "The Paataatus are our partners in Mid Captain Samakro's appropriately named light show."

He looked at Samakro. "We've discussed the possible combinations of Paataatus and Vagaari," he said. "Historically, the Vagaari borrow their victims' technology but seldom take their ships without visible modification." He gestured toward the orbiting cruisers and frigate, still traveling in their close-knit defensive cluster. "But we *do* know someone who is happy to commandeer ships directly, either taking over their crews or replacing them with their own."

Samakro looked at the cluster, then back at the fighters pretending to attack and to be attacked in turn. Someone who directly commandeered ships . . .

He stiffened as the fighters' attack pattern suddenly registered. *And* someone to whom Thrawn's very name was an instant incitement to violence. "The *Nikardun*?"

"I believe so," Thrawn said. "I've long suspected General Yiv was trying to make a connection with the Paataatus, either as allies or subjects. If my reading of the current situation is correct, it's the latter." He smiled tightly. "I further believe the Paataatus have realized that our arrival offers a chance to get rid of them."

Samakro thought it over. Fighters who used non-Paataatus tactics and formations, and then only pretended to attack. An official who initiated a conversation, made a big loud show of antagonism, but then asked specifically if the *Springhawk* intended a threat against the Paataatus. Thrawn, assuring the prince that he came in peace, but also threatening to show the full might of the Chiss Ascendancy.

No. Not *threatening*.

*Promising*.

"And you think the Nikardun are listening?" he asked.

"The Prince Militaire's supposedly hostile words to us strongly suggest that." Thrawn cocked an eyebrow. "So tell me: Where are they?"

Samakro looked at the tactical. How in the world could he answer that? The Nikardun could be anywhere on the ground, anywhere in space, anywhere even in the whole of Paataatus territory.

He didn't much like these guessing games of Thrawn's even when things were calm. Here, at the front end of a battle, he liked them even less.

"Remember the cruisers," Thrawn murmured.

Samakro frowned at the formation on the tactical, thinking back to their switch to defensive posture. "They're in the ventral cruiser," he said. "The one riding beneath the frigate."

"How do you know?"

"Because that's the one that started out directly behind the frigate. Which I assume is the ship the Prince Militaire is aboard?"

"Unproven, but likely," Thrawn agreed. "I suspect we interrupted an exercise in Nikardun tactics, with that particular cruiser threatening the frigate should there be any resistance. When we appeared, the cruiser quickly moved to a spot where it could maintain that threat while also being the best-protected ship in the group. Anything else?"

"Only the fact that you just pointed out, sir," Samakro said. "The cluster is in mid-orbit, with nothing likely to come at them from that direction. Why would the prince need a ship to protect against an attack from his own world?"

"Why, indeed," Thrawn said. "Very good, Mid Captain. Azmordi, I believe it's time to make our move. Start us inward toward the frigate."

"Yes, sir," Azmordi said. The planet and starscape shifted as the *Springhawk* turned a few degrees and began accelerating. "Sir, there are two groups of fighters between us and the cluster."

"They'll move aside," Thrawn said calmly. "Afpriuh, shift low-power lasers to the nearest of the two blocking groups and open fire. Maintain near-misses and glancing blows—no damage."

"You think the Nikardun can see us?" Samakro asked. "Their view is being blocked by two other ships."

"If they had no way of seeing us, the Paataatus would have no need for an elaborately counterfeit attack," Thrawn pointed out. "They may be tapping into the sensors from the other ships, but we must assume they're monitoring our activities."

And in the meantime, there were a cruiser and a frigate, not to mention several fighters, between the *Springhawk* and its target. "How are we going to get the Paataatus ships to move?"

"Unfortunately, we can't," Thrawn said. "I have a plan, but a successful resolution will rest on the Prince Militaire's shoulders. We can only trust that he's as quick and perceptive as I believe him to be."

"First fighter group moving aside," Dalvu called. "Second fighter group pulling back toward the warship cluster."

"Excellent," Thrawn said. "As anticipated. Afpriuh, set up two breacher missiles, with four plasma spheres to follow. They'll be launched in a straight line—no spread—aimed and timed for impact on the frigate."

"Yes, sir," Afpriuh said, his fingers skating across his board. "Time until attack?"

"Whenever the launchers are ready."

"Yes, sir." Afpriuh hesitated. "May I remind the captain that if we launch too soon, the Paataatus will see them coming and have time to evade?"

"And that second fighter group is also still in the way," Dalvu added. "They'll be in position to intercept and block."

"Understood," Thrawn said. "Brisch, prepare to resume communications. Afpriuh, are the missiles ready?"

Afpriuh nodded. "Ready and targeted."

"Open communications," Thrawn said, keying his control. "Prince Militaire of the Paataatus, this is Senior Captain Thrawn. Your actions have been noted, and your intent toward us is clear. Are you prepared to witness the might of the Chiss Ascendancy?"

"Your actions are likewise noted," Prince Militaire said. "We are prepared. Do your worst." The comm keyed off.

"A challenge?" Samakro suggested.

"A request," Thrawn corrected him grimly. "Afpriuh: Launch breachers."

On the tactical the breacher missiles appeared, arrowing from their tubes. A moment later they became visible out the viewport as they burned through space toward the planet below. Samakro checked the data list, confirmed that Afpriuh had correctly taken the warship cluster's own orbital velocity into account with the attack trajectory. The group of Paataatus fighters fell back before the missiles, heading toward the cluster but holding station between the missiles and the warships. The countdown mark on the plasma spheres edged toward zero . . .

"Launch spheres," Thrawn ordered.

There was a subtle jolt as the four plasma spheres shot away from the *Springhawk* and chased after the missiles. The Paataatus fighters were still falling back, Samakro saw, but they weren't nearly as fast as the missiles and were rapidly losing ground. For a bad moment, he thought the prince had misunderstood what Thrawn was doing and would let the fighters take the impacts—

"Fighter maneuvering thrusters activated," Dalvu called. "Veering aside . . . fighters clear. Missiles clear to target."

"Should you warn him?" Samakro asked.

"The Nikardun may hear," Thrawn said. His voice was steady, but Samakro could hear his commander's tension. If the prince wasn't as smart and alert as Thrawn was banking on, the *Springhawk* was about to abandon this shadowboxing and open real hostilities. "Afpriuh, cease laserfire."

The sky went back to starlit darkness as the *Springhawk* and then the Paataatus fighters ceased their sham battle. The breachers were nearly to the warships, the plasma spheres right on their tails. Samakro held his breath, feeling an odd sense that everyone else, Chiss and Paataatus alike, was doing likewise . . .

And on the sensor display, the top cruiser of the stack veered violently to starboard, moving clear of the incoming missiles. The frigate beneath it, its larger size and mass making that particular maneuver impossible, instead executed a portside roll, pitching up on its left side and getting clear of the missiles' path. Samakro got a glimpse of the cruiser beneath it, flying on its back with its missile tubes pointed in clear threat at the prince's ship as the breachers blazed past the frigate and slammed into it.

The missiles were still splashing the cruiser with acid, burning away electrostatic barrier nodes and missile control circuits, when the plasma spheres impacted. The concentrated bursts of ions added their destruction to that of the breachers, wrecking control systems and turning the cruiser into a paralyzed mass of metal and ceramic.

And as the last running light on the cruiser winked out, the frigate and the rest of the cruisers opened fire.

Not with low-power weapons, as the fighters had against the *Springhawk*. The whole area blazed with light as seemingly every laser on the Paataatus ships targeted the disabled cruiser, blasting away huge chunks of hull and inner structure, shattering section after section after section. Superheated liquids and gases spewed outward, secondary explosions of missiles and laser capacitors racked the remaining structure.

And then, with one final barrage, it was over.

For a long moment, the *Springhawk*'s bridge was silent. Samakro stared at the drifting debris that had once been a warship, feeling a little sick despite himself. He'd seen death and destruction, but seldom seen such cold and absolute fury.

Across the bridge, Brisch cleared his throat. "Senior Captain? The Prince Militaire is signaling."

"Thank you." Thrawn touched the switch. "This is Senior Captain Thrawn," he said. "I trust all is in hand?"

"All is in hand, Senior Captain," the Prince Militaire said. His voice, Samakro noted, was completely calm, in eerie contrast with the ferocity of the attack. "Our would-be Nikardun enslavers are dead."

"They were all in the enhanced cruiser?"

"All those that mattered. The leaders, and those who directly threatened my life in trade for the cooperation of all the Hiveborn. Those who remain on the hive-home will be dealt with." The prince paused. "*Are* dealt with," he corrected, still calm. "There are tales that the Chiss Ascendancy has dealt with all other Nikardun?"

"There may yet be small pockets of resistance," Thrawn said. "But they will not last much longer. Nor are they likely to extend their reach to Paataatus space."

"They certainly will not," the prince said, and Samakro could hear both promise and threat in his voice. "In past days the Hiveborn have faced you to their regret, Senior Captain Thrawn. It was a unique experience to have you as an ally."

"The Ascendancy was glad it could be of service," Thrawn said. "The Nikardun have been a blot upon the Chaos for too long. Then we are finished here?"

"By no means, Senior Captain Thrawn," the prince said. "By no means."

Samakro looked at the tactical, a tingle on the back of his neck. Those Paataatus fighters were still out there, many of them still in combat range. A quick retuning of their lasers to full power . . .

"You said you had a question," the prince continued. "If the Paataatus can answer it, we will be honored to do so."

# MEMORIES V

The Grand Migration on Shihon was a confluence of a dozen or more bird species, each crossing migration paths with the others in a large area of fields, ponds, and rolling hills. Most of the birds stayed for a while, eating and resting until the next wave of incoming travelers pushed them out. The whole event took a full month, turning the place into a wonderland for serious bird-watchers.

As Haplif had predicted, they arrived a day late for the event, shortly after the first vanguard scouts from the incoming flocks arrived, but well before the flocks themselves were due to make their appearance. Hopefully, Yomie would be content with that.

The Agbui ship was assigned a spot on one of the landing fields a few kilometers from the edge of the migration assembly site. An hour later, attendance chits and maps in hand, Yoponek and Yomie joined the other bird enthusiasts on the railcar system that would take everyone within walking distance of the event.

With the two Chiss finally gone, it was time for Haplif's meeting with Jixtus.

No one was standing guard at the freighter's entrance when Haplif arrived. The hatch opened at a twist of the release handle, and he took a couple of steps into the air lock to get out of view from outside. There he paused and pulled back his hood. "Haplif of the Agbui, reporting as ordered," he announced to the empty room.

In response, the inner hatch slid open, revealing a long corridor heading forward. As Haplif started walking, another hatch a few meters ahead also slid open, soft light from the room behind it spilling out into the corridor. Bracing himself, he walked to the hatchway and stepped through it.

He'd expected to find himself in an office. Instead, the room was a meditation center, with colored drift tendrils intertwining around floating light globes over thick tactile carpet and self-contouring anatomic chairs. Jixtus was nestled into one of the chairs, hidden beneath his usual robe, hood, and veil. One of his gloved hands was making small movements in time with the quiet music playing in the background. "Haplif of the Agbui," he said in greeting, the waving hand interrupting its rhythm long enough to point to one of the other chairs. "Sit."

"Thank you, my lord," Haplif said, easing down into the indicated chair. Like all anatomic chairs, this one looked like it would be easier to get into than out of.

"Tell me, do you find this Grand Migration fascinating?" Jixtus asked.

"We only came here because our Chiss guides wanted to," he said, trying not to sound too defensive. "We have to accommodate them or they might not—"

"Yes, so Shimkif informed me," Jixtus said. "But that's not what I asked. I asked if you found the confluence fascinating." He cocked his head, that side of the hood opening slightly to show more of the veil behind it. "I certainly do."

Haplif stared. "You *do*?"

"Without a doubt," Jixtus said. "Did you know that, while most of the birds here feed on seeds and insects, there are several larger predator birds as well?"

"I would think that would make the seed-eaters uncomfortable."

"Yes, one would assume that," Jixtus agreed. "But these particular predators eat rodents and fish, not other birds." He lifted a finger in emphasis. "Here's the interesting part. There are other land and water animals nearby that *do* target the smaller birds. The predator birds' response is to take settlement grounds along the edges of the main migration fields, up against the surrounding tree line and into the trees themselves."

Haplif shook his head. "I don't understand."

"Don't you?" Jixtus said. "The predator birds, with beaks and talons designed for combat, are creating a protective zone around the more vulnerable species, thus discouraging attacks while the flocks rest up to continue their journeys." He made a sort of chuckling sound. "Rather analogous to Chiss society in general, though one must be careful not to carry metaphors too far. Did you bring your report?"

"Yes," Haplif said, pulling the datastick from inside his robe. He leaned forward as far as he could in the anatomic chair, just managing to get the stick to Jixtus's casually outstretched hand. "The majority of the information was gleaned from conversations with our guides," he added as he returned to a more comfortable position. "One of them, Yoponek, fancies himself a scholar of Chiss history, while his social life-cravings require at least a basic knowledge of current family relationships. Other details I was able to fill in on my own."

"Excellent," Jixtus said, setting the datastick aside. "That should prove most useful. What's your current schedule for this journey to Celwis?"

"Yomie, the other Chiss, wants to spend another four weeks watching the migration," Haplif said. "If we leave right after that—"

"You have three weeks."

Haplif felt his mouth quiver. "Excuse me?"

"The various pieces are coming together," Jixtus said. "If you're convinced this Councilor Lakuviv is the one, you must make contact with him in no more than three weeks."

"I see," Haplif said. Looking away from the masked figure, he let his eyes drift around the room, watching the tendrils as he tried to think.

Option one was to simply dump Yoponek and his annoying betrothed. But as he'd told Shimkif, there was no guarantee he could find someone else to introduce them to Lakuviv. Option two was to give Yomie three more weeks of bird-watching, then lock her into the ship and head for Celwis whether she liked it or not. She would be a windstorm to live with for a while, but he could get through that. The question then would be how badly her attitude would affect Yoponek's own enthusiasm for meeting Celwis's top Xodlak officials.

Option three . . .

He looked back at Jixtus. The veiled face was still pointed at him, and Haplif had the eerie sense of an unblinking stare behind it. "All right," he said. "Three weeks it is."

"Excellent," Jixtus said, his voice giving Haplif the impression that the other was beaming. "I knew I could rely on you. Now, once you've properly prepared Lakuviv, you're going to need a navigator."

"I assumed we would use the navigator we already have," Haplif said, a brief chill running through him. He didn't know what part of the Chaos these so-called Attendants came from—he'd never seen anyone like them except the pair in Jixtus's personal service. But they were clearly from someplace far away, and their purple robes and eerie eye lenses were as unsettling as their perpetual silence.

"Impossible," Jixtus said. "He must remain hidden from everyone in this part of the Chiss Ascendancy. But I'll find you someone suitable, possibly a Farseeker or Void Guide."

"Or a Pathfinder," Haplif suggested. "They do a lot of work with the Chiss, especially at the Celwis end of the Ascendancy."

"So they do," Jixtus agreed, sounding thoughtful. "Now that you mention them, I believe I know the perfect one for this task. Excellent." He picked up a datarec from beside his chair and tapped it. "Meet me at this location in twenty days."

"That's just one day before you want me on Celwis," Haplif warned, pulling out his own datarec and checking the location Jixtus had just sent. "Never mind," he added as he saw how close together the two locations were. "That should be no trouble."

"Good," Jixtus said. "That will be all for now. I'll have more information when I deliver your Pathfinder."

"Yes, my lord," Haplif said. Tucking his datarec away, he rolled to the side, hoping that particular move would allow him to quickly exit his chair while still maintaining some dignity. He was right on the first, not so much on the second. "I'll see you in twenty days."

"Good." Jixtus gestured in the direction of the distant migratory fields. "If you have time, I encourage you to take a moment and observe the birds. It will be as instructive to your mind as it is good for your soul."

"If I have time," Haplif said. "If not, I expect my soul is as good now as it's ever going to get."

Shimkif was gone when Haplif returned. She'd left no message beyond a brief statement that she'd be back when she'd fixed their problem.

For three days nothing changed. Yoponek and Yomie

headed off each morning for their bird-watching and came back each evening tired but happy. If they noticed Shimkif's absence, they didn't ask about it.

On the fourth day, the two Chiss returned barely two hours after leaving.

And this time they weren't happy at all.

"What's the matter?" Haplif asked, intercepting them just inside the air lock. "Did you forget something?"

Yomie didn't answer. She just glared at him and pushed past, stomping down the corridor toward her room. "Yoponek?" Haplif prompted.

The boy's lips tightened. "It's over," he said. "I don't know how or why, but somehow it's over."

"What's over?" Haplif asked, frowning.

"The Grand Migration." Yoponek sighed. "The birds are just . . . I don't know. Gone. There are still a couple of flocks coming in, but all the rest have picked up and gone elsewhere."

"That's bizarre," Haplif said, peering down the corridor where Yomie had disappeared. "I gather Yomie is disappointed?"

"*Disappointed* is hardly the word," Yoponek said sourly. "Amazing, isn't it? A thousand years running, and the stupid birds pick *our* wandering year to change their pattern."

"Maybe they'll be back," Haplif said. "We have this landing slot for the full month. Maybe whatever disturbed them will be gone in a couple of days and they'll be back."

"The docents we talked to don't think so," Yoponek said. "They say that, for whatever reason, this part of the migration is over for the year."

"I'm so sorry," Haplif said, brushing his fingers comfortingly across the side of Yoponek's head. There was mostly frustration there, mixed with concern, confusion, and more than a bit of relief.

The frustration and confusion were obvious. The concern was probably for Yomie and her disappointment. Was the relief because they could now abandon this whole migration nonsense and go to Celwis?

Time for a gentle probe. "You know, there must also be bird migrations on Celwis," he pointed out. "Not to mention the waterfalls Shimkif talked about. In fact, with all that water around, it's likely there would be plenty of birds and animals for Yomie to watch."

"Maybe," Yoponek said.

"And while Shimkif and Yomie go see the birds and waterfalls," Haplif continued, "you and I can contact Councilor Lakuviv. A few hours—half a day at the most—and you'll rejoin your betrothed having solidified your glorious future with the Coduyo family."

"That would be wonderful," Yoponek said wistfully. "But I'm starting to think that's never going to happen."

"Yoponek?" Yomie's voice came from down the corridor.

They turned. Yomie was striding toward them, questis in hand, a determined look on her face. "All right, so the Grand Migration is over," she said, coming to a halt in front of them. "There are two other migrations going on at other sites. We can go see one of them. Maybe both—we'll have time."

"Excuse me?" Haplif asked, staring at her. No—she couldn't be serious.

"You heard me," she said, swiveling the questis around and holding it up in front of him and Yoponek. "The one along the Panopyl Mountains is closest and it's supposed to start in two days. If we hurry, we can get a good landing slot before everyone else here figures it out and heads in that direction."

Yoponek threw Haplif a sideways look. "Yomie, we agreed we were going to Celwis, remember?" he reminded her gently.

"*After* the Grand Migration."

"The migration is over."

"We wrote a month for it into our schedule," Yomie said firmly. "There are still three weeks left."

"Yomie, be reasonable—"

"I *am* being reasonable," she shot back. "You all want to go talk to some stuffy number-squinter on Celwis? Fine. Leave me here and come get me when you're done."

Yoponek tensed, and even without touching him Haplif could see that he was about to say something stupid or irrevocable. Time for a more diplomatic voice to chime in. "Please don't be angry, Yomie," he said, using his most soothing tone. "Of course we're not going to leave you here all alone. But our supply of spices is dwindling, and we need to find somewhere to start a new crop."

"So start one while we're watching the birds," Yomie said. "You said you can get a crop in a couple of weeks."

"*If* the soil and climate are suitable," Haplif said. "The proper combination for that is exceedingly rare. And the mountain climate you're suggesting won't work at all."

"What about these?" she asked, tapping the brooch pinned to her tunic. "You could sell these instead of your spices."

"The jewelry is more difficult to produce and requires a supply of the metals."

"But it doesn't require special dirt or humidity or whatever," Yomie countered. "What are you saving them for, somebody's starday?"

Behind his earnest smile, Haplif ground his teeth. He'd known right from the start that giving Yomie that brooch was a bad idea. "They're only for very special people."

"Well, then, maybe you should take this one back," Yomie said, reaching behind the brooch to unfasten the clasp.

"Yomie, that's not fair," Yoponek chided.

Yomie hesitated, then lowered her hand. "You're right," she said reluctantly. "I'm sorry, Haplif." She wiggled the questis again at Yoponek. "But you *did* say we could stay until the migration was over. Can't we at least go to the Panopyl Mountains for a few days?"

"If it's this important to you, sure," Yoponek said. "But it's not fair to make the Agbui stay here when they need to move on. Maybe it's time we parted ways."

"I would hate for our relationship to end in such un-pleasantness," Haplif protested. "Let me make a sugges-tion. When Shimkif returns, we'll go to the mountains and see what's happening with that other migration. At that point we'll discuss it again, and hopefully come to a mutu-ally acceptable time to travel to Celwis. Is that agreeable?"

"It is to me," Yoponek said, quiet relief in his voice that they didn't have to have this out here and now. "Yomie?"

"All right," Yomie said, a bit more reluctantly, probably realizing that Haplif's proposal was still only half a victory. "Where did Shimkif go?"

"I don't know," Haplif said with complete honesty. "But I'm sure she'll be back soon. There's food in the salon if you're hungry."

"Thank you," Yoponek said. "Come on, Yomie. You can tell me about these other migrations while we eat."

Three hours later, Shimkif finally returned. "Are they back?" she asked as she walked into Haplif's room.

"Yes, a few hours ago," he said. Her clothing was stained with dirt, perspiration, and something that looked like plant residue, but she was clearly very satisfied with her-self. "I understand the Grand Migration has moved. How did you pull that off?"

"Quite easily, actually," she said, dropping her back-pack on the deck and lowering herself gingerly into one of the chairs. "I poisoned some of the areas—not lethally, just enough to make the birds sick—so they would avoid them. Then I captured some other birds and took them to an area where I'd laid in extra food supplies. Once both groups passed the word to the other birds—however the Chaos they do that—enough of the flocks shifted location that the whole thing was thrown off balance."

Haplif nodded. "Nice."

"*I* thought so," Shimkif said "We gearing up to leave?"

"Small problem," Haplif said, scowling. "Yomie's found another migration halfway around the planet she wants to go to."

Shimkif's forehead skin crinkled. "What?" she asked, her voice suddenly gone still and ominous.

"You heard me," Haplif said. "At the moment, I've only promised we'll go for a couple of days before we reopen the Celwis discussion. I assume your trick will work as well there as it did here?"

"You assume wrong," Shimkif growled. "The Grand Migration is well documented, and I had time on the way here to work out the details on the birds and their feeding habits. Not a chance I can do it again on the fly."

"That's unfortunate," Haplif said, glowering. "Well, then, we'll have to come up with some other way to stop it."

"Yes," Shimkif said, her voice grim and thoughtful. "I suppose we will."

# CHAPTER FOURTEEN

"Yes, Lakbulbup, I realize it's early morning there," Lakphro said patiently into the house comm. "It's not exactly prime talking time here, either."

"What time is—? Oh, I see," Lakbulbup said, and Lakphro could visualize his cousin's familiar squint as he peered at his display's readouts. "Why in the world are you calling at this hour?"

"I need a favor," Lakphro said, making sure to keep his voice low. "I'm calling now because Lakansu and Lakris are still asleep, and I don't want either of them to know about it."

"Must be *some* favor," Lakbulbup said. "If you're thinking about running away from home and enlisting in the Expansionary Defense Fleet, forget it. We have *some* standards, you know. Anyway, after seventeen years of marriage, there can't be much fight left in you."

"You might be surprised," Lakphro said, rolling his eyes. Lakbulbup's attempts at humor were legendary at family get-togethers. "Listen, I have a piece of jewelry an alien gave me. I need to know—"

"An *alien*? Who?"

"They're called Agbui, but I doubt you've ever heard of them," Lakphro said. "This particular group says they're cultural nomads traveling the Chaos looking for new cultures and insights and some such."

"Sounds like a mass wandering year."

"Could be," Lakphro said. "Maybe Agbui do wandering decades. No idea. The point is that they gave my wife and daughter fancy brooches they'd made out of thin metal wires. Sort of as an apology for—well, that doesn't matter."

"What kind of metal is it?"

"I don't know," Lakphro said, fishing Lakris's brooch out of his pocket and peering at it. "There are four different types: gold, silver, red, and blue. The point is that when I showed Lakansu's to the senior aide to our local Xodlak Councilor, she snatched it right out of my hand, ordered me not to tell anyone about it or let my family tell anyone about it, and then left with it in her pocket."

"Interesting," Lakbulbup said, his earlier annoyance at the hour of the call fading away. If there was one thing the man liked, it was a good puzzle. "I don't suppose you have a way of testing for radioactivity?"

"Actually, I do," Lakphro said, "and no, it's not. It's also not magnetic or prismatic or microwave-responsive. It's also not particularly heavy."

"That cuts out a lot of the exotics, anyway. Have you tried running a current through it?"

"I'm afraid to," Lakphro admitted. "I've already lost Lakansu's. If I fry Lakris's, I'm going to be in very serious trouble here."

"Sounds like you're already in serious trouble," Lakbulbup said. "Or don't I count as one of the people you're not supposed to talk to about this?"

"I know," Lakphro said with a sigh. "But it's driving me crazy, and I had to talk to *someone.* I've looked at this thing until I was crosseyed, and I can't figure out why Lakjiip went completely airborne when she saw it."

"Who can tell with politicians?" Lakbulbup said. "I presume you didn't call just to get this off your chest."

Lakphro braced himself. "I want to send it to you," he said. "Your wife's a scientist, and she knows other scientists. Maybe she can get someone to run tests that I can't and see things I can't."

"You *do* know her lab is biological, right?" Lakbulbup reminded him. "What you need is someone in metallurgy, or maybe just a professional jeweler."

"Which I hoped Dilpram could find for me. Can she?"

"Probably," Lakbulbup said. "But I'm wondering why you're sending it halfway across the Ascendancy when there are a thousand people on Celwis who could do the same job."

"A thousand people who might happen to bump into Councilor Lakuviv or his aide?"

"What, do people just casually bump into family officials on Celwis?"

"Redhill's a folksy province, and Lakuviv's angling for higher office," Lakphro said. "And all it would take is one."

"I suppose." Lakbulbup's sigh was audible over the comm. "Okay. I'll ask her to make a list of people who might be interested. How soon can you get it to me?"

"I can send it out tomorrow morning," Lakphro said. "Later this morning, rather. If I ship it standard parcel, the schedule says it should reach Naporar in six to eight days."

"Or you could send it express."

"Have you checked those rates lately?"

"Point," Lakbulbup conceded. "Okay, go ahead and toss it in the mail. While I'm waiting for it to get here, I'll talk to a few people. Discreetly, of course."

"Thanks, Lakbulbup," Lakphro said. "And make sure *they* know they have to be discreet, too."

"I'll only approach the ones I know I can trust," Lakbulbup promised. "Actually, the whole thing's starting to sound quite intriguing. Very shifty-eyes-and-dark-shadows and all."

"You've been watching too many dramas."

"Excuse me; *I've* been watching too many?" Lakbulbup countered drily. "I'm not the one shipping contraband jewelry across the Ascendancy in the dead of night."

"Whatever," Lakphro said. "Thanks, Lakbulbup. I owe you one."

"No problem," Lakbulbup said. "Say hi to Lakansu and Lakris for me. Well, when you *can* say hi. I assume we're also not talking about this conversation?"

"Not for the moment, no," Lakphro said. "Thanks again, and I'm sorry I woke you."

"Oh, I wasn't asleep," Lakbulbup said innocently. "But there's nothing like an early-morning grouse to set the proper mood for the day. Anyway, I had to let the growzer out. Talk to you later, cousin."

"You too."

For a long minute after Lakphro clicked off the comm, he sat at his desk, cupping Lakris's brooch in his palm. It still wasn't too late to give the jewelry back to his daughter, he knew. He could make up some story about how she must have dropped it in the feedlot, and how he'd found it. Then he could go back to being a rancher and forget the whole thing.

But he couldn't. Lakjiip had stolen his wife's brooch, and Lakphro was going to find out why. Whatever it cost him, he was going to find out why.

As a Pathfinder, one of the gifted few who could achieve the trance state that allowed the Great Presence to guide him through the tortured and ever-changing paths of hyperspace, Qilori of Uandualon had spent most of his life in ships or in navigator concourses. He'd seen planets from afar, and actually landed on a number of them, but they'd never felt like home.

Still, as the Chiss pilot flew the Xodlak patrol ship inward, staying behind and to the side of the Agbui freighter it had been escorting, Qilori could see how people who liked nature and planetary life might be impressed by the place.

Wide-open vistas dotted with sparkling blue lakes and rivers. Forest and grassland, rugged mountains, and only occasional swaths of desert. No cities, no construction, untouched by war or pestilence or civilization. Just woodland creatures, and peace and quiet.

Until, of course, those same woodland creatures decided they didn't want anyone disturbing their land. At that point, any would-be colonists had better hope they were armed.

All in all, Qilori preferred the more ordered life of space.

"Did I hear the Agbui captain call the planet Hoxim?" a voice came from behind him.

Qilori turned, feeling his cheek winglets press flat against his skin. He'd navigated his fair share of Chiss ships, mostly diplomatic vessels but also occasional merchants who needed to get across the Chaos in a hurry and didn't mind paying the price for a good navigator. Never in all of those missions had he met a single blueskin with even a shred of humor.

But this one, this Senior Aide Lakjiip, was in a class by herself. Her expression seemed to be set in a permanently intense half scowl, her questions were clipped and precise, and he never saw her interact with any of the other Chiss aboard unless she was giving orders or asking for information.

She was on the bridge every time Qilori came out of his trance, looking at him as if wondering what he needed a rest break for. She was there when he left for his brief sleep periods, and she was there when he returned. If the Chiss ever decided to develop mechanical robots, she would probably be the template.

But her personality defects really didn't matter. She was here, Qilori was here, and his job was to answer her questions. "That's what the Agbui call it," he said. "I don't know if the word means anything in their language or is just a pair of random syllables."

"What do the natives call it?"

"There aren't any," Qilori said. "No natives, no colonists, not even any observation bases. The Agbui wouldn't be here if they thought they were intruding on someone else's territory." He offered her a small smile. "They're very conscientious about such things."

If she was impressed by Agbui conscientiousness, she didn't show it. "You've been here more than once, I gather?"

"A few times, yes," he said. Actually, of course, he'd never even seen the place before today. "It was Haplif's turn—let me see—about ten months ago to come by to drop off supplies for the workers and collect the processed metal strands to take for his own group and any others who might happen to pass nearby. Like this freighter just did with Haplif's group."

"So there aren't any regular supply runs?"

"I don't think anything down there is that organized," Qilori said. "But to be honest, I really don't know. I've gone outside to look around a couple of times, but I frankly prefer the cleanliness of a ship to the untidiness of planetary life."

"How long have the Agbui been coming here?" Lakjiip asked. "Specifically, how long have they been working these mines?"

"I don't know," Qilori said. "Long enough to erect a permanent settlement and a couple of electroextraction processing units. Not more than a few decades at the most, though."

"And no one else has ever found the place?"

"There are an immense number of worlds in the Chaos," Qilori reminded her. "This one in particular isn't close to any of the local civilizations and is also far off the usual travel pathways. There's really no reason for anyone to come here."

"Except cultural nomads seeking knowledge, making new friends, and expanding the width and breadth of their lives," Lakjiip said.

Qilori looked at her in surprise. "That's very poetic, Senior Aide."

"It's what Haplif told Councilor Lakuviv when he first arrived at Redhill," she said. "I understand the payment for your services is some of their jewelry?"

"And room and board, of course," Qilori said, feeling his cheek winglets doing a small flutter. This was the delicate part. "Plus the chance to share in the cultural aspects of their travels."

"Yet you rarely leave the ship," Lakjiip said.

Qilori shrugged. "As I said, I prefer shipboard life. But I'm able to share in the various local foods they bring in, and can peruse the electronic entertainment and educational options from my quarters."

"Mm." Lakjiip looked back out the viewport. "There are a few things I'll want to check when we get down there. Perhaps you'd be good enough to show me around."

Qilori felt another twitch of his winglets. Showing her around a place he'd never been to. "Of course," he said. "I'd be honored."

---

Haplif had carefully and thoroughly prepped Qilori for what he'd be heading into. Even so, the Agbui settlement was surprisingly impressive.

The main part was a modest, two-story building to the left of the mine entrance, consisting of a pair of sleeping room wings attached to a combination cafeteria and relaxation center. The two ore processing plants to the right of the mine were marvels of compact design, with power and water sources off to the side and neat stacks of compacted waste material a couple of hundred meters farther on where it wouldn't bother either the work or the workers. The mine entrance itself was built into the rock face of a mountain, the center section of a spine of volcanic peaks cutting across this part of the planet and fading into the mists in both directions. Groups of Agbui moved briskly back and forth, transferring crates of supplies from the freighter to the residence building and taking smaller crates from a storage shed near the refinery back to the ship.

Qilori had seen the maps, floor plans, and technical specs, of course. But none of them had done the place justice. If the goal had been to make it a combination of efficient, resourceful, and simple, they'd succeeded beautifully.

"At least now we know why no one else bothered with this place," Lakjiip said from behind him.

Qilori turned. The woman was squatting down beside one of a row of bushes, peering at a shoulder-slung multi-analyzer. "Pardon?" he asked.

"The soil," she said, straightening up and showing him the display. "Quite acidic. Too acidic for any Chiss food plant to grow. Probably equally hostile to most of the alien foodstuffs in this part of the Chaos. If the whole planet is like this, it's useless for any large-scale colonization."

"I assume the acidity means you can't eat the native plants, either?"

"Probably not." Lakjiip leaned over the bush for a closer look. "I'll take a few samples back to Celwis, but most alien plants aren't useful to us even when the soil is better. You *did* say the other nomad groups bring in supplies for the miners, didn't you?"

"Yes," Qilori said. "Though the Agbui might have figured out how to process the local plants. Someone in the cafeteria could probably tell us."

"Later." Lakjiip nodded toward the mine. "I want to look in there."

They were nearly to the mine entrance, and Qilori could see the darkened tunnel stretching back into the mountain, when an Agbui suddenly popped up in front of them. "I'm sorry, gentlebeings," he said in a tone that made it clear he genuinely *was* sorry. "No outsiders are permitted in the mine. There are dangers within."

"What kind of dangers?" Lakjiip asked.

"Those that exist in all mines," the Agbui told her. "Unsafe footing. The chance of rocks breaking from walls and ceilings. Uncertain air, with occasional outgassings of unhealthy or even toxic fumes."

Aboard ship, Qilori had noted that Lakjiip was accustomed to getting her own way, and for that first half second he thought she might actually demand the alien step aside. But the moment passed, and she simply nodded. "I understand," she said. "Perhaps on my next visit." She half turned and pointed at the refinery. "May I look in there?"

"Sadly, that area is also deemed dangerous to the unwary and unprepared." The Agbui brightened. "But we can look in through the windows, if you'd like. I would be happy to describe to you the equipment and processes within."

"That would be helpful," Lakjiip said. "Lead on."

They spent the next hour looking in through various of the refinery's windows while the Agbui gave a running description of what his six fellows inside were doing. Lakjiip asked occasional questions but was mostly content to let him talk.

Qilori spent little of his own time on either the view or the commentary. Most of his attention was spent avoiding a group of large flying insects that seemed to have taken an interest in him. Between his furtive efforts to shoo them away, he kept a wary eye on some

beady-eyed lizards squatting beneath one of the nearer bushes, creatures that also seemed inordinately interested in the strangers. It was
to his immense relief when Lakjiip finally finished her inspection
tour and gave him permission to return to the ship.

They spent the rest of the day there, slept overnight in the patrol
ship, and left the next morning in convoy with the Agbui freighter.
The aliens weren't going back to Celwis, or even to another world in
the Ascendancy, but Lakjiip had agreed to escort them out of the
system to make sure some passing pirate didn't get ideas. One of the
peculiarities of their hyperdrive, the Agbui had explained to Lakjiip,
was that their ships needed to be farther out of a planetary gravity
well than those of most species before they could enter hyperspace.
That greater distance, along with the time it took to cross it, made
them especially vulnerable to attack.

Given how much of the rest of the Agbui story was false, Qilori
normally would have assumed that was also a lie. But given that he'd
already witnessed the longer approach time during his brief association with Haplif, he was inclined to believe it.

Should he ever need to make a quick escape in an Agbui ship, he
made a note to himself, he would need to keep that in mind.

He was in the navigational chair, making one final adjustment to
his sensory-deprivation headset, when he heard the captain's voice
behind him. "Did you accomplish everything you set out to do here,
Senior Aide?"

"Yes," Lakjiip said, and even through her precise professional tone
Qilori could hear her underlying satisfaction. "Yes, I did."

Qilori smiled. She had accomplished what she wanted. In that
case, so had Haplif.

And so had Jixtus.

Still smiling, he settled the helmet on his head and prepared to
once again join the Great Presence.


Once again, Thurfian was already waiting at the agreed-upon spot in
the March of Silence when Zistalmu arrived.

Only this time, instead of using the time to observe and brood and plan, Thurfian used it to seethe.

*How* did Thrawn keep pulling these things out of the fire?

"You're late," he snapped as Zistalmu stepped into conversational range. "I've been waiting fifteen minutes."

"My apologies," Zistalmu said, inclining his head.

Which made Thurfian even angrier. Getting snapped back at would have given him an excuse to verbally lay into the man, and he really, *really* wanted to lay into someone right now. "I assume you have some kind of excuse?"

"I was working out the details of a contingency plan," Zistalmu said, still with that maddening calm.

"Oh, so now *you* have a plan?" Thurfian said scornfully.

"Yes, I do," Zistalmu said, some of the coolness starting to crack. "Because it certainly looks like yours has run straight into the ground."

Thurfian took a deep breath, preparing a crushing retort—

And paradoxically, the seething rage faded back into a corner of his mind.

Because Zistalmu was right. Sending Thrawn against the Vagaari *had* been his idea. And it certainly wasn't the Irizi's fault that it hadn't worked. "It does, doesn't it?" he conceded. "My apologies for my words and my tone. I was just so furious . . . I assume you've read the report?"

"Twice," Zistalmu said sourly. "*And* listened to the diplomatic corps try to decide if they were outraged or salivating at this first real break in relations with the Paataatus."

"*And* no doubt listened to General Ba'kif point out oh-so-sincerely that because the ship he attacked was Nikardun, it didn't even violate the preemptive-strike prohibition."

"That too," Zistalmu said. "Also listened to Ba'kif explain that just because the message came in via a Paataatus triad transmitter doesn't mean it might be some trick. Not when it came wrapped in a military encryption with Thrawn's personal confirmation overlay."

"And the fact that they were willing to send it from one of their triads just underscores their gratitude toward him."

"Indeed," Zistalmu said. "All of which just adds another layer of glory on the Mitth. Are you *sure* you want to take him down?"

"Are we going to have to go through this every single time?" Thurfian growled. "What if he'd misread the Paataatus, or they'd misread him? What if he'd missed with that breacher and plasma sphere barrage? What if he'd not only missed the Nikardun but hit the Prince Militaire's ship? We'd be at war, Thrawn would be up on charges, and there might well be only *Eight* Ruling Families."

"I think you're overstating the case a bit," Zistalmu said. "But only a bit. The question now is, since Thrawn seems to be on another winning streak, what do we do about it?"

Thurfian eyed the other, belatedly remembering that this whole conversation had started with Zistalmu stating he had a plan. "I assume you have a way to stop him?"

"My sense right now is that, realistically, he can't be stopped," Zistalmu said. "If the suggestions the Paataatus gave him about possible Vagaari whereabouts prove false, then he returns empty-handed. But he still returns a hero on the diplomatic front. If there *are* still a few Vagaari out there, odds are he'll destroy them."

"Assuming the Paataatus are right about there being only a small remnant at most," Thurfian said.

"That *is* the Paataatus backyard," Zistalmu reminded him. "If anyone would know about a major pirate gang operating there, it's them."

"Assuming they didn't lie to Thrawn just to get rid of him."

"There's that, of course," Zistalmu agreed. "To get back to the plan. My thought is that if we can't stop Thrawn from picking up some glory, maybe we can at least make him share it."

Thurfian frowned. "How?"

"We send him some help," Zistalmu said. "Obviously, we can't send one of our ships." He smiled tightly. "Even more obviously, we can't send one of yours. So. How does a Xodlak ship sound?"

Thurfian thought back. Hadn't it been a Xodlak representative who'd made Zistalmu late to their last meeting? "Do they even *have* any warships?"

"Technically, all they have are their various planetary defense forces," Zistalmu conceded. "Though some of their planetary patrol ships probably edge toward warship class. They also have some larger ships in reserve, though again they're technically not allowed to fly them."

"Until and unless they regain Ruling Family status."

"Right. But no, I was talking about an Expansionary Defense Fleet ship commanded by a Xodlak. If the Mitth get the glory from Thrawn's exploits, surely the Xodlak will get equal credit if one of theirs is in command."

"Seems reasonable," Thurfian said. "And since the Xodlak are allies of the Irizi . . . ?"

"We might get a bit of the glow," Zistalmu conceded. "But the Mitth will get all of Thrawn's, so what are you worried about?"

"I suppose you're right," Thurfian said, a bit reluctantly. Clearly, Zistalmu was hoping the Irizi would get more than just a glow off a Xodlak captain's success.

Still, Thurfian could hardly expect Zistalmu's cooperation on this if he didn't get *something* out of the deal. "You have a ship in mind?"

"That was the research that made me late." Zistalmu pulled out his questis and handed it over. "Our best bet is the *Grayshrike*, commanded by Senior Captain Xodlak'in'daro. She's part of Admiral Ar'alani's task force, so she and Thrawn have worked together, which makes her a logical person to send to assist him."

"You think Ba'kif and Supreme Admiral Ja'fosk will go for that?"

"Why not? The *Springhawk*'s off in unknown territory. The Paataatus are behind him, possible Vagaari forces are in front of him, and there are no allies or resources anywhere nearby. It's only prudent to send help, and the *Grayshrike* is the ideal option."

Thurfian skimmed the data Zistalmu had compiled. It did indeed look like the *Grayshrike* would be an excellent choice. "What about this Captain Lakinda? Is she going to fall under Thrawn's spell like Ba'kif and Ar'alani?"

"Not a chance," Zistalmu assured him. "I've spoken with a Xodlak on Naporar who deals with the Expansionary Defense Fleet officer corps. He says she's ambitious, competent, and that even as a senior officer she's very family-focused. Given the Xodlak relationship with the Irizi, and the tensions we have with you Mitth, she's going to be completely resistant to anything he throws at her."

"All right," Thurfian said. There were still potential pitfalls to all this, he knew. But there were pitfalls to everything he and Zistalmu had been doing ever since they made this private alliance. "How do you want to do this?"

"I'm ready to submit the proposal to Ba'kif and Ja'fosk," Zistalmu said. "The *Grayshrike*'s somewhere out of the Ascendancy at the moment, but Csilla ought to be able to reach it with a triad message. Given Thrawn's legendary thoroughness, it's unlikely he'll finish his survey before Lakinda can get out there to assist him."

Thurfian hesitated. So many uncertainties . . . but it was certain that if they didn't do something, Thrawn would eventually crash and burn, and possibly take the Mitth down with him.

And if Zistalmu was hoping the *Grayshrike* could share in the glory, Lakinda should also be able to share in the blame if that happened. "All right, let's do it," he said. He lifted a warning finger. "But this had better work."

"It will," Zistalmu promised. "Lakinda wants the Xodlak to be one of the Ruling Families again. Thrawn and the Mitth can't get that for her. The Irizi can.

"Whatever we need her to do, she'll do it."

# CHAPTER FIFTEEN

Ar'alani had planned their arrival at Sunrise very carefully, making sure the *Vigilant* and *Grayshrike* arrived in the planet's orbital shadow and a sufficient distance out that they could make a quick exit into hyperspace if the Battle Dreadnought Thrawn and Lakinda had tangled with had sent another warship to take its place.

But as far as she could see from the *Vigilant*'s position, the black disk of the planet was alone.

She gazed at the darkened world in front of them, an unpleasant chill running through her. Civilized worlds generally had lighting patterns that were visible at night, either navigational aids or just the lights of traveling vehicles. On a handful of special worlds like Csilla, those lights were few and far between, but they were still there.

But on Sunrise's nighttime surface, there was nothing. Either the war had utterly devastated the planet, or the survivors were cowering in the darkness, afraid to show anything that might attract their enemies.

Wutroow, standing beside Ar'alani's command chair, had clearly seen the same absolute darkness and come to the same conclusion. "And Thrawn calls this place *Sunrise*?" she asked.

"So he does," Ar'alani said, wincing a little. "Whether he believes the name is appropriate is a different question." She keyed her comm, double-checking that it was set on a tight beam that wouldn't leak out to any eavesdroppers who might be lurking in the area. "Captain Lakinda, this is Admiral Ar'alani," she said. "Opinion?"

"Our sensors aren't showing any ships or other power sources in the area," Lakinda's voice came over the speaker. "However, that isn't necessarily conclusive. The region the warship was guarding was on the other side of the planet. If there's really something there that the aliens are interested in, that's probably where it will be."

"Agreed," Ar'alani said. "On the other hand, if your skirmish worried its masters enough to send more than one replacement, they should be positioned so as to watch all approaches, including our current one. The fact that neither of us is picking up anything suggests—"

"Movement, Admiral," Biclian cut in from the sensor station. "Coming around the starboard edge of the planet."

"Get me a reading," Ar'alani ordered, peering at the sensor display. The object was *big*, easily big enough to be a major warship. But it was moving along in an almost leisurely way, apparently not in any hurry. Had it failed to spot the two Chiss ships out here? "Passive sensors only. Captain Lakinda?"

"We're scanning it now, ma'am," Lakinda said.

"Belay that," Ar'alani said. "Shift your scans to aft and flanking. I don't want something sneaking up on us while we're all gawking."

There was just the slightest hesitation. "Yes, ma'am."

"She *does* so hate to be left out of the action," Wutroow muttered.

"I don't think running out of things to do is going to be a problem," Ar'alani replied. "Biclian?"

"Analysis coming up now, Admiral," Biclian said. "It's about the *Vigilant*'s size, irregularly shaped, not any warship configuration we've seen before. Surface albedo suggests rough rock with admixed iron and other metals. Orbital path is constant, no evidence of motive power."

"I'll be damned," Wutroow said suddenly. "Admiral, it's a *moon.*"

"Senior Captain Wutroow is correct," Biclian confirmed. "A very small moon, or possibly an asteroid."

"Interesting," Ar'alani said. The last time she and her bridge crew had had a conversation about an asteroid . . . "Give me a reading on orbital eccentricity."

"One moment, ma'am." Biclian paused, eyeing his displays. "Preliminary reading is point zero zero five."

"Practically circular," Wutroow said darkly. "Probably not a random gravitational capture, then. Are you thinking what I'm thinking, Admiral?"

"Very likely," Ar'alani said. "Captain Lakinda, there wasn't anything like this asteroid in your battle records. Could it have been in that orbit the entire time you were here, out of your view on the wrong side of the planet? Or is it something new?"

"We're reviewing the records now, Admiral," Lakinda said, and Ar'alani could visualize the senior captain's eyes narrowed in concentration. "Given the limited length of time we were here, it *is* possible that we just never saw it. A precise time-line analysis might be able to backtrack the asteroid's orbit to be certain, but that will take time."

"Which we may not have," Wutroow warned. "I trust you've had a chance to review our report from that last Nikardun base?"

"Yes, ma'am, we have," Lakinda said. "Are you thinking this might be another of the camouflaged missile launchers that the attackers used there?"

"I think it very likely," Ar'alani said.

"If it is, it has to have some kind of sensor array to know when to launch," Wutroow pointed out. "In which case, it may have already spotted us."

"It may," Ar'alani agreed, gazing at the unpretentious blob floating across the sensor display. "Or it may not. Wutroow, we've got Thrawn's records of the *Springhawk*'s and *Grayshrike*'s battle here, don't we?"

"I think so," Wutroow said, punching keys on her questis. "Yes, we do."

"He came in on a different vector than the *Grayshrike* did," Ar'alani said. "Run the sensor data and see if you can spot that asteroid anywhere. Maybe at the corner of one of the scans, where no one was looking."

"He *was* conducting a battle at the time," Wutroow pointed out as she continued to work the questis, "so there's a good chance that even if it was there he'd have missed it."

"A *fair* chance, anyway," Ar'alani corrected. "Even in the middle of a battle, there's very little that gets past him."

"Well, given that it would have been drifting around the opposite side of the planet from where the battle was taking place, I promise not to tease him if it did." Wutroow put the questis away. "I've got the sensor techs working on it."

Ar'alani nodded. "Biclian?"

"Still reading as a fairly normal asteroid, ma'am," Biclian said. "Unfortunately, the data profile from passive sensors is limited. If there's a missile launcher hidden inside, there's no way we're going to pick up on it."

"Which may be something we can use to our advantage," Ar'alani said thoughtfully. If that really was a weapon that had been brought in since the last skirmish . . . and if there was another unfriendly warship lurking on the other side of the planet . . . "Continue passive sensors. Captain Lakinda, are you game to try something dangerous?"

"As opposed to just being part of the Expansionary Defense Fleet," Wutroow added.

"Yes, ma'am, of course," Lakinda said, sounding a bit uncomfortable with Wutroow's dry humor.

"Good," Ar'alani said. "Here's what we're going to do."

Across the *Grayshrike*'s bridge, Wikivv gave her helm controls one last check. "We're ready, ma'am," she said, looking over her shoulder at Lakinda.

"Acknowledged," Lakinda said, eyeing the data on the helm display and mentally crossing her fingers. She would put Wikivv up against any pilot in the Expansionary Defense Fleet, but the kind of precision Lakinda was asking from her this time was beyond anything Wikivv had ever done before.

But Ar'alani wanted it, and Wikivv had assured them she could do it, and so here they were. "Shrent, inform the *Vigilant* that we're ready," she ordered, looking over at the combat status display. Whatever the next few minutes brought, the *Grayshrike* was ready for battle.

"*Vigilant* acknowledges," Shrent reported. "Admiral Ar'alani says we can go at your convenience."

"Acknowledge," Lakinda said, consciously bracing herself. "Wikivv: Three, two, *one*."

There was the usual visual and mental jerkiness as the *Grayshrike* performed Wikivv's in-system jump. The black disk of Sunrise abruptly filled half the viewport, and the hyperdrive status indicators changed as the planet began pulling the ship deeper into its gravity well.

Thirty degrees to portside, barely a kilometer distant and moving away from the *Grayshrike* along its orbit, was the asteroid.

"Portside yaw thirty degrees," Lakinda ordered. "Slow and casual. Don't try to close, just ease up into following position behind it."

"Yes, ma'am."

The *Grayshrike* began its yaw turn, and Lakinda focused her full attention on the irregular mass of rock. If Ar'alani was right about this being the same weapon used against the Nikardun base, and if whoever was monitoring the sensors assumed the asteroid was about to come under Chiss attack, Lakinda's only warning would be the massive explosion as the shell disintegrated and cleared the weapon to fire. If that happened, the *Grayshrike* would have only that small handful of seconds to get in the first shot.

But whoever was controlling the weapon was evidently not the nervous sort. The *Grayshrike* finished its turn, lining itself up with the asteroid, without sparking any reaction. "Wikivv, increase speed to match," Lakinda ordered. "Excellent job with the jump."

"Thank you, ma'am," Wikivv said. "Increasing speed . . . matching, and holding distance."

"When do you want to start closing the gap?" Apros asked from beside Lakinda's command chair.

"We'll wait until Ar'alani's in position," she told him. "Vimsk, any sign of the *Vigilant*?"

"Not yet—yes; there it is," the sensor officer interrupted herself.

"I see it," Lakinda said, eyeing the tactical display. The *Vigilant* had emerged into view a quarter of the way around the planet ahead of them, farther out of the gravity well, in a similar position to the spot the *Grayshrike* itself had held during the previous skirmish. If the aliens had sent another ship, and if it was again positioned to monitor the same section of the planet, it now ought to be in full view. The secondary sensor display lit up as the *Vigilant* began sending visual and sensor telemetry—

And there it was. A Battle Dreadnought of the same configuration as the one she and Thrawn had tangled with two weeks ago.

Lakinda frowned. No, not just another warship. It was the *same* warship. The battle scars from Thrawn's breacher and laser attack on its port side were unmistakable.

Apros spotted it, too. "So they just sent it *back*? I'd have expected them to at least slap a fresh coat of paint over the damage before they let it out again."

"Apparently not," Lakinda said.

"Unidentified warship, this is Admiral Ar'alani aboard the Chiss Expansionary Defense Fleet warship *Vigilant*," Ar'alani's Taarja words came over the bridge speaker. "Please identify yourselves."

"Should we let the *Vigilant* know it's the same ship?" Apros suggested.

Lakinda shook her head. "I'm sure Ar'alani's already figured it out."

"Chiss warship, you intrude in an area where you're not wanted," a harsh voice came back. "Leave immediately or face severe consequences."

Lakinda straightened in her chair, peripherally aware that a ripple of sudden interest was running through her bridge. None of the ships they'd faced here earlier, not the Battle Dreadnought or any of the gunboats, had responded to their hails. For them to suddenly be talking was a new wrinkle.

More than that, it strongly suggested that Ar'alani's plan was working. The enemy commander, secure in the knowledge that his asteroid missile could deal a death blow to the *Grayshrike* at any moment, was hoping to worm a little information out of Ar'alani before he destroyed both ships. At the same time, with the *Grayshrike* supposedly sneaking up on the main confrontation from behind the asteroid, Ar'alani's mirror plan to gather data before springing her own surprise attack would also be obvious to him.

Some commanders, Lakinda reflected, would have accepted the simple military value of their perceived advantage and merely used it to overwhelm the opponent. This one was cooler and more ambitious.

The enemy knew he had the upper hand because he had a secret weapon. Ar'alani knew *she* had the upper hand because she knew about the asteroid, and the enemy didn't know she knew.

Mentally, Lakinda shook her head. Even Thrawn might have trouble following this one.

"Wikivv, start easing us toward the asteroid," she ordered. "Not too close, and not too fast. Make it look like we're making sure we'll be completely hidden behind it once we come into the Battle Dreadnought's view."

"Unidentified warship, this is Admiral Ar'alani," Ar'alani replied. "Please clarify. Who exactly is it who doesn't want us here?"

"This world has been devastated by an attack from an evil that calls itself the Nikardun Destiny," the alien said, still in that same severe tone. "We were begged by the survivors to stand guard and protect them, lest the Nikardun or other scavengers take advantage of their weakness and plunder the few remaining scraps."

Lakinda frowned. Unless he was lying—which was certainly possible—then there *were* still some people alive down there. The question would be whether there were enough of them to persuade the Magys not to go through with her mass suicide plan.

But that would be Thrawn's problem. Lakinda's current problem was sitting rather closer to hand.

"An interesting coincidence," Ar'alani told the alien. "As it happens, we're here for the same reason. Perhaps we can join forces."

"*We* were begged for help by the survivors."

"Yes, I heard you," Ar'alani said. "Can you give me the name of your contact on the planet?"

There was a sound that sounded like tearing metal. "Do you think me a fool?" the alien demanded. "I will not offer useful information to an intruder."

"I'm sorry to hear that," Ar'alani said. "*We* were invited by the Magys. You may have heard of her."

"What is a Magys?" the alien sneered. "A small local dignitary? *My* mandate arises from the planetary leaders themselves."

"Their names?"

"I do not need to offer you any defense for my presence."

"Their names?" Ar'alani repeated.

"Captain, the asteroid is rotating," Vimsk spoke up. "Very slowly, but the changes in reflection from the surface stone are unmistakable."

Getting into position to target the *Grayshrike*? "Ghaloksu, I need a way to disable that thing," she said, muting the conversation between the *Vigilant* and the alien commander. "How do we do that?"

"I'm not sure we can, ma'am," the weapons officer said hesitantly. "Not until the shell is open."

"So let's figure out how to open it," Lakinda said. "What do we know?"

"The shards the *Vigilant* found at the Nikardun base didn't have any scoring or residue," Ghaloksu said. "That suggests the shell wasn't blown off explosively but rather via mechanical means. The bits of metal dug into the shards suggests a spherical isokinetic framework, initially contracted under pressure around the launcher. When the pressure's released, the framework expands violently outward, with prongs or struts attached to it pushing against the sections of the shell and shoving them apart."

"You can see the fracture zone lines on the surface where the breakage will happen," Vimsk added. She touched a key, and an overlay appeared across the asteroid's sensor display image. "They're too regular to be anything but deliberate."

Lakinda scowled. She'd assumed the shell would be blown by

shaped charges scattered around the surface, charges they could either prematurely detonate with lasers or disable with plasma spheres. But if the entire mechanism was deep inside the shell, there was probably no way to get at it from the outside. "What about command transmissions?" she asked. "Someone ordered the asteroid to rotate, and someone has to order the shell to splinter and the missile to launch. Can we jam the signals or disable the receiver?"

"We could if we knew where the receiver was," Ghaloksu said. "Problem is, we don't."

"Actually, with something this size, they'll probably have multiple receivers," Shrent put in. "Scattered around the surface so that there would be one in range no matter what the asteroid's position or angle was."

And there was no way they could saturate the entire surface with plasma spheres. Even if they had enough fluid, they didn't have enough time. "All right," Lakinda said, gazing at the fracture line map. Vimsk was right—they were extremely regular, forming rough hexagons on the surface.

She felt her eyes narrow. Rough, *small* hexagons. "Ghaloksu, are those sections big enough to fire a missile through? If not, there must be an area where they're bigger."

"Which would mark the spot where the internal framework is more open," Ghaloksu said, nodding. "In which case, we'll know when it's nearly in firing position."

"Vimsk?" Lakinda asked.

"Setting up a search pattern now, ma'am," the sensor officer confirmed.

"Good," Lakinda said. "Make it fast."

"Once we find it, what do we do?" Apros asked.

"For starters, we don't let it get fully lined up on us," Lakinda said, thinking quickly. Part of Ar'alani's plan had been for Lakinda to find a way to disable and capture the hidden weapon while the *Vigilant* kept the larger warship busy. But she'd also made it clear that if Lakinda had to destroy the asteroid to protect her ship, she shouldn't hesitate to do so.

Unless . . .

"Ghaloksu, ready all weapons," she said. "I'm going to want lasers, breachers, and spheres, in that order. Vimsk, let me know as soon as you see something that looks like one of your larger shell sections coming around toward us. Wikivv, get ready to fire full reverse thrusters."

There was a brief chorus of confirmations from the other officers. "As soon as one of the larger sections comes into view, we're going to try to laser it open," Lakinda continued. "Once we've got access to the inside, we'll send in breachers to burn through a section of the isokinetic framework, hopefully messing up the expansion mechanism, followed by spheres to shut down the missile launcher's electronics. If we do everything fast enough—" she glanced at the tactical, confirming that the *Vigilant* and alien warship were still squared off against each other "—and if Ar'alani can keep their attention on her, we may be able to disable it before they realize what we've done."

"Worth a try," Apros agreed. "At which point, we'll have to hope we can take down the Battle Dreadnought before they can destroy it like they did the gunboats our last time around."

"They won't get a chance this time," Lakinda told him, "because as soon as we've disabled it we'll circle to the other side and take out any missiles they try to throw at it."

Apros's forehead creased slightly. "Sounds a little risky."

"The admiral wants the asteroid missile," Lakinda said. "I intend to get it for her. Any questions?"

His lip twitched, but he shook his head. "No, ma'am."

"Then get over to Ghaloksu," she said, nodding toward the weapons station. "He'll be busy coordinating the attack and may need an extra set of hands."

"Yes, ma'am." With a nod, Apros crossed to the weapons console.

"Vimsk?" Lakinda prompted.

"Still scanning, ma'am," the sensor officer said, leaning close to her displays. "The sections are still running the same size."

"Captain, I think the battle's about to start," Shrent spoke up from the comm station.

Lakinda keyed the comm back on: "—or we will have no option but to do whatever is necessary to drive you from this system," the alien was saying.

"Everyone look sharp," Lakinda called. "The launch area must be coming up—they wouldn't want to open hostilities with the *Vigilant* unless they were ready to take us out. Shrent, did the alien say anything useful when I wasn't listening?"

"There were one or two things, ma'am," Shrent said, his voice a little strained. "With all due respect, I don't think this is the time—"

"There!" Vimsk cut in. "Larger section coming into view."

"Ghaloksu, there's your target," Lakinda said. "Wait until enough of it is in range, then open fire."

"Yes, ma'am," Ghaloksu said. "Ten more seconds should do it."

Lakinda looked at the weapons officer's tactical setup. He had the spectrum lasers split into groups, each group programmed to start at one of the section's vertices and then sweep both directions along the fracture zones. By the time they'd finished with the nearest set of lines the far edge of the section should have rotated into range and be ready for the same treatment. If the zones were thin enough, the whole section should be free in five to ten seconds.

If the rock was thicker, they might still be at it when the Battle Dreadnought woke up to the danger and launched countermeasures.

Ghaloksu's timing countdown was nearly there. "Stand by to fire," Lakinda called. "Three, two, *one*."

Through the viewport the lasers blazed out, their beams marked by slightly fuzzy glows where they ionized or vaporized the bits of gas and dust between the *Grayshrike* and the asteroid. The energy beams dug into the rocky surface, started their coordinated sweeps along the fracture zones—

And without warning the entire asteroid exploded, hurling shards of stone outward in all directions.

# CHAPTER SIXTEEN

"Full reverse!" Lakinda barked, flinching reflexively as several large fragments flew straight toward them. An instant later the spectacle was cut off as the viewport blast shields automatically slammed shut. There was a forward twitch of unbalanced deceleration as Wikivv threw power to the forward thrusters, trying to kill their forward momentum and send the ship backward.

But the *Grayshrike* was massive, and it had been moving at orbital speeds behind the asteroid, and there was simply too much inertia involved to come to a quick stop. As the compensators caught up and smoothed out the *Grayshrike*'s movement, the ship lurched with multiple impacts from high-speed pieces of the asteroid shell slamming into its bow and flank extensions.

"Orders?" Ghaloksu called out.

Lakinda focused on the sensor display. The asteroid's internal framework had opened to full extension, a few bits of stone still clinging to the struts that had slammed outward and forced the shell apart. In the center of the framework, rotating faster now that it no longer had to contend with the shell's extra mass, was the missile, its nose peeking out from the thick casing that was the launcher. "Launch spheres," she ordered. "Wikivv, all ahead full—get us in close."

"Launching spheres," Ghaloksu said.

"Accelerating to close approach," Wikivv added.

With the viewport still blocked by the blast shields, there was no direct view available. But between the sensor and tactical displays, the situation was more than clear.

Clear, and ominous. The framework hadn't rotated completely around yet to line up the missile on the *Grayshrike,* which left the tighter lattice sections forming a barrier between the cruiser and the missile launcher. On top of that, the framework was still rotating. The combination of those two factors was going to make it extremely difficult for Ghaloksu to get even a single plasma sphere through any of the gaps intact.

But he was giving it his best shot. Lakinda watched tensely as sphere after sphere hit a lattice strut and exploded in a burst of ionic energy, or occasionally slipped through a gap only to miss the launcher and shoot across to explode on the framework's other side. Peripherally, she saw that with the aliens' ambush having failed, the Battle Dreadnought had opened fire on the *Vigilant.* The space between the two massive warships had erupted in laserfire and the thruster trails of missiles.

"*Grayshrike,* report," Ar'alani's taut voice came over the speaker.

Lakinda keyed her comm. "Enemy launcher open to attack," she called back. "Engaging it with spheres."

"Good. Make it fast."

"Yes, ma'am," Lakinda said, frowning as the barrage of plasma spheres abruptly stopped. "Ghaloksu?"

"Launch window section of the lattice is coming up, ma'am," Ghaloksu said. "I'm holding back until we have a clearer shot."

Lakinda felt her stomach tighten. A clear shot at the launcher was all well and good . . . except that a clear sight line worked in both directions. If the launcher hadn't been completely disabled, the missile could end up coming straight down the *Grayshrike*'s throat.

She took a quick look at the tactical data display. Despite the obstacles, Ghaloksu had managed to get three completely on-target impacts. Even if the launcher was still partially functional, that should be enough to at least slow it down. "Understood," she told him. "Don't miss." The opening rotated into position—

And the *Grayshrike*'s entire forward plasma battery opened up, raining a fresh barrage of spheres at the launcher, their ion bursts creating a spectacular display of coronal fire as they spattered against the target. Lakinda watched the display, looking closely for any signs of activity. So far, nothing. "Vimsk?" she prompted

"I think we got it, ma'am," Vimsk reported. "No electronic or electrical activity registering. It's dead."

"Or at least sleeping very soundly," Apros added. "Captain, spheres are down to less than sixty percent."

"Ghaloksu, belay sphere launches," Lakinda ordered, looking at the display showing the distant battle. The *Vigilant* was still standing its ground, but if the flickers of explosions were any indication, the alien's missiles were getting steadily closer before Ar'alani's spectrum lasers could take them out. She keyed the comm—"Admiral, we've neutralized the missile launcher."

"Good," Ar'alani said. "Lock on a tractor beam and get over here."

Lakinda frowned. She understood that Ar'alani wanted the launcher captured intact for study. But with the *Vigilant* going toe-to-toe with a Battle Dreadnought, the launcher didn't seem like it should be the *Grayshrike*'s first priority. She keyed the mute—"Ghaloksu, how fast can you get the launcher free?" she asked.

"Not very, ma'am," Ghaloksu said. "It's tethered to the lattice with sixteen guy wires. The lasers should be able to cut them, but they're so thin they're going to be hard to hit. And of course, some of them are currently behind the launcher."

"Understood," Lakinda said, looking back at the battle. Ar'alani's prize was just going to have to wait. "Wikivv, get us moving—full attack vector."

"Yes, ma'am," the pilot said, and there was another slightly uncompensated jerk as she angled the *Grayshrike* around the side of the lattice and threw full power to the thrusters.

"Keep us on the enemy's portside flank," Lakinda continued. "Better chance of sneaking up on it that way."

"Even if they haven't fixed the overall damage, they may still have replaced some of those sensors," Apros pointed out. "Do you want to hit them with a sphere barrage first to knock out whatever's there?"

"No, we'll risk it," Lakinda said, studying the tactical. The Battle Dreadnought was nose-on to the *Vigilant*, both ships attacking with their flank and shoulder weapons clusters. If the alien ship was still even partially blind on its port side, the *Grayshrike* should be able to get into attack range before it was spotted. "Even if the sensors are still gone, a sphere barrage will alert them that we're coming."

"Understood," Apros said. "What's your plan?"

"We're going to try to take out the hyperdrive or the main thrusters or both," Lakinda said. "Ghaloksu, set up breacher attacks midships and aft, using your best guess as to where those two systems are centered. Once the breachers have hit, follow up with laser barrages."

"Yes, ma'am," Ghaloksu said.

"Whether we manage that or not, we'll keep going," Lakinda continued, "sweeping over the warship's dorsal surface and strafing with spheres, breachers, and lasers. Once past, Wikivv, you'll run us a one-eighty yaw turn to face the alien's starboard side, and we'll continue the attack. Questions?"

There was a brief silence. "Then get to it," Lakinda said. "Vimsk, grab every bit of data you can about that ship, both to assist Ghaloksu in targeting and also for future analysis."

"Yes, ma'am," the sensor officer said.

"Good." Lakinda took a deep breath. "The *Vigilant*'s in trouble. Let's even the odds a little."

The Battle Dreadnought had first fired two missiles, then four missiles, then six. Now the latest salvo—eight missiles—was on its way.

"Could they *be* any more obvious?" Wutroow muttered.

"Perfectly straightforward way to find the limits of an enemy's defenses," Ar'alani pointed out.

"Straightforward, maybe, but pretty expensive," Wutroow said as the *Vigilant*'s spectrum lasers took out the first two incoming missiles. "They'd have done better to just throw a single massive volley and see how many of them we couldn't stop."

"Alien minds, alien logic," Ar'alani said. "Oeskym?"

"We're handling it," the *Vigilant*'s weapons officer said. "Breachers are reset if you want to try those again."

"Admiral, the *Grayshrike*'s headed this way," Biclian cut in before Ar'alani could answer.

Ar'alani looked at the tactical. The cruiser was indeed on the move, accelerating at full power toward the battle.

Only it was coming alone, without the lattice and hidden missile launcher Ar'alani had specifically told Lakinda to bring with her.

She hissed out a quiet curse. Her plan had been for the *Grayshrike* to tow the launcher in close and then propel it into the combat zone between the two ships. If the *Vigilant*'s electronics people were lucky, they might be able to trigger the launcher and send the missile at the Battle Dreadnought. If not, Ar'alani could try to detonate the missile in place in the hope of scoring some blast damage against the enemy. Now both those options were gone.

Unfortunately, she couldn't order Lakinda to go back and get the launcher. The *Grayshrike* was already too far along, and accelerating too hard, for that to be practical.

"Launch two breachers," she ordered Oeskym. "Try running a laser spread around them, see if that will keep the dibbers away."

"Yes, ma'am."

Ar'alani shifted her attention to the tactical, watching as Oeskym launched the breacher missiles. The enemy had come up with a new tactic since their encounter with Thrawn and Lakinda: small, nimble missiles that Wutroow had dubbed *dibbers,* probably originally designed for use against gunboats and other small fighters. Unfortunately, the tiny missiles were also effective against breachers, and had successfully blasted all but two of the ones the *Vigilant* had launched against the alien.

Destroying the breachers didn't stop the wave of released acid, of course, and the dibber swarm always paid the price. But so far they were hitting the breachers far enough out that the acid globs expanded and dissipated into uselessness by the time they reached the alien warship itself.

Even worse, the dibbers had proven surprisingly effective against the plasma spheres, their impacts puncturing the spheres' self-focusing sheaths and dissipating the compressed ion clusters packed inside. The fact that the attacking dibber itself was instantly disabled was of little consolation, since the question at that point was whether the *Vigilant* would run out of sphere fluid before the Battle Dreadnought ran out of dibbers.

Given the recklessness with which the aliens were spending the little missiles, Ar'alani wouldn't bet either way.

"What is she *doing*?" Wutroow said under her breath. "Is she looking to *ram* them?"

Ar'alani frowned. The *Grayshrike* was still accelerating toward the enemy warship, with no indication Lakinda was planning to slow down. "She must be trying to get in a flank attack before they know she's there."

"*Trying* being the operative word," Wutroow growled. "What makes her think they haven't replaced their portside sensors?"

"Probably figures it's her best shot," Ar'alani said, thinking quickly. Unless the Battle Dreadnought was still completely blind on that side, the *Grayshrike*'s only hope was for the *Vigilant* to create some sort of distraction. And given the alien commander's obvious goal in his missile attacks . . .

Ar'alani looked back at the main tactical. The two breachers Oeskym had sent had now been destroyed, though having the lasers burning through the space around them as they flew had interfered with the dibber response enough that the missiles had made it closer than any of the previous attempts. Something to keep in mind for the future.

But for right now—"Oeskym, cease all offensive fire," she ordered. "Continue with defensive fire only. Prep a volley of six breachers, targeted on sensor and weapons clusters along the starboard flank, with three spheres ready to fire behind each. Launch breachers on my command, spheres five seconds later."

"Admiral?" Wutroow asked cautiously.

"Just watch," Ar'alani said as she keyed her comm. If she was reading the enemy commander correctly, this should work. "This is Admiral Ar'alani," she called. "Interesting preliminaries. So. Now that I know how to destroy you, shall we return to our respective peoples and deliver our reports?"

There was no response. The final enemy missile of the current salvo disintegrated under Chiss laserfire.

And then, to Ar'alani's quiet relief, the Battle Dreadnought's own lasers went silent. "Your statement lacks accuracy," the alien commander said scornfully. "It is *I* who knows how to destroy *you*."

"Hardly," Ar'alani said, watching the *Grayshrike*'s approach out of the corner of her eye. She'd hoped Lakinda would pick up on the gambit, or at least realize that with hostilities temporarily stopped there was a greater chance the alien would notice her approach toward his portside flank.

Lakinda had. The *Grayshrike*, which had been driving at full acceleration, abruptly shut down its thrusters, leaving it coasting at high speed along its vector. Even better, the cruiser's lights and emissions went dark as Lakinda put her ship into stealth mode.

And with that, Ar'alani's hoped-for stage was set.

"No, you've seen what I wanted you to see," she told the alien. "I, on the other hand, know exactly what your weak spot is and how to exploit it. So run home if you want. We'll easily win the next battle."

The alien spat out something in his own language. "You have not yet finished with *this* one," he snarled. "I will destroy you all—"

"Launch," Ar'alani said quietly.

The breacher missiles tore from their tubes, separating from their original formation as they followed Oeskym's tracking toward six spots along the Battle Dreadnought's starboard flank. The alien responded instantly, firing a burst of dibbers at each missile. The dibbers converged on their targets, slamming into the missiles and destroying them, sending their payloads into space. Even as the thick waves of acid slowly expanded, shimmering as they continued toward their original targets, the plasma spheres appeared, burning through space behind them. Another salvo of dibbers shot from the Battle Dreadnought, zeroing in on the spheres—

And disintegrated in midflight as their intercept courses took them straight through the acid globs flowing ahead of them.

"Lasers!" Ar'alani snapped. "Target bridge and dibber launchers."

The *Vigilant*'s lasers tore at the alien's hull. Simultaneously, the Battle Dreadnought's lasers also opened fire, raking across the Chiss electrostatic barriers. Ar'alani watched as the plasma spheres completed their journey unhindered, delivering their paralyzing ion loads into the enemy's starboard side. She shifted her attention to the *Grayshrike*—

Just in time to see the heavy cruiser launch twin clusters of breachers at the battle cruiser's portside flank.

Belatedly, the alien warship opened defensive fire with a handful of spectrum lasers, probably all it had left on that side. But it was too little too late. The breachers slammed into the hull, their acid loads digging farther into the damage already there. The additional corrosion was eating through the metal when the *Grayshrike*'s own lasers opened fire, digging even deeper into the alien ship.

"Getting a drop in energy emissions," Biclian called. "Power levels down thirty percent. I think the *Grayshrike* got one of their reactors."

"They may have taken out the hyperdrive, too," Wutroow added, pointing at one of the data displays. "Particle emission profile just dropped off the curve." She looked back at Ar'alani. "Time to call on them to surrender?"

"Missile launch toward the *Grayshrike*!" Oeskym snapped.

Ar'alani winced. It was a *big* missile, bigger than any of the ones she'd yet seen the Battle Dreadnought use. Reflexively, she opened her mouth to shout a warning to Lakinda—

And closed it again. The missile had settled onto its final trajectory, and that vector wasn't targeting the *Grayshrike*.

It was targeting the asteroid missile launcher.

Lakinda saw it, too. But there was nothing she could do. The *Grayshrike*'s lasers lanced out, trying to take out the weapon as it swept past. But it was too well armored, and going too fast, and in the end she could do nothing except join Ar'alani in watching it slam into the lattice and launcher and obliterate both.

And with that task completed—

Ar'alani caught her breath with sudden premonition. "Lakinda, veer off!" she snapped. "Get out of there *now*."

The *Grayshrike* had pitched upward in response to Ar'alani's order and was driving away from the enemy when the Battle Dreadnought disintegrated in a coordinated series of violent explosions.

"Wikivv, get us out of here," Ar'alani ordered.

"Yes, Admiral."

A moment later, even as the *Vigilant* started pulling away, the first wave of debris spattered across its hull. Ar'alani tensed, but the impacts were far gentler even than those they'd suffered from destroyed enemy missiles. Clearly, the Battle Dreadnought's self-destruct system had been designed to shred everything into very small pieces.

And with that, it was over.

"*Grayshrike*?" Ar'alani called. "Report."

"Minor damage only, Admiral," Lakinda's voice came back.

"Same here," Ar'alani said, running her eye over the *Vigilant*'s damage report. "Fortunately for us, he was more interested in learning our tactics and weak spots than in outright destroying us. Come back around—we'll rendezvous and see how much of this we can sort out."

"Acknowledged, Admiral."

Ar'alani keyed off. "Senior Captain Wutroow, go to the sensor station and assist Biclian in looking for any dibbers that might still be incapacitated after running through one of our spheres," she ordered. "If you find one, get a shuttle out there to bring it back for study."

"After making sure it *stays* incapacitated, I assume?" Wutroow asked, gesturing the order over to Biclian.

"Absolutely," Ar'alani confirmed. "The last thing we want is to bring a weapon aboard that might go boom. Better idea: Rig one of the shuttles with disassembly and analysis equipment, and they can do the preliminary work out there."

"Yes, ma'am," Wutroow said. "Whether or not they found *our* weak spots, at least we found theirs."

"Which is?" Ar'alani asked.

Wutroow frowned slightly. "The mixed breacher-and-sphere attack. Right?"

Ar'alani shook her head. "That was a useful tactic. But it's not their underlying weakness." She gestured to the tactical. "At their earlier encounter, the *Grayshrike* blinded their portside flank sensors with spheres, opening the way for Thrawn to launch an attack against that side. Here, with the *Grayshrike* coming up on that same side, we threw spheres at their starboard flank."

"Ah," Wutroow said, nodding. "Which they then assumed was a precursor to an attack over on that side. Possibly from a third ship about to come at them out of hyperspace."

"Right," Ar'alani said. "Notice, too, that all of that reaction came after the asteroid's inbuilt self-defense system blew the shell when it sensed it was being attacked."

"Is that what happened to it?"

"I assume so," Ar'alani said. "We'll study the *Grayshrike*'s records, but it's the only thing that makes sense. At any rate, the Battle Dreadnought's commander saw the explosion, and with the lack of good sensors on that side he assumed the *Grayshrike* was at least temporarily out of the battle."

"I see," Wutroow said. "So their weakness is making assumptions and not confirming them?"

"And perhaps being too easily distracted." Ar'alani gestured to the sensor station. "Get busy on that dibber hunt. The aliens worked very hard to make sure there weren't any souvenirs for us to take home. Let's see if we can find something they missed."


"I'm sorry, Admiral," Lakinda said, trying not to wince. Even in a private meeting, facing a superior officer required a certain degree of decorum. "I assumed you meant to bring just the launcher, and I was told we couldn't get it free quickly enough."

"It's all right," Ar'alani soothed from the other end of the conference table. "My scenario would also have ended with the missile destroyed, so it's not as if we could have salvaged it for study anyway."

"No, ma'am." The admiral was being nice about it, but there was no way Lakinda could avoid feeling like a fool.

What made it even worse was the nagging suspicion that Thrawn wouldn't have missed the intent of Ar'alani's quick order.

"I presume you've heard we weren't able to get to any of the dibbers before they also self-destructed," Ar'alani continued. "Whoever these aliens are, they're *very* determined to keep as many of their secrets as they can."

"It would appear so," Lakinda agreed.

Of course, the battle itself had provided *some* data. They had the enemy's laser spectra and intensities, plus their overall missile blast profiles. The *Grayshrike* also had the form and design of the metal lattice they'd used in the asteroid weapon.

Unfortunately, none of that would go very far in figuring out who these aliens were or where they came from.

"Still, the commander was more careless than he might have been with his language," Ar'alani said. "The term he used—*generalirius*—when he was referring to General Yiv, for example. Of course, he *was* expecting to destroy both of us before we could send word elsewhere."

"Yes, I saw that in your report," Lakinda said. "Do you know what it means?"

"No, but the term *generalissimo* is supposedly used by a couple of nations out past the Tarleev," Ar'alani said. "It refers to someone who's both the chief military commander and the chief civilian leader. *Generalirius* might be related to that term."

"Interesting," Lakinda said. Or, of course, it might not be related to anything at all. "If they're from that part of the Chaos, they traveled quite a distance to get here."

"Which would raise interesting questions as to what they're doing here," Ar'alani agreed soberly. "First Yiv, and now these unknowns, all coming out of nowhere to sniff around the Ascendancy's borders. Two data points is hardly a pattern, but even so I don't like the trend."

"On the other hand, unless someone else uses the same asteroid trap, these are the same ones who took out those Nikardun bases," Lakinda pointed out. "It's possible they came here solely to chase down Yiv, and now that he's gone they might simply leave."

"That would be very convenient," Ar'alani said. "Though if all they wanted was Yiv, why take a poke at us?"

Lakinda felt her lip twitch. "I don't know," she admitted. "Alien minds; alien logic."

"An all-too-common excuse for lack of knowledge," Ar'alani said. "Unfortunately, also very true. Well. We don't know if any of their other ships or bases were close enough for the commander to send his battle data before he self-destructed. If they were, we may have a tougher fight the next time we go up against one of them."

"I suppose we'll find out," Lakinda said, eyeing Ar'alani closely. So far there'd been nothing in this conversation that couldn't have been said via ship-to-ship comm. Why had the admiral invited her over to the *Vigilant*?

"I suppose we will," Ar'alani agreed, something in her tone suggesting this part of the meeting was over. "That covers the official briefing, the part that will go on the record. Now the real reason I asked you here. I trust you've had time to read your most recent message from Csilla?"

"Yes, ma'am," Lakinda said, keeping her voice and face studiously neutral. The transmission had come in via the Schesa triad only an hour ago, and a full hour's worth of thought and puzzlement had still left her unable to make top or bottom of it. "I assume you also received a copy?"

"I did," Ar'alani said. "Let's start with the question of whether or not you want to go."

Lakinda frowned. "The orders seemed abundantly clear," she said, trying to read Ar'alani's face. Unfortunately for her, the admiral was even better at being studiously neutral than she was. "I'm to proceed immediately to Csilla to rearm and repair as necessary, then join the *Springhawk* in Senior Captain Thrawn's search for the Vagaari pirates."

"The orders are indeed clear," Ar'alani agreed. "But as your commander and the flag officer on the scene, I can countermand any and all orders as I see fit. So again: Do you want to go?"

"I'm sorry, Admiral, but I don't understand the question," Lakinda said, feeling even more like a fool. What exactly was Ar'alani getting at here? "Why would I not want to go assist the *Springhawk*?"

"First, because I could use you here, should our new friends send more ships." Ar'alani looked her straight in the eye. "And second, because you have a problem with Thrawn."

Lakinda felt her throat tighten. "I'm not sure I know what you mean, ma'am."

"I think you do," Ar'alani said. "Every time you and Thrawn are together, there's an underlying prickliness in your face and voice. Nothing blatant, certainly nothing anyone else would probably notice. But it's there."

"Admiral—"

She stopped as Ar'alani held up a hand. "I don't know what the issue is, and I don't care. Family problems, personality conflicts, or whatever. It's also certainly not unique in the fleet—there are whole sections of senior officers' profiles devoted to who they work well with and who they should probably never be paired with again."

Lakinda took a deep breath. "I don't have a problem with Senior Captain Thrawn, ma'am," she repeated. "Even if I did, I would never let personal feelings get in the way of working with him or any other of my fellow officers or warriors. Unless you need me to stay and assist with the ground survey, I'll return to the *Grayshrike* and prepare for our departure."

"Very good, Senior Captain," Ar'alani said, her voice going to full formal. "At your convenience, and on your schedule. If I can assist in any way, don't hesitate to let me know."

"Thank you, Admiral," Lakinda said. "One thought. Since I'm heading directly back to the Ascendancy, I suggest we transfer the *Grayshrike*'s remaining breachers and plasma fluid to the *Vigilant*. It won't bring you up to a full complement of either, but it would be helpful if you end up in further combat."

"It would indeed," Ar'alani said. "Thank you for the offer. I'll get Senior Captain Wutroow on it immediately."

By the time Lakinda was back on her shuttle, she'd alerted Apros to get started on the weapons transfer from his end. Apros hadn't been happy at the *Grayshrike*'s new orders, and his response to her order made it clear he was equally unhappy that Lakinda hadn't asked Ar'alani to countermand Csilla on this one.

Lakinda couldn't disagree. Even with the alien warship that apparently had been assigned to the system now destroyed, it was a serious risk for the *Vigilant* to stay here alone to search for the reasons for its presence. Two ships were always better than one, and the fact that Supreme Admiral Ja'fosk apparently thought Ar'alani would do better alone than Thrawn would was of small comfort.

Still, the *Vigilant* was a powerful warship and Ar'alani an extremely capable commander. If the aliens sent more ships, they would likely end up the same way the Battle Dreadnought had. Certainly Ar'alani's plan had shown she shared Thrawn's fondness for layered tactics.

Lakinda frowned as an odd thought struck her. Ar'alani was three years older than Thrawn, and she'd known him at Taharim Academy. Since that time the two of them had worked together on a number of missions.

So was it, in fact, Thrawn's tactical genius that Ar'alani had learned from? Or was it the other way around? Could Thrawn have simply adopted Ar'alani's methods and run with them? In that case, maybe he got all the attention because he was brash enough to go full-bore into situations where Ar'alani's innate prudence suggested a slower approach.

If Thrawn really wasn't as good as everyone thought, then maybe Lakinda wasn't as much in his shadow as she thought.

Something to consider. In the meantime, she had a ship to prepare, weapons to off-load, and Thrawn's latest reports to study. Whatever was going on with the *Springhawk*, the *Grayshrike* would likely be seeing more combat. Probably very soon.

# MEMORIES VI

The Panopyl Mountains were nice enough if one liked mountains. The bird migration was interesting enough if one liked birds.

Haplif liked neither and was getting damn tired of having to put up with them.

"There's just so little here that can take you to your future," he reminded Yoponek as he poured the boy another drink. "Bird migrations are for those who prefer the stillness of the past. Your path lies forward, toward the excitement of honor and recognition."

"I can't disagree," Yoponek said, taking a sip from his cup. "You understand me, Haplif, better even than Yomie does. But my path also includes my betrothed, and this is where she's happy."

"Of course, of course," Haplif said, brushing his fingertips across the side of Yoponek's head as he pretended to push back a stray strand of hair. The boy's feelings for Yomie were still there, unfortunately. But they seemed weaker now than they'd been when he'd first met the couple. Maybe the seeds of discontent he'd been planting were finally starting to take root. "You've certainly done all you can to make her happy," he continued. "But does giving her short-term happiness require you to give up your long-term hopes and dreams?"

"I haven't given them up," Yoponek said stubbornly. "They're just postponed."

"Perhaps," Haplif said, putting some darkness into his tone. "But the Agbui have a saying: *An opportunity postponed is an opportunity lost.* Who knows whether or not Councilor Lakuviv will be available to speak to you in a month? Or in two months, or in three?"

"Who knows if he'll be available in two weeks?" Yoponek countered. "Even if we left today—" He broke off, staring into his cup. "Look, Haplif. If you say that Lakuviv is the one to see, I believe you. But he isn't the only Xodlak Councilor in the Ascendancy, or even on Celwis. If we can't see him, maybe someone else will do."

Haplif curled his fingers in frustration. Maybe someone else would work for Yoponek, but no one else would work for *him.* "But Councilor Lakuviv is the only one whose land is suitable for our spice harvests," he said. "He and Redhill province are where our two desires and needs coincide."

"I'd forgotten that," Yoponek admitted. "But right now, the Panopyls are where Yomie's desires and needs coincide."

And they were back where they'd started. "All I'm asking is that you talk to her," Haplif said. "There are surely bird migrations everywhere, even on Celwis."

"I can try," Yoponek said doubtfully. "But I make no promises."

"I ask none," Haplif said. *Damn* the boy and his utter spinelessness. "Thank you, and sleep well. You'll be heading out early tomorrow as usual?"

"Yes," Yoponek said, setting down his cup and moving to the hatch. "We'll try not to wake anyone when we leave. Good night, Haplif."

"Good night."

For a few minutes Haplif sat motionless, thinking and brooding. The Panopyl migration was smaller, less concentrated, and therefore less interesting than the one Shimkif had so artfully disrupted. The contrast was strong enough that he'd hoped Yomie would quickly tire of it and be ready to move on.

But they were now in their fourth day, and the girl was still going strong. Either she was genuinely excited, despite the tameness of the event, or she was just too stubborn to admit she'd been wrong.

Or else this was some kind of power game she was deliberately playing against Haplif.

He muttered a curse. Her cloud journal drawings might hold some clues to that, but he'd searched her room thoroughly during the past two days without finding them. Clearly, she'd taken to carrying the pages with her when she and Yoponek headed out to watch the birds.

In the meantime, Jixtus's deadline was ticking ever closer.

Haplif stared at the far wall, mentally running the numbers again. If they got out of here in the next three or four days, they could easily manage the rendezvous with Jixtus and the new navigator he'd promised. Five days would be marginal. Six would be impossible.

None of which meant disaster for the mission, of course. Long experience in these things had taught Haplif to build a margin for error into his plans and time lines. But making Jixtus wait at the rendezvous would be a bad idea.

Yoponek had promised to talk to Yomie. But at this point, Haplif's best hope was Shimkif. Once again, she'd slipped out shortly after their arrival and hadn't been seen since. Hopefully, this migration was also about to come to an abrupt end.

The next morning dawned clear and bright. Yoponek and Yomie left the ship just before sunrise with all their bird-watching gear. Two hours later they unexpectedly returned.

But not in the same shape as they'd left. Yomie was nearly unconscious, Yoponek was drenched in sweat as he half carried, half dragged her alongside him.

"I don't know what's wrong," Yoponek panted as the two Agbui who'd hurried out at his plaintive call carried Yomie to her room. The Chiss girl's eyes were unfocused, Haplif saw as they passed him, her breathing labored. "She said she wasn't feeling well, and we started back. Halfway down the path, she suddenly became too weak to walk."

"You should have called," Haplif said, taking the boy's arm and leading him into the ship behind the others. Yoponek made as if to follow Yomie; Haplif turned him instead to the salon and sat him down in one of the chairs. "We would have come to help you."

"We couldn't," Yoponek said. He was on the edge of exhaustion, Haplif could see, his legs wobbling from the grueling task of getting his betrothed back to the ship. "Comm emissions confuse the birds, so that whole area is under a suppression blanket."

"I see," Haplif said, pouring him a drink. Was Yomie's sudden illness pure coincidence? Or was it Shimkif's doing? "We need to call a doctor. Our medical knowledge of your people is very limited."

"An emergency team is on the way," Yoponek said, drinking deeply and handing the cup back for a refill. "I waited to call until we were in sight of the ship so I could tell them where to come."

Haplif frowned. "Did you think we might have left?"

Yoponek gave a little shrug. "I don't know. The way you

talked last night . . . you need to do what's right for you and your people. I understand that."

"That may be," Haplif said. "But we would never leave our companions. Certainly not without talking about it."

"Haplif?" someone called from the corridor. "The Chiss medics are here."

"Show them to Yomie's room," Haplif said, standing up and offering Yoponek a helping hand. "Come."

"A *greenstripe?*" Yomie asked weakly from her bed, frowning up at Yoponek and Haplif. "But I never felt a sting or even a bite."

"You wouldn't have," Yoponek said, his hand resting reassuringly on her shoulder. "The medics said they're one of the few venomous insects that don't bite or sting. They spit their venom onto the skin to be absorbed into the rest of the body. The ones here in the mountains have to defend against bigger animals, so their toxin is particularly nasty."

"First the Grand Migration, now this," Yomie murmured. "I don't seem to be having much luck these days."

"The good news is that now that you've been exposed, the antitoxins in your body will make sure you won't ever have another reaction this extreme," Yoponek went on. "Even better, you should be pretty much recovered in a day or two."

"So are we heading for Celwis now?" Yomie asked, a hint of resignation in her voice.

Haplif and Yoponek exchanged looks. "I thought you wanted to stay here and watch the migration," Yoponek said.

"I thought *you* wanted to go to Celwis," Yomie countered.

"We can discuss all that later," Haplif put in quickly. The last thing he wanted was to have Yomie making demands when Yoponek's emotions were all tangled up in her illness. "Right now, as Yoponek said, you need rest."

"All right," Yomie said, closing her eyes. "We'll talk tomorrow."

"Tomorrow," Yoponek promised, squeezing her hand once and then turning to the hatch. Haplif gave her an encouraging smile and followed.

Yoponek had retired to his room to think—and, knowing him, probably worry—when Shimkif finally returned.

"I couldn't find a way to disrupt the migration this time," she said, sinking into a chair and taking the drink Haplif handed her. "So I did the next best thing and disrupted *her*. Hopefully, that will be the end of it."

"Maybe," Haplif said doubtfully. "We'll see what she has to say in the morning."

"You don't understand," Shimkif said. "I dropped in on her before coming in here. You know how twitchy she is about being touched? Well, not right now she isn't."

Haplif crinkled his forehead skin. "You realize readings taken while the subject is asleep aren't reliable."

"Ah, but she *wasn't* asleep," Shimkif said. "That's the point. She was a little dozy, but conscious. It turns out we were wrong." She considered. "Or I was, anyway. See, she doesn't want Yoponek to give up all his hopes and dreams for her. She just wants him to be *willing* to give them up. Once she's satisfied that he would do that for her, he can go charging on to fame and fortune on Celwis, and she'll stand by smiling and being all proud of him."

"That's great," Haplif said, sifting rapidly through the possibilities. If he could maneuver Yoponek into making that commitment clear to her, they could be out of here by tomorrow.

"*Maybe* it's great," Shimkif cautioned. "The problem is that we don't know what it'll take to persuade her. Theoretically, Yoponek should be the best source of information, but to be honest I'm not convinced he knows his betrothed any better than we do."

"Maybe I can get something from him in the morning," Haplif said. "Or maybe from her."

"Just be careful not to push them," Shimkif said, draining her drink. "The girl especially. She's smarter than she seems—I'll guarantee you that. If she even suspects we're trying to slip something past her, she'll pull them both out so fast you'll wonder if they need a navigator for the trip."

"I'll be careful," Haplif promised. "Go get some rest. With luck, tomorrow—or the day after at the latest—we'll be off this miserable planet."

Yomie was sitting up in bed, working with her questis, when Haplif arrived. "Good morning," he said cheerfully as he stepped into the compartment. "How are you feeling?"

"Much better," she said, looking at him over the top of the questis. "I was just reading up on greenstripes. It says they almost never attack Chiss."

"That's what the medics said, too," Haplif agreed. "They told us attacks are rare, but they happen a couple of times a year." He smiled as he stepped closer. "That means you're one in a million, which of course we've always known. Where's Yoponek?"

"I sent him to the viewing grounds," Yomie said, still eyeing him. "No sense both of us missing out on the day." She lowered her gaze, focusing again on the questis. "I was searching for other migrations on Shihon. Turns out there are more than I realized."

"Interesting," Haplif said, taking a final step to put himself beside her bed. "Maybe after we've visited Celwis we can come back and watch one or two of them."

"Maybe." Yomie closed her eyes and stretched back, as if adjusting her spine and neck. Haplif reached forward and brushed her head with his fingertips.

*Hatred!*

He jerked the hand away, the unexpected flash of emotion nearly knocking him back off his feet. He blinked away the sensation and looked back at Yomie.

To find her staring hard at him, the hatred and revulsion he'd just felt now plastered across her face.

And there was something else there, too: understanding and a bitter-edged validation. "I knew it," she said, her voice digging into Haplif like shards of broken ceramic. "I *knew* it. You're telepathic. You're *all* telepathic."

"I don't know what you're talking about," Haplif insisted.

But the words were pure reflex and far, far too late. Her little trap had nailed him, all right. Nailed him right to the deck.

"You've been manipulating us ever since we met, haven't you?" she accused, ignoring his protest. "Making us jump to your music. Leading us by the nose." Her face went suddenly rigid. "No. Leading *Yoponek* by the nose. Why? What possible use is he to you?"

"I don't know what you're talking about," Haplif repeated. "Yomie—this is the toxin talking. You're not well. You're—"

"And who made me that way?" Yomie snapped. "Who poisoned—" She broke off, her eyes going wide. "The Grand Migration. Did you poison *that*, too?"

"Yomie—"

"Never mind," she said, dropping the questis onto her lap and snagging her comm from the side table. "No more lies. As soon as I tell Yoponek—"

And with that, of course, Haplif no longer had a choice. *Option three.*

"She left?" Yoponek asked, frowning at the message Haplif had given him. "Just . . . *left*?"

"Not permanently," Haplif hastened to assure him, brushing his fingertips across the boy's head. Yoponek was surprised, confused, and unhappy. But there was no suspicion. "As you see, she's just going to spend some time at the migration and two or three of the others in the area, then connect up with us again once we return from Celwis."

"But that could be months," Yoponek protested. "How can she leave when she hasn't even recovered from her poisoning?"

"It won't be months before we're back," Haplif soothed. "Six weeks, eight at the most. And the medics came by again while you were gone and checked her out. I've got their report right here, if you want to read it. Don't worry, she's fine."

"I suppose," Yoponek said, still frowning.

"And even on Celwis we'll only be a few days' journey from here," Haplif pointed out. "If she starts feeling bad, or wants to leave, she can message you and we'll send the ship back to get her while our spices are growing."

"I know," Yoponek said. "It's just . . . leaving me behind doesn't sound like something she'd do."

"How little we truly know other people," Haplif said philosophically. "Did you realize she was this interested in bird migrations, for example? I didn't think so. No, I think she's been looking for a way she could watch her birds while you met with Councilor Lakuviv, and this was her solution. Now both your hopes and dreams will be satisfied." He shook his head in admiration. "Very clever girl."

"She is that," Yoponek said, his face clearing. "Well, if that's what she wants, I guess she's old enough to make that decision. When do we head for Celwis?"

"We can leave within the hour," Haplif said, brushing the boy's head again. Some of the unhappiness lingered, but it was rapidly fading into a guarded eagerness at this sudden and unexpected opportunity to finally take the first step toward his future glory.

Never mind that Haplif's story was gossamer-thin. Yoponek wanted to believe it, and so he did. "And of course, the sooner we leave, the sooner we can complete our business on Celwis and reunite the two of you."

"That makes sense," Yoponek said. "Well. I need to get cleaned up before dinner."

"I'll meet you in the salon at seven," Haplif said. "Oh— one more thing. She left this for you." He held out the brooch he'd given the girl.

"She left it?" Yoponek asked, frowning as he picked it up off Haplif's palm.

"She said it was her promise you'd be together again," Haplif said. "She said to keep it until you can pin it back on her." He smiled. "Perhaps at your wedding?"

"Absolutely at our wedding," the boy said. He gazed at the brooch another moment, then slipped it carefully into his pocket. "Thank you."

"You're welcome," Haplif said. "Now go clean up. By the time dinner is served, we'll be on our way." He smiled. "To Celwis and your future."

Six hours later, when Haplif was sure Yoponek was fast asleep in his room, he had the ship leave hyperspace just long enough to release Yomie's body into the vast emptiness of the universe.

He made damn sure that all the pretty pictures of her cloud journal, the fancy oh-so-clever drawings where she'd been secretly recording everything she knew about him and the Agbui, went with her.

# CHAPTER SEVENTEEN

"So it really *is* there," Councilor Lakuviv said, feeling a strange sense of unreality as he gently stroked the three metal wires.

"It really is," Lakjiip confirmed from the chair across his office desk. "And the fools have no idea what they're sitting on."

"So it would seem," Lakuviv agreed. "They just *gave* these to you?"

"Voluntarily and unhesitatingly," Lakjiip said. "They said the metal has no particular value of its own. It's the skill with which the artists turn it into jewelry that's important."

Lakuviv shook his head. "Idiots."

Lakjiip shrugged. "In general, I suppose that's mostly true of art. Give an artist a hundred Univers to spend on paint and a presentation board, and out pops a picture someone else will spend thousands for. It's just that in this specific case the whole thing is reversed."

"If you ask me, everything about the art world is just barely controlled anarchy," Lakuviv said. "But that's not our problem. When is Haplif due in?"

"Anytime now," Lakjiip said. "I talked to the pilot a few minutes ago, and he said he was on schedule." Her lip twisted. "Oh, and he's bringing Yoponek with him."

"Who?"

"Yoponek," Lakjiip repeated. "That Coduyo midager on his wandering year. He was the one who first brought Haplif in to meet you."

"Right," Lakuviv said, frowning as he tried to remember the boy's face. "He's still here?"

"He's still on Celwis, if that's what you mean," Lakjiip said, eyeing him curiously. "He's also been at Redhill Hall five or six times since they all arrived last month. You hadn't noticed him?"

"I've had more important things on my mind," Lakuviv reminded her. Though now that she mentioned it, he did remember seeing a strange midager chatting with some of the aides and lower officials in the building's corridors. "What did he want?"

"Here at the hall?" Lakjiip shrugged. "I really don't know. I think he mostly wants to make as many connections with the Xodlak family as he can. Probably just playing politics and pretending he's someone who matters. Most of the aides he's been pestering have been willing enough to humor him."

"Or else he has some grand notion of scoring a position as a Coduyo-Xodlak liaison someday," Lakuviv said. "Well, when he and Haplif arrive he's welcome to wait somewhere else."

"Understood," Lakjiip said. "Do you have a plan for how to proceed?"

"First, we need more details on this mining area," Lakuviv said, looking back at the wires. "That's why I want Haplif. Just because you only saw Agbui there doesn't mean there aren't other alien groups involved."

"We did a half orbit on the way out, with full sensors running," Lakjiip said. "There was nothing anywhere but pristine, unoccupied wilderness."

"I'm not doubting you," Lakuviv said. "But just because there's no one there *now* doesn't mean someone else might not drop by on occasion. There could be aliens working offworld in the supply or distribution chains. There could be several species sharing the mines, each one having control of them and the refineries for a couple of months at a time before the next group moves in and takes over. Like a sublet on a home or business."

"I doubt that's the case," Lakjiip said, her eyes distant in thought. "I can't see anyone except the Agbui failing to recognize the significance of a nyix mine that rich. And if anyone else knew, the word would have gotten out long ago."

"Probably, but not necessarily," Lakuviv said. "You can build commercial freighters and transports perfectly well without nyix—in fact, both we and the Agbui do exactly that with our civilian craft. It's only when you upgrade to warships that you need something stronger."

"Any culture that doesn't have warships doesn't last very long out there," Lakjiip countered. "But I suppose you could be right," she added, holding up a hand to forestall further argument. "And the Agbui seem to be mostly nomadic. Aliens who can always just pick up and run wouldn't need to know how to fight."

"Exactly," Lakuviv said. "So. As I said, we first confirm the Agbui are the only ones involved. After that . . ." He paused. After that, protocol would require him to contact Patriel Lakooni and lay everything in front of her. She would then decide how or even whether to send the information further up the family hierarchy.

And that could be a sticking point. Lakuviv and Lakooni had had their disagreements over the years, and he wasn't at all sure he could trust her to believe him on this, at least not without doing extensive investigations of her own. Even if she was willing to move more quickly, it would be far too easy for her to work herself into getting all the credit while he got nothing but a side note. For that matter, she could even paint over him and Redhill completely, and there would be little or nothing he could do about it.

"After that, we'll see," he told Lakjiip. "This might be important enough to take directly to the Patriarch."

"Patriel Lakooni won't be happy if you bypass her," Lakjiip warned.

"Lakooni's pride isn't the issue here," Lakuviv said stiffly. "Getting hold of this planet for the Xodlak family is. Depending on what Haplif says, we may not have time to go through local channels."

Lakjiip started to speak, stopped and looked at her comm. "They're here," she said. "Where do you want them?"

"I'll see Haplif at the Judgment Seat," Lakuviv said. "From here on, we might as well keep everything strictly official. You can leave the Coduyo boy in the reception area."

Haplif was waiting in front of the white chair when Lakuviv and Lakjiip arrived. "I greet you, Councilor Lakuviv," Haplif said cheerfully as they walked toward him. "May I express our appreciation for your generosity in escorting our freighter to and from our mining world. Pathfinder Qilori reported that the freighter captain was most effusive in his praise."

"You're more than welcome," Lakuviv said, catching the eyes of the two guards who'd brought Haplif in and nodding toward the reception room. The guards nodded acknowledgment in turn and headed toward the door. "Thank you for making the time to meet with us today."

"It is my privilege and pleasure," Haplif said. "How may I serve you?"

"I had a few questions about your facility," Lakuviv said, watching as the guards filed through the doorway and closed it behind them. "Senior Aide Lakjiip was most impressed with your operation, but we were both curious about whether or not you have any other workers there."

"I don't understand," Haplif said, the slit of a mouth puckering in the midst of all that wrinkled facial skin. "We have many workers: miners, refiners, extrusion operators, and food preparers. What others would we need?"

"I was actually asking whether you might have hired other species for some of those tasks," Lakuviv said, watching the alien carefully. "There are aliens particularly suited to underground mining, for instance, short and stocky with lower oxygen requirements and the ability to see in low-light settings."

"Oh, no, we couldn't employ anyone like that," Haplif protested, a whole-body shiver running through him. "We could never trust anyone so thoroughly as to allow them access to the mines. Our jewelry and spices are the sole sources of our livelihood. If we were to lose our source of inexpensive metals, our very survival would be in danger."

"Yet you let *us* see the operation," Lakjiip pointed out.

"But you are different," Haplif said, sounding puzzled. "You are the Chiss, noble and honorable and courageous. You treat us as you treat all others, as fellow travelers in this grand journey through life."

Despite himself, Lakuviv winced a bit. Was Haplif *really* that naïve? "You have a great deal of trust, Haplif."

"It is born of experience and insight," Haplif said firmly. "For three months we have traveled with Yoponek of the Coduyo. He has been first our companion and then our friend. Through him I have learned to understand the Chiss heart, the Chiss soul, and the Chiss nobility. I would trust you with my life, Councilor Lakuviv of the Xodlak."

His face seemed to cloud over. "And indeed, I may very soon have to turn that trust into action. As you are aware, pirates have attacked us once. Who can say if they will do so again? Who can say if they will then find their way to our mines?"

"You think that's possible?" Lakuviv asked, feeling his heart starting to beat a little faster. This was the very opening he needed, the opening he'd been trying to figure out how to engineer. Now Haplif had unwittingly done it for him.

"Nothing in this universe is impossible," Haplif said solemnly. "As I'm certain Senior Aide Lakjiip has told you, the Agbui have no way to stop an aggressor determined to slaughter our people and take or destroy what we've worked so hard to build."

"Yes, indeed," Lakuviv agreed. As if anyone in their right mind would actually *destroy* a nyix mine. But of course he couldn't say that. "Is there anything we can do to help you?"

"The Xodlak family has mighty warships circling this world," Haplif said, pointing one of those long fingers toward the ceiling. "Even mightier than the one you sent to escort our freighter. I know; I've seen them. If one could be sent to guard our world . . . but I recall the difficulty you had wresting even a simple patrol craft from the hands of your Patriel. This would be a much harder task."

"As you yourself said, nothing in the universe is impossible," Lakuviv said. "I'll put a call into the Patriel's office immediately."

"Oh," Haplif said with a distinct lack of enthusiasm. "Yes. That would be wonderful."

"You sound unhappy," Lakuviv said. "Is there a problem?"

"No," Haplif said in that same neutral tone. "Please don't take this as a criticism, Councilor Lakuviv. The Xodlak family has been wonderfully gracious to us. It's just that . . . I'm not certain the Patriel can be fully trusted. I don't mean she can't be trusted with the safety of the Agbui," he hastened to add. "I'm sure she would never betray us. I'm merely concerned that she may usurp any commendations or thanks that would come to you from the determined and selfless defense of our world. I would hate to see your work pushed to the side and your initiative buried beneath another's claims."

"So would I," Lakuviv said grimly. So it wasn't just him who thought Lakooni was a glory-thief. Haplif had seen that in her, too. "More important than any commendations, though, is the question of whether we have time to go through the proper protocol. Under the circumstances, perhaps I should contact the Patriarch directly with this matter."

The loose skin of Haplif's face piled itself into a bunch. "You can do that?" he asked with obvious amazement. "You can speak directly to the exalted head of the Xodlak family?"

"Of course," Lakuviv said. It wasn't nearly that easy, of course. He would have to go through at least a couple of layers of homestead officials before he even reached the Patriarch's office, let alone the Patriarch himself.

But this was important enough, and urgent enough, that he was confident he would be passed through those obstacles with minimal delay. "I'll start the procedure at once."

"Thank you for coming," Lakjiip put in. "I'll have your driver take you back to Lakphro's ranch. We'll contact you again as soon as Councilor Lakuviv has news."

"You are gracious, Senior Aide Lakjiip," Haplif said. "However, would it not be better for me to remain here and available for any questions your Patriarch might have? There may be details that only I can supply."

"Possibly," Lakjiip said, looking questioningly at Lakuviv. She knew as well as he did the kind of bureaucratic maze he was casually promising to walk his way through, and how long things of that sort normally took. "But it might not be right away."

"I am content to wait," Haplif said. "The sooner we have Xodlak defenders over our world, the sooner all Agbui will be able to rest."

"If you're willing, it's all right with me," Lakuviv said. "Senior Aide Lakjiip will instruct the guards outside to find you a place where you can rest, and arrange for some refreshment."

"Once again, I am in your debt," Haplif said. "Your name will forever be blessed among the Agbui people."

"Thank you," Lakuviv said. Now if only his name could move up the Xodlak family hierarchy, *that* would be the real miracle.

Lakuviv's call to the Patriarch went about as well as he should have expected.

He connected to the family homestead on Csilla without difficulty. Identifying himself as a Councilor on Celwis got him through the first two layers of screening, while his insistence that the matter was vital to Xodlak interests got him through a third layer. Barely an hour after beginning the call he was finally to the Patriarch's office, talking with the Patriarch's third aide.

And there the whole thing ground to a halt.

"He said that there was nothing interesting or amusing, let alone vital, that a Councilor could possibly bring to the Patriarch's attention," he fumed to Lakjiip, glaring at the comm display on his office desk.

The *blank* comm display. The cursed aide had said a brief goodbye, told him to go through proper channels next time, and cut him off.

"Maybe Patriel Lakooni would have better luck," Lakjiip suggested.

"Lakooni doesn't know anything about this," Lakuviv reminded her.

"Maybe it's time she did."

Lakuviv clenched his teeth. Unfortunately, she was right. Without the Patriel's approval, he wouldn't even be able to get another patrol ship to send to the Agbui, let alone the dormant frigate or one of the cruisers.

Not that any of the warships would do much good anyway. Without full crews, they were really only useful for the cruisers' current job as defensive weapons platforms.

Still, even a couple of patrol ships would be better than nothing. At least that would give the Xodlak some claim to the mines and their output when they eventually brought this to the Syndicure. "Fine," he said with a sigh as he keyed the comm again.

The Patriel didn't have nearly as many layers of screening as the Patriarch, and there were far fewer officials below her clamoring for her attention. Ten minutes after Lakuviv initiated the call, Lakooni was on.

"I should inform you right up front," Lakooni said after the standard greetings, "that I've already heard from the Patriarch's office. I am *not* pleased you went over my authority that way."

"I'm sorry if you feel slighted," Lakuviv said, working hard to hold on to what was left of his temper. No concern for anything but rigid structure and her own petty authority. "But a situation has unexpectedly arisen, one that could either bring great profit and renown to the Xodlak or mean disaster for the entire Ascendancy."

"I also don't appreciate theatrics, Councilor," Lakooni growled. "Fine. You have two minutes to tell me what's going on."

"It concerns the Agbui cultural nomads who arrived in Redhill province a month ago," Lakuviv said. "I can't say more than that on the comm."

"This is a secure connection."

"We can't rely on that," Lakuviv countered. "I need you to come to Redhill Hall, where I can give you the full story."

"Are you *insane*?" Lakooni demanded. "If you want a face-to-face, you can come here."

"There are reports and resources here that I can't bring with me," Lakuviv said. "Resources that rival family representatives in Brickwalk might notice and wonder about."

"So let them gawk," Lakooni said impatiently. "What could they possibly see that would be a problem?"

Lakuviv clenched his hands into fists. Could she not even take a hint when it was dropped straight in front of her? "I told you this is something that could bring renown to the Xodlak," he said. "It would bring equal renown to any other family that got to it first. *And* to whoever the liaison was who brought it to that family's attention."

There was a brief silence. "You thought this was worth taking directly to the Patriarch," Lakooni said. "Taking past *me* to the Patriarch."

"Only because the timing here is critical," Lakuviv said. "If we don't get moving quickly, we may not be able to move at all."

Another silence, a longer one this time. Lakooni knew even better than he did how family rivalries swirled through the upper echelons of Ascendancy life. "Fine," she said reluctantly. "Whatever it is, I still think you're way off vector here. But fine. I was going to head to Fissure Lake tomorrow for a few days anyway. I'll leave now instead and swing by Redhill on my way."

"Thank you, Patriel," Lakuviv said, breathing a silent sigh of relief. If he could convince Lakooni, maybe together they could get the Patriarch moving in time to get some ships out there and take possession of the mines. "You won't be disappointed."

"I had better not be," Lakooni warned. "I'll be there in three hours. Be ready to amaze me."

She broke the connection. Lakuviv gazed at the display another moment, then looked across the desk at Lakjiip. "She's coming," he said.

"So I gathered," Lakjiip said. "Whether she'll agree to take it to the Patriarch is a different question."

"She will," Lakuviv said. "She's quite predictable when she thinks there's something in it for her."

"Putting her in a special class with—well, with almost everyone else," Lakjiip said. "Are you going to keep Haplif and Yoponek in the hall until she arrives?"

"We have to keep Haplif, anyway," Lakuviv said, standing up. Once again, he'd almost forgotten the Coduyo boy was even here. "If Yoponek wants to go back to the Agbui ship, we'll have someone take him."

They found Haplif and Yoponek in one of the conference rooms, talking earnestly over the remains of the meal that had been sent in to them. "Ah—Councilor Lakuviv," Haplif said brightly as he spotted the newcomers. "And Senior Aide Lakjiip. Do you bring good news?"

"I hope so," Lakuviv said. "I've persuaded Patriel Lakooni to come here and discuss the matter with me. She may have some questions for you, as well, so I trust you're still willing to stay?"

"Absolutely," Haplif said. "If she approves of your request for Xodlak family assistance, what will be the next step?"

"We go to the Patriarch and ask him to authorize military action," Lakuviv said. "The Xodlak family still has a small fleet from our time as one of the Ruling Families, though the major warships are understaffed and have been repurposed as planetary defense platforms."

"Like the warships circling Celwis?" Haplif asked.

"The light cruisers, yes," Lakuviv said, nodding. "There's also a frigate in the system that's essentially dormant. At any rate, if the Patriarch agrees the next step will be to gather Xodlak reservists from our various worlds to fully crew whatever ships he decides to send."

Yoponek cleared his throat. "That sounds like it will take time," he said.

"*Everything* takes time, Yoponek," Lakuviv said, pinning the midager with a glare. What was the boy interrupting for? None of this had anything to do with him or the Coduyo family. "Would you prefer waiting for the next class of graduates from Taharim Academy?"

"Well . . ." Yoponek looked at Haplif.

"Go ahead," the Agbui urged. "It was your thought and insight."

"All right." Yoponek turned back to Lakuviv. "Unless the Xodlak work differently from everyone else in the Ascendancy, you could declare a family emergency and bring some officers and warriors directly from the Expansionary Defense Fleet."

Lakuviv stared at him. "What are you talking about?"

"I'm talking about bringing in people from the fleet," Yoponek repeated. "I mean *real* officers and warriors, not reservists like you were talking about. I mean, reservists might not have been aboard a ship for years. You can call up as many as—let's see; I think it's—"

"Never mind the numbers," Lakuviv interrupted. "What do you mean by a family emergency?"

"It's something any of the Forty can do if they were ever one of the Ruling Families and have an undercrewed family fleet," Yoponek said. "I studied this a while back—thought the whole concept was fascinating. It was, oh, about thirty years ago that some breakaway alien sect was threatening to move in on Coduyo holdings on Massoss. The family declared an emergency, but the Defense Force was busy with something somewhere else and couldn't spare us any ships. So we got some of our family members off their ships—"

"Yes, yes, I get the gist," Lakuviv interrupted, looking at Lakjiip. "Senior Aide?"

"Found it," Lakjiip said, peering at her questis. "It was thirty-two years ago. The Coduyo had an old—a *very* old—light cruiser at Massoss—"

"It was a hundred years since we'd been one of the Ruling Families, so of course it was old," Yoponek interjected.

"—which three hundred officers and warriors from the Defense Force were quickly brought in to crew," Lakjiip said, ignoring the interruption. "By the time the aliens arrived in force, the cruiser was reactivated and able to quickly drive them off."

"But that was a security issue," Lakuviv pointed out. "That's not what we've got here."

"I don't think the declaration has any specific requirements," Lakjiip said, tapping back and forth between pages.

"No, it doesn't," Yoponek confirmed.

"The Patriel just has to declare an emergency," Lakjiip continued, ignoring the boy's interruption, "and send a message out to all Defense Force and Expansionary Defense Fleet personnel."

"And their captains just let them go?" Lakuviv asked, feeling a sudden stirring. So the Patriarch's office wasn't even involved in the procedure?

Lakjiip shrugged. "Unless a ship is engaged in combat or what's called an imminent threat situation, the commander has to authorize fifteen days' leave to anyone who's called to answer such a summons."

"Extraordinary," Haplif said, shaking his head. "I've never heard of such an arrangement anywhere else the Agbui have visited."

"If a particular ship is close enough to the declaring planet and there are enough family personnel to justify it, the commander may agree to swing by and drop them off," Lakjiip said. "But most of them will be dropped at the nearest planet and required to make their own way."

"Does the family then reimburse them for that expense?" Haplif asked, his forehead skin bunching again.

"That, or they use travel passes," Lakuviv said, his mind spinning with possibilities. Celwis had the warships, and with a family emergency declaration they would have the officers and warriors to crew them. All he needed was the Patriel's approval, and the nyix mine was as good as theirs. "Those are permits that allow them to travel free on any civilian transport within the Ascendancy. Most of the Forty Great Families give them to their military personnel."

"The Coduyo do," Yoponek put in.

"So do the Xodlak," Lakuviv said.

"I see." Haplif tilted his head a bit. "Do I take it from the expression on your face that you have a plan?"

"You take it correctly," Lakuviv said. "Thank you, Yoponek, for bringing that bit of history to my attention. I don't think I'd ever heard of that arrangement before."

"You're welcome," Yoponek said. "Of course, the last time it was used *was* three decades ago, so it's not surprising you hadn't heard of it."

Which could have been a subtle insult, Lakuviv knew: a high-ranking official of another family being unaware of important political history and law. But right now, he couldn't be bothered even to resent the boy's audacity. "I think now that you and Yoponek won't be needed tonight, after all," he went on. "If you'll collect anything you brought, I'll have the driver meet you at the skycar and fly you back to Lakphro's ranch."

"Now?" Haplif asked, sounding suddenly wary. "But you said Patriel Lakooni was on her way. What if you need me to talk to her?"

"Don't worry, I'll convince her," Lakuviv assured him. "It's getting late, and I'm sure you have work to do tomorrow. Spices to harvest, or something of that sort."

"Very well," Haplif said. He seemed still uneasy but willing to go along. "Come, Yoponek. Thank you for your hospitality, Councilor Lakuviv."

"The guard outside will escort you to the skycar," Lakuviv said as the alien and Chiss midager headed for the door. "I'll let you know if and when I have good news."

"You will have it," Haplif promised. "Great rewards emerge like gloriosi from the silken sheaths of great risks. Whatever risks you take on behalf of the Agbui, they will be repaid a thousandfold."

"I'm sure they will," Lakuviv said.

He watched in silence until the door had closed behind them, then turned to Lakjiip. "I want the names and ship assignments of all Xodlak members in the Expansionary Defense Fleet," he said. "Also see if you can get a listing of what officer and crew positions we'll need to fill on the frigate and cruisers."

"Understood," Lakjiip said, working her questis. "I wouldn't worry too much about the positions, though. It's still Xodlak policy that family members who join the fleet must also become familiar with our own warships and their operation. Everyone we get should be able to step into any shipboard position with a few hours' orientation."

"Let's hope so," Lakuviv said. "Regardless, that'll be for them to work out. Do we have a comm specialist on staff?"

"We have two."

"Get me one of them. Make it the one who's best at keeping secrets."

"Yes, sir," Lakjiip said, eyeing him. "What happens if you can't persuade the Patriel?"

"I'll persuade her," Lakuviv promised grimly. "Trust me. I'll persuade her."

# CHAPTER EIGHTEEN

"Yes, I got the brooch yesterday," Lakbulbup's voice came over the comm. "Pretty little bauble, isn't it?"

"Yes, it is," Lakphro said, a little tartly. Finally. Lakris had been going crazy trying to find her "lost" jewelry, and he was running out of ways to deflect her questions and veiled accusations about whether he might have done something with it.

Even worse, he was running out of ways to suggest she not tell that Agbui girl, Frosif, about the disappearance. The sooner Lakbulbup got this project up and running, the better. "Did you find someone to analyze it?" he asked.

"Yes, I've got a couple of names," Lakbulbup said. "But while it was still on its way here I had another thought. Have you ever heard of an Expansionary Defense Fleet officer named Senior Captain Mitth-'raw'nuruodo?"

"I don't think so," Lakphro said, searching his memory. The name *did* sound a little familiar, though, now that he thought about it.

"He was one of the minor players in the battle against the Nikardun over the Vak homeworld of Primea about three months ago."

"Ah," Lakphro said. "Three months ago we were having a calving crisis. You keep track of these military affairs better than I do."

"I would hope so, seeing as it's part of my job," Lakbulbup said. "My point is that Senior Captain Thrawn has a reputation for knowing a lot about alien art and artworks."

"I'm happy for him," Lakphro said, looking furtively at the door.

At this hour his daughter probably wouldn't walk in on the conversation, but his wife might, and she would want to know who he was talking to on Naporar and why. "But I don't need an art critic. I need a metals specialist."

"I know that's what you asked for," Lakbulbup said. "Here's the thing. I'm wondering if Thrawn might be able to tell us something else about the brooch, just as it is. Maybe something important."

"Like what?"

"No idea," Lakbulbup admitted. "But once we take it apart for testing, even a little bit apart, that chance is gone."

"I don't know what he could possibly see that we can't," Lakphro said. "It's a bunch of metal threads, and they're woven together in a pattern. End of story."

"Like I said, I don't know, either," Lakbulbup said. "But I remember hearing a show once where a music critic who'd just listened to half a minute of a new recording was able to pop out with the piece, the conductor, *and* the ensemble playing it. If he could do that from the sound alone, who knows what someone like Thrawn could do with just a look?"

Lakphro scratched at his cheek. Sending the brooch who knew where would surely be a colossal waste of time. But Lakbulbup had the brooch, and Lakphro could tell his cousin's mind was already made up. "Where is Thrawn now?"

"He's on a pirate-hunting expedition out past the Paataatus," Lakbulbup said. "But I'm sure he'll be returning to base sometime soon."

"*How* soon?"

"I don't know," Lakbulbup said. "After he's found and dealt with whatever's out there, I suppose. He's also got a reputation for thoroughness."

"Did you miss the part about this being important?"

"Calm down, cousin," Lakbulbup soothed. "This Haplif fellow has been there, what, you said a month? That's a lot of time for nothing to have happened, isn't it?"

"Maybe," Lakphro said. "But what if—"

"But nothing," Lakbulbup said firmly. "Trust me, Lakphro. I've heard stories about this Thrawn fellow, and I truly think it's worth running the brooch past him."

"There's not much I can do to argue you out of it *now*, is there?" Lakphro ground out.

"Hey, you wanted me to use my professional contacts, right?" Lakbulbup reminded him. "That's what I'm doing. Look, it's really no big deal. There are a couple of Xodlak on Thrawn's ship. As soon as the *Springhawk* gets back, I'll send it to one of them and he'll pass it on to Thrawn. Nothing to it."

"And if his pirate hunt goes on for the next two months?"

Lakbulbup's sigh was audible over the comm. "All right. Compromise. I'll hold the brooch for Thrawn for . . . mm . . . let's say ten days. If he's not back by then, we'll go with your plan and I'll get the metals analyzed. Fair enough?"

Lakphro shook his head in resignation. "Make it seven and it's a deal."

Lakbulbup's sigh was louder this time. "Fine," he said. "Seven days."

"Thanks," Lakphro said. "Sorry to be so pushy, but this is digging at me, and I need to get it resolved."

"I understand," Lakbulbup said, sounding a bit more sympathetic. "But it'll be all right. I mean, let's be honest—this is all happening on Celwis. Really, cousin, what kind of crisis could possibly happen on Celwis?"


Lakuviv had expected Patriel Lakooni to be on time. She was. He expected her to listen to his description of the Agbui mines and mining world without comment. She did. He hoped she would accept his proposal for taking the planet and its riches for the Xodlak.

She didn't.

"Do you even hear what you're saying?" she demanded when he'd finished his presentation. "You want to involve the Xodlak in this insane project on nothing but a whim and a wink?"

"Excuse me, Patriel Lakooni, but it's hardly as haphazard as you suggest," Lakuviv said stiffly.

"Isn't it?" she countered. "These Agbui pop in out of nowhere, they just *happen* to land in your province, they just *happen* to have a nyix mine that no one else in the Chaos has ever heard of, and it just *happens* to be completely open and undefended? That doesn't sound insane to you?"

"Just because you haven't taken the time to talk to and study the Agbui doesn't mean I haven't," Lakuviv said. "I know these people. I know who they are and what they want. Haplif thinks very much as I do"—including sharing Lakuviv's assessment that the Patriel was a pompous glory-thief—"and we both understand the danger the Agbui people face."

"And somehow these sophisticated aliens have never heard of nyix?"

"Why should they have?" Lakuviv asked. "They don't use it—all their ships are civilian. But you saw the analysis of the wires in their jewelry."

Lakooni shook her head. "No," she said. "This can't be as it seems. Somehow, this Haplif is playing you for who knows what purpose. There's no way this mine could have escaped everyone's attention. I'm not going to add another layer of gullibility on top of yours. The conversation is over."

Lakuviv took a careful breath. He'd hoped it would end with her giving her support. But he'd been prepared for the alternative. "If that's your final word, so be it," he said. "Just be aware that if the Xodlak don't move, the Coduyo will."

Lakooni's eyes narrowed. "Meaning?"

"Meaning one of Haplif's traveling companions is a Coduyo scholar," Lakuviv said. "You probably knew that once, though I suppose you've forgotten. The point is that he's already contacted his Patriarch and they're in the process of moving on the Agbui mines."

"Impossible," Lakooni insisted, eyeing him closely. "The Coduyo barely have functional patrol ships, let alone anything suitable for actual combat. Are they seriously planning to move on an entire world with a couple of century-old cruisers?"

"Not at all," Lakuviv said. "They're going to use ours."

"Are you—?" Lakooni broke off, the narrowed eyes widening. "You mean . . . *our* warships? The frigate and cruisers here at Celwis?"

"Exactly," Lakuviv said. "They're already gathering Coduyo officers and warriors from the fleet. When they arrive at Celwis, they'll have emergency authorization certificates allowing them to come aboard our ships and raise them to a war footing."

"Will they, now." Lakooni stood up from the office guest chair and waved Lakuviv away from his desk. "Move, Councilor," she ordered. "I need your secure comm."

"I doubt the Coduyo Patriarch will take your call," he warned, standing up and moving aside.

"Oh, he'll be getting a call, all right," Lakooni said grimly as she brushed past him. "And he *will* take it. But that will come later. Right now, I'm going to guarantee the security of my warships." She dropped down into his chair and waved him toward the door. "Wait outside. This may take a few minutes."

"Yes, Patriel," Lakuviv said. He'd expected her to make this call, and to want privacy for it.

In fact, he'd counted on it.


He was standing outside his office when Lakooni emerged fifteen minutes later. "*There* you are," she growled, standing in the doorway and beckoning imperiously to him. "Your comm has gone dead. You need to get someone in here to fix it."

"I'll see to it right away," Lakuviv promised as he walked into the office. "Did you make your call?" he added as she followed him inside.

"I made *one* of them," she said acidly as he reached past her and closed the door. "And then the comm went down. As I just told you." She frowned, looking at the desk and then back at him. "What are you just standing there for? I told you to get someone to fix this."

"Not right now," Lakuviv said, feeling his heart thudding in his chest. It still wasn't too late to back down, he knew. Almost, but not quite. "That was a smart move, calling the warships' commander and telling him under no circumstances to allow any non-Xodlak personnel aboard without consulting you first. That should block even an emergency order from Csilla or Naporar, at least temporarily."

Lakooni's face had gone rigid. "What are you talking about?" she demanded. "How did—? You were listening *in*?"

"Not exactly," Lakuviv said. "Well, yes and no. You see, I was the junior officer you just spoke to. The one who promised to give your message to the commander."

Lakooni's mouth dropped open, a stunned look on her face. "What are you talking about?" she repeated, more mechanically this time.

"We need this, Patriel Lakooni," Lakuviv said, hearing a slight tremor in his voice. Tension or passion, he wasn't sure which. Maybe both. "The Xodlak need these mines, and the riches and renown that will come with them. It's the only way we'll ever regain the Ruling Family status that was once rightfully ours. To do that, we need to call in fleet officers and warriors, to activate the warships that were also once rightfully ours."

"Councilor Lakuviv—"

"But what I needed in order to do that," Lakuviv said, nodding toward the decorative pendant around Lakooni's neck, "was a real-time recording of the rolling authorization codes with which you begin and end all orders and directives." He paused. "Such as the order to seal our warships against non-Xodlak."

For a handful of heartbeats Lakooni stared at him in taut silence. "What order did you give, Councilor?" she said at last, her voice dark.

"I already told you," Lakuviv said. "I called—rather, you, Patriel Lakooni, called—for officers and warriors to respond to a family emergency situation on Celwis. From the Coduyo experience thirty years ago I estimate four days to gather all the personnel we need, plus a maximum of two more to get the ships ready to go. Six days, and they'll be on their way to the Agbui mining world."

"No," Lakooni said flatly. "You'll take me to a secure comm—*now*—so I can countermand—"

She broke off, freezing in place, her eyes again going wide at the sight of the charric gripped in Lakuviv's hand and pointed at her. "Are you *insane*?" she breathed.

"You've told your office you're going to your Fissure Lake retreat," Lakuviv said, fighting the trembling in his hand as he stepped forward and took her comm from her belt. And now it *was* too late to back down. "You'll be my guest here instead. By the time anyone wonders why you haven't checked in, the operation will be under way."

"You'll lose everything for this," Lakooni bit out. "Your position, your family, your freedom, possibly your life. You have one chance—*one*—to end this before it's too late."

"The Patriarch himself will thank me when the mines become ours," Lakuviv said. "It's not too late for you to join in. There are riches and glory and honor to be had, Patriel Lakooni, for us and the family—"

"No," Lakooni cut him off. "If you want to indulge in this insanity, you'll do it alone."

"As you wish." Lakuviv opened the door and stepped out into the hallway, looking both ways to confirm they were alone. "This way, please. I'm afraid you'll have to stay in my private suite for the next few days. I've already set it up for you."

With one final ice-edged look, she stepped from the office and turned in the indicated direction. Lakuviv stayed close behind her, his hand shaking openly now. *Great rewards emerge like gloriosi from the silken sheaths of great risks:* Haplif's words echoed through his mind. The risk here was indeed great.

But the rewards would be far, far greater.

"The last of the plasma fluid's been transferred aboard and the tanks sealed," Apros reported, his voice nearly inaudible above the grinding hum of the weapons bay lifters. "There are three more breachers to be loaded, and that'll be it."

"Good," Lakinda said, looking at her chrono. Supreme Admiral Ja'fosk wanted the *Grayshrike* to be on its way as soon as the rearming and reprovisioning was complete, which should now be another hour at the most. Thrawn had been told via triad that Lakinda was on her way, but given that the *Springhawk* was far out of range of return communication there was no way of knowing if he'd received the message.

And that could be a problem. Thrawn had transmitted his proposed search pattern to Naporar when he left Paataatus space ten days ago, but there were any number of situations that could have forced him off that path. Lakinda wouldn't know for sure until she arrived at the system that was her best estimate for a rendezvous. If the *Springhawk* wasn't there and wasn't within ship-to-ship comm range, she would have to start her own search pattern and hope she could track him down.

It would help if Thrawn could persuade the Paataatus to relay a message back to the Ascendancy with their own triad transmitter. But that further assumed the aliens were still feeling kindly enough toward him to allow it, and Lakinda couldn't afford to rely on that.

Which led directly to a more ominous unknown. Lakinda had read Thrawn's brief report on his encounter with the Paataatus, and she could understand the aliens being grateful for getting the last remaining Nikardun threat off their backs. But in her experience, gratitude between bitter enemies didn't last longer than a good dinner party. Once she passed their territory, they would be at her back. Not the kind of tactical position she liked to be in.

A tone from her comm interrupted her musings, and she keyed it on. "Senior Captain Lakinda."

"This is Lieutenant Commander Lakwurn; hyperdrive tech," an unfamiliar and hesitant voice came over the speaker. "I have a—well, an unusual request that's just been handed to me. May I have permission to come to the bridge?"

Lakinda looked at her office's bridge monitor. Sky-walker Bet'nih was at the navigation station, with Caregiver Soomret standing behind her. Their presence meant no non-bridge personnel were permitted. "Where are you?" she asked Lakwurn.

"Hyperdrive Two, ma'am."

"I'll be right there," Lakinda said, standing up. One of the senior officers needed to check the hyperdrive before they left anyway. This would save Apros or Ovinon a trip.

The hyperdrive chamber was a buzz of activity when Lakinda arrived, with the techs and operators running through the usual preflight tests. A young man was fidgeting near the entrance, a small box in one hand and his comm in the other. He was frowning at the latter, she noticed as she approached. "Lieutenant Commander Lakwurn?" she asked.

"Yes, Senior Captain," he said with the slight breathlessness of someone unaccustomed to speaking directly with the ship's commander. "My apologies for dragging you all the way down here, ma'am."

"Not a problem," Lakinda said. "You said you had a request?"

"Yes, ma'am," Lakwurn said. "I don't, exactly, but—" He thrust out the box. "Here, ma'am. One of the HQ personnel sent this up with instructions for me to give it to one of the *Springhawk*'s officers when we rendezvoused with them, which he would then give to Senior Captain Thrawn. But since this came in—" He held up his comm with a sort of helpless look on his face. "I hoped you'd be willing to give it to Senior Captain Thrawn for me."

"What is it?" she asked, taking the box. It wasn't sealed, she noted, which suggested it wasn't too personal. Besides, it was aboard *her* ship, which gave her every right to open it. Working her fingers under the edge of the lid, she pulled it off.

Inside, nestled inside a wad of padding, was a striking brooch made of intertwined metal wires. "This is for Senior Captain *Thrawn*?" she asked.

"Yes, ma'am," Lakwurn said, sounding a little awed as he gazed into the box. Clearly, he hadn't opened it himself. "That's . . . non-regulation, isn't it?"

Lakinda had to smile at that. "Decidedly so, Lieutenant Commander." She replaced the lid and offered the box back. "But I don't see the problem. Is there some reason you can't deliver this to him yourself?"

"But—" he waved his comm again. "I have to leave. Don't I?"

Lakinda frowned. "What are you talking about?"

"I'm—" He turned the comm around and offered it to her. "This. It just came in."

Lakinda peered at the note on the display.

From: Xodlak'oo'nifis, Patriel of Celwis
To: all Xodlak Expansionary Defense Fleet officers and warriors

A Xodlak family emergency has been declared for Celwis. All officers and warriors not currently engaged in combat operations or imminent threat situations are to take immediate leave and assemble at Celwis for vital military operations.

"It came in under the family encryption," Lakwurn said. "I'm not sure exactly what I'm supposed to do."

"The summons seems clear enough," Lakinda said, handing him back his comm and pulling out her own. If Lakwurn had gotten a summons, why hadn't she?

She had. She'd just been too busy to notice it.

She'd read about family emergency protocol at the academy, she remembered now. But even then it had seemed like something ancient, even quaint, a procedure that harked back to the Ascendancy's early days. Apparently, it was still active.

And Lakwurn's question was a damn good one.

The *Grayshrike* wasn't engaged in combat or in an imminent threat situation. True, it was on its way to assist the *Springhawk*, and at some point her ship might end up in one or both of those categories. But the protocol didn't consider vague future possibilities.

Where did her loyalties lie? She'd sworn an oath to the fleet and the Ascendancy, but she was also a member of the Xodlak family. A case could also be made that a crisis in the Xodlak also contained within it a crisis in the Ascendancy as a whole. Without knowing any of the emergency's specifics, there was no way to judge where her skills and rank were most needed and could be used most effectively.

Her family needed her. So did Thrawn and the fleet.

Which imperative did she obey?

She felt her stomach tighten. No. Thrawn needed the *Grayshrike*. He didn't necessarily need Lakinda herself.

And if the fleet didn't expect its officers and warriors to respond to family emergencies like this, this protocol shouldn't still be in force.

"Your leave is hereby granted," she told Lakwurn. "Get your kit and report to the weapons hatch."

"Yes, Senior Captain," Lakwurn said, sounding uncertain. "Will I need to—how do I arrange transport to Celwis?"

"I'll make the arrangements," Lakinda said. "Meet me there in ten."

His eyes widened. "Meet *you*? I—" He stiffened again. "Yes, ma'am."

"And give me that," she added, plucking the box from his hand. "I'll instruct Mid Captain Apros to give it to Thrawn. Go on—move."

"Yes, ma'am." Lakwurn slipped past her to the hatch and hurried out into the passageway. Lakinda followed more slowly, her mind running through everything that would need to be done before she left. First on that list would be to inform Mid Captain Apros that he was now in command of her ship.

"I tell you, Syndic Thurfian, the UAG is a menace," the Obbic emissary insisted in a voice that was equal parts passion, fear, and persuasion.

"More than just a menace," the Clarr sitting beside her added. His tone, Thurfian noted, wasn't nearly as nuanced as the Obbic's. "I've told you what it's done to the lake fish. What do you think it's doing to the people of Sposia?"

Thurfian sighed to himself. The two delegates from Sposia—he'd already forgotten their names in the roiling turmoil of their presentation—had talked for nearly an hour straight, their accusations and unsupported innuendo abating only when one of them paused to send yet another chart or list to his questis. Amid the flurry of words, he still hadn't heard a single hard fact to support their contention that the Universal Analysis Group was a threat to them, to Sposia, or the Ascendancy as a whole. Or even to the fish.

He had to hear them out, of course. The Obbic were allies of the Mitth, which guaranteed them a fair hearing. The Clarr weren't allies of any of the other Ruling Families in particular, but they'd always shown a leaning toward the Irizi. Thurfian's attentiveness to their concerns might help prevent them from moving any closer.

But he'd listened, and he'd studied their charts, and none of the alliances and non-alliances in the Ascendancy required him to sacrifice any more of his day to this nonsense.

"I understand your concerns," he said in his most conciliatory tone when the recitation finally tapered off. "But I can assure you that you have nothing to worry about. The Universal Analysis Group has operated under the auspices of the Stybla for decades without any mishaps."

"Then why are they so secretive about their operation?" the Obbic demanded. "Sposia is our world. Why can't we get in to see what they're doing?"

"And what about the fish?" the Clarr added.

"First of all, Sposia is not *your* world," Thurfian said. "Your four families may dominate, but there are thousands of other families and millions of other Chiss living there."

The Obbic gave a snort. "*Lesser* families," she muttered.

"The Ascendancy is home to all," Thurfian reminded her firmly, trying not to let his irritation show. The Obbic had always tended to look down on everyone who wasn't of the Nine or the Forty; and while Thurfian may have had some of that same attitude when he was a midager, at least he'd grown out of it. "Furthermore, just because the Stybla oversee the facility doesn't mean there aren't personnel from the other Ruling Families involved. There are."

"What about the *fish*?" the Clarr pressed.

"The fish aren't disappearing because of runoff or anything else from the facility," Thurfian said. "They're disappearing because the people are overfishing the lake."

"Impossible," the Clarr insisted. "We have strict guidelines in place."

"Best guess is that you also have poachers in place."

The Clarr drew himself up. "Syndic Thurfian—"

"However, just because there haven't been any incidents in the past doesn't mean there might not be some in the future," Thurfian continued. "I'll make some inquiries as to the current safety protocols and see if they need to be modified or enhanced. If such is needed, I'll make sure the changes are implemented."

The Obbic and Clarr exchanged looks, and Thurfian braced himself. But apparently they'd run out of words, or perhaps merely out of expectations. "Thank you for your time, Syndic," the Clarr said, rising from his chair and motioning his companion to do likewise. "We'll look forward to your report on those protocols."

"You'll have it within three months," Thurfian promised. "Good day."

"Good day."

They'd been gone for ten minutes, and Thurfian was finalizing the wording of a memo to send to the Universal Analysis Group, when his door opened.

And to his surprise, Speaker Thyklo walked in.

"Speaker," Thurfian greeted her, scrambling to his feet. For Thyklo to come to the Syndic Prime's office instead of summoning Thurfian to hers was nearly unheard of. "What can I do for you?"

"I just wanted to congratulate you on your handling of the Sposia complaint commission," Thyklo said, waving Thurfian back down as she carefully eased herself into the seat the Obbic had just vacated. She'd been a vigorous and effective fighter for family interests for many years, but Thurfian had noted that age was finally starting to catch up with her. "I spoke to them briefly on their way out."

"I had the impression they weren't exactly pleased by my response," Thurfian said.

"No, but they weren't nearly as displeased as they might have been," Thyklo said. "In fact, they said you'd been more helpful than any of the other syndics they'd spoken to."

"I'm not surprised," Thurfian said. "They sound like crazed yubals."

"A common reaction to anything kept out of the public eye, sadly," Thyklo said. "But you handled it well." She cocked her head slightly. "If I may say so, you remind me a little of Syndic Thrass. He was also good at appearing to give people what they wanted while simultaneously doing what needed to be done."

"Really," Thurfian said, feeling a stirring inside him. "I assume that's a compliment."

"Very much so," Thyklo said with a smile. "Thrass wasn't as skilled at it as you are, but he definitely had the talent. A terrible shame that we lost him."

"Yes. To Thrawn."

"Or to circumstances," Thyklo said. "It's easy to place blame, but it's not always productive. Or always accurate." She stood up, keeping one hand on the armrest for balance as she did so. "I'll let you get back to work now. I just wanted to stop by and express my appreciation." She smiled lopsidedly. "Along with everything else, you saved *me* having to sit for an hour and listen to them." With a friendly nod, she turned and left the office.

For a moment Thurfian stared at the closed door, his mind spinning. Thyklo coming to his office; Thyklo complimenting him on his negotiation skill; Thyklo even comparing him to Thrass, whose memory was still achingly fresh for many of the Aristocra.

And then, there were the rumors. Rumors that Thyklo was growing weary of the stress of being Speaker. Rumors that she was looking to retire, or to be named as Patriel on one of the quieter Ascendancy worlds. Rumors that at least two Patriels were also looking to retire. If all those rumors happened to come together . . .

Firmly, Thurfian put the thought out of his mind. Right now, his only goal was to prove that he would be a good and competent Speaker. The timing of that opening, whenever it happened, would take care of itself.

Picking up his questis, he got back to work.

# CHAPTER NINETEEN

"Breakout in thirty seconds," Samakro called from his position behind the *Springhawk*'s weapons station.

Standing behind Che'ri, Thalias stifled a yawn. Most of their search pattern had been short flights, but this particular one had been long enough that Thrawn had opted to use their sky-walker instead of the slower jump-by-jump method.

Which was all to the good as far as Thalias was concerned. Ever since they'd left the Paataatus behind and started their pirate search, Che'ri had mostly been sitting around the suite with nothing to do but eat, sleep, do her lessons, play, and slowly go stir-crazy.

On most of the *Springhawk*'s trips, Thalias's largest problem was coping with their sky-walker's fatigue and stress. Dealing with a ten-year-old's boredom was an entirely different challenge.

What made it worse was that there was no defined end in sight. The Chaos was a huge place, and even with information from the Paataatus narrowing it down there were hundreds of star systems where a pirate gang could lurk. Thrawn's decision to confine their search to systems containing planets the Vagaari could live on narrowed things down enormously, but even Thalias knew that choice was largely arbitrary. She could understand the advantage of having someplace available nearby to retreat to if something suddenly went sour, but there was no guarantee the Vagaari thought that same way.

Eventually, of course, Thrawn would have to give up and return to the Ascendancy. The question was whether he would admit defeat before Che'ri got hold of a tool kit and started taking apart all their furniture.

Che'ri inhaled sharply in her Third Sight trance, her hands moving seemingly of their own volition across the controls. Thalias looked down as the girl shut down the hyperdrive and pulled them back into space-normal. Resting her hands reassuringly on Che'ri's shoulders, Thalias looked up at the starscape that once again surrounded the ship—

"Laserfire!" Afpriuh snapped from the weapons console.

—and the space battle blazing in the near distance almost directly ahead of them.

"Stand by weapons," Thrawn said calmly from his command chair. "Dalvu?"

"I make it four ships," Dalvu called, hunching over her displays. "Three fighter-class attackers, probably gunships; one medium-sized defender, probably a freighter. All configurations unknown, but they don't look Paataatus to me."

"I agree," Thrawn said. "Though they do bear some resemblance to ancient artifacts we've uncovered from the region northeast-zenith of here."

"Captain, we're being hailed," Brisch spoke up. "The freighter captain is requesting assistance."

Thrawn didn't answer. Thalias looked over her shoulder, to see that he was leaning forward as he gazed out the viewport at the battle, his eyes narrowed, his forehead creased in thought. Thalias looked at Samakro, found he was also watching Thrawn. The first officer's expression, in contrast with his commander's, was not so much thoughtful as slightly puzzled.

"Sir?" Brisch prompted hesitantly.

"I heard you," Thrawn said. For another moment he continued to watch the battle. Then, with a microscopic nod, he leaned back in his chair and touched the comm key.

"—urgently needed," a wheezing voice rattled off in the Minnisiat trade language. "Repeat: Unknown warship, this is Captain Fsir aboard the freighter *Saltbarrel*. We have come under attack by violent and evil marauders. Please, your aid is urgently needed."

"Sir," Samakro said, a hint of warning in his voice.

Thrawn inclined his head in acknowledgment, and Thalias thought she spotted a hint of a smile as he keyed the mike. "This is Senior Captain Thrawn of the Chiss Expansionary Defense Fleet warship *Springhawk*," he said in Minnisiat. "My apologies, but we are engaged in a vital mission that forbids us to stop and assist others."

Thalias frowned. Engaged in a vital mission? She'd never heard that rule before.

From the look on Samakro's face, neither had he. "Senior Captain?" he murmured.

Thrawn muted the mike. "I have a suspicion, Mid Captain," he said, nodding toward the distant battle. "Let's see what they do."

The wait wasn't long. Even as Samakro also turned to the viewport, one of the gunboats broke off its attack on the freighter and headed for the *Springhawk*. "As I expected," Thrawn said. "Afpriuh, prepare spectrum lasers for return fire."

"Yes, sir," Afpriuh said. "Should I prep spheres and breachers?"

"I think not," Thrawn said. "The lasers should be sufficient."

Che'ri muttered something, and Thalias felt the shoulder muscles under her hands tense up. The girl hadn't seen a lot of combat, but she'd seen enough to know that the standard Chiss three-layer response was usually necessary to take out even a warship as small as a gunboat.

But Thrawn wasn't going to do that. What did he know, Thalias wondered, that she didn't?

The gunboat reached combat range and opened fire, raking the *Springhawk* with a pair of heavy lasers as it simultaneously made a hard turn to evade return fire. "Sir?" Afpriuh asked, his hands poised on the firing controls.

"A moment, Senior Commander," Thrawn said. The gunboat curved around and again fired, its lasers again skittering across the *Springhawk*'s hull. It started to turn again as it had before—

"Fire," Thrawn said.

The gunboat's lasers had slashed across the *Springhawk* instead of focusing on a single spot, a tactic that seemed odd to Thalias. Perhaps the fighter's crew was inexperienced, or perhaps they were hoping luck and a scattergun approach would allow them to hit something vital and unprotected.

If that was their plan, it failed. Thalias could see the electrostatic barrier status board from where she was standing, and the *Springhawk*'s defensive sheath was holding up quite well against the attack.

Unfortunately for the attackers, Afpriuh was fully experienced and probably hadn't relied on luck since he was eight. As the gunboat again swung around he fired a full salvo of the *Springhawk*'s lasers, all of them centered on the aft thruster section, all of them tracking with the target's movement. Thalias held her breath, visualizing the focused energy tearing into and through the hull metal . . .

And with a burst of flame and smoke, the gunboat exploded.

Thalias blinked. *That* was fast. Much faster than the *Springhawk*'s usual battles, in fact. Apparently, Thrawn had been right not to bother with breachers and plasma spheres. The debris cloud expanded into the vacuum, and as it dissipated Thalias saw that the other two gunboats had abandoned their attack on the freighter and were now moving toward the *Springhawk*.

"Afpriuh, fire at will," Thrawn ordered. "Again, limit your response to lasers."

"Yes, sir," Afpriuh said, and Thalias caught his tight smile as he bent over his controls. Of all the bridge officers, she'd often thought, he seemed to take the most pure joy from his job.

The *Springhawk*'s lasers flashed, and again, and again. The gunboats returned fire as best they could, but they'd started too far away for the range of their weapons, and their attacks were as ineffective as the first fighter's had been. They were just starting to reach the distance where the first attack had occurred when the *Springhawk*'s lasers finished digging through their hulls.

And once again, the serene starry background was marred by the violence of explosions.

Thrawn waited until the twin firestorms burned out into expanding spheres of blackened and half-melted wreckage. Then he again touched his mike key. "This is Senior Captain Thrawn," he said. "Captain Fsir, please report your status."

"Much more promising now, Senior Captain Thrawn," the alien's wheezing voice came back. "My passengers and I offer our humble gratitude for your timely assistance. How may we repay you?"

"You may begin with information," Thrawn said. "Who are your people, where do you come from, and what is your purpose here?"

"We are the Watith," Fsir said, his voice suddenly hesitant. "We come from a system far away. May I ask why you wish its location?"

"Merely to add to my general knowledge of the Chaos," Thrawn said. "Certainly the Chiss have no territorial ambitions beyond our borders."

"Yet you identify yourself as an *expansionary* fleet."

"The title also includes the word *defense*," Thrawn pointed out. "But no matter. Tell me why you're here."

"A safer question," Fsir said, his caution fading. "We came to this system to study the possibility of setting up a long-range communications relay station."

"A triad transmitter?"

"Is that what the Chiss call it?" Fsir asked. "Oh, yes, of course—an obvious name. Three poles—triad—yes, that makes sense. At any rate, as you know if you've spent much time in this region, the nations here are few in number, small in size, and great in separation. The nearest relay station is controlled by the Paataatus, who never allow others to use it."

Thalias smiled to herself. If the Paataatus were really that miserly with their triad, it made their willingness to let Thrawn use it even more of an honor than she'd thought. They must *really* have wanted their Nikardun oppressors eliminated.

"Our leaders thought a relay station of our own could be a good investment," Fsir continued. "It would be available to all—for a suitable fee, of course—set up on an unclaimed world that could nevertheless support the necessary operational crew and their families."

"Interesting," Thrawn said. "I presume you've now decided to remove this system from your list?"

"Why do you say that?" Fsir asked. "Our study shows the planet is perfectly suitable for our needs."

"Except that someone doesn't want you here."

"Someone—? Oh. Those fighters?" Fsir made a rude-sounding noise. "Hardly a statement of warning. They were merely a group of pirates pausing for a navigational recalibration before returning to their base. They obviously saw us as an opportunity and decided to take it."

Thalias caught her breath. Pirates? *Vagaari* pirates?

"Had they succeeded in capturing us, they would have been sorely disappointed by our banquet of specialized electronic equipment and our famine of marketable goods," Fsir said. "Though perhaps they were seeking captives. All the more reason to be grateful for your intervention."

"You said they were pirates," Thrawn said, and Thalias could hear the studied nonchalance in his voice. "Do you know which group they're from?"

"Don't misunderstand, please," Fsir cautioned. "I don't know for a fact that these were any raiders in particular. I simply assumed their identity and purpose because of our current proximity to the Vagaari pirate base."

A quiet stir ran through the bridge. Thalias looked back at Thrawn, noting that the small smile she'd seen earlier was back. "Interesting," he said. "As it happens, the Vagaari are the exact group we're looking for."

"Remarkable!" Fsir said. "Then we are well met, indeed. The universe has seen fit to reward you for your courage and kindness to the Watith. That is . . ." He paused. "May I ask what your purpose is in seeking out the Vagaari? You do not wish to join them, do you?"

"Hardly," Thrawn assured him. "We're here to assess whether or not they pose a continuing threat to this region."

"Ah," Fsir said, not sounding entirely convinced. "Well. In that case, perhaps I may offer my services as a guide to their base?"

"It would be enough to give us the coordinates," Thrawn said. "There's no reason you need to expose yourself to danger by leading us there yourself."

"I would like nothing more than to avoid further danger," Fsir said. "Unfortunately, our coordinate system likely varies greatly from that of the Chiss, and I don't trust my directions to lead you there with accuracy. Also, to be perfectly honest, right now I think remaining in your company will be our best way of avoiding danger. There may be other pirate stragglers about, and you saw how poorly equipped we are to face such threats."

"I understand," Thrawn said. "I welcome your company and your guidance."

"Thank you," Fsir said. "We can depart as soon as is convenient for you."

"That will be a short while yet," Thrawn said. "Before we travel to the Vagaari base, I wish to examine the wreckage of these gunboats."

"The—?" Fsir actually sputtered. "The *wreckage*? Senior Captain Thrawn, are you perhaps blind? There is no wreckage, only dust."

"On the contrary," Thrawn said. "We are tracking several larger pieces of debris. More than that, even small bits can be valuable. The gunboats' violent explosions, for example, strongly suggest their weaponry included missiles as well as lasers. There may be chemical deposits that will help us learn what sort of missiles they were, including the propellant-and-explosive mix used. Fragments of their electronics might similarly offer clues as to the ships' origin or their computer and communications systems."

"You are indeed wizards if you can glean so much from so little," Fsir said. "Very well. Can you estimate how long this examination will take?"

"Five days at the most," Thrawn said. "Likely only three or four. In the meantime, you're free to continue your planetary survey."

"Our survey was largely complete," Fsir said, sounding doubtful. "Still, I suppose we could fill the time by beginning the follow-up study to find a suitable location for the transmitter. A more immediate concern, and the reason I asked for your time line, is that with the failure of these ships to return the Vagaari may send out a search party."

"If they do, we'll deal with them."

"Yes," Fsir said, his voice sounding uncertain. "I merely thought a wiser strategy might be to attack their base quickly, before they were alerted that there may be trouble."

"In general, that is indeed a good strategy," Thrawn agreed. "In this case, knowing as much about the enemy as possible offers a potentially better advantage even than surprise."

"I yield to your deeper knowledge of such things," Fsir said. "Very well, we shall wait until you are ready. Nevertheless, I urge you to move as quickly on your studies as possible."

"We'll get to it immediately," Thrawn promised. "While my people are working on that, perhaps you could give me a tour of your vessel."

"Why would you want such a thing?" Fsir asked, his voice suddenly guarded.

"I want to meet your crew and technicians," Thrawn explained. "We'll be going into a likely combat situation, and I need to assess your capabilities."

"Combat is *your* venue, Senior Captain," Fsir said. "We have no intention of getting near any battles."

"The Vagaari may have other ideas," Thrawn said drily. "Regardless, I need to know what your ship and people are capable of in order to properly plan my tactics."

"I doubt we're capable of anything, really," Fsir admitted. "More to the point, we have a great deal of proprietary equipment aboard for our work on the relay station. My superiors would be highly displeased if any of our secrets were deciphered and appropriated."

"In my experience, there is little that can be learned from simply observing the casings of electronic equipment," Thrawn said. "Particularly since the labeling will all be in your script, which undoubtedly is unknown to us. Your navigational equipment can of course be shrouded to prevent me from obtaining any clues to your world's location."

"I suppose," Fsir said, still sounding hesitant.

"Perhaps your superiors could be persuaded to look upon it as payment for our rescue of their people and secrets," Thrawn suggested. "In addition, a visit would give you the opportunity to see if your legends of the Chiss are accurate."

"Who suggested we even *have* legends of the Chiss?"

Thrawn smiled. "Come now, Captain. *Everyone* in the near reaches of the Chaos has legends of the Chiss."

Fsir sighed. "Very well, Senior Captain. Give me some time to prepare and coordinate with my people. I'll contact you when we're ready."

"I'll await your call," Thrawn said. "In the meantime, we'll begin our work on the battle debris. Farewell."

He tapped off his mike. "Mid Captain Samakro, have Shuttle One prepped and arrange for four armed guards to meet me there."

"Are you sure four will be enough?" Samakro asked, pulling out his questis and logging the orders. "And do you want any other officers along?"

"Four guards will be sufficient," Thrawn said. "And including other officers would make Fsir think we had ulterior motives in coming aboard."

Thalias smiled to herself. Of course there were no ulterior motives. Certainly none Fsir and his fellow Watith would suspect. Not even Thrawn's fellow Chiss really understood how much of a people's culture and society he could glean merely by looking at their clothing and their ship's décor.

"Also organize three shuttle crews to begin collecting debris," Thrawn continued. "They're to focus on larger pieces, but also gather samples of dust."

"And bodies?" Samakro asked.

"Yes, if there are any," Thrawn said. "Though I didn't see anything in the explosions' aftermath that looked intact. Mid Commander Dalvu?"

"I saw no bodies, either, Senior Captain," the sensor officer concurred. "But even if nothing survived intact, there should be fragments."

"Agreed," Thrawn said. "If so, Mid Captain, make sure the collection crews watch for them."

"Yes, sir," Samakro said, still working his questis. "Is there anything in particular you want the analysts to look for?"

"Begin with the missile debris and electronics I mentioned to Captain Fsir," Thrawn said. "Body fragments are to be analyzed for genetic material."

He looked out the viewport to the distant Watith ship. "I want to know if Vagaari were flying those gunboats," he added. "And if not, who was."

Senior Aide Lakjiip's eyes went a little wider as she read Lakinda's personnel profile from her questis. "Senior Captain Xodlak'in'daro," she said, sounding both surprised and a little bit in awe. "*Senior* Captain. Excuse me, but I confess I hadn't expected anyone of your rank and status to answer the family summons."

"I don't know why not," Lakinda said. "I'm as much Xodlak as you are."

"Yes, of course you are," Lakjiip said hastily. "I just . . . apologies, Senior Captain. We've been highly gratified by the response already, and your presence is a fantastic additional bonus to the operation. It underlines the immense pride we all have in our family."

"I'm glad we're all working together," Lakinda said, studying the other woman. The emergency summons had come from Patriel Lakooni, and Lakinda had naturally expected that someone from the Patriel's office would be in charge here. Why was a mere Councilor's senior aide passing out the duty assignments? "What exactly is this all about?"

"I note that the ship you command, the *Grayshrike,* is a heavy cruiser," Lakjiip continued, still peering at her questis. "As you may know, we have an old family frigate, the *Midsummer,* which has been stored here for the past fifty years. We'd be honored if you would agree to be its commander."

"I'm happy to serve wherever Patriel Lakooni deems best," Lakinda said. "What's the *Midsummer*'s current status?"

"About ninety percent," Lakjiip said. "Our local crews have been working on bringing it up ever since Patriel Lakooni sent out the emergency call three days ago. And as other officers and warriors began arriving, those work parties were of course steadily expanded." Her lip twitched. "Unfortunately, it doesn't look like we'll have the time and personnel to give you both cruisers. However, the *Apogee* is the better of the two, and the overseers estimate both it and the *Midsummer* will be ready to fly within the next ten to twelve hours."

"I see I made it just in time," Lakinda said. "May I ask where Patriel Lakooni is right now?"

"She and Councilor Lakuviv are coordinating the operation from Councilor Lakuviv's office," Lakjiip said. "I'm sure she'll be available to offer some words of encouragement before things heat up."

"That's the second time you've used the word *operation*," Lakinda said. "Not counting its use in the original summons. What exactly is going on?"

"Well . . ." Lakjiip hesitated. "At the moment that's classified," she said. "But as one of the ship commanders, you of course have both a right and a need to know. All right. It all started when a group of aliens—the Agbui—arrived on Celwis . . ."

Lakinda listened in silence and growing amazement as Lakjiip laid out the story of aliens and jewelry and all-but-untouched nyix mines. "That's . . . just a little bit unbelievable," she said when the senior aide had finished. "Are you sure you're reading all this correctly?"

"I've seen the mines myself," Lakjiip assured her. "The entire world is pristine, untouched, and unoccupied. Probably even unknown." She dug into a pocket. "I also brought back souvenirs."

"You're sure that's nyix?" Lakinda asked, studying the piece of wire.

"Absolutely," Lakjiip said. "Every sample we've obtained has been carefully analyzed." Her lip twitched. "Including one we borrowed from a citizen."

Lakinda nodded. The possibilities here were tremendous.

But they were also ominous.

She studied Lakjiip's face. There was an enthusiasm half hidden beneath that calm expression, determined and hard-edged. "This will certainly be of huge benefit to the family," Lakinda said. "But it seems to me that a resource like this ought to belong to the Syndicure and the fleet."

"Absolutely," Lakjiip said, as if that was obvious. "The Xodlak family merely wishes the honor and triumph of its discovery."

"Honor, and perhaps a petition for reinstatement into the Ruling Families?"

Lakjiip gave a nonchalant sort of shrug. "That would only seem fair."

"Yes," Lakinda murmured. Like the shrug, the words had also been casual.

But it seemed to Lakinda that the enthusiasm in the senior aide's eyes went just a little bit stronger and harder. She wanted a return to the Xodlak days of glory, all right. Wanted it very badly.

But then, didn't every member of the family? And really, if everything Lakjiip said was true, didn't they deserve it?

"In the meantime, we need to get you to your ship," Lakjiip continued. "Come. I'll walk you to the shuttle."

# MEMORIES VII

The two ships Qilori had been told to expect were already waiting at the rendezvous when he arrived.

Qilori studied them as he approached the pulsing lights that marked the starboard access hatch on the smaller of the two. Neither ship was a design he recognized, though the smaller ship was configured like a yacht while the larger looked more like a freighter or possibly a low-rent passenger transport. The smaller one, he decided, was probably Jixtus's.

He inhaled deeply, his cheek winglets fluttering with anxiety. Jixtus's summons had come much sooner after their initial meeting than he'd expected, right in the middle of a job he couldn't back out of. He'd had to sweat pinefruit to get here on the alien's schedule, and he'd almost not made it.

But there the two ships were, already linked together by boarding tunnels, their thrusters showing no residual heat. By Qilori's estimate that meant they'd been waiting for at least six hours, possibly longer. Possibly a *lot* longer.

At their first meeting, Jixtus had threatened to leave Qilori stranded in the vast emptiness between stars if he didn't cooperate. Jixtus's chosen rendezvous was in very much that same grade of nowhere.

The summons had instructed him to not announce himself by comm, but to dock directly with the smaller ship when he arrived. Maneuvering carefully—the last thing he needed was to put a dent in Jixtus's hull—he floated up to the marked hatch and attached his landing tube and a trio of maglock tethering cables. He shut down his systems to standby and headed to the hatch, sternly telling his cheek winglets to behave themselves.

He'd expected Jixtus to be waiting impatiently on the other side of the hatch. Instead there was an unfamiliar alien standing there, his wrinkled facial skin a mix of dark red and dirty white, his lipless mouth almost invisible within those folds, his bright black eyes gazing unblinkingly at Qilori. "I am Qilori of Uandualon," Qilori identified himself in Taarja as he closed the hatch behind him.

"Good day, Pathfinder," the alien replied in Minnisiat. "I am Haplif of the Agbui. We've been waiting for you. Come."

He turned and strode down the corridor. Again trying to calm his winglets, Qilori followed.

The room Haplif led them to was something of a shock. It wasn't an office or command center, but more of a meditation room, with soft carpet underfoot and floating threads and light globes overhead. Seated in what appeared to be a self-contouring chair at the far side of the room was Jixtus.

At least Qilori assumed it was Jixtus. With his face concealed by a black veil, his hands encased in gloves, and a loose robe and hood covering everything else, he might have been any other biped alien. Or for that matter, a statue, a mannequin, or even one of the mechanical robotics of Lesser Space legends.

"Welcome, Qilori of Uandualon," the figure said, lifting a hand and gesturing to a pair of chairs facing him. "Be seated, both of you."

It was Jixtus's voice, and the hand movement proved at least that the hooded figure wasn't a statue or mannequin. It could still be a robotic, though. "Thank you," Qilori said, walking to one of the chairs and easing himself gingerly down into it. Self-contouring, all right. "I want to apologize for being late," he continued as Haplif sat down in the other chair. "I was on a job, and I thought that abandoning it would bring attention you probably wouldn't want."

"As well as damaging your professional reputation?" Jixtus suggested.

"My reputation is important," Qilori said. "Not just to me, but to you as well. Any future jobs you want me to do—"

"Any future jobs will depend on how well you complete this one," Jixtus interrupted calmly. "So will any future. You understand?"

Qilori's cheek winglets twitched. "I would very much like to have a future," he managed.

"Good," Jixtus said. "Then we shall have no problems with motivation." He paused as if considering. "And you were not late. Haplif and I were merely early."

Qilori felt some of the tension trickling away. The damn hooded alien could have said that in the first place.

"Your part is twofold," Jixtus continued. "First, you will travel with Haplif and his group, pretending to be his navigator."

"*Pretending?*" Qilori asked, frowning.

"Also remaining out of sight of his passenger," Jixtus went on, ignoring the interruption. "When the time is right, Haplif will offer your services to his mark, and you will navigate their ship to a planet whose coordinates he will give you. You will pretend you've been there before, and provide answers to any questions they may have about it."

"Answers that will be supplied by me," Haplif said. "Don't worry, we'll have plenty of time to go over the whole story."

"What if they ask a question you haven't covered?" Qilori asked.

"In that case, you'll just tell them you don't know," Haplif said. "You're only a navigator, after all. There's no reason they should expect you to know everything."

"All right," Qilori said. So far, this seemed simple enough. "Do I then bring them back, or take them somewhere else?"

"Of course you'll bring them back," Haplif said, the skin of his face wrinkling even more. "I'm weaving a path to their destruction. Why would I settle for one dead when I can have all of them?"

"It was just a question," Qilori said hastily. For all his bland and almost comical appearance, this Haplif creature had a definite blood streak in him. "I don't know anything about this sort of thing. Who will I be navigating for?"

"A minor Chiss official from a minor Chiss world," Haplif said. "That's all you need to know."

Qilori tensed again, feeling his winglets flatten across his cheeks. "May I ask if you anticipate any military action?"

Haplif snorted. "What's the problem, Pathfinder? Are you afraid of a little laserfire?"

"I'm afraid of professionals who think they can casually stray out of their area of expertise," Qilori shot back. "You talk of weaving a path to destruction. Fine. This is obviously some sort of con game, and I have no doubt you know what you're doing. I just don't want it to morph into warfare you might not be ready for. Especially since *I'll* be squarely in the middle of it."

"There will indeed be military action, Pathfinder," Jixtus said. "But it won't involve Haplif, and you won't be anywhere near it. Is that good enough?"

Qilori felt his winglets quiver. Arguing with Jixtus was undoubtedly dangerous. But walking into a Chiss battle would be worse. "With all due respect, sir, that depends on who's doing the shooting," he said carefully. "There are Chiss I would never face if there were any other alternatives."

"Yes, yes, we know all about them," Haplif said impatiently. "Supreme General Ba'kif, Admiral Ar'alani, one or two of the younger commodores—"

"And Senior Captain Thrawn," Qilori interrupted.

Haplif made a rude sound. "A *senior captain*? You must be joking. My lord, we're wasting time—"

"Patience, Haplif of the Agbui," Jixtus said, a note of curiosity in his voice. "You've mentioned that name to me before, Pathfinder, have you not?"

"I have," Qilori confirmed. "He was the one who took down General Yiv."

"Nonsense," Haplif said. "I've seen the reports. It was Ar'alani who led the battle over Primea from the *Vigilant,* assisted by Senior Captain Lakinda of the *Grayshrike* and Mid Captain Samakro of the *Springhawk.*"

"I didn't say he defeated the Nikardun," Qilori said stiffly. "I said he took down Yiv. That he, *personally,* took down General Yiv."

"Yiv had his own Battle Dreadnought," Jixtus said mildly.

"Thrawn had a one-person freighter," Qilori said. "Are you starting to understand who this Chiss is?"

Haplif shook his head. "No. I don't believe it."

"I was there, Haplif," Qilori said. "I saw it; and on one level *I* don't even believe it. But it happened." He looked back at Jixtus. "Again with respect, sir, if you listen to me on anything, please listen to me on this. If Thrawn gets involved in this operation, it's over. And not in a good way."

For a long moment, the room was silent. Qilori waited, his cheek winglets fluttering. *In the vast emptiness between stars.* If Jixtus decided to take offense at Qilori's words or his tone . . .

"I had wondered why the officially listed commander of

the *Springhawk* wasn't named in the rolls of the battle," Jixtus said at last, his voice more thoughtful than angry. "Perhaps it would be wise to arrange for this Senior Captain Thrawn to be elsewhere when Haplif's web-weaving comes to its completion. Would that make you happy, Qilori of Uandualon?"

"Yes, sir," Qilori said, feeling his winglets settle down a bit. "Though I'd be happier if he could be eliminated entirely."

"What, a military man who can defeat a Battle Dreadnought with a freighter?" Jixtus asked drily. "Still, another good thought. I'll see what I can arrange."

"Thank you, sir," Qilori said. "What do you want me to do to help?"

"You?" From behind Jixtus's veil came an amused chuckle. "Please. If General Yiv couldn't handle Thrawn, I doubt you can."

"Besides, I thought you wanted to stay clear of the shooting," Haplif muttered.

"At any rate, you have your assignments," Jixtus said. "And no, Pathfinder, I'll make my own arrangements for this Thrawn. Hints and rumors in the right ears should remove him a sufficient distance from Haplif's web." He gestured, a wave that encompassed both Qilori and Haplif. "You may go."

"Thank you, sir," Qilori said. He worked his way out of his chair, looking sideways at Haplif as he did so. If the Agbui resented the fact that Jixtus had taken Qilori's side of the argument, there could be trouble once they were together and out of Jixtus's sight.

But there was nothing ominous he could see in Haplif's expression. Apparently, he was the kind of good soldier who didn't let his pride get in the way of following his commander's decisions.

That, or he was too busy getting out of his own chair right now to worry about such things.

"You will leave your ship here, Qilori," Jixtus continued. "Haplif will bring you back to retrieve it when the job is finished."

"Yes, sir," Qilori said, trying to keep his winglets steady. He'd taken the ship out on a recompensed favor, and there would be livid hell to pay back at the concourse if he held on to it too long.

But he'd survived one argument with Jixtus. He had no intention of risking a second. Out of the corner of his eye he saw that Haplif, now back on his feet, had given Jixtus a little bow. Qilori did likewise, then turned to follow Haplif toward the hatch—

"One more thing, Qilori," Jixtus said.

Qilori turned back, his winglets twitching. "Yes?"

"You've navigated many Chiss ships, have you not?" Jixtus asked.

"Yes, sir," Qilori said. More of them than he'd ever wanted to, actually.

"Freighters and long-range transports?"

"Some," Qilori said, wondering where the hooded alien was going with this. "A few diplomatic ships, as well."

"Any warships?"

"One or two." Qilori winced at the memory. "Thrawn hired me to navigate for him a couple of times."

"And yet, it appears that most Chiss military craft don't hire navigators at all," Jixtus said. "Would you agree?"

"I don't know," Qilori said, his winglets fluttering again. "I can only speak from my own experience. Though now that you mention it, I don't recall other Pathfinders talking about such jobs."

"That leaves two possibilities," Jixtus said. "Either the Chiss have their own group of navigators, some aliens hidden on an obscure world of the Ascendancy..." He paused. "*Or* they have a means of finding their way through the Chaos without navigator assistance."

Qilori frowned. "What other means could there be?"

"It is said that millennia ago, the Chiss adventured into Lesser Space, taking part in wars between two hostile factions over vast and ever-shifting regions," Jixtus said, his voice again thoughtful. "Those factions reportedly had special navigational techniques that involved computers or mechanical constructs. Even now, those in that part of the galaxy use such techniques."

"I see," Qilori said as he saw where Jixtus was going. "You think the Chiss may have brought some of those devices back when they got tired of the wars and withdrew to the Ascendancy?"

"Possibly," Jixtus said. "And no, I don't expect you to solve this mystery for me at this time. But be aware that the mystery exists, and be watchful." He gestured toward the hatch. "Now go."

"Yes, my lord," Haplif said. With another bow, he turned again and left the meditation room. Qilori did the same, then hurried to catch up.

"We'll go back to your ship and get whatever luggage you need," Haplif said as they walked together down the corridor. "Shut everything down good, because we won't be back for a while."

"Understood," Qilori said, his mind spinning with possibilities. If the Chiss *were* using something electronic—and if the device could be stolen or copied—space travel would suddenly be opened up in a way that hadn't been possible for thousands of years. Whoever owned such a device could dictate to the entire Chaos, gaining immense wealth and power along the way.

Except that it would be Jixtus, not him, who had that

wealth and power. Qilori himself would have nothing. Not even his job.

Possibly not even his life.

He felt his winglets give one last flutter before settling against his cheeks. Yes, he would look for clues to the navigational device. But he would think long and hard before giving those clues to Jixtus. Or for that matter, to anyone else.

# CHAPTER TWENTY

Thrawn had promised Captain Fsir that the *Springhawk* would be ready to move on the Vagaari within five days. For the first three of those days Thalias barely saw the commander as he worked with the debris analysts, held conferences with Samakro and the other senior officers, and made at least two trips across to the Watith ship. Clearly, he was incredibly busy.

It was therefore something of a shock when Thalias opened the sky-walker suite hatch late on the third day to find Thrawn standing there. "Good evening, Caregiver Thalias," he said formally. "May I come in?"

"Certainly, Senior Captain Thrawn," Thalias said, hastily stepping aside. "Do you need to talk to Che'ri? She's taking a nap, but I can wake her if you want."

"No, this isn't about her," Thrawn said. He stepped inside, sealing the hatch behind him. "I came to look in on your roommate."

"But Che'ri is—oh," Thalias said, wincing. She'd gotten so used to the hibernation chamber in her sleeping room, especially since draping a blanket over it, that she'd almost forgotten there was a living being inside. "*That* roommate. Are you going to—uh—"

"Wake her?" Thrawn shook his head as he walked across the day-room and opened the hatch to her sleeping room. "No. I merely wanted to remind myself of her style of clothing."

"Her clothing?" Thalias echoed, frowning as she followed him. "Anything in particular you're looking for?"

"A connection between her people and the Watith," Thrawn said over his shoulder. Stepping up to the hibernation chamber, he pulled off the blanket Thalias had put there.

For a long minute he just gazed through the canopy at the sleeping Magys. Thalias stayed where she was, afraid to move lest she break his concentration.

Finally, he stirred. "No," he said, as if talking to himself. He put the blanket back and turned to Thalias. "I can see no connection."

"Did you expect one?" Thalias asked, stepping out of his way as he came back to the dayroom. "We're a long way from their world."

"Agreed," Thrawn said. "It was just a thought. Thank you for your time."

He started toward the exit. Thalias was quicker, stepping between him and the hatch. "Sorry, Senior Captain, but you can't just leave me with strange questions like that. Can't you at least tell me what's going on?"

"You're not one of my officers," Thrawn reminded her.

"No, but I'm responsible for the care of your sky-walker," she said. "Officer or not, that makes me one of the most important people on this ship. More than that—"

She hesitated, wondering if she should tell him. The Patriarch had told her all this in confidence, after all.

Still, he hadn't said it was to be kept a secret, at least not from Thrawn. More important, the better she could convince him she was part of his inner circle—whether or not including her had been his idea—the likelier it was that she could get information out of him instead of continually being kept in the dark. "More than that, when I was at the Mitth family homestead on Csilla a few months ago the Patriarch asked me to look after you."

Thrawn raised his eyebrows. "Did he, now," he said with a smile. "I was unaware I needed looking after."

"Everyone needs *some* looking after," Thalias said. "He mostly wanted me to run interference for you as best I could against your enemies."

"I assumed lasers, breachers, and plasma spheres were my primary tools against such people."

"You know what I mean," she said. "Your *political* enemies."

His smile faded. "Yes." He hesitated, then gestured her toward the couch. "Very well. I can tell you some of it. Not all."

Trying not to look too eager, Thalias settled herself on the couch. Thrawn took one of the chairs facing it, eyeing her as if trying to decide exactly how much she needed to know. "Interesting that you spoke of enemies," he said. "I believe the *Springhawk* is currently in the middle of a trap."

Thalias felt her eyes go wide. "I presume Mid Captain Samakro and the others are aware of that?" she asked, forcing her voice to stay calm.

Thrawn shrugged slightly. "They accept my word for it. I don't think all of them see it for themselves."

"What are they missing?"

"The battle between the Watith freighter and the three gunboats was staged," Thrawn said. "The attackers were making a great deal of noise and fury, but they were causing only superficial damage."

"Maybe they were trying to herd the freighter deeper into the gravity well," Thalias suggested.

"I also had that thought," he said. "That's why I watched the battle a few moments before answering Captain Fsir's call. Again, all four ships were creating an impressive show, but the gunboats' containment box wasn't nearly solid enough to keep an experienced captain trapped if he wanted to escape."

"I see," Thalias said, trying to think it through. Though if Fsir *wasn't* all that experienced . . .

"But that was only the first part," Thrawn said. "You saw how one of the gunboats—and *only* one—moved to attack us, as if they knew the Syndicure's prohibition against preemptive attacks and were offering us the necessary excuse to fight back."

"I wondered why you used such an odd reason for not helping him," Thalias said. "I don't think I'd ever heard that one."

"You hadn't heard it because I made it up," Thrawn said. "If the freighter had been in genuine danger, I expected Fsir to argue the point. But he didn't even mention it."

"Because they already had their plan, knew it would draw us in, and stuck with it," Thalias said, nodding.

"Exactly," Thrawn said. "But there's more. After the battle came Fsir's curious and convoluted reason for not giving us the Vagaari base coordinates. That suggests he wants to control the time and place of our arrival there. It brought to mind how the navigator on the Paccian refugee ship also controlled their arrival at Dioya."

"Yes," Thalias said, shivering at the memory of that incident. The navigator whom the refugees had hired had deliberately steered the ship into an ambush that had killed them all. "But if this is a trap, what are they waiting for? We've been sitting here for three days. Surely Fsir could have called them by now and brought them down on us." She frowned as a sudden thought struck her. "Unless they're far enough away that they're out of his comm range?"

"Unlikely." Thrawn again raised his eyebrows. "Tell me why."

Thalias puckered her lips. Another of his little teaching moments. Sometimes she enjoyed these challenges. But with mental images of enemy warships blazing at them out of hyperspace, this didn't seem like the time and place for such games.

She took a deep breath, trying to think it through. "He wouldn't be worried about the Vagaari if they were that far away?" she suggested. "Or maybe he wouldn't even know about them?"

"Perhaps," Thrawn said. "And?"

"There probably wouldn't be stragglers coming here from a base that far out?"

"Perhaps. And?"

Thalias scowled at him. What else could there be?

And then she had it. "There's something in the system they need for the battle," she said. "An orbiting weapons platform, or maybe a warship that can still fight but can't leave for some reason. Maybe with a damaged hyperdrive?"

"Or perhaps the warship is simply too undercrewed for some reason," Thrawn said. "Ironically enough, the Ascendancy itself has a precedent for such things: The warships of former Ruling Families can be used for local system defense but cannot be sent elsewhere except under special circumstances. Whatever the reason, though, I think you're right. Fsir intends to lure us into range of something large and powerful, and must wait until we're ready to oblige him."

"That doesn't sound good," Thalias said. "What are you going to do?"

"I'm going to see it through," Thrawn said, his voice dark. "If this was orchestrated by the Vagaari, we need to find them and deal a final, killing blow. If it was set up by a hitherto unknown threat, we need to assess their danger to the Ascendancy."

"Even if it's a trap?"

Thrawn smiled. "*Especially* if it's a trap," he said. "An enemy bold enough to stage a deliberate attack on a Chiss warship needs to be identified." He gave a small shrug. "That's the primary mission of the Expansionary Defense Fleet, after all."

"Yes," Thalias agreed reluctantly. "When?"

"Within the next two hours," Thrawn said, standing up. "We've gleaned as much information from our analysis as we're likely to get, and other conditions are also right. Time to move on to the next stage." He paused, eyeing her. "You will, of course, keep this conversation to yourself."

"Certainly," Thalias promised. "What other conditions are also right?"

"I mean *entirely* to yourself," Thrawn said, ignoring her question. "I don't want Che'ri worrying about what we may be heading into."

"I understand," Thalias said. She remembered all too well the effect that excessive worrying could have on Third Sight. A panicked sky-walker was the last thing the *Springhawk* needed. "I'll keep it private. What other conditions?"

"We'll be doing a jump-by-jump to match Fsir's route, but I'll want you and Che'ri on station in case we need to move quickly," Thrawn said. "Mid Captain Samakro will come get you when we're ready." With a final nod, he started across the dayroom.

"What about the body parts?" Thalias called after him as a belated thought occurred to her. "You said the analysis was complete. Was there Vagaari genetic material in the body parts?"

"Interesting you should ask," Thrawn said, pausing beside the hatch. "We found no body parts at all amid the wreckage."

Thalias frowned. "*None?*"

"None," Thrawn said. "That may mean nothing, of course. Explosions as violent as those that destroyed the gunboats scatter debris throughout a large volume of space. It could be that the bodies were thrown too far to be detected before we began our collection. We *did* find some genetic material, but the results were inconclusive."

"I see," Thalias said. "I just . . . I remember hearing stories that the Vagaari sometimes put captives in special pods on their warships' hulls to discourage counterattacks."

"Those weren't merely stories," Thrawn said grimly. "Are you thinking they may have done something similar here, with enslaved pilots' bodies wired with explosives in case of defeat so that their species couldn't be identified?"

"Something like that," Thalias said. A horrific idea, with an equally horrific mental image accompanying it.

"From what I saw of the Vagaari, that's certainly possible," Thrawn said. "All the more reason to let Fsir take us to the source of the perpetrators."

"So that we can destroy them?"

"So that we can," Thrawn said, "and so that we will."

"As you leave Celwis on your path to making Xodlak family history," Councilor Lakuviv's voice came over the *Midsummer*'s bridge speaker, "I wish to offer one final note of encouragement and admonition. For reasons of security, only your commanders know your true task, which they'll share with you when the time is right. But know with confidence that the end goal will be well worth all your efforts. From this moment forward your performance will either bring honor and glory to the family, or send it reeling into disaster."

Seated in her command chair, Lakinda felt anticipation tugging at her. She'd had a few doubts along the way, but Lakuviv's sheer enthusiasm, like Senior Aide Lakjiip's, was infectious. A Xodlak-owned nyix mine that could provide warship hulls to the fleet for years to come would certainly bring glory to the family.

And if there was any justice in the Syndicure, there would once again be Ten Ruling Families.

Taking possession of the mines should be easy enough, provided Lakuviv had been right about no other aliens knowing about the mines. If that assumption was wrong—if the Xodlak warships arrived to find other forces waiting for them—they would have to earn back their family's position the hard way.

But they would do it. They were Xodlak warriors, and their family was counting on them. They would win through.

"You'll be traveling jump-by-jump for the next few days, which I know can be wearying," Lakuviv continued. "But be assured that expert pilots and navigators have mapped out your route, and the path you've been given is the best and most efficient one available."

Lakinda nodded to herself. She'd received the route a few hours ago, and had run it past the *Midsummer*'s pilot, who'd most recently been third pilot on a destroyer. He'd confirmed that it seemed reasonable, and further promised to check it against local conditions at each of the task force's recalibration and repositioning stops. If he found a better route midway along their journey, they could always switch to that one.

She winced a little. The *pilot.* The *first officer,* the *second officer,* the other bridge officers. She'd been so busy getting the ship ready that she hadn't had a chance to memorize anyone's name or even their rank. With all the work yet to do in fine-tuning the ship's equipment, it was unlikely she could change that social deficiency before they reached their goal, either. Certainly not with her chronic bad memory for names.

Officially, that wasn't a problem. First, Second, Helm, Weapons, Comm—all such titles and descriptives were legitimate usage for a captain when requesting information or giving orders. But Admiral Ar'alani made it a point to know and use her officers' names, and ever since the *Grayshrike* was first attached to Ar'alani's task force Lakinda had made a point of emulating her superior's style.

"I emphasize one more time the vital secrecy required," Lakuviv continued. "There are those who may try to learn details of your mission, and others who may attempt to subvert it. I've therefore instructed your comm officers to ignore any and all transmissions except those originating from this office and carrying this protocol."

Lakinda sat up a little straighter. Neither Councilor Lakuviv nor Senior Aide Lakjiip had said anything about such complete comm silence.

In fact, she wasn't even sure such an order was legal. These might be Xodlak warships, but they were mostly crewed by Expansionary Defense Fleet officers and warriors. Standing orders specified that ships of the fleet were to be open to official communications at all times except under extraordinary situations.

Not replying to a transmission was one thing. Given the current situation, she had no problem with that. Refusing to even log incoming messages was something else entirely.

For that matter, the fact that Patriel Lakooni had never shown up to be part of the conversations or planning for this mission still lurked in the dark corners of her mind. Could something have happened to her? Illness, or some other emergency? It was strange and just a little ominous.

"Farewell, then, all of you," Lakuviv finished. "May the honor and dignity of the Xodlak family travel before you, behind you, and at your right and left." There was a soft tone, and the transmission ended.

"Comm sealed as ordered, Senior Captain," the comm officer called.

"Hyperdrive ready," the pilot added. "First vector locked in."

"And onward to glory we go," the first officer commented as he stepped to Lakinda's side, his voice colored with suppressed excitement. "Your force is ready, Senior Captain Lakinda."

"Acknowledged, First," Lakinda said, wincing again. The bridge officers had at least taken the time to learn *her* name. "Comm, inform the *Apogee* that it may jump to hyperspace when ready."

"Yes, ma'am," the comm officer said. Lakinda leaned forward, peering out the bridge viewport, watching as the cruiser flickered and vanished.

"*Apogee* has jumped," Sensors confirmed.

"Acknowledged," Lakinda said. "Helm, follow on my mark. Three, two, *one*."

The stars became star-flares became the hyperspace swirl. "On our way, Senior Captain," Helm said. "Vector looks good."

"Orders, ma'am?" the first officer asked.

"Have the engineering crew continue with their work, focusing especially on the computer upgrades," Lakinda told him. "I want reports every hour until everything is fully functional. Weapons, go down to secondary command and start running your crews through combat drills. Also hourly reports."

"Yes, Senior Captain," the weapons officer said. Unstrapping from his seat, he squeezed between the consoles and strode toward the hatch.

"Anything else, Senior Captain?" First asked.

Lakinda hesitated. "Yes," she said. "Comm, you'll alert me at once if there are any incoming transmissions."

"You mean transmissions from Councilor Lakuviv?" Comm asked.

"I mean *any* transmissions," Lakinda said. "You won't acknowledge or reply without further orders, but you *will* inform me when anything comes in."

Comm looked questioningly at First. First cleared his throat. "Those weren't our orders, ma'am," he said.

"I'm the commander on the scene," Lakinda reminded him. "I can adjust or even countermand orders where I see fit." She looked him in the eye. "Do I need to quote from the standing orders?"

First's lip twitched. "No, Senior Captain."

Lakinda turned back to the communications officer. "Comm?" she invited.

Comm didn't look at all happy. But his nod was firm enough. "Understood, ma'am," he said.

"Good." Lakinda settled back into her seat. "Helm: time to first repositioning stop?"

"Two hours, Senior Captain," the pilot reported. His voice sounded a little tense, but there was no hesitation in his reply. "After that, we'll be effectively out of the Ascendancy and the jumps will be shorter."

"Thank you." Lakinda looked up at her first officer. "In a mission like this, First, all information is important," she said, making sure her voice would be audible across the entire bridge. "Councilor Lakuviv said there might be efforts to subvert our mission. If there are, I want to know what they are, when they happen, and who's behind them."

"Understood, ma'am," First said, sounding calmer. "That seems reasonable." His eyes narrowed slightly. "I assume that you *will* be following Councilor Lakuviv's order not to reply to such transmissions?"

"I see no reason why not," Lakinda said. "Carry on, First."

"Yes, ma'am."

He moved away, pausing at each console along his path to check on the station's status. Lakinda watched him for a moment, then turned back to her chair's display and started her own run-through of the *Midsummer*'s flight and combat capabilities. If someone out in the Chaos wanted her mission to fail, they might well be willing to go beyond simply sending a few transmissions.

She had no intention of making it easy on them.

# CHAPTER TWENTY-ONE

On most of the *Springhawk*'s voyages, Thrawn had used Che'ri and her Third Sight to navigate through the Chaos. Traveling via jump-by-jump had only been utilized for the last leg or two, and then only when Che'ri needed rest. As a result, Thalias had never participated in a prolonged jump-by-jump trip.

It was, she quickly discovered, excruciatingly boring.

Jump to a system. Come out of hyperspace. Confirm position. Move through space-normal to the departure point necessary to line up for the next jump. Recheck possible hyperspace anomalies between points. Jump to the next point on the list, which was seldom more than five or six star systems away. Come out of hyperspace. Repeat.

And repeat, and repeat, and repeat.

There was really nothing anyone could do about it. They had to follow the Watith freighter in order to get to the Vagaari base, or whatever was at the end of this game, and since Fsir had no navigator that meant traveling jump-by-jump.

Unfortunately, the expected trap might not wait to the end, but could be sprung at any of the midpoints where the victim might be expected to be less alert. If that happened, Thrawn might decide on a quick exit and would need Che'ri ready and waiting.

At least Thrawn had set them up in secondary control, where procedure and etiquette were a bit looser than on the bridge. Here Che'ri could get up and stretch her legs during their periods in hyperspace without bothering anyone. Senior Commander Kharill, again in charge of secondary command, had even relaxed his usual stiffness enough to have a cot brought in and squeezed into the back where Che'ri could take a quick nap during the longer hyperspace legs if she needed one.

Thalias's biggest fear was that the whole journey would take longer than a few hours. If it stretched to the point where Che'ri needed a sleep period, the *Springhawk* would be flying at risk during the hours where their sky-walker wasn't available.

Unfortunately, they couldn't simply stop for those few hours, as Chiss warships sometimes did when their sky-walkers needed sleep. A delay like that would be hard to explain to Fsir, since a normal jump-by-jump could theoretically run for several days straight as long as there were enough pilots available to rotate the helm duty. Fsir would never believe the *Springhawk* didn't have enough personnel to handle a round-the-clock flight, and they couldn't afford to let him become suspicious.

Thrawn had told Thalias and Che'ri that his reading of Fsir's crew indicated only one of the twenty-three Watith aboard had any pilot training. Theoretically, that meant a journey longer than a day would also require Fsir to suspend their jump-by-jump so that his pilot could rest, which would then give Che'ri the sleep time she needed. But as the hours dragged on, and Fsir showed no signs of stopping, Thalias wondered if Thrawn had been wrong.

Fortunately, he hadn't. Ten hours after their departure, they reached the final leg of the journey.

"This is Senior Captain Thrawn," Thrawn's voice came from the secondary command room's bridge monitor. "Captain Fsir informs me that one final twelve-minute jump will take us to the Vagaari base. I consider it likely that we'll emerge into a combat situation. All officers and warriors stand ready." There was a click as the comm shifted from ship-wide mode to the private link between the bridge and secondary command. "Status, Senior Commander Kharill?"

"Secondary command is ready, Senior Captain," Kharill said. "Skywalker is in position."

"Acknowledged," Thrawn said. "Hopefully, we won't need her. Lieutenant Commander Brisch?"

"Yes, Senior Captain," the comm officer said. "Signal sent; confirmation received. All is ready, sir."

"Very good," Thrawn said. "Lieutenant Commander Azmordi, on my mark: Three, two, *one*."

The star-flares erupted, then settled into the hyperspace swirl.

Beside Thalias, Che'ri hunched her shoulders forward and settled her hands on the controls. Her profile looked tense, Thalias saw, her cheek muscles clenching and unclenching. At the station on Che'ri's other side, Laknym was sitting just as rigidly at his weapons console, his eyes narrowed in concentration. He seemed to sense Thalias's eyes on him, and turned his head. For a moment their eyes met.

And to her mild surprise Thalias realized that what she'd taken to be concern was instead a grimly eager anticipation.

Small wonder. The *Springhawk* was about to go into battle, likely a battle for its very life. This was Laknym's chance to prove himself in the eyes of Thrawn and Kharill, his chance to show that he was indeed worthy of continued fleet advancement. He flashed Thalias a smile, then returned his full attention to his board.

Thalias turned back to the bridge monitor, watching the chrono count down the time to arrival. She looked at Che'ri, who seemed slightly less tense now. The timer ran to zero—

With a flash of star-flares, the *Springhawk* emerged from hyperspace.

"Mid Commander Dalvu?" Thrawn prompted.

"Combat range clear," the sensor officer reported. "Mid-range . . . there they are, sir. Twenty fighters, gunboat size, drifting in ultrahigh planetary orbit. No power emanations detected. Far range . . . nothing else visible between us and the planet."

"Did we catch them sleeping?" Che'ri whispered.

"Not necessarily," Laknym said. "At this range, standby and complete shutdown look pretty much the same to passive sensors. They could be wide awake and just sitting back with their feet up, watching for trouble."

Thalias peered surreptitiously over her shoulder. Speaking of trouble, if Kharill caught the civilians talking . . .

But Kharill wasn't glaring at Thalias or looking ready to reprimand Laknym. His full attention was on the visual display, his eyes narrowed, his expression intense.

And in the middle of that concentration Thalias thought she could see a small smile.

"There," Dalvu said sharply. "There they go, sir."

Thalias looked back at the display. The silent, darkened gunboats were starting to come to life: running lights coming on, some of them drifting out of their orbits as thrusters ramped up, attitude positions changing as they turned one by one to face the incoming Chiss cruiser.

"They see us!" Fsir's panicked voice came over the speaker. "Senior Captain Thrawn, they *see* us!"

"So they do," Thrawn said. "Unfortunately for them, they have nowhere to go."

"Don't be a fool!" Fsir pleaded, his wheezing voice almost managing a screech. "If they send word to the base—there!" He gasped as two of the gunboats spun around and blasted off in the direction of the planet. "You must stop them!"

"There's no base back there, Captain Fsir," Thrawn said.

"Fool!" Fsir spat again, sounding even more frantic. "The base is an orbiting weapons platform—you can't see it because it's on the far side of the planet. But it's there, and it's horribly powerful and dangerous. If you don't stop those fighters before they can sound the alert, neither your people nor mine will ever see another moonrise."

Thalias felt a hard knot form in her stomach. Good tactical advice . . . except that the two fleeing gunboats were well to the rear of their companions. The only way for the *Springhawk* to get to them would be to first fight its way through the other eighteen. With all the gunboats now alert and fully powered up, even Thrawn couldn't handle odds like that.

And then, to her amazement, she heard a sound from behind her. A rumble that sounded suspiciously like a chuckle.

She turned. The small smile she'd seen on Kharill a minute ago had become a full-grown smirk.

Was he actually *glad* that Thrawn was facing impossible odds?

But that made no sense. Back when Thalias had first come aboard the *Springhawk,* Mid Captain Samakro had accused her of being a spy, and for a long time after that she'd sensed reluctance and even hostility toward Thrawn from some of the other officers. But surely by now they'd realized their commander knew what he was doing, and that they could trust him.

Especially since a failure on Thrawn's part here would take *all* their lives, including those of Kharill and any other naysayer.

The gunboats were spreading out from their orbital paths now, expanding outward toward the *Springhawk* like a blossoming flower. "Afpriuh, target the two closest gunboats," Thrawn said, his voice showing no signs of tension. "Lasers only. Kharill?"

"Yes, sir?" Kharill called.

"You'll be handling plasma spheres," Thrawn said. "I'll want a full spread, targeted on all but the leading two gunboats. They'll be moving and obscured when you fire, so Laknym will have to use his best judgment."

"Understood," Kharill said. The smile, Thalias noted, was still there. "Laknym?"

"Ready, sir," Laknym said confidently.

"Launch at my command," Thrawn said. "Afpriuh, lasers on my mark. Three, two, *one.*"

On the visual display, the *Springhawk*'s spectrum lasers flashed out, spraying light and vaporized metal from the two leading gunboats. Out of the corner of her eye, Thalias saw Laknym working feverishly at his board, his eyes flicking across the displays as he set up his targeting. The two gunboats under attack tried to dodge out of the way of Afpriuh's lasers, but they were still sluggish, and their hulls continued to boil away. They made one final attempt to dodge—

An instant later both of them exploded into roiling blasts of fire.

"Spheres: *Fire,*" Thrawn ordered.

Laknym's fingers jabbed into the launch controls. Thalias looked at the visual, then at the tactical, trying to see through the smoke and expanding clouds of debris. The view cleared as the dust and fragments spread out into the darkness.

Belatedly revealing to the gunboats the plasma spheres blazing toward them.

But the enemy had apparently anticipated the *Springhawk*'s attack. Even before the obscuring material thinned Thalias could see that the gunboats were on the move, angling away from the incoming spheres. Only two of them were caught by Laknym's spread, and those only with glancing blows that left them limping but still functional.

Thalias winced. Two gunboats destroyed. Two more partially disabled. Fourteen still alive, armed, and heading for the *Springhawk*.

"Did you see it, Mid Captain Samakro?" Thrawn asked.

"Yes, sir, I did," Samakro confirmed. "I suggest we finish it before they get in range."

"Agreed," Thrawn said. "Senior Commander Kharill, five more spheres, targeted on the Watith freighter."

Thalias frowned. On the *freighter*?

"Yes, sir," Kharill said. "Laknym?"

"Already set, Senior Commander," Laknym said.

"At my command," Thrawn said. "Brisch, give the word."

"Yes, sir," the comm officer said briskly. On the bridge monitor, Thalias saw him key a single switch . . .

And suddenly another warship flashed into view behind and above the gunboats. Thalias heard Che'ri gasp in surprise—

"This is Mid Captain Apros, commanding the Chiss Expansionary Defense Fleet warship *Grayshrike*," Apros said over the speaker. "Enemy gunboats, surrender or be destroyed."

"Launch spheres," Thrawn said quietly.

Again, Laknym's fingers tapped the controls. Thalias looked at the tactical.

To see the Watith freighter pitching up and away from the *Springhawk*, its thrusters abruptly blazing at full power, apparently and inexplicably making a run for it.

But it was too late. The freighter was barely into its turn when Laknym's plasma spheres slammed into it, impacting with brilliant splashes of released ionic energy. The thrusters abruptly failed, and the running lights went dark, and the entire vessel began drifting along its last vector.

"Watith freighter is down," Dalvu announced.

"So are the gunboats," Afpriuh said.

Thalias frowned at the tactical. He was right. Every one of the fighters had gone as silent and dark as the freighter, drifting in exactly the same way. Even the two that had been racing toward the planet seemed to be dead in space.

"You were right, Senior Captain," Samakro said, and on the bridge monitor Thalias saw him shaking his head. "I forthrightly admit I didn't believe it. But you were right."

"Thank you, Mid Captain," Thrawn said, tapping his comm key. "Boarding party: Go. Make sure all personnel are secured before you shut down their remote piloting systems."

Thalias blinked. Remote *piloting* systems?

"And the day may not yet be over," Thrawn continued. "*Grayshrike*, we were told there was a weapons platform currently in the planetary shadow. Did you have a view of that area while you were setting up your jump?"

"We did, Senior Captain," Apros said, "and you were misinformed. There's nothing at all in orbit over there, weapons platform or otherwise."

"Good," Thrawn said. "I expected that would be the case, but there was always a chance." He turned to Samakro. "In that case, Mid Captain, the day *is* over."

"Perhaps not, sir," Apros said before Samakro could reply. "There's a matter I urgently need to discuss with you. Request permission to come aboard."

"Of course, Mid Captain," Thrawn said. "At your convenience. Before you leave, I'd appreciate you instructing your officers to assist us in gathering up the gunboats. I want to examine as many as I can, and I don't want them drifting out of convenient reach."

"Understood, sir," Apros said. "The orders are given."

"Thank you," Thrawn said. "I'll await your arrival."

The comm keyed off. Listening with half an ear as Thrawn began giving orders to the *Springhawk*'s shuttle crews and tractor beam operators, Thalias gave Che'ri a smile. "And now," she said, "I think it's time we both got some sleep. Some *real* sleep."

"It's all over?" Che'ri asked, not sounding like she believed it.

"It's all over," Thalias said. She looked past the girl and raised her eyebrows at Laknym. "It is, right?"

"Yes," Laknym said, giving her a tight smile. Whatever he'd been hoping to prove today, he was clearly satisfied with the outcome.

"But I don't understand," Che'ri said as she started to unstrap. "Senior Commander Kharill? What happened out there?"

Thalias turned around. Kharill was busy with his questis. "Senior Commander?" she prompted.

He looked up long enough to scowl at her, then returned his attention to his questis. "Lieutenant Commander Laknym will fill you in," he said.

"Yes, sir." Laknym turned to Thalias. "We always expected this would be a trap. Well, Senior Captain Thrawn and the other senior officers did, anyway. From their analysis of our earlier battle, they suspected that the whole thing was staged and that the Watith were actually controlling the gunboats from the freighter."

"You mean like people playing a game?" Che'ri asked.

"Exactly," Laknym said. "When Senior Captain Thrawn visited the freighter, he counted twenty Watith who Fsir called passengers, plus what looked like twenty control consoles. When we arrived here and saw twenty gunboats waiting for us, it looked like he was right."

"Which was why there were no bodies or body parts on those other gunboats," Thalias murmured. *And*, she realized now, why Kharill had been smiling right there at the beginning. He'd seen that the gunboat count matched with Thrawn's, and realized his commander's analysis had been right.

"Right," Laknym said. "The clincher was when Senior Commander Afpriuh blew up two of the gunboats and put a debris cloud in front of the others. You saw me launch my spheres; but you also saw that the gunboats were moving to evade them before they could possibly see them coming."

"Because the operators were on the freighter," Thalias said, nodding, "and they *could* see the spheres."

"Exactly," Laknym said. "We'd already made contact with the *Grayshrike* before we left the last system—I guess it had been sent out to assist us and was following the search pattern Senior Captain Thrawn had sent Csilla—and Senior Captain Thrawn had them shadow us here. Once we knew the freighter was controlling the gunboats, he brought them in to keep Fsir distracted while our spheres disabled it."

"And they were trying to get away," Che'ri said eagerly. "I saw them trying to get away."

"Yes, they were," Laknym agreed, smiling at the girl. "Which all by itself would have shown they were part of the trap."

"I see," Thalias said. "Thank you, Lieutenant Commander. We'll get out of your way now. Come on, Che'ri."

"We get to sleep now?" Che'ri asked as she unstrapped from her seat.

"Yes," Thalias said. "Unless you want some dinner first."

"I don't know," Che'ri said, her forehead wrinkling with concentration.

"When *will* you know?"

Che'ri stood up and stretched. "When I know what you're thinking about making."

"Another small town coming up," Senior Warrior Yopring's voice came over the *Vigilant*'s bridge speaker. As usual, the words were hard to understand through the roar of the airflow buffeting the shuttle as it flew across the planetary surface far below. "Or it could be another industrial complex."

"Great," Wutroow muttered from Ar'alani's side. "One more of either and we'll have completed yet another double zigzig card."

"Acknowledged," Ar'alani said, ignoring the comment. "Might as well take a closer look."

"Yes, ma'am."

Ar'alani gazed out the viewport, stifling a yawn. Not that she didn't sympathize with Wutroow's boredom. They'd spent the past two weeks running a search pattern of the area the Magys had suggested was the one the alien Battle Dreadnought had been guarding. So far they'd turned up four decent-sized cities, three of them in ruins and the fourth mostly so; twenty-two industrial centers with roughly the same percent of destruction; five mines, all of them apparently deserted; and any number of small towns, villages, and farming homesteads.

The good news was that, despite the widespread devastation across Sunrise, there were definitely survivors. The search party had spotted only dribs and drabs, mostly people working the fields who weren't able to get under cover fast enough. But the shuttle's heat sensors had painted a different picture, a view of a society slowly but definitely coming back from the carnage. Much of it was underground or otherwise hidden—not unlike Csilla itself, Ar'alani noted—but it was coming back nonetheless.

If all the Magys cared about was that there were indeed survivors, that ought to be enough evidence to convince her to bring her refugees back to Sunrise. But if there were other criteria—quality of life, probability of long-term survival, or some critical numerical threshold she was looking for—she might still decide to go with the death-by-Beyond choice.

But at least now Ar'alani had data with which to argue the point.

"My mistake, Admiral," Yopring corrected. "It's not a town, but a mine, nestled up against the side of the mountains."

"Anything moving?" Ar'alani asked.

"This one . . . actually, yes," Yopring said. "In fact . . . whoa. It's active, all right. There are dozens of workers down there. Maybe even hundreds."

"Well, *that's* a good marker of civilization," Wutroow commented.

"Most people don't waste effort running mines until everyone's got food and shelter."

"If that's the case, this place must be swimming in borjory sauce," Yopring said. "I see people, some long buildings—probably communal barracks—tracks for mine carts, a landing area big enough for— *damn!*"

"What is it?" Ar'alani demanded. Silence. "Biclian?" she snapped.

"On it, Admiral," the sensor officer said, peering at his displays. Out of the corner of her eye, Ar'alani saw Wutroow leave her spot beside the command chair and hurry toward the currently uncrewed weapons console. "Tracking two skycars south of Yopring's position—"

"Sorry, ma'am." Yopring's voice came back, sounding a little breathless. "I was just startled, that's all. Two skycars popped up out of nowhere, and I had to dodge to get around them—"

"Watch it—they're on your tail," Biclian warned.

"Four more coming in from the north and west," Wutroow added, sliding into the weapons seat. "Looks like they're trying to cut you off."

"I'll take your word for it," Yopring said. "I don't see them yet."

"You will in about a minute," Wutroow said, keying the overhead view up onto the tactical. "Admiral?"

"I'm on it," Ar'alani said, frowning at the display. The two skycars from the south had forced the Chiss shuttle away from the mine and now appeared to be trying to drive it toward the other four.

"Offhand, I'd say the miners don't like company," Yopring said calmly. "Orders, Admiral?"

"Hold your course," Ar'alani said. "Let them think they're winning. Biclian, pull up the shuttle's telemetry, see if the skycars look space-capable."

"They're certainly big enough to be," Biclian said. "They're also heavily armored. And I'm pretty sure I see a pair of lasers racked under the altitude stubs."

Ar'alani grimaced. Armored *and* armed. Terrific.

And with the whole depth of Sunrise's atmosphere between the skycars and the *Vigilant,* she doubted even her spectrum lasers could punch through that much air with enough left over to take out armored skycraft. Certainly not fast enough to keep them from nailing Yopring first.

They would just have to try something else.

"All right, Yopring, here's what you do," she said, pulling up a copy of the tactical on her questis and tapping a spot. "Hold course to the point I've marked. Wutroow, when he arrives, you'll fire a full-bore laser salvo into *these* two spots." She tapped two more marks. "You think you can hit them simultaneously?"

"No problem, ma'am," Wutroow said. "Ah. Nice."

"Yopring?" Ar'alani asked.

"Got it, ma'am," he said. "Up?"

Ar'alani looked at the racing skycars. If they were combat-trained, and quick enough . . . "No," she said. Behind her, the bridge hatch slid open and Oeskym hurried in, making for the weapons console. Ar'alani caught his eye and waved him back. Wutroow was already in position, and there was no time for them to swap out. "Not up, but down and sideways. *Then* up, but only when you judge it to be safe. Ready?"

"Ready, ma'am."

"Wutroow?"

"Ready, ma'am."

"Stand by." Ar'alani watched the tactical, focusing on the shuttle and counting down the seconds . . . "Three, two, *one*."

And as Yopring reached the spot between the two converging rivers that Ar'alani had marked, the *Vigilant*'s lasers flashed out, burning through and roiling the atmosphere as they blazed into the flowing water on both sides of the shuttle.

The sudden energy discharge sent massive clouds of steam and condensing water vapor billowing into the air. Ar'alani held her breath . . .

Whoever was commanding the skycars was indeed trained and quick. The obscuring clouds were the perfect opportunity for the intruder to claw for the safety of the sky, as Yopring himself had suggested as his next move. Even as the *Vigilant* continued firing into the water, all six skycars pitched sharply upward in an attempt to intercept the shuttle's presumed escape vector and take him down.

But Yopring wasn't there. Instead, as per Ar'alani's order, he'd dropped the shuttle to treetop level, spun a hard ninety-degree yaw turn to his left, and raced off across the landscape.

He was a good three kilometers away before the skycars reached the top of the cloud and realized he'd slipped their encirclement. By the time they were dropping back toward the ground Yopring was on the ascent, driving toward space as fast as the shuttle's thrusters could take him.

For a moment Ar'alani thought the skycars would continue the chase. But they made only a halfhearted attempt at a fresh pursuit before breaking off. The shuttle was now too far away for a quick catch, and the higher they went into the thinning atmosphere the better the chance that the *Vigilant*'s lasers could take them with a single shot each. They would have to be content with chasing the intruder away.

In that, at least, they'd succeeded. The *Vigilant* didn't have the ground-force capability to go back down with enough warriors and firepower to challenge the mining complex's security. Whatever was down there would have to wait until another day.

"Nicely done, Admiral," Wutroow said as she handed the weapons station back to Oeskym. "What now?"

"We got what we came for, Senior Captain," Ar'alani told her. "We know there are survivors, lots of them, and that the society is starting to grow back from the ashes."

"Yes, ma'am," Wutroow said. "*And* that there's something down there someone is *very* interested in keeping to themselves. I assume we're not going to let them?"

"If that someone is one of the native inhabitants, the Ascendancy will have no say in the matter," Ar'alani reminded her.

"If they're not?"

Ar'alani looked back at the tactical, watching the skycars heading back to their lairs. Skycars whose design was radically different from any of the hundreds of wrecked air vehicles the shuttle's survey runs had recorded. Skycars whose guardian Battle Dreadnought had done its best to destroy the *Vigilant* and two Chiss heavy cruisers.

"If they're not, we'll find a way to make them sorry they came here," she told Wutroow softly. "*Very* sorry."

# CHAPTER TWENTY-TWO

"I find this extremely unsettling," Thrawn said, pinning a clearly uncomfortable Mid Captain Apros to his conference room chair with a hard-edged glare. "What kind of family emergency could make Senior Captain Lakinda leave her post?"

"I don't know, sir," Apros said. His eyes shifted away from Thrawn's gaze to Samakro, as if hoping to find support or at least sympathy.

Samakro kept his face expressionless. If that was what Apros wanted, he was out of luck. Family and family politics be damned—as far as Samakro was concerned, abandoning a command post was unthinkable.

And for Apros to have stood by and let her go without trying to stop her was equally unthinkable.

"Did she give you any hints?" Thrawn asked.

"No, sir," Apros said, reluctantly bringing his eyes back to the senior captain. "I'm not sure she even knew at that point. The message said the Xodlak family members were to assemble at Celwis. If it said any more, she didn't share it with me."

"Did you at least try to talk her out of it?" Samakro demanded.

"I talked as hard as I could for the three minutes she allowed me," Apros shot back. He didn't dare show anger to a superior officer like Thrawn, but he apparently figured another mid captain like Samakro was fair game. "She and Lakwurn were gone before I could do anything else."

"Lakwurn?" Thrawn asked.

"Hyperdrive specialist," Apros said. "He got the same message Senior Captain Lakinda did."

"So the Xodlak aren't merely seeking command officers," Thrawn said, his tone turning thoughtful. "They want *all* military personnel."

"So it would seem," Apros said. "I did some checking along the way. The Xodlak warships at Celwis consist of two partially crewed light cruisers on an orbital defense station and an uncrewed reserve frigate."

"What are they doing, setting up for a battle?" Samakro asked, frowning.

"That's what I'm afraid of," Apros said grimly. "Because during one of our sky-walker breaks on our way to meet you we got another set of transmissions, two of them in family codes. Our weapons officer, Senior Commander Erighal'ok'sumf, subsequently informed me that he and the other two Erighal aboard had received family emergency summons of their own."

"Did you let *them* go, too?" Samakro growled.

"Of course not," Apros said stiffly. "Nor did Ghaloksu ask. We were engaged in an imminent threat situation, which rendered the summons void. But given Senior Captain Lakinda's abrupt departure, he thought I should know about it."

"Were the Erighal also supposed to rendezvous at Celwis?" Thrawn asked.

"No, at Copero," Apros said. "But it gets stranger. After Ghaloksu came to me, I made some inquiries and discovered that the Pommrio had also sent out an emergency summons."

Samakro felt his eyes narrow. *Three* of them?

"They were to assemble at Sarvchi," Apros continued. He gave a small, helpless-looking shrug. "I don't know what it all means, sir. But I don't like it."

"Nor should you," Thrawn said, his eyes narrowed slightly. "Celwis, Copero, Sarvchi. All systems at the Ascendancy's east and southeast sectors. Tell me, Mid Captain, was there any indication that Csilla or Naporar had been alerted?"

"There were no transmissions to me or to the *Grayshrike* proper,"

Apros said. "And as I mentioned, the others came in under family encryptions. Whatever's going on, it seems to only involve those three families."

"Unless there are others not represented among your officers and warriors," Thrawn pointed out. "Without access to those encryptions, you wouldn't know of those summons."

Apros's lip twitched. "Yes, sir. That's true."

"Regardless, the lack of any official alerts indicates that the Ascendancy as a whole isn't facing a threat," Thrawn continued. "That would seem to rule out an invasion or any kind of widespread natural disaster." He turned to Samakro. "Mid Commander Samakro. Thoughts?"

"I don't know, sir," Samakro admitted. "I note that all three families are of the Forty, which might imply some sort of joint operation. Perhaps a salvage or rescue mission."

"If they're just looking for people to crew their ships, I would assume they would exclude combat command officers from the summons," Thrawn said. "For that matter, why call on the fleet at all? Surely there are enough family members in the merchant services to handle a nonmilitary situation."

"Could it have something to do with your mission?" Apros asked. "We're currently to the southeast-nadir of the Ascendancy. Could the families have heard something about the Vagaari, maybe not solid enough to call in the Defense Force, but solid enough to warrant extra security for those three systems?"

"Security in the form of antiquated ships?" Samakro scoffed. "Anyway, as Senior Captain Thrawn pointed out, in that case why *not* call the Defense Force? Planetary security is what they're there for."

"Plus the Vagaari rumors appear to be unfounded," Thrawn said. "I've spoken to Captain Fsir, and he claims he was merely hired to engage the *Springhawk* in battle."

Samakro frowned. He'd known Thrawn had had a brief conversation with Fsir, but he'd been so busy monitoring the collection of the wayward gunboats that he hadn't had a chance to learn the results of that interrogation. "But not hired by the Vagaari?"

"Apparently not," Thrawn said. "Nor was he hired by the Paataatus, if that was your next question. He claims he was contacted by an unknown alien, given the region we would likely be searching, and told to destroy us or, if that wasn't possible, to at least keep us occupied. Since then he has been moving between the likely systems, hoping he would hit one at the same time we did."

Samakro nodded. And once he'd made contact, he could lure them into the trap he'd already set up with the rest of his gunboats.

It was just his bad luck that his target had been Thrawn and the *Springhawk*. "Did he describe this seriously overconfident alien?" he asked.

"Only that he was robed and hooded with a veil obscuring his face," Thrawn said, picking up his questis. "A more complete interrogation will have to wait until we can return to Csilla. Mid Captain Apros, how many of those gunboats do you think you can carry, either towed or anchored to the *Grayshrike*'s hull?"

"I thought you were going to examine them here," Apros said, frowning.

"There's no time," Thrawn said. "Whatever's happening in the Ascendancy's southeast sectors, we need to identify it and see if we're needed to help resolve it."

"It doesn't sound like the Expansionary Defense Fleet was invited," Samakro pointed out.

"Do you care?" Thrawn asked.

Samakro looked at Apros. Command officers abandoning their ships . . . "Not really."

"Neither do I," Thrawn said. "Mid Captain Apros?"

"I'm not sure," Apros said, his forehead wrinkling in concentration. "Probably eight or nine."

"Make it nine," Thrawn said. "Mid Captain Samakro?"

"Assuming you also want to bring the freighter, we should be able to handle it plus five gunboats."

"I agree," Thrawn said. "We'll leave the pair still heading for the planet and the two that Lieutenant Commander Laknym hit with his plasma spheres. That gives us fourteen in good shape. Mid Captain

Apros, you'll return to the *Grayshrike* at once to oversee your part of the anchoring operation and to prepare your ship for departure."

"Yes, sir," Apros said, tapping on his questis. Samakro beat him to the punch, getting his own order logged before Apros finished with his. "Orders logged and my people on it." A brief and slightly pained expression flickered across Apros's face. "One more thing, Senior Captain, if I may." He dug into a pocket and pulled out a small, cloth-wrapped item, which he set on the table in front of Thrawn. "I was asked to give you this, sir."

"What is it?" Samakro asked, craning his neck as Thrawn unwrapped it.

"A piece of jewelry," Thrawn said, sounding bemused. He held it up, and Samakro saw that it was a delicate brooch made of interlocked metal threads.

"There's a note with it," Apros said, pointing to the data cylinder nestled against the side of the brooch. "My apologies, sir—with everything that's happened today I almost forgot. It was given to a Xodlak rancher, sent to another family member on Naporar, then on to Senior Captain Lakinda."

"Who entrusted it to you," Thrawn said, setting down the brooch and slipping the cylinder into his questis.

"The rancher obtained it from an alien group called the Agbui. Apparently, it's stirred up a great deal of official interest." He looked at Samakro. "On Celwis."

Samakro felt his eyes narrow. The planet where Xodlak officers and warriors were currently flocking. "Enough interest to warrant an emergency summons?" he asked.

"If not, we're looking at a remarkable coincidence," Thrawn agreed. "Thank you, Mid Captain Apros. Return to your ship and do all you can to expedite our departure."

"Yes, sir," Apros said, standing up. "I'm sorry I couldn't be more helpful." Nodding to Thrawn, then to Samakro, he left the conference room.

"I wish he could have been more helpful, too, sir," Samakro said, scowling at the brooch. "A bit of jewelry isn't much to go on."

"Perhaps more than he realizes," Thrawn said. "We know now that three families are involved—perhaps more, but three at least. We know all three are from the Forty Great Families."

"And that all of them are allied to different Ruling Families," Samakro added.

Thrawn's forehead creased briefly. "I was unaware of that."

"Yes, sir," Samakro said, wincing. Once again, Thrawn's ignorance of political realities was peeking through. "The Xodlak are allied with the Irizi, the Pommrio are supporters of the Plikh, and the Erighal are with the Dasklo." He nodded toward the brooch. "I assume we're going to start with Celwis?"

For a moment Thrawn didn't answer, but gazed in silence at the brooch. He turned it over in his hands, his fingers tracing the intricate pattern. "No, I think we'll start somewhere closer to home," he told Samakro, standing up. "Come with me, Mid Captain. I have a thought."

Che'ri had decided that she was too tired to eat a full meal, but too hungry to take a nap. They compromised, with Thalias making her a snack to ease her rumbling stomach and then packing her off to bed.

Thalias was finishing up her own snack and mentally tucking herself into her own bed when the door signaled a visitor.

"Good day, Caregiver," Thrawn said, nodding to her. "My apologies for the intrusion."

"No problem, Senior Captain," Thalias said, stepping back and letting him and Samakro come in. The first officer looked puzzled, she noted, while Thrawn looked unusually grim. "Has something happened?"

"I assume Sky-walker Che'ri is asleep?" Thrawn asked, looking at the closed hatch to the girl's sleeping room.

"She went down about ten minutes ago, so probably," Thalias said. The last time he'd come here and asked about privacy—"Is this about my—uh—other roommate?"

"Yes," Thrawn said, crossing toward Thalias's room. "This time, I also need to talk to her."

"Of course," Thalias said automatically. To *talk* to her? She glanced again at the growing understanding and uneasiness on Samakro's face, then hurried to catch up with Thrawn.

He'd removed the blanket from the hibernation chamber and was studying the control panel when she and Samakro entered. "Do you know how to operate that, sir?" Samakro asked.

"The procedure is quite straightforward," Thrawn said. Lifting a protective cover, he pressed the button beneath it. "This may take a few minutes," he added. "Perhaps you'd prefer to wait in the day-room, Caregiver?"

"I'm fine," Thalias said, wincing as the indicator lights began running a slow sequence. "May I ask what this is about?"

"I want her to look at this." Thrawn showed her a rather beautiful brooch made of metal wires. "I want to know if she recognizes the design."

"I thought Apros said it came from aliens called the Agbui," Samakro said.

"So he did," Thrawn said. "But look at the Magys's clothing. You can see for yourself the style similarities between the pattern and the brooch."

Samakro peered through the canopy, then looked questioningly at Thalias. She shook her head and gave him a small shrug. Whatever Thrawn was seeing, it wasn't obvious to her, either. "Are you saying the Agbui are some of the Magys's people?" she asked.

"Not at all," Thrawn said. "The note included pictures, and the two species are quite different." He looked at her. "Let me tell you about the conversation we've just had with Mid Captain Apros."

By the time he'd finished the tale of family emergencies, aliens with fancy jewelry, and attempts to destroy the *Springhawk,* the hibernation chamber had finished its cycle and the Magys was awake.

And she was not happy.

"How do you do this to me?" she demanded, stumbling over the Taarja words as she struggled into a sitting position in the chamber. "How dare you deny me the right and weight of leadership? Do you betray me and my people with no guilt or consequence?"

"Would *you* betray your people for no reason?" Thrawn countered. "Or are guilt and consequence only for others?"

"I do not betray," the Magys shot back. "My people are gone. I and my remnant have no right of lingering survival."

"We don't yet have proof of that," Thrawn said. "At any rate, that is a question and a decision for another day. For the moment, I need you to look at—"

"The decision is *now*," the Magys spat. "You wish to seclude me from my remnant? You seek to make them wait in vain for my word and my decision?" She drew herself up. "So be it. I lay down my leadership. They may touch the Beyond in their own stead and time, as I myself will now do."

Thalias tensed. The Magys's companion, she remembered, had killed himself at her order, without the use of any obvious weapon. If she could do the same thing—"What if your people *aren't* gone?" she spoke up.

"You speak words of which you know nothing," the Magys bit out.

"And you do?" Thalias retorted. "You saw your world from space. From *space*. You have no way of knowing what's really going on down there."

"If I do not know, neither do you."

"Or maybe I do," Thalias said, her heart pounding. She was taking a horrible risk here, and there was no way of knowing whether pushing the Magys would do anything except hasten her death. But she had to try *something*. "What if your people are even now rebuilding their homes and their cities? What if they're growing food and putting your civilization back together? What if your remnant, far from following the rest of your people into death, would in fact be *leading* them there?"

"You know nothing about it," the Magys insisted.

"Don't I?" Thalias demanded. "Do people look for luxury when they're starving? Do they build amusement centers when they have no homes? Do they make *these*—" She plucked the brooch from Thrawn's hand and slapped it into the Magys's. "—when they don't even have basic clothing?"

The Magys's eyes widened as she stared at the brooch. "Where did you get this?"

"Where do you think?" Thalias countered, watching her closely.

"From my world," the Magys whispered, her anger and frustration suddenly gone. "My world."

"Then you *do* recognize it?" Thrawn asked.

"Of course," the Magys said, her voice almost reverent. "It is the style of the Southern Mountain artisans. Only they can create such beauty from wires of metal. I feared they were dead with all others." She looked up at Thalias. "But surely this cannot be new. Surely it was found abandoned in the rubble of destruction."

"Of course it's new," Thalias said. "Do you see any stains of age or war on it?"

The Magys again lowered her eyes to the brooch. Opened her mouth, closed it again. "What will you do now?" she asked.

"The question is, what will *you* do," Thrawn countered.

"The warships we saw," she said, still gazing at the brooch. "They were not settlers."

"No," Thrawn said. "They were invaders."

"Trying to take your world from your people," Thalias added. "Are you going to let them?"

The Magys rubbed her thumbs gently over the brooch. "When all are gone, we have no future but to touch the Beyond," she said. "But when our people are invaded and enslaved—"

She looked up at Thrawn, and Thalias saw a new set to her jaws. "You must take me to my people."

"I will," Thrawn said. "But not immediately. I'm afraid you'll have to sleep a little longer."

"No," the Magys insisted. "I have slept enough. My people need me."

"Which is precisely why you must return to your sleep," Thrawn said. "No one outside this room knows you are still aboard, and we must keep them from finding out."

"Why?"

"Because if you're seen, my superiors will call me back home,"

Thrawn said. "They will place you in confinement for study and begin an investigation of my actions which will delay your return."

"What if I stay in here?" the Magys countered, waving a slightly shaky arm around the room. "No one will see me here."

"They may," Thrawn said. "Others come in at times to perform maintenance and resupply. We cannot take the risk."

"I do not wish—"

Abruptly she broke off, and Thalias saw a subtle shift in her expression. Her eyes flicked to the side, then back to Thrawn. A flick of her eyes to Thalias . . .

"Very well," the alien said, her voice also subtly changed. "If you insist, I will sleep." She looked again at Thalias. "You will stay with me?"

"I will," Thalias promised. "As much as I can."

"Very well," the Magys said again. She looked at the brooch still clutched in her hand. "You will want this back," she added, offering it toward Thalias.

"Perhaps you'd like to hold on to it?" Thalias asked.

"I cannot ask it," the Magys said.

"But I may offer it," Thrawn said. "Lie down now, please. When you next wake, it will be to the sight of your people."

The alien nodded, turning her eyes to Thalias. "Thank you," she said, and laid back down. Thrawn closed the canopy, and again keyed the chamber. A minute later, the alien was back in hibernation.

Under the circumstances, Thalias knew, she'd better get in the first word. "My apologies, Senior Captain," she said. "My behavior over the past few minutes has been severely disrespectful."

"But equally productive," Thrawn said. To Thalias's relief, there didn't seem to be any anger or even annoyance in his voice. "Certainly you should know by now I consider results far more valuable than etiquette. Mid Captain Samakro? Thoughts?"

"Only that the whole thing seems bizarre," Samakro said. "Why in the world are these Agbui stealing jewelry from the Magys's people and passing it off as their own? What does that gain them?"

"I don't know," Thrawn said, starting for the hatch. "Let's find out."

"How?" Thalias asked.

"By asking the one person we can hope will have the answers," Thrawn said. "Thank you for your help, Caregiver. Rest well."

A minute later he and Samakro were gone, the suite's hatch closed behind them. Thalias returned to her sleeping room, replaced the blanket over the hibernation chamber, and lay down on her bed.

And tried to figure out what exactly had just happened.

The Magys didn't want to go back to sleep. That much was abundantly clear. Thrawn had presented good arguments for why it needed to be, warnings that Thalias had no doubt were legitimate. But the Magys had still been ready to argue the point.

And then, without warning, she'd given in.

So what had changed?

It was only as Thalias was finally falling asleep that she remembered the sideways look the Magys had made, the glance that had seemed to end her arguments and resistance.

The look she'd sent across the suite . . . in Che'ri's direction.

# CHAPTER TWENTY-THREE

Lakinda was sound asleep in her cabin when the comm chimed. Blinking her eyes open, she fumbled for the switch. "Lakinda," she said.

"Comm here, Senior Captain," the second comm officer's voice came hesitantly from the speaker.

Lakinda felt a twinge of embarrassment. The primary bridge officers had quickly realized she didn't have their names down, and had switched to identifying themselves only by their position descriptives. Clearly, the word had passed to the officers of the other two watches, as well.

So now *everyone* knew their captain was an idler with a bad memory for names. Terrific. "Yes?"

"You asked to be informed immediately when a transmission came through," the officer reminded her, sounding even more hesitant. "I didn't see an exception logged for if you were asleep."

"No, there wasn't," Lakinda said. Though she probably should have put one in. Every time the *Midsummer* stopped for a repositioning there was a message or two waiting for it. Most were from the Expansionary Defense Fleet headquarters on Naporar, but there'd also been a couple of general notices from the Defense Force command on Csilla, along with two private notices wrapped in some family's private encryption. At this point, given their distance, everything was being pumped through the triad on Colonial Station Chaf, though how long that would last she didn't know. "What do we have?"

"It's not from Naporar this time," Comm said. "It's a signal from Mid Captain Csap'ro'strob aboard the *Grayshrike*."

Lakinda sat up in her bed, the haze of sleep vanishing. *Apros* was calling her? "Put him through," she ordered.

"Ah . . . may I remind the senior captain that contact with anyone except Councilor Lakuviv's office has been forbidden?"

"So noted," Lakinda said, putting some ice into her voice. Apros knew she'd been called to a family emergency. He wouldn't be trying to reach her unless his ship—*her* ship—was in serious danger. "Put him through."

There was a moment of silence. Then—

"This is Mid Captain Csap'ro'strob aboard the Expansionary Defense Fleet warship *Grayshrike*," Apros said. "I urgently need to speak with Senior Captain Xodlak'in'daro, current location unknown. Repeating—"

Lakinda tapped the mike key. "This is Lakinda," she said. "Go ahead, *Grayshrike*."

"—aboard the Expan—" the voice broke off as the recorded loop was deactivated. "Senior Captain, this is Mid Captain Apros. Can you please boost your signal? We're a bit far apart."

"One moment." Lakinda keyed for more power. "What's the matter? Why are you calling me?"

"We need information, ma'am," Apros said. "We also have information—vital information—that you may need."

"*We* meaning the *Grayshrike*?"

"*We* meaning myself and Senior Captain Thrawn," Apros said.

"We need to know where you're going and the nature of your mission," Thrawn's voice came in.

"That's confidential," Lakinda said shortly. So her ship *wasn't* in danger? "It's family business," she added, reaching for the mike switch. "I'm sorry, but I can't—"

"Were you aware that two other families have also called emergencies?" Thrawn interrupted. "And that all three of your family assembly points are in the Ascendancy's south and southeast sectors?"

Lakinda paused, her finger hovering over the key. "Which families?"

"The Erighal and Pommrio," Apros said. "I'm guessing you *didn't* know that?"

"No," Lakinda said, her stomach tightening. Those two encrypted family transmissions . . . and of course, there were no Erighal or Pommrio aboard the *Midsummer* to receive and decrypt them. Had those been the same general summons she'd answered from the Xodlak? "Do you know what they're up to?"

"No, but the fact that everyone's assembling in the same region strongly suggests a connection," Apros said.

"Yes, it does," Lakinda had to concede. Could word of the Agbui mine have leaked out somehow? Were those other two families trying to get there before the Xodlak force? "I'm sorry, but I can't say anything more," she said, again reaching for the mike key. First thing to do would be to boost her task force's speed, perhaps shaving the safety margins of hyperspace travel a little—

"One more question, Senior Captain," Apros said. "Does your mission have anything to do with alien jewelry?"

Lakinda froze. What the *hell*? "What alien jewelry?"

"Jewelry that a species called the Agbui have been handing out on Celwis," Apros said. "They claim they're the ones who created it, but they aren't. It comes from Sunrise, the world of the Magys and her refugees."

Lakinda's chest suddenly went tight. "Is it just the jewelry?" she asked carefully. "Or does the metal also come from there?"

"I . . . don't know," Apros said, sounding a little confused. "I assume it's made with local materials, but I don't know for sure. Is that important?"

"Vitally important." Lakinda braced herself. "The Agbui claim to have a mine on an uninhabited world. We're on our way to claim it and the planet for the Xodlak. I'm guessing the Erighal and Pommrio have the same goal in mind."

"Really?" Apros said. "That seems a little odd."

"Not at all," Lakinda said between clenched teeth. "One of the metals in the weave is nyix."

She'd expected Apros and Thrawn to go silent at that one. She was right.

"Not just nyix, but nyix that's apparently abundant enough to be wasted in fancy jewelry," she continued. "What the *hell* is going on?"

"They're scamming you," Thrawn said. "You and the other families. They're mining nyix from Sunrise—"

"Having possibly incited a civil war there in order to gain better access," Apros put in.

"In retrospect, I'd say that's almost a certainty," Thrawn agreed darkly. "They then created the illusion they were mining the metal from an entirely different world."

"Complete with a mine, miners, and refining facilities," Lakinda said, remembering Lakjiip's assurance that she'd personally seen the place. "Building up a lure so enticing that the entire Xodlak family jumped at it."

"What I don't understand is what they hope to get out of it," Apros said. "Have you paid them for this so-called mining world?"

"They don't want money," Lakinda said. The whole, horrible thing suddenly made sense. "They're getting exactly what they want. Three of the Forty Great Families are preparing to fight to the death to own a worthless piece of rock."

"And each of the three is allied to one of the Ruling Families," Apros said grimly. "They're trying to start a civil war."

"And they're damn well likely to succeed," Lakinda said bitterly. "I don't know about the other families, but I have a frigate and a light cruiser. Even with thrown-together crews, that represents a *lot* of firepower."

"I suspect the other families have only patrol ships," Thrawn said. "But depending on how far their leaders were willing to strip away their planetary defenses, they could bring a fairly comparable number of lasers to the scene."

"Yes," Lakinda agreed. "But how did they pull it off? As far as I know, the Agbui never left Celwis."

"Maybe *that* group didn't," Apros said. "But it's starting to look like they had other groups scattered around the Ascendancy spinning their own little poison webs."

"I agree," Thrawn said. "A coordinated operation, exquisitely planned and timed."

"Never mind the artistic beauty of it all," Lakinda snarled. "We need to send a warning to Csilla right away."

"We're already too far out for a clear signal," Apros said. "Besides, it's too late for them to send anyone to stop it."

"Mid Captain Apros is right," Thrawn said. "However, there may be something the three of us can do. Senior Captain Lakinda, how much do your officers and warriors know about your mission?"

"Nothing, really," Lakinda said. "Certainly not the end goal. I don't give them those details until we reach the planet."

"Good," Thrawn said. "At least that buys us some time. Here's what I have in mind."

Lakinda and Apros listened in silence while he laid out his plan. It was, to Lakinda's mind, about as crazy a scheme as she'd ever heard.

But it might work. And at the moment, she didn't have anything better to offer.

"Understood," she said when he'd finished. "We'll go with that for now. But I reserve the right to revisit it if we come up with something better by the time we arrive."

"I'm open to suggestions," Thrawn said. "Assuming there's time to reconfigure for an altered plan."

"There *is* that," Lakinda conceded. "All right. What do you need from me?"

"First of all, we need to know where we're going," Apros said. "Can you send us the location?"

"Of course." Lakinda snagged her questis, punched up the mining planet's coordinates, and keyed them into the transmission. "You should have it now."

"Confirmed," Apros said. "Senior Captain Thrawn?"

"Yes, I have it," Thrawn said. "I assume, Senior Captain Lakinda, that you don't have any sky-walkers with you?"

"No, we're traveling jump-by-jump."

"Good," Thrawn said. "Then Mid Captain Apros and I should be able to arrive ahead of you and the other families' forces."

"Assuming those warships also don't have sky-walkers," Apros warned.

"I can't imagine they do," Lakinda said. "But I suppose it's possible. Do you want me to try to speed up and get there a little sooner? I may be able to shave a few hours from my timetable."

"That would be helpful," Apros said. "But only if you can do it safely."

"And without arousing any suspicions," Thrawn added.

"I'll do what I can," Lakinda said. "Shall I try to contact you again along the way?"

"I doubt you'll be able to," Thrawn said. "From now on we'll be spending as much time in hyperspace as our sky-walkers can handle. Good luck, Senior Captain."

"And to you two, as well," Lakinda said. "There's one more thing. Mid Captain Apros?"

"Yes, ma'am?" Apros said.

Lakinda took a deep breath. She'd so badly wanted this. So badly wanted to bring honor to the Xodlak family, and in doing so bring honor onto herself. Instead, she was poised to bring ruin on everything.

Not now. Not anymore. "Your mission," she told him, "is to keep whatever happens from escalating into a civil war. If accomplishing that mission requires the destruction of my two ships, understand clearly that we—*and* I—are expendable."

"Senior Captain—"

"No argument, Apros," she said. "Or from you, Thrawn."

"I wasn't going to offer one, Senior Captain," Thrawn said mildly. "Be assured in turn that we'll do everything we can to avoid any such sacrifices."

"I appreciate that," Lakinda said. "But I'm serious."

"So are we," Apros said. "We'll see you in a few days, Senior Captain. Good luck."

The comm keyed off. Lakinda laid back down, and for a minute stared at the ceiling. A massive deception and manipulation. A possible civil war.

And only the *Grayshrike* and *Springhawk* poised to defuse it.

Two heavy cruisers, and Thrawn's plan.

She'd been wrong earlier, she realized now. It wasn't Thrawn who'd borrowed tactics and strategies from Admiral Ar'alani, but Ar'alani who'd observed and adapted Thrawn's methods for herself. Thrawn's methods were Thrawn's, all the way.

Because Ar'alani would *never* try something this insane.

Neither, for that matter, would Lakinda herself. Maybe Thrawn had merely been lucky all these years, his victories as much a product of that luck as they were of his plans. Or maybe there was something inherent in his way of thinking that drew his opponents into his schemes at precisely the times and places where he needed them.

But that didn't mean he was better than Lakinda. *Better* and *worse* were artificial and meaningless concepts. He'd had his victories; she'd had hers.

No *better* or *worse*. Just *different*.

Propping herself up again, she tapped for the bridge. "Duty Officer, this is Senior Captain Lakinda," she identified herself. "I'll be there in fifteen minutes. In the meantime, the pilot is to start running some numbers. He has until I arrive to figure out how to speed up our passage. And alert the *Apogee* that I'll want the captain and first officer available to talk in one hour."

She got a confirmation and keyed off the comm, the words again racing through her mind. *Deception . . . civil war . . .*

*Expendable.*

Was Thrawn willing to die for the Ascendancy? She didn't know. Maybe that was yet another way the two of them were different.

Hopefully, neither of them would have to find out over a worthless piece of rock.

Swinging her legs over the side of the bed, she grabbed her uniform from the valet stand and started getting dressed.

---

The two Xodlak warships had left. Haplif couldn't see them from Lakphro's ranch, but he knew by the sudden decrease in local comm activity that they were gone. Gone on their mission to bring glory to the Xodlak family and Councilor Lakuviv.

And with that, it was over.

At least Haplif's part was. The coming battle, the fury and death, the destruction and screams of betrayal, the descent into confusion and civil war—all those of course were yet to come.

But they were inevitable. Just because the Chiss Ascendancy didn't yet realize its doom had been sealed didn't mean there was any way for them to escape it.

It was over. Now, finally, Jixtus would let him go home.

There were still a few random seedlings left in the spice plot, he saw as he finished the last row. But suddenly he didn't care whether he got them all or not. Yoponek was off the ship on some errand Shimkif had contrived for him, all the rest of the equipment and people were packed up, and Shimkif had the crew working on launch prep. Haplif's original plan called for them to leave in half an hour, but there really was no reason they couldn't lift off right now. He straightened up, closing the box of seedlings and looping the strap over his shoulder—

"I hear you're leaving," a voice came from behind him.

He turned. Focused on the spices and his own musings, he hadn't heard Lakphro come up behind him. "Yes, it's time for us to move on," he told the rancher, keeping his voice cheerful. "New worlds, new vistas, new experiences. An exciting time in our continuing journey through the universe. I want to thank you for your hospitality in letting us use part of your land."

"That's it?" Lakphro asked. "Just a few random words of thanks?"

Haplif crinkled his forehead skin, taking another look at the rancher. The Chiss was dressed differently than usual, with heavier boots and coveralls. Instead of his usual light jacket, he was wearing a checkered brown monstrosity with a big brass-tooth sealer down the front. His usual electric-jolt animal-control stick was holstered to his right thigh, but today he was also wearing a second lurestick on his left. His feet were spread slightly apart, as if he was preparing for a fight, and his glowing red eyes were narrowed with suspicion.

"I'm sorry if our thanks were inadequate," Haplif said, still keeping his tone light. "Would an epic poem be more to your liking? Perhaps a musical interweave in five-part harmony?"

"Don't be sarcastic," Lakphro said. "It doesn't fit your public image. No, I was thinking maybe more of your precious wire jewelry."

Haplif's mouth started to quiver with surprise. Ruthlessly, he forced it shut. "Our jewelry?" he asked carefully.

"Oh, no, of course not," Lakphro said. "I forgot. Those are just for bribes, aren't they?"

And with that, Haplif realized he was going to have to kill him.

He'd hoped to avoid any more killing. Not for any moral reasons, but because it was such an unpleasant feeling to wrap his fingers around someone's throat and feel their fear and hopelessness as he drained the life from them.

On the other hand, he'd never really liked Lakphro. The rancher had always held himself aloof from his guests, suspicious and unfriendly and way too inquisitive about what the Agbui were doing. This killing he might actually enjoy.

"You see, you made a mistake," Lakphro went on. "You forgot who we were."

"Who, the grand and mighty Chiss?" Haplif scoffed, starting to ease toward the other. "Don't make me laugh. You have the same weaknesses and passions as everyone else in the Chaos, and are just as easy to manipulate." He snorted. "If anything, this insane family setup of yours makes it even easier. All that ambition and infighting and suspicion are perfect for my kind of operation."

"And that's where you made your mistake," Lakphro said softly. "You're right about the ambition and infighting parts. But you never understood the family part."

"Hardly," Haplif said, still drifting forward. The rancher was almost within grabbing range now. "Family is genetics and bloodlines and annoying relatives. Nothing more."

"You're wrong," Lakphro said. "It's also friendship, loyalty, support, and communication." He raised his eyebrows. "*Especially* communication. We talk to one another, the Xodlak do. Our leaders may wallow in ambition, but the rest of us talk to one another. We talk here in Redhill, we talk elsewhere around the planet, and we even talk to relatives on Naporar."

Haplif frowned. "Naporar?"

"Where the headquarters of the Expansionary Defense Fleet is located," Lakphro said. "I sent Lakris's brooch there to be analyzed. In return, my cousin told me that the whole fleet has been turned upside down, with Xodlak family officers and warriors summoned here to Celwis."

So someone outside of Councilor Lakuviv's circle knew about that. Unfortunate, but hardly calamitous. Nothing Lakphro could do could change any of it. "What does that have to do with me?" he asked.

"Don't play stupid," Lakphro said scornfully. "It doesn't work any better than the sarcasm. You hand out jewelry, you spend hours with Councilor Lakuviv, Patriel Lakooni vanishes for days at a time, ships full of warriors assemble here."

The rancher shook his head, drawing his right-hand lurestick and pulling down the tab of his jacket. Frosif had been right, the odd thought occurred to Haplif; the sealer *did* sound like a flat-blast artillery shell coming at them. "This sort of thing doesn't happen on Celwis," Lakphro continued. "Not unless there's some alien in our midst pulling on our strings."

"I have no idea what you're talking about," Haplif insisted. Almost there . . .

"I think you do," Lakphro said. He thumbed the lurestick's switch, and Haplif heard the faint, high-pitched warning whine of the device's full-power setting.

Haplif had seen Lakphro's daughter take down a full-grown yubal with that setting. He had no interest in seeing what it would do to him.

Fortunately, he wouldn't have to. One leap forward, and the rancher would be his.

"And pretty soon everyone else will know it, too," Lakphro said. He ran the sealer tab back up again, as if he'd belatedly noticed that the air out here was a little chilly. He started to step back, as if also belatedly realizing how close Haplif had come.

And then, it was too late.

Haplif leapt across the gap separating them, his left hand flashing out to slap at the side of the lurestick. Lakphro's feet stumbled as he tried to back up, his left hand fumbling for the second lurestick holstered on that hip.

But he didn't have a chance. Haplif caught the man's neck in his right hand, wrapping his long fingers around the throat as he took a half step to the side to crowd against Lakphro's arm and keep him from drawing the second weapon. The rancher's emotions flooded across his mind, ripples of anger and betrayal and determination. Haplif clenched his hand tighter, savoring the feel of the raw emotion, waiting for the fear and hopelessness that would soon spread across the anger—

The racing footsteps had just registered in his ears and mind when something slammed into his side and a stabbing pain exploded through his right arm.

The impact threw him to the side, the agony in his arm tearing his grip off Lakphro's throat. He twisted his head around as he fought for balance against the sudden weight trying to drag him to the ground.

To find one of the growzer border hounds clinging to him, its white teeth clenched solidly around his arm, its hind legs making little furrows in the dirt, a low snarl rumbling from its throat.

Haplif cursed, staggering back against the animal. He grabbed at the upper jaw with his left hand, trying to pry the damn mouth open. Out of the corner of his eye, he saw the rancher had recovered from his partial strangulation and was coming toward him, lurestick raised high.

Despite the pain, Haplif smiled. Lakphro might think he was helpless, but in calling the growzer down on him the fool had just handed him a weapon he would never even think of. He watched as Lakphro moved closer, still prying at the animal's jaw, judging his timing . . .

And as Lakphro stretched out the lurestick Haplif heaved his shoulder and hips around, putting his full weight into swinging the growzer that was hanging from his arm around to slam into the rancher's side. Lakphro staggered, the lurestick swinging wide.

It was only then that Haplif saw the second lurestick ready in Lakphro's left hand.

But again, the rancher was too late. With a supreme effort, Haplif broke the growzer's momentum and started it swinging back toward Lakphro. Electric weapons, he knew, normally required a few seconds to recover from a discharge. If he could get Lakphro to waste that first shot, he would still have him. The lurestick was reaching out toward him—

With a snarl of triumph Haplif slammed the growzer into the weapon's tip. There was a small flash, a half-seen burst of coronal energy, and the animal's body went rigid.

And Haplif screamed as the creature's jaws convulsively tightened around his arm, the teeth tearing through skin and muscle, snapping bone and severing artery and vein.

He was on his back on the ground, still screaming, when the shadow of his ship passed over him.

Perhaps Shimkif had seen that he couldn't be rescued. Perhaps that was merely her excuse for abandoning him here. Perhaps his death had always been part of her plan.

It didn't matter. Nothing mattered. Not anymore.

Because he'd won. Whatever happened to him now, the Chiss ships were on their way, and their civil war had begun.

The last thing he saw before the darkness took him was Lakphro's glowing red eyes gazing down at him.

# CHAPTER TWENTY-FOUR

All was ready.

The *Springhawk* and *Grayshrike* were in position. Their crews and personnel were as prepared as Thrawn and Samakro and Apros could make them.

And in the end, Samakro thought with a vague sense of gathering doom, it was all going to come down to the actions of fourteen of those officers and warriors.

Fourteen.

All of them were from the *Springhawk,* not from any partiality or seniority, but by simple necessity. As the two warships raced to reach the Agbui planet ahead of the three incoming family task forces, and as a result spent as much time in hyperspace as their sky-walkers could handle, the *Springhawk*'s officers and warriors were the only ones who could easily access the Watith freighter strapped to the cruiser's underside.

Fourteen.

Lakinda had told them the Xodlak force consisted of a frigate and light cruiser. Even if she could pull her punches without her senior officers noticing and calling her on it, it was still questionable whether the *Springhawk* and *Grayshrike* could stand up to them. The fact that two more family forces were also on the way tilted the odds even further.

Only now it was no longer just the two cruisers in the calculation.

Now there were also the fourteen remote-controlled gunboats salvaged from the Watith attack.

Samakro didn't especially like Thrawn's plan. Neither did Apros, and Senior Captain Lakinda hadn't sounded very enthusiastic about it, either. But Samakro had thought long and hard over the past couple of days, and he'd been unable to come up with anything better.

And so now here he was, pacing slowly up and down the narrow aisle between the twenty remote-control consoles in the Watith freighter, putting the fourteen men and women through yet another hour of practice, drills, and simulated combat. Making sure they were as prepared for what was to come as they could possibly be.

"Mid Captain Samakro?"

Samakro paused. Laknym, seated halfway down the aisle, was looking toward him. The plasma sphere specialist's hand was half raised, and his expression was troubled. "A question, Lieutenant Commander?" Samakro asked as he walked over to him.

"Yes, sir," Laknym said. He paused, waiting until Samakro was standing over him. "I understand the reasons for this, sir," he said, lowering his voice. "I understand that I'm under orders—"

"You volunteered for this job, did you not?" Samakro asked.

"Yes, sir, I did," Laknym said. "But Senior Captain Thrawn is my commander. I consider a request from him, even if it's for volunteers, to be the same thing as an order."

"I see," Samakro said. That was exactly the kind of attitude of loyalty, commitment, and obedience the fleet liked to see in their officers and warriors. "What's your question?"

He saw Laknym's throat work. "Sir . . . I'm being asked to fire on my own family's ships."

"Yes, you are," Samakro agreed. "And you know the reason for that. You and the other Xodlak on this team are the ones most familiar with your ships' weaponry and defenses."

"Yes, sir, and I understand that." He hesitated again. "Here's my problem, sir. The Xodlak are allies of the Irizi. Senior Captain Thrawn is of the Mitth, rivals of the Irizi. I'm wondering . . . do you think there might be . . . could there be a political aspect to this?"

"An excellent question," Samakro agreed. "Let me give you a simple answer: no."

Laknym frowned. "*No,* sir?"

"No," Samakro repeated. "I understand your concern, especially under the circumstances. But the truth is . . ."

He paused, looking down the aisle at the other men and women working busily on their drills. "The truth, Laknym, is that I've been Thrawn's first officer since he came aboard. I've watched him in battles, in preparation for battles, in the aftermath of battles, and dealing with Aristocra and senior officers."

He looked back at Laknym. "And I have never—*never*—seen anyone as utterly incompetent at politics as he is."

For a moment Laknym just frowned up at him. Then slowly, the frown relaxed. "You're saying, sir, that Senior Captain Thrawn isn't playing politics here because he never plays politics?"

"I'm saying," Samakro corrected, "that Senior Captain Thrawn never plays politics because he doesn't know *how* to play politics." He took a deep breath, huffed it out. "Bottom line. When Thrawn comes up with a plan, it's strictly military. Nothing more, nothing less."

"Yes, sir," Laknym said. "I understand."

"And this *is* a good plan," Samakro added. "It'll work, and it'll work well." He inclined his head. "And now I believe you have some drills to run?"

"Yes, sir, I do," Laknym said. "Thank you, sir." He gave Samakro a brisk nod and turned back to his console.

For another moment Samakro watched over Laknym's shoulder as he jumped back into his part of the simulation.

And realized to his mild surprise that his pep talk had worked better than he'd expected. Not only had he convinced Laknym that Thrawn's plan would succeed, he'd actually convinced himself.

But only if these fourteen men and women did their job.

Stepping away from Laknym's console, he resumed his slow walk down the aisle, watching each of them in turn, ready to offer advice or correction or encouragement.

Because, really, a plan was only as good as the people executing it.

And Samakro had no intention of letting these fourteen fail because of him.

The star-flares faded into stars, and the *Midsummer* had arrived.

"Sensors, full scan," Lakinda ordered, doing a quick visual through the viewport. Time to see if shaving a few hours off their journey had paid off.

"Combat range clear, Senior Captain," the sensor officer reported. "Mid-range clear. Far range . . . clear."

"Acknowledged," Lakinda said, breathing a little easier. The extra work had indeed paid off. Just as she'd hoped, the Xodlak ships had beaten the other two families here. "Continue scan. Helm, take us in."

From his position beside Lakinda's command chair, the first officer cleared his throat. "I believe, Senior Captain, that Councilor Lakuviv said you were to announce our mission at this point."

"Yes, First, he did," Lakinda said, looking casually at the tactical display. It was still filling in as the sensors continued to collect data, but so far there was nothing out there. "It was reported to Councilor Lakuviv that this planet may be home to one or more mines and rare ore deposits. Our mission is to locate those mines and assess their value."

"To assess a *mining* operation?" First asked, staring at her. "Forgive me, Senior Captain, but that strikes me as not only flimsy but also ludicrous."

"I'm just telling you what Senior Aide Lakjiip told me," Lakinda said, meeting and holding his gaze.

"I don't believe it," First said flatly. "No Patriel would haul in family members from all over the Ascendancy for something that trivial."

"*Or* activate a frigate and cruiser to bring us all here," the second officer added, his face just as suspicious as First's. "There has to be more to it than that, Senior Captain."

"And we want to know what it is, ma'am," First said. "*All* of it."

"Or?" Lakinda asked, layering some ice beneath her calmness. Thrawn had said the *Springhawk* would be waiting for them. Where was he?

First didn't even twitch. "You're the commander, Senior Captain," he said with the same icy calmness. "You can refuse to tell us. But if you do, there *will* be consequences down the line."

"Are you threatening me, First?" Lakinda asked, still keeping her tone calm. If Thrawn didn't get in here fast—

"Not at all, ma'am." He drew himself up. "But bear in mind that while I may be only a junior captain, I *am* Xodlak blood."

"So noted," Lakinda said, her heart sinking a little. In the fleet, such distinctions in family rank were meaningless.

But at this time and place they weren't Ascendancy officers. This was a Xodlak operation, and First's status meant he would have receptive ears in the Patriarch's office that would be closed to Lakinda. If this whole thing turned belly-up—

"Contact!" Sensors spoke up sharply. "Multiple contacts. Five . . . no, six. Six incoming ships. Two groups, each with three ships."

"Acknowledged," Lakinda said, looking at the tactical. The Erighal and Pommrio, undoubtedly. Fortunately, they hadn't jumped in right on top of each other. Or on top of the *Midsummer* and *Apogee*, either.

Possibly by design. Along with providing the planetary coordinates, the Agbui on Celwis had presumably assisted Lakuviv's people in mapping out the jump-by-jump pattern that the Xodlak ships had followed, which had partially defined which part of space they'd arrived in. Maybe Haplif's accomplices in this con game had done the same for the other two families' ships, making sure they arrived slightly separated from each other. Not only would that avoid potential snarls, but it would give everyone time to realize they weren't the only ones going for the prize and, perhaps, decide just how hard they were going to fight for it.

"Do we have IDs on them?" First asked.

"Configuration marks them as Chiss," Sensors said, frowning at his displays. "But—"

"Senior Captain, I'm getting transmissions," Comm cut in. "The ships . . ." She touched a key.

"—is Expeditionary Force Alpha," a haughty voice came over the bridge speaker. "I'm serving formal notice that we are claiming this world and all its resources for the Erighal family of the Chiss Ascendancy."

"Unacceptable, Erighal task force," a new voice came, just as haughty as the first, and this one carrying an edge of anger. "Kindly identify yourself and your ships."

"I am Force Alpha, operating under the auspices of the Erighal family," the Alpha commander said in an even, precise voice. "That's all you need to know."

"Is it, now," the second voice bit out. "Fine. Be aware that *I* am also a military task force, traveling under the auspices of the Pommrio family, and I formally challenge your claim."

"What *is* this?" First growled. "Senior Captain? What's going on here?"

"I already told you," Lakinda said. She tapped her comm key. "This is Task Force Xodlak," she called, "since we all seem reluctant to give our actual names."

"Names are irrelevant," the Erighal said. "All that matters is that the Erighal now own this world."

"The Pommrio challenge that claim," the Pommrio commander repeated.

Lakinda looked at her first officer. He was staring out the viewport, his face rigid, his eyes blazing. He still didn't know what was down there, but he now knew that two other families badly wanted it.

And that was suddenly all that mattered. He was Xodlak blood, and he would be damned if he would let the Erighal or Pommrio take something he already considered to be his. Whatever it took— whether threats or demands, combat or death—the planet and its mines were going to belong to the Xodlak.

And with a sinking heart, Lakinda realized Apros and Thrawn had been right. There was going to be a battle today, and when the dust settled the Ascendancy could very well be balanced on the edge of civil war. Only she and Thrawn stood in the way of that disaster.

In the meantime, she had a role to play out. "The Xodlak challenge both your claims," she said. "I'll also point out that we were here before either of you."

"Who was here first is irrelevant," the Erighal said. "All that matters is who is here *last*."

Beside Lakinda, the first officer made a rumbling sound in his throat. "Senior Captain, I recommend we go to full combat stations."

"Agreed," Lakinda said, keying the ship-wide alert. "How are you at a weapons console?"

"I spent over a year at one."

"Excellent," Lakinda said. "Take that station and ready your weapons."

"Yes, ma'am." He headed briskly across the bridge.

"New contact, Senior Captain," Sensors called. "Just coming around the curve of the planet."

"Wonderful," First growled over his shoulder. "Which family is it *now*?"

"No family, sir," Sensors said. "It's the *Springhawk*." He half turned to look at Lakinda. "And they're in trouble."

"There they are," Dalvu's voice came over the speaker in the Watith freighter's control room. "Got the Xodlak ships . . . there are the Erighal . . . and there on the far starboard are the Pommrio. Looks like everyone's here, Senior Captain."

"Very good, Mid Commander," Thrawn's voice came. "Mid Captain Samakro, are you ready?"

"We're ready, sir," Samakro said. "Officers and warriors: Go."

There were nods and muttered acknowledgments up and down the aisle as the fourteen men and women activated their gunboats.

"Make it look good," Thrawn reminded them. "Remember, the *Springhawk* is in serious trouble."

Samakro looked over at the repeater displays that had been set up above the forward hatch. Thrawn was putting on an amazingly realistic show, he saw, with the *Springhawk* squirming back and forth as it tried to shake away the gunboats swarming around it and throw off the freighter attached to its underside. The repeaters didn't show it, but Samakro knew the cruiser's lights and power levels were also flickering, its thrusters firing only intermittently, and its electrostatic barrier completely gone. As far as any of the family ships out there could tell, the *Springhawk* was going down fast.

Only now, with their sudden arrival, it had been given a reprieve. Shifting his gaze to the tactical, Samakro saw the fourteen gunboats that had supposedly been harassing the cruiser abandon their formation and accelerate toward the newcomers.

And family commanders who'd been ramping up for a squabble among themselves were suddenly facing an unexpected challenge.

A very *serious* challenge, too. Dalvu had the profiles up now, and adding in the two Xodlak ships the total count came to one frigate, two light cruisers, and five patrol ships. With fourteen gunboats bearing down on them, the smart move would be for them to escape back into hyperspace and come back when they had more firepower.

But they wouldn't. The lure of the imaginary nyix mine was too strong, the risk to family honor and prestige too great. Maybe the last remaining ship would run, if it was still able to do so. But until then, they would all stand and fight.

Which was, after all, exactly what Thrawn was counting on.

"Incoming, Senior Captain," Sensors announced, his voice tight. "I make it fourteen fighter-class warships, probably gunboats."

"Acknowledged, Sensors," Lakinda said. "Erighal and Pommrio ships, I strongly recommend you get out while you still can. If these gunboats were able to bring a Chiss heavy cruiser to the edge, they're way more than either of you can handle."

"Negative on that, Xodlak," the Erighal commander growled. "We're not leaving."

"Not with an Expansionary Defense Fleet ship and crew in danger," the Pommrio added. "If we leave now, they'll just go back and finish off the *Springhawk*."

Lakinda breathed a silent sigh of relief. She'd been pretty sure they wouldn't run, but there'd always been that chance. More important, their oaths to the Ascendancy were starting to push against their loyalties to their families. "As you will," she said. "In that case, we need to put together a joint battle front, anchored by my frigate and our two cruisers. Erighal, you're currently in the middle, so the Pommrio ships and I will move in and form up on you." She gestured to the pilot. "Helm, get us over there. *Apogee,* stay on our flank until we reach the Erighal."

"Just a moment, Xodlak," the Erighal said. "I agree on a joint battle front. I don't necessarily agree that you should be in command."

"I have the frigate," Lakinda reminded him. "More important, I'm a senior captain. Your rank?"

There was a pause. "Mid captain," he said reluctantly.

"Pommrio?" Lakinda prompted.

"Also mid captain," the other replied. "Very well, Xodlak. The Pommrio cede command to you. But be warned: If I see you slanting this operation to favor your family over ours, I reserve the right to withdraw my support and my ships."

"As do I," the Erighal said.

"So noted," Lakinda said. "Let's focus on rescuing the *Springhawk* and keeping ourselves alive, shall we? All right. We'll start with a modified double-wing formation: frigate in the center, Xodlak cruiser to starboard, Pommrio cruiser to portside. Patrol ships fill in the wings, staying far enough back to be partially shielded, far enough forward to deliver laserfire. Once the gunboats split their attack formation, you'll all be largely on your own, but I suggest the patrol ships stay close to one of the larger warships. Questions?"

"No, Senior Captain," the Pommrio said.

"Repositioning my ships and awaiting your arrival," the Erighal added. "And don't dawdle—those gunboats are moving up fast."

"Acknowledged," Lakinda said. "Helm, boost our speed fifteen percent. First?"

"Weapons crews running pre-combat checks," First reported from the weapons console. "We'll be ready once they open fire."

Lakinda felt her lip twist. *Once they open fire.* Even here, facing a clear and present threat, the rules against preemptive strikes persisted. "Good," she said. "*Midsummer* officers and warriors: Prepare for battle."

"This is it," Samakro said, gazing at the *Springhawk*'s tactical repeater as he strode down the control room aisle. The eight family ships had finished gathering into a modified double-wing, and their formation was poised to meet the incoming gunboats.

Fortunately, from the transmissions the *Springhawk* had been able to eavesdrop on, it looked like Lakinda was in overall command. The plan would probably still work if one of the other commanders had claimed that position, but it might have made things trickier.

"Remember your orders," he added, pausing behind Laknym's station. "And watch yourselves—we don't want this ending too quickly."

He leaned over Laknym's shoulder. "You ready, Lieutenant Commander?" he asked softly.

"Yes, sir," Laknym said.

"Good," Samakro said. Whatever the young man's uncertainties had been about firing on his own family's ships, he'd apparently been able to put them aside. "First shot coming up. Make it count."

Laknym nodded. The gunboats reached firing distance . . .

Ahead, in nearly perfect unison, the wall of gunboats erupted with laserfire.

"Three hits!" Sensors snapped. "Ventral bow, dorsal port side, ventral port side."

"Weapons, open fire," Lakinda ordered. "Target the ones that shot at us. Damage?"

"Barrier down twenty percent," Sensors reported as the *Midsummer*'s lasers opened fire, raking across the gunboats. "Targeting Sensors One and Five down twenty percent; switching to manual targeting to compensate. No nodes hit, weapons clusters undamaged."

"Acknowledged," Lakinda said, feeling some of her tension draining away. Samakro had done it. He and his team of gunboat controllers were actually making this look real. "Weapons?"

"Two hits," First reported. "One on dorsal bow—no clear damage indicated—second a possible kill shot on portside laser."

The starscape ahead of them had become a blaze of laserfire as the gunboats and Chiss warships dueled. The gunboats delivered one final salvo and then broke off, their intertwined attack formation suddenly blossoming outward. "Watch it—they're shifting to single combat," Lakinda warned. "Patrol ships, stay sheltered as best you can."

"Belay that, Force Alpha," the Erighal commander cut in. "The Erighal do not hide like children. Engage at will, and engage fully."

"Nor do the Pommrio abandon others to fight in their stead," the Pommrio commander added. "Patrol ships, form up on my flanks."

Lakinda grimaced. But she should have expected that. Capturing the nyix mines might not be as important as it was an hour ago, but maintaining family honor was always a priority.

And practically speaking, once a battle devolved into one-on-one, it really was every ship for itself. She should be happy the tentative alliance had lasted this long.

"As you wish," she said to the other commanders. "But stay together, guard one another's backs, and set up kill shots wherever you can."

"Set up shots among our own ships, or with the others?" First asked pointedly.

*Family first:* The words whispered through Lakinda's mind. Words that had been with her since childhood. Words that had colored every thought and been a background to every decision. Words that had become even more important after she was raised from her obscure origins and made a part of the Xodlak.

And right now, words that could do nothing but get in her way. "With whichever damn ship is in position," Lakinda said tartly. "Just remember that we're all Chiss. Xodlak, Erighal, Pommrio—we're all Chiss."

"So we are," the Pommrio said with quiet menace. "Let us make these aliens *very* sorry they ever crossed our path."

"Multiple hits on family ships," Dalvu reported. "Minor hull damage on two of the Erighal patrol ships, minor hull damage and one laser inoperative on Pommrio cruiser, targeting sensors inoperative on Xodlak and Pommrio cruisers and all three Erighal patrol ships. Reduction in barrier strength on all vessels. No other damage detected."

Samakro exhaled a breath he hadn't realized he'd been holding. "Well done," he called to the fourteen men and women at their control consoles. "Open up your formation. Time to go to one-on-one."

He touched Laknym on the shoulder. "And *that*," he reminded the other, "is why you're all shooting at your own family's ships."

"Yes, sir," Laknym said, sounding marginally calmer.

Samakro focused on Laknym's displays, watching the starscape twist violently as he maneuvered his gunboat around and between the answering laser blasts. This aspect had been just one more point of genius in Thrawn's plan.

Because each family's warships had their own set of unique differences, specifications, and peculiarities, and each family made a point of training its fleet warriors in those details. That meant that those warriors, and *only* those warriors, knew how and where to attack their family's ships with a maximum of ferocity and a minimum of actual damage.

The battle raged on. The gunboats continued to swarm the Chiss warships, firing madly and as ineffectively as possible, focusing on targeting sensors and empty sections of hull. Their opponents, with no such restrictions to slow them down, fired back with lasers and occasional breachers, steadily grinding away at their attackers' numbers.

As each gunboat was destroyed, its control panel went dark, and its operator was finished. They all reacted differently to that endpoint, Samakro noted: some clenching their fists in frustration, others just slumping back in their seats in relief, others making tension-relieving small talk with neighbors who had similarly been idled. The number of gunboats dropped to eleven, then nine, then eight—

"Senior Captain, we have a tight-beam transmission from the *Midsummer*," Brisch suddenly said over the speaker. "Senior Captain Lakinda says we have a problem."

# CHAPTER TWENTY-FIVE

The gunboats continued their attack, blasting away at the family ships and taking fire in return. Lakinda kept a close eye on the *Midsummer*'s status boards, watching for the inevitable mistake on the part of whoever was targeting her ship, bracing herself for the laser shot that would take out a barrier node or accidentally blast through a weak part of the hull and kill whoever was on station behind it, or the misjudged approach that would slam the gunship itself into her.

But so far that hadn't happened. Whoever Thrawn had assigned to handle the gunboats, they were doing their jobs well.

The enemy was down to eight when, like a brick slapping her in the face, she saw the terrible flaw in the entire scheme.

For a long minute she just sat there, gripping the armrests of her command chair as the battle raged around her ships, her brain racing to sort through the problem and find a solution. If she did . . . no. If someone on the *Springhawk* did . . . no. If Thrawn had already spotted the flaw and worked it into his plans . . .

She dug her fingers a little harder into her armrests. No. There was no way Thrawn could have caught this one. Not with his blindness to family politics. He would continue on, bring the scenario to a triumphant end . . . and then watch helplessly as that triumph collapsed. *Deception . . . civil war . . .*

She had to warn him. But that wouldn't be easy. Even if she could risk her own officers listening in, standard battle protocol required her bridge comm to remain open to all the other ships of her task force. She would have to make an excuse to leave the bridge and go to the duty office.

Another laser shot slammed into the *Midsummer*'s hull. "Damage to Number Eight Targeting Sensor," First reported.

"Acknowledged," Lakinda said, standing up and crossing over to him. "Assessment?"

"They're enthusiastic enough," he said, sending another pair of laser blasts chasing after one of the gunboats. "Lucky for us, they're not very good at picking their targets."

"Indeed," Lakinda said, noting in passing the irony there. In truth, the gunboats were hitting *exactly* what they were aiming for. "I need you to take command for a few minutes," she added, lowering her voice. "I'm going to try to get a message to the *Springhawk*."

First craned his neck to look up at her, his eyes narrowed. "Why?"

"Sensors indicate they've gone partially dormant," she said. "That tells me they were already tangling with these gunboats before we arrived. They may have picked up useful information on them."

The eyes narrowed a little more. "I don't think a private conversation is a good idea," he warned. "We're in a precarious enough relationship with the Erighal and Pommrio. We don't want to look like we're going behind their backs." He gave a derisive snort. "Besides, considering the shape the *Springhawk*'s in, what kind of useful information could Thrawn possibly have?"

"I wasn't asking for your advice or opinions, First," Lakinda said. "I'm giving you notice and an order. Maintain pressure on the gunboats, and keep an eye on the *Apogee*. I'll be back as soon as I can."

She retraced her steps across the bridge, continuing past her command chair to the far side and slipping through the duty office hatchway. She sealed the hatch and sat down at the desk, keying on the equipment and punching in her private code. Most ship transmissions went through the bridge comm station, but there was an independent system available for the commander's private use.

On Expansionary Defense Fleet ships, that system was inaccessible to the comm officer. There was no way to know if Xodlak family warships followed the same etiquette.

The *Springhawk* was a fair distance away, and it took her nearly a minute to get a tight beam set up and aimed. Finally, she was ready. "*Springhawk,* this is Senior Captain Lakinda," she said. "We have a problem."

She paused a second until it occurred to her that Thrawn couldn't reply, even with a tight beam, without the risk that one or more of the other family ships would be able to pick it up. "Once this is over, the Erighal and Pommrio are going to insist on going down to examine the mines," she continued. "When they see the entire setup is a fraud, it'll spark a huge degree of embarrassment. You can't hide something like that forever, and once it's out in the open there will be a public uproar, with anger, recriminations, massive efforts to find someone to blame—"

She broke off. By this point, even Thrawn should have gotten the message. "The end result won't be much better than if they'd come to physical blows," she said. "I don't know how you're going to prevent that, but you have to find a way."

She swallowed hard. *Expendable* . . . "I think someone's going to have to crash the Watith freighter into the fake mine. I know it's hard, but if that's the price we have to pay, then we have to pay it."

She paused, wondering if there was anything else she should say. But she'd said enough. "I have to get back to the battle now. Good luck."

She closed down the tight beam and the comm, locking the log so that the next duty officer couldn't just sit down and pull up the transmission record. She stood up, returned to the hatch, and tapped the release.

To find the second officer standing outside waiting for her, his face rigid. Standing a pace behind him were two warriors with charrics belted at their sides.

"Senior Captain Xodlak'in'daro," Second said, his tone painfully formal, "I am hereby informing you that, for crimes and offenses against the Xodlak family, the senior officers of the Xodlak frigate *Midsummer* have removed you from command."

"What are you talking about?" Lakinda demanded, her pulse suddenly pounding. "*What* crimes?"

"Betrayal of Xodlak family interests," Second said. "Disregard for Xodlak family orders and instructions. Communicating and consorting with the enemy."

"The Mitth are not our enemy," she insisted, feeling a sudden catch in her lungs. *Communicating with the enemy.* Had they tapped somehow into her message? Had someone figured out that the *Springhawk* was controlling the gunboats, and that speaking with them really *was* talking to the *Midsummer*'s attackers?

"They're not our allies, either," Second countered.

"Did you learn anything about the gunboats?" the first officer called from the weapons console.

Called at full volume, Lakinda noted, without any attempt to keep the question confidential. Apparently, it wasn't just the senior officers, but the entire bridge crew who were in on this. "Senior Captain Thrawn was unable to respond," she said.

"Of course," First said scornfully. "But I assume you were able to talk to him?"

A laser blast flashed past the viewport, briefly illuminating the bridge. "In case you hadn't noticed, First, we're in the middle of a battle," Lakinda said. "We don't have time for this."

"Agreed," Second said. "You are therefore to be confined to quarters until a proper investigation can be completed."

Lakinda straightened up. They had no legitimate right to do this, she knew. Hearsay, innuendo, assumption, deduction—none of those were sufficient grounds to relieve an officer of her post. Every one of her officers, from First on down, must certainly know that.

But as she herself had said, they didn't have time for this.

"This isn't the end of this matter," she warned, stepping out of the office.

"Indeed it isn't," Second agreed. He moved out of her path and gestured to the two warriors. "Warriors?"

The first warrior turned and headed for the hatch. The second waited until Lakinda had followed, then fell in behind her.

And with that, the entire plan was suddenly balanced on a wobbling edge. Thrawn had counted on her being in command of the

Xodlak ships through the whole battle, ready to make any last-minute moves or adjustments that might be needed. Now that advantage was gone.

Only Thrawn didn't know it. And he never would. Not until it was too late.

For a long moment no one in the freighter command room spoke. Not because everyone was too busy—only seven of the gunboats were still in action—but because everyone understood the repercussions of Senior Captain Lakinda's suggestion.

Disconnecting the Watith freighter would be easy enough, Samakro knew. It would also be possible to set it on a course that would crash it into the bogus mining area. Thrawn had already planned to cut the freighter loose and destroy it once all the gunboats had been eliminated anyway.

But that destruction was supposed to happen quick and close, before any of the distant family ships could tell that the freighter wasn't operational. Sending it instead to a crash-landing on the planet would give the observers way too much time to analyze its course and realize it wasn't under power or command. Especially since at that point they would no longer be distracted by the confusion of a battle.

The obvious plan would be to evacuate the controllers back to the *Springhawk* right now and send the freighter on its way while the battle was still in progress. Only that wouldn't work. As soon as the controllers left their posts the remaining gunboats would go inactive, drifting along the way they'd done back at the ambush system when Thrawn had disabled the freighter. At that point, no one could fail to realize something peculiar was going on, and all it would take would be a quick tractoring and examination of one of the gunboats to rip the scheme wide open.

They couldn't send the freighter now. They couldn't send it after the battle.

Or rather, as Lakinda had already hinted, they couldn't send it alone.

Laknym was the first to speak. "Sir?" he said, his eyes still on his displays as he continued his attack on the Xodlak warships. "Senior Captain Lakinda was right. You're going to need someone to pilot the freighter to the surface. I volunteer for the job."

"I appreciate that, Lieutenant Commander," Samakro said, looking around at the control consoles and the other men and women. If they could disassemble one of the gunboat consoles and take it aboard the *Springhawk* . . . but they'd already looked at that possibility during the voyage here and concluded the equipment was too complicated and too integrated into the freighter's own systems. If they could rig up a remote control for the freighter itself . . . but there was nothing in the *Springhawk*'s stores they could use for something like that, and they didn't have time to create one on the fly.

"Sir?" Laknym prompted.

"I heard you," Samakro growled. "If and when the job comes open, I'll let you know."

Could they turn one of the gunboats around now and send it at the planet? A gunboat would survive the trip through the atmosphere as well as the freighter would and destroy the mining area as well.

But after so many of the other fighters had been destroyed in battle, would that look to the family commanders like uncharacteristic and suspicious cowardice? How much suspicion would it take to bring this whole thing down and precipitate the vicious infighting Lakinda had warned them about?

"Mid Captain Samakro?" Thrawn's voice came from the speaker.

"Yes, sir," Samakro said with a heavy sigh. "Sir, I think Senior Captain Lakinda is right. The only way to make this work is for someone to stay behind and control the freighter on its last flight. Lieutenant Commander Laknym has volunteered."

"Thank you, Lieutenant Commander," Thrawn said. "You're right, Mid Captain, that the freighter needs to be seen as being under command."

Samakro looked down at Laknym. The other's throat was tight as he continued to operate his gunboat, but there was no regret in his eyes or his face. "Understood, sir."

"I don't think you do, Mid Captain," Thrawn said calmly. "I said it needed to be *seen* as being under command. I never said it needed to be piloted."

Samakro frowned. "Sir?"

"Continue your attack," Thrawn said. "But make sure you hold one gunboat in reserve for my use."

"Yes, sir." Still frowning, Samakro touched Laknym's shoulder. "That was for you, Lieutenant Commander. Senior Captain Thrawn wants you to keep your gunboat alive."

He didn't know what Thrawn was planning. He could only hope that Laknym, too, could be kept alive.


Thalias and Che'ri were playing a game in the sky-walker suite when they got the urgent summons.

Thrawn was standing behind the comm station as the warriors escorted the woman and girl onto the bridge. "Apologies for my silence," he was saying. "But we were temporarily disabled and briefly boarded, and have only now regained full control of the ship. I understand Senior Captain Lakinda attempted a transmission, but we were unable to properly receive it. Can she take a moment to repeat her message?"

"Captain Lakinda is no longer in command of Task Force Xodlak," an unfamiliar male voice ground out.

"Has she been injured?"

"She is no longer in command," the other repeated, "and I have no time to discuss it further. As you can see, we're engaged in combat."

"Yes, with the same group of warships that attacked us," Thrawn said. "May warrior's fortune smile on your efforts."

He gestured to the comm officer, who touched a key. "Transmission ended, sir," he confirmed.

Thrawn nodded and turned back. He spotted Thalias and Che'ri and motioned them toward his command chair.

"Thank you for coming," he said as the three of them gathered around the chair. "One moment." He touched the chair's mike key. "Mid Captain Samakro, are you ready?"

"Yes, sir," Samakro's voice came from the chair's speaker. "The thrusters are primed and the acceleration vector and profile have been triple-checked. Most of my people are already back in the *Springhawk,* and the rest can be out of here in thirty seconds."

"Good. Stand by." Thrawn looked over his shoulder at the comm officer. "Brisch, signal to the *Grayshrike.* Message: *Now.*"

"Yes, sir," Brisch said. "Message sent."

Thrawn turned back to Thalias and Che'ri. "We have a problem that I'm hoping you can help us fix."

"We'll do whatever we can, sir," Thalias said, taking a step toward the navigator's station. "Come on, Che'ri."

"Not there," Thrawn said, putting out a hand to stop them. "I need you at the weapons station."

"The *weapons* station?" Thalias asked, looking down at Che'ri. "Sir, we don't know anything about weapons or defenses."

"Actually, Che'ri *does* have some experience with decoys and decoy deployment," Thrawn said. "But don't worry, this isn't anything like that."

"Sir, the *Grayshrike* is here," Dalvu announced.

"Thank you," Thrawn said, turning to the tactical display. "Samakro, stand by."

Thalias followed his gaze. Whatever was going on out there, it was an absolute mess. The tactical showed about a dozen ships clustered together in the far distance, all of them maneuvering and firing at one another. Eight of them, mostly grouped in the center of the display, were marked with Chiss logos, while those marked as enemies swarmed around them. At the far edge of the display, a fair distance away from the battle and even farther from the *Springhawk,* a flashing image indicated the newly arrived *Grayshrike.* Even as Thalias watched, the newcomer swiveled toward the mass of other ships and opened fire on the attackers.

Thalias looked down at Che'ri. The girl was also staring at the tactical. But where Thalias felt mostly confusion, Che'ri's expression was one of concentration and curiosity.

"Gunboats: Disengage and run," Thrawn ordered.

On the display, the five enemy ships abruptly broke off their attack on the Chiss warships and swung around toward the planet, accelerating hard and regrouping into a cluster of their own as they ran. The Chiss behind them continued firing, their lasers joined by fire from the *Grayshrike* angling in from the far side.

Actually, Thalias saw now, given the way the various ships were positioned, the enemy ships would move a little closer to the *Grayshrike* before they passed that point and began opening up the distance again. That point of closest approach would be the cruiser's best chance to take them out.

Unfortunately for the *Grayshrike,* it had been in the middle of a yaw turn toward the main battle and was out of position to give chase. All it could do was continue the barrage from its portside lasers, an attack that was now joined by a stream of plasma spheres.

But the enemy ships were still too far away and were cutting rapidly across the field of fire. Combined with their evasive maneuvering, that was keeping them mostly clear of the bombardment. Thalias winced as she watched them successfully pass the *Grayshrike* and continue on, wondering if all five were going to make it to safety.

But there was just too much laserfire coming in for them to dodge it forever. Seconds later, in rapid succession, three of the five were hit with killing shots from the *Grayshrike* and disintegrated in massive explosions. The two survivors kept going, finally passing out of range and leaving the attackers behind. The *Grayshrike* made one last try with another wave of plasma spheres, but the ships were going too fast and the spheres fell behind.

"Final two gunboats are clear," Samakro announced.

"Clear the freighter, and activate thrusters," Thrawn ordered.

"Freighter cleared, Senior Captain," Samakro's voice came from the command chair speaker. "Activating thrusters: *now.*"

Thalias twitched as the deck abruptly began shaking beneath her. "Thalias?" Che'ri gasped, her hand grabbing Thalias's for balance.

"It's all right," Thrawn calmed her. "The vibration's coming from the Watith freighter. It's still tethered to the *Springhawk,* but its thrusters are now running at full power and it's trying to get away." The shaking continued, perhaps growing a little stronger—

"Aboard," Samakro called, sounding a little breathless. "Hatch sealed."

"Release freighter," Thrawn ordered.

With a final jolt, the deck vibration vanished. Thalias peered out the viewport and saw the freighter racing away, its vector cutting across the *Springhawk*'s orbit as it headed toward the edge of the planet.

"Afpriuh, stand by lasers," Thrawn ordered. He had his questis out and was tapping on it. "These spots: here, here, and here. Weave them into a general pattern of near-misses."

"Yes, sir," the weapons officer said, keying his board. A flurry of laser shots lanced out from the *Springhawk,* blazing around and past the fleeing freighter. Midway through the barrage the freighter seemed to realize it was under attack, twitching first to portside, then to starboard, then to starboard again as it tried to evade the cruiser's fire.

"Excellent," Thrawn said, nodding. "Continue firing, again making it look like your targeting systems are still not fully functional."

"Yes, sir."

The laserfire resumed. This time, as far as Thalias could tell, none of the shots had any effect.

Thrawn turned back to Thalias and Che'ri. "And now for you, Skywalker," he said. "Let me explain the situation."

He waved out the viewport. "We have an abandoned freighter and two empty gunboats heading toward a collision over the planet, all of which has been carefully laid out to end with them crashing onto a specific spot on the surface. What we need to do—"

"Wait a minute," Thalias interrupted. "You said the freighter was *abandoned*? I just saw it maneuver."

"What you saw was a set of precise laser shots hitting the maneuvering jets and releasing bursts of compressed gas," Thrawn told her. "In the short run, I expect that the Chiss warships observing the drama will see that and also assume the freighter is under power and control."

His lips tightened. "Unfortunately, they're almost certainly recording everything, which will allow them to carefully and leisurely examine all that has happened and all that is about to happen."

He turned to the tactical. "It may be that those future analysts will also conclude, as you just did, that the freighter was under command at that point," he said, his voice low and almost contemplative. "They may further conclude that the reason the two remaining gunboats are no longer running evasive maneuvers is that the *Grayshrike*'s failure to reach them with lasers and plasma spheres showed such maneuvering to be unnecessary. The problem is that we can't rely on the analysts to reach those conclusions."

He turned back. "What we need is to convince those future viewers that what happened here today—even just one aspect of it—is something the *Springhawk* couldn't possibly have engineered."

He held out a hand to Che'ri. "That's where you come in, Skywalker Che'ri. Come with me."

He led her forward a couple of steps, stopping her beside the weapons officer. "This is Senior Commander Afpriuh," he said, identifying the man.

"I know," Che'ri said, nodding to him. "Hello, Senior Commander."

"Hello, Sky-walker," Afpriuh said, nodding to her.

"We're going to try something I don't believe has ever been tried before," Thrawn said. "In approximately two minutes the freighter will reach a critical point in its journey. At that time it will also be nearly to the edge of tractor beam range, and our current orbit will also have moved us to a point where we'll have a partial view of its portside flank."

He pointed out the viewport. "What we're going to do is attempt to use the tractor beam to turn it slightly to portside, in the direction away from the planet."

Thalias looked at Afpriuh. The weapons officer was staring straight ahead, his profile giving no hint of his thoughts. "Is that even possible, Senior Commander?" she asked.

Afpriuh gave a small shrug. "Theoretically, yes," he said. "It just requires a particularly narrow beam and a target point forward of the freighter's center of mass." He turned to look up at her. "But it also requires that we get it right on our first try."

"Because . . . ?"

"Because otherwise the visual record will show twitching in the freighter's movement as we try to make the right connection," Thrawn said. "Those movements will be read, correctly, as additional tractor connections."

"Interference from the *Springhawk*," Thalias said, nodding. "Which you already said we don't want."

"Exactly." Thrawn looked down at Che'ri. "What we're going to do is have Afpriuh attempt to lock on with the tractor beam, using a low enough setting that it won't have any visible effect. You, Sky-walker Che'ri, will be watching the sensor display, using Third Sight to see a few seconds into the future. If and when—"

"Wait a minute," Thalias cut in as she suddenly understood what he had in mind. "You're not serious."

"Your hand will be on top of Afpriuh's," Thrawn continued, ignoring the interruption. "If and when you see the freighter make the yaw turn we're looking for, you'll indicate that by tapping or pressing down on his hand. When that happens, he'll run the tractor beam to full power before he activates it."

"That can't work," Thalias insisted. "Che'ri can't see something and then influence it to become something else."

"Third Sight can show her what the senior commander is about to do," Thrawn said. "In this case, that vision will be of the microscopic movement the freighter would experience if he'd left the beam on low power. As long as he's in control and she's not directly changing the event, it should work."

"But—"

"Thalias," Che'ri said quietly.

Thalias broke off, looking at her. "Che'ri, I'm not sure this is a good idea," she warned.

"But it's sort of like what I do all the time," Che'ri pointed out. "I see what the *Springhawk* might run into and change its direction so that it doesn't."

"It's not the same," Thalias insisted. "Remember, I used to do all that, too. When you're a navigator, you see something that's about to happen and make it not happen. What Senior Captain Thrawn is talking about is seeing something that *isn't* going to happen and making it happen anyway."

Che'ri shook her head. "I don't see the difference."

Thalias clenched her teeth. On one level, she wasn't sure she saw a difference, either.

But her gut instincts were still screaming that it was radically different. Warning her that this was uncharted and potentially dangerous territory; further warning her that pushing Third Sight this way might affect Che'ri in ways they couldn't predict.

"I don't know if it'll work," Che'ri went on. "But shouldn't we at least try?"

Thalias looked at Thrawn. "What happens if she doesn't do this?"

"Perhaps nothing," Thrawn said. "The analysts may not find anything suspicious, and then all will be well. If they do, there may be trouble among some of the families. Perhaps serious trouble. But those are only possibilities. If you're uncomfortable with this, you don't have to do it."

Che'ri squared her shoulders. "No," she said. Her voice was shaking a little, but there was no hesitation in it. "I didn't think I could learn to fly a spaceship. You said I could, and I did. If you say I can do this, I can. Where do you want me?"

"Right here," Thrawn said, moving her a few centimeters closer to Afpriuh. "This display—the one right here—is the one you'll watch. I'll keep it lined up on the freighter. Put your hand here—" he took her left hand and laid it, palm downward, on top of Afpriuh's right hand "—and press or tap as soon as you see the freighter move. All right?"

She nodded. "I'm ready."

Thrawn touched her shoulder, gave Thalias a brief look, then nodded. "Begin."

For a long moment nothing happened. Thalias stared at the display, feeling her heart thudding, wondering if this was going to work. Beside Che'ri, Afpriuh's hands moved delicately on his controls, his left hand making small adjustments, his right tapping every few seconds on a recessed button.

The *Springhawk*'s bridge had gone silent. Out of the corners of her eyes Thalias could see the rest of the officers sitting motionlessly, as if afraid of breaking a spell.

Were they worried about Che'ri? Or were they thinking about the consequences of failure? Thalias didn't know exactly what was going on, but this level of quiet tension suggested the situation might be more serious than Thrawn had let on.

*Trouble among some of the families*, he'd said. What did that even mean? Complaints filed with the Syndicure? Trade disagreements?

Che'ri seemed to be swaying a bit, one of her signs of fatigue or stress. Stepping close behind her, Thalias rested her hands on the girl's shoulders, steadying her and offering silent support.

Abruptly, Che'ri's fingers spasmed on the back of Afpriuh's hand.

Thalias snapped her attention back to the display, her hands squeezing Che'ri's shoulders. For another second nothing happened.

And then, there it was: The movement Thrawn had hoped for. The distant freighter shifted position, its bow turning a few degrees to portside. Thalias took a deep breath, let it out in a relieved huff—

And jerked backward as the image exploded into fire.

She looked up and peered through the viewport. In the far distance she could see the small spark of flame that had been amplified by the telescopics of the display, a spark now visibly angling toward the planet looming off to starboard.

What the *hell* had just happened?

"Collision confirmed, sir," Dalvu reported crisply from the sensor station. "Remaining gunboats have rammed the freighter. New combined vector . . . looks good, sir. Surface impact should be on target."

"Acknowledged," Thrawn said. "Caregiver?"

"Yes?" Thalias asked.

Thrawn nodded toward Che'ri. Frowning, Thalias focused on the girl.

The girl hadn't moved. She was still standing, her shoulders suddenly tense beneath Thalias's hands, her eyes fixed on the console.

Or maybe fixed on nothing at all. "Che'ri?" Thalias prompted.

No reply. No response. Carefully, Thalias gently turned the girl back around toward her. "Che'ri?"

For another moment Che'ri just stood there, her expression blank. Then she shook herself. Her eyes blinked twice and then came back to focus. "Did it work?" she asked.

"Yes, it did," Thalias assured her. "Are you all right?"

"I think so," Che'ri said, frowning. "Yes, I'm all right. That was just . . . it felt kind of backward."

Thrawn looked toward the rear of the bridge. "Warriors?" he called, beckoning to the pair who'd escorted Thalias and Che'ri in from their suite. "Take Sky-walker Che'ri to the medcenter for a full examination."

"You don't have to do that," Che'ri protested. "I'm fine."

"It's just a precaution," Thalias soothed. "Besides, you haven't been checked out for a while. The medics have probably missed you."

"No, they haven't," Che'ri grumbled. "What about our game?"

"The game will keep," Thalias said. "Come on, now—no fussing allowed. This needs to be done."

"Fine," Che'ri muttered again. Still not happy, but she let Thalias lead her to the hatch without further argument.

"Thank you, Sky-walker," Thrawn called after them. "And you, Caregiver. Thank you both."

Thalias looked sideways at Che'ri. Yes, their game would wait until they were back in the suite. And then later this afternoon, maybe an hour or two after they returned, it would be over.

Thrawn was clearly playing some sort of game, too. The question on Thalias's mind now was whether it, too, was over.

Somehow, she doubted it.

# CHAPTER TWENTY-SIX

"'m sorry Patriel Lakooni," Lakphro said, giving the woman a helpless shrug. "I really don't know anything more about Haplif or the other Agbui than I've already told your investigators."

"Yes, I understand that's your position," Lakooni said, her eyes boring into Lakphro's like she was trying to see into the back of his brain. "All I'm asking is that you rethink everything. That you rethink it very, very hard."

Lakphro forced himself to meet that gaze, some anger starting to mix into his frustration and nervousness. That was his *position*? What was *that* supposed to mean? "I've already told you everything," he said. "If you want more, you'll have to ask Councilor Lakuviv or Senior Aide Lakjiip."

"Thank you," the Patriel said, her voice going even colder than it had already been. Whatever dislike she had toward Lakphro, she was carrying a triple dose of it toward the others. "Be assured that the *former* Councilor"—she leaned heavily on the word—"and his aide are being questioned even more thoroughly than you are."

"Did they mention the Agbui had a Coduyo midager and a Pathfinder with them?" Lakphro offered. "I never met them, but I heard a couple of people talking."

"The Pathfinder disappeared with the alien ship," Lakooni said. "The midager will be interviewed elsewhere at a future date."

"Right," Lakphro muttered. But not yet, and probably not as intensely as Lakphro and his family had been. The Xodlak and Coduyo were allies, and both were allies of the Irizi. Word had probably come down from above to go easy on the kid.

Allies got special treatment. Normal everyday citizens, the ones who would never be part of the family's upper echelons, not so much. "Can I go now?" he asked. "I have a ranch to run."

Lakooni pursed her lips. "For the moment," she said reluctantly. "But keep yourself available in case we need to talk to you again."

"I'm running a ranch," he growled, standing up. "Where would I go?"

"The Ascendancy is a big place," Lakooni countered. "One last thing. Your daughter mentioned that a piece of jewelry the Agbui had given her had been lost. Was it ever found?"

"No," Lakphro said without hesitation. After all, he'd lied about it so often to Lakris that the words now came out without any effort at all.

This time, at least, unlike the times he said that to his wife and daughter, there was no accompanying flicker of guilt.

"Too bad," Lakooni said, her eyes again boring into his. "You'll let us know if it is."

"Of course," Lakphro said. "You'll be the first."


"I'm sorry, Supreme General," Mid Captain Samakro said. "There's really nothing more I can tell you."

"I understand," Ba'kif said, glowering across his desk at the man. Not surprisingly, every one of Thrawn's officers had offered the same story: The *Springhawk* was attacked, it was partially disabled and briefly boarded, and the timely arrival of the *Grayshrike* and the Xodlak, Erighal, and Pommrio family warships had been the only thing that saved it from destruction. The boarders had subsequently been found dead in the *Springhawk*'s brig, victims of small doomsday devices planted inside their bodies by their unknown employer.

The *Grayshrike*'s commander, Mid Captain Apros, had been lionized by all three families for his actions. Apros in turn had thanked the families publicly and enthusiastically for their timely arrival at the scene in time to pluck the *Springhawk* from disaster. The families had accepted the gratitude with grace and had reminded everyone that they were Chiss first and Xodlak, Erighal, or Pommrio second. At that point, as far as everyone was concerned, the incident was over.

Somehow, no one got around to explaining what they were all doing that far out of Ascendancy territory in the first place.

The worst part was that Ba'kif would probably never be able to get the complete truth. Ever since the deployment of sky-walkers aboard Ascendancy ships and the veil of secrecy wrapped around them, there had been a curious but necessary dichotomy in law and regulations. Bridge officers who knew about the sky-walkers were forbidden to speak about anything the girls were involved with, not even to others who shared the secret. The rest of the officers and warriors aboard were expected to obey all orders, to accept whatever happened without question, and generally to do their jobs and mind their own business.

For whatever reason, Thrawn had brought his sky-walker into the events over that distant and unremarkable planet. The result was that only Thrawn was free to give Ba'kif the truth about those events.

Under normal circumstances, Ba'kif would have hauled the other into his office to demand exactly that. But in yet one more bizarre twist to this story, all three of the affected families, along with their assorted allies in the Syndicure, seemed to be actively blocking any inquiry by the fleet in general and Ba'kif in particular. Their own accounts of the abortive attack on their family warships, and an escaping enemy freighter that tried too late to turn out of the path of a pair of fleeing gunboats, had matched perfectly with the statements from the *Springhawk*'s officers. The Syndicure had declared the matter closed and clearly intended it to remain so.

Allies of the Irizi, Dasklo, and Plikh, all doing their damnedest to keep a Mitth senior captain from testifying before the fleet and likely getting in trouble. A Mitth officer, moreover, that many of them disliked to the point of hatred.

Paradox atop riddle atop mystery.

"Would it help if I promised anything you say would be treated as confidential?" Ba'kif asked, trying one last time.

"I'm sorry, Supreme General," Samakro said evenly. "There are standing orders I have no choice but to obey. You'll have to ask Senior Captain Thrawn."

Ba'kif eyed him. There'd been something in his tone . . . "You don't like Thrawn, do you, Mid Captain?"

Samakro hesitated. "Permission to speak honestly, sir?"

"Certainly."

"No, sir, I don't," Samakro said. "I don't think he understands how anything outside the fleet works, and I don't think he's very good at inspiring his officers and warriors. He pushes things to the edge, takes liberties with orders, and generally acts in a manner that previous generations of fleet officers would find disgraceful."

He seemed to brace himself. "But that doesn't really matter. He's an excellent commander, and he knows how to handle his ship. Even his most outrageous hunches are generally proved correct, and he always brings us through whatever storms we find ourselves in. *Always.*"

"You sound like a good first officer," Ba'kif commented.

"Which is also the point, sir," Samakro said. "I'm the *Springhawk*'s first officer. Senior Captain Thrawn is the *Springhawk*'s commander. Whatever I might personally think of him is completely irrelevant. I'm an officer of the fleet, he's my commander, and I will follow him and obey his orders to the best of my ability. Period."

Ba'kif inclined his head. "As I said, Mid Captain: a good first officer." He waved toward the door. "You're dismissed. Thank you for your time."

For a few moments after Samakro left, Ba'kif gazed thoughtfully at the closed door. Yes, he would certainly ask Thrawn about it.

But not yet. Not until things had quieted down, or there was a new threat or internal scandal to distract the Syndicure's attention.

For the moment, it was more vital that they gather further information on these Agbui cultural nomads who seemed to be somehow at the center of everything. The Council needed to know who they were, where they came from, who if anyone they were working for, and what their intentions were. Unfortunately, at the moment all of those investigations were being conducted by the three affected families.

But that was about to change. Fleet forces had also been involved, which made it only reasonable that the Council invited themselves into the game.

The families probably wouldn't like it. Neither would the Syndicure.

Ba'kif didn't especially care.

It could have gone better, Samakro realized soberly as he made his way from Ba'kif's office toward the main shuttle landing area. But it could also have gone much, much worse.

His claim of silence based on Che'ri's presence on the *Springhawk*'s bridge was pure fantasy, of course. It adhered to the strict form of that regulation, certainly, but it was light-years out of the creators' intent. If Ba'kif had chosen to demand an answer, and Samakro had continued to refuse, he would be on his way to a small detention cell right now.

But he'd been pretty sure Ba'kif wouldn't press the issue. Right now, the Syndicure was in self-defense mode, determined to sweep whatever had happened out the door, and the Council was just as clearly not interested in sweeping any of it back in. Maybe later, after the families moved on to other matters, but not now.

What was bothering him more was that, as far as he could tell, there hadn't been a peep out of anyone regarding the nonsense story he'd given Thalias.

And there should have been. The soap bubble he'd spun to her about Sunrise being the last-stand fortress for the Nikardun remnant should have been screamed from the Assembly Cupola by now. There should have been outrage and scorn and syndics calling for Thrawn's head in a bucket for ever entertaining such a ridiculous notion.

Instead, there was nothing. Did that mean that Thalias wasn't a spy, after all?

Samakro scowled. Of course not. All it meant was that she or her controller had decided to sit on the story, waiting for a better opportunity to hang it around Thrawn's neck.

But that time would come. And when it did, Thalias would finally be unmasked.

And she would very much regret it.

Because her betrayal wouldn't just be an attack on Thrawn. It would be an attack on the entire Expansionary Defense Fleet, on all the officers and warriors who risked their lives daily to protect the people of the Chiss Ascendancy. That was something that simply could not be allowed to happen.

So let them wait. Let them plot and scheme. Let them choose the time and the place.

Whenever it was, wherever it was, Samakro would be waiting.

When the assignment Qilori was handed identified his job as guiding an unnamed person in an unflagged ship, he was pretty sure what was going to happen somewhere along the way.

He was right.

"I'm sorry I can't deliver a better report," he apologized when he finally ran out of words.

"Calm yourself, Pathfinder," Jixtus said, his gloved fingers tapping gently on the edge of his contour chair. "I never expected this to mark the end of the Chiss Ascendancy. They're more resilient than that." He paused, and Qilori had the sense of an evil smile behind the black veil. "Though perhaps not nearly as resilient as they think."

Jixtus paused, the robed shoulders giving a little shrug. "You were right to be concerned about this Chiss officer, though. I'll be sure to add Senior Captain Thrawn into our calculations in the future."

"I would definitely recommend that," Qilori said, his cheek winglets twitching. "I wish I could offer some hints on how to defeat him."

"Defeat isn't always necessary," Jixtus said. "Isolation and neutralization can be equally effective. My more immediate concern is the fact that you left Haplif's body behind for the Chiss to examine."

"That wasn't my decision," Qilori said hastily, feeling his winglets starting to flutter. "Shimkif saw that the Xodlak rancher had killed him and ordered the pilot to get clear."

"Again, Pathfinder, calm yourself," Jixtus said, more severely this time. "The Grysks lay blame only where it's deserved, and only on those who fail us. Each of our servants is responsible solely for his own decisions and actions, not for another's."

"Yes, sir," Qilori said, feeling his winglets and his tension subsiding. *Grysks.* He'd never heard of a species by that name.

Or a faction, if that's what they were. Or a combine, or a gang, or something else entirely. A name by itself really didn't contain much information.

But at least now he had a name to put to the manipulators behind all this. "Is it over?" he asked. "I mean, are you going to need me for anything else?"

"Really, Pathfinder, you surprise me," Jixtus said. "Have you forgotten your other mandate?"

Qilori frowned. "Sir?"

"I told you to learn for me how exactly the Chiss navigate through the Chaos," Jixtus reminded him. "*That* is what I need you for, and *that* is the task you will accomplish."

"Yes, sir," Qilori said. The weight on his heart, which had been starting to lift, now came crashing back down. "I'll do my best."

"Yes, you will," Jixtus agreed calmly. "Because as I said, we lay blame on those who fail us."


"I'm told, Senior Captain Lakinda," Syndic Zistalmu said, his voice studiously casual, "that your family is unhappy with you."

"I've heard similar reports, Syndic Zistalmu," Lakinda said, long practice allowing her to keep her face and voice expressionless. "You'll understand that I can't comment on such things."

"Of course," Zistalmu said. "I understand."

Lakinda nodded. She would just bet he did.

The Xodlak weren't just unhappy with her. They were furious. The Patriarch himself had sent a message castigating her for failing to secure the nyix mine for them. That, despite the fact that the Celwis Patriel's own internal investigation had surely by now uncovered evidence that the whole thing had been a fraud from the beginning.

Lakinda herself would probably never know the final results of any such inquiry. The fog of secrecy that had been spread over this thing was both awesome and more than a little frightening. Under the circumstances, she probably didn't want to know what was going on right now between the Xodlak and their allies.

Only she might not have a choice about that. The Irizi were one of the Xodlak's strongest allies, and her presence today in Syndic Zistalmu's office might well be part of the fallout from those backroom deals and maneuverings.

If he demanded she tell him everything she knew, could she refuse him? There were limitations on such things in the fleet, but she'd been on a family mission and under family auspices. Did fleet rules even apply?

"Naturally, I commend both your loyalty and your discretion," Zistalmu continued. He picked up his questis and gestured to it. "I'm also quite impressed by your list of recent successes," he continued. "Your campaigns with Admiral Ar'alani's task force have been most impressive."

"Thank you, sir," Lakinda said. "I'll remind you that much of the credit for those victories goes to the admiral and her capable leadership."

"Again, loyalty and discretion," Zistalmu said, inclining his head to her. "We of the Irizi value both qualities. You're, what, a Xodlak merit adoptive?"

"Yes," Lakinda said, a sour taste in her mouth. The first officer on the *Midsummer,* trying to stare her down because he was blood and she wasn't.

Though that gulf might soon evaporate, and not in a good way.

Along with the anger and frustration radiating from the Patriarch's office had come calls for Lakinda to be detached from the family entirely. At the moment those calls weren't loud, but it seemed to her that they were slowly growing in both number and volume.

What would happen to her if it came to that? Would she be rematched to her old family, back in the obscure Oyokal farming community that she'd escaped from when she joined the fleet? More worrying, if she was no longer Xodlak, what would be the Defense Hierarchy Council's response? Theoretically, she would still keep her rank; but would they decide she could no longer be an effective ship's commander? "Though family status doesn't matter in the fleet," she added, as much to herself as to Zistalmu.

"Of course not," Zistalmu agreed. "Nor should it. On the other hand, it never hurts to have a strong family position, whether to leverage for future endeavors or just as a bit of cushioning against the general surprises of life." He raised his eyebrows. "Tell me, Senior Captain: How would you like to move up from merit adoptive to full Trial-born?"

Lakinda felt her eyes widen. She'd assumed Zistalmu's purpose in calling her in was to either coax out some additional details of the nyix fiasco or else simply to offer moral support for her family problems. Suggesting he was willing to push through an advancement was the last thing she could have expected. "Can you *do* that?" she asked. "I need the Patriarch's approval to even start the Trials, and as you just said the whole family is unhappy with me."

Zistalmu chuckled. "Oh, I doubt even our Patriarch could convince yours to change his mind on anything," he conceded. "The Xodlak have been good allies, but your current Patriarch is a stiffnecked old groundlion. No, Senior Captain, you misunderstand. I'm not encouraging you to take the Xodlak family Trials. I'm offering you the chance to become a Trial-born of the Irizi."

"Oh," Lakinda managed. All right; so Zistalmu offering to nudge the Xodlak on her behalf was the *second* to last thing she could have expected. "I . . . don't know what to say."

"You don't need to answer right now," Zistalmu said. "In fact, I'd be a little concerned if you *didn't* take some time to think about the offer. But be assured that it's genuine, it's eagerly and wholeheartedly given, and it's completely open-ended. Take all the time you need, and contact me when you've made a decision."

"I will," Lakinda said. "Understand in turn that whether or not I accept, I'm flattered and humbled by the offer."

"We wouldn't make it if we didn't feel you deserved it," Zistalmu said. "At any rate, I'm sure you have other matters that require your attention, so I'll say farewell. For now."

"Thank you, Syndic," Lakinda said, standing up. "I'll make a decision as quickly as I can."

"At your own pace, Senior Captain," Zistalmu said. "Good day."

A moment later Lakinda was striding down the corridor, her head spinning. *Trial-born of the Irizi.* Not in the farthest reaches of her imagination would such a possibility ever have occurred to her.

Yes, she would consider it. She would consider it *very* seriously. As an old man back home had once jokingly told her as he picked himself up off the ground, *When you see the saddlebull is about to throw you, jump off.*

And really, *Senior Captain Ziinda* had a nice and rather exotic ring to it.

The call came late at night. As, Thurfian thought to himself, all such calls should come.

"He passed early this morning," Speaker Thyklo told him, her voice tired and strained. "Peacefully, and with his family in attendance. I know that was the way he would have wanted to go."

"As would we all," Thurfian said. "I'm sorry to hear that he's gone."

They were the standard words spoken at such news, Thurfian knew. But unlike some who would be repeating that sentiment in the coming days, he genuinely meant it. He and Patriarch Thooraki had had their clashes over the years, and Thurfian was pretty sure the old man had disliked him. But Thooraki had guided the Mitth well and with a firm hand, and the family had grown stronger and deeper under his leadership. And that, truly, was what mattered. "Have you and the Patriels chosen his successor yet?" he asked Thyklo.

"We have," the Speaker said. "We've chosen you."

Thurfian felt his mouth drop open, the last lingering tendrils of sleep fog vanishing. "*Me?*"

"You," Thyklo confirmed. "I know that traditionally the Patriarch is chosen from among the ranks of the Patriels, but the confusion surrounding the recent military incident has underscored the need to keep firm control of family dealings at the planetary level. None of them felt confident that they could leave matters in the hands of their deputies while new Patriels were chosen."

"Yes, that makes sense," Thurfian said, still feeling the hammer blow of the news bouncing around his brain. He'd been working hard these past few weeks in an effort to angle himself higher in the family's ranks.

But his goal had really been just for Speaker Thyklo's position. Never in his wildest dreams had he expected to jump directly to Patriarch.

Speaking of Thyklo, he'd better make sure that avenue hadn't been inadvertently overlooked. "What about you, ma'am?" he asked. "The Speaker is also traditionally a viable candidate for Patriarch."

"It is," Thyklo agreed. "And the position was indeed offered to me. But the network of contacts and friendships I've established in the Syndicure can't simply be handed over to someone else. Not even you. No offense meant."

"None taken," Thurfian said. So this was really happening. *Patriarch of the Mitth* . . . It was a huge step.

But he could do it. He knew he could. The Patriarch had a whole squad of deputies and aides to help oversee the swirling hive that constituted the Mitth family. They would handle the details, leaving him free to consider and then enact the broader policy decisions.

In fact, as he thought about it, he realized that Thyklo's position as Speaker would actually have been harder for him to step into. That role was even more dependent on personal connections and relationships, on favors given and received, on quiet deals and unspoken promises.

As Patriarch, Thurfian would have to take on some of those same tasks, of course. But now those challenges would be with his own family members and the other family Patriarchs, not the roiling mess that was the Syndicure.

Yes. He could do it. "If you and the Patriels believe I can serve the family best in that capacity," he said gravely, "I accept your offer with thanks and humility. I will strive, with your support and counsel, to maintain and advance the honor, glory, and power of the Mitth."

"As will we all," Thyklo said. "And now you're expected at the homestead. Senior Aide Mitth'iv'iklo and an escort are on their way to your home, and should be there within twenty minutes. Bring whatever you like, but don't worry about packing—that will be handled later today. The office and staff will be informed while you're en route, and the Patriels will be waiting to speak to you via conference call when you arrive. Any questions?"

"Not at this time," Thurfian said. "Though as long as Senior Aide Thivik is still on his way, I might as well start the packing. I presume I'll be speaking with you later, as well?"

"At your convenience," Thyklo said. "Congratulations, Patriarch Thurfian. May the Mitth flourish under your guidance."

*Patriarch Thurfian.* The words echoed through Thurfian's mind as he pulled on his clothing. *Patriarch Thurfian.* He'd once wondered with private amusement what Zistalmu would think if he knew Thurfian had been elevated to Syndic Prime. He could only imagine the Irizi's expression when he learned Thurfian was now the Mitth Patriarch. Zistalmu's expression would be priceless.

So, when the time was right, would Thrawn's.

Thurfian didn't have a lot of keepsakes, but most of them were items he didn't trust to some random moving crew. The twenty minutes were nearly up, and he'd finished packing the relics into sturdy travel boxes, when there was a tone from the door.

He opened it to find Senior Aide Thivik waiting, a group of four

Mitth guards spread out protectively in the corridor behind him. "Good evening, Senior Aide," Thurfian greeted him gravely, stepping aside to let him in. "Thank you for coming, and my condolences on the passing of your master and our beloved Patriarch."

"Thank you, Syndic Prime," Thivik said gravely as he stepped past Thurfian into the suite, closing the door on the other Mitth. "Patriarch Thurfian, I should say. I trust you're ready?"

"I am," Thurfian said, eyeing him closely. Thivik always looked old and gaunt, but tonight he looked even older. Patriarch Thooraki's death had clearly hit him hard. "I have a few things we'll want to take with us."

"Yes," Thivik said, turning to look at the boxes Thurfian had packed. "You're quite pleased with yourself, aren't you?"

"Pleased?" Thurfian asked cautiously.

"Pleased that you've been granted the highest position in the Mitth family," Thivik said, still looking at the boxes. "Pleased that you now have more power than you've ever dreamed possible. Pleased that your hopes and goals, whatever they might be, are about to be realized."

"Should I instead cower in fear and false modesty?" Thurfian countered. "Yes, I'm pleased. Pleased, humbled, and awestruck. Should one who has been placed at the head of the greatest and noblest family of the Chiss Ascendancy be otherwise?"

"The greatest?" Thivik said, his tone suddenly gone odd. "Perhaps. That determination is for future historians. But the noblest?"

He turned around, and Thurfian had to stifle a sudden urge to take a step backward. The sudden intensity in the other's face . . . "We shall travel to the homestead, Patriarch Thurfian," Thivik said quietly. "We shall speak with the Patriels, and your staff, and we shall settle you into your new home. You shall have a good night's rest, and a filling breakfast."

Thivik's eyes seemed to glitter. "And then," he said, his voice taking on an edge of long distant pain, "I will tell you of the ancient history of the Mitth. The *true* history, so long suppressed.

"And I will tell you of a terrible alien weapon known as Starflash."

Read on for an excerpt from the epic conclusion
to The Ascendancy Trilogy:

# THRAWN
## ASCENDANCY
### LESSER EVIL

**BY TIMOTHY ZAHN**

# PROLOGUE

"**P**repare for breakout." Senior Captain Mitth'raw'nuruodo's voice echoed across the *Springhawk*'s bridge. "All officers and warriors stand prepared. We're not here to start trouble, but I intend to be ready for it."

First Officer Mid Captain Ufsa'mak'ro scowled to himself. Of course Senior Captain Thrawn didn't plan to start trouble. He never did. Yet somehow trouble always seemed to happen.

If that pattern was determined to continue, it couldn't have picked a better spot for it.

Bad enough that Zyzek was an alien system. Worse that Chiss records had nothing about it beyond its location and that it was a trading center for several of the small nations to the east and southeast of the Chiss Ascendancy. Even worse that Thrawn believed this to be the system where Captain Fsir and his fellow Watith had been recruited to launch their ambush attack on his ship.

Worst of all that no one else knew the *Springhawk* was here.

They should have gone straight back to the Ascendancy. They should have left the planet Hoxim and the skirmish Samakro had privately dubbed the Battle of the Three Families and headed back to Csilla for repairs, debriefing, and what was likely to be a memorable job of sweeping the whole mess out the door. All the other Chiss warships, the ones crewed exclusively by members of the Xodlak, Erighal, and Pommrio families, had done exactly that, making the slow jump-by-jump back home while their commanders no doubt struggled to write all this up in their logs.

But not the *Springhawk*. The hours Thrawn had spent studying the Watith freighter before its destruction had somehow convinced him that Zyzek was where Fsir had come from. From there, it was only a small leap of tactical logic to swinging by that system on their way home and taking a look.

Samakro understood the strategy. On one level, he even agreed with it. The *Springhawk* had sky-walker Che'ri to speed it on its way through the twisting hyperspace pathways of the Chaos, while any observer who'd been lurking around to report on the battle would have some lesser navigator or none at all. The fact that Thrawn could get to Zyzek ahead of that news could be a major advantage in information gathering.

But that was one small plus, and it was piled on top of a whole stack of minuses.

"Breakout: Three, two, *one*."

The star-flares collapsed into stars, and the *Springhawk* had arrived.

"Full scan," Thrawn ordered. "Pay special attention to the ships in the various orbits. I'll want as complete a catalog of ship types as possible, along with where in the orbital stack they are."

"Yes, Senior Captain," Mid Commander Elod'al'vumic acknowledged from the sensor station.

"Kharill, assist her with the cataloging," Thrawn added.

"Yes, sir." The voice of Senior Commander Plikh'ar'illmorf came over the speaker from secondary command. "Dalvu, mark which sectors you want us to handle from here."

"Yes, Senior Commander," Dalvu said. "Marking them now."

"Watch for movement, either inward as an attempt to hide from us or outward in an attempt to flee," Thrawn said. "We're here to see if we can create a reaction." He nodded toward the helm. "Azmordi, start moving us inward. Sky-walker Che'ri, stand ready in case we need to leave quickly."

"Yes, sir," Lieutenant Commander Tumaz'mor'diamir said from the helm.

"Yes, Senior Captain," sky-walker Che'ri's caregiver Mitth'ali'astov echoed.

Samakro let his eyes sweep slowly across the bridge. Dalvu, Kharill, Azmordi. Officers he'd served with a long time, dating back to when he'd commanded the *Springhawk* and continuing through Thrawn's current tenure as captain. He knew them and their abilities and trusted them with his life.

Thalias, on the other hand . . .

He focused on the caregiver as she turned back to the viewport, her hand resting reassuringly on Che'ri's shoulder. Thalias was still far too much of a mystery to him, with uncertainties and doubts swirling around her.

Worse, from Samakro's point of view, she carried the stench of family politics. Syndic Mitth'urf'ianico had done some fancy maneuvering in order to get her aboard the *Springhawk,* and Samakro still didn't know what Thurfian's game was.

But he would find out. He'd already planted the seeds, feeding Thalias a story and conspiracy theory that painted Thrawn in a bad light, a story he knew she would eventually spill to Thurfian or possibly to someone else. When she did—when she betrayed that confidence—he would finally have proof that she was a spy sent to destroy or at least damage the *Springhawk*'s commander. Then, maybe, he'd be able to convince Thrawn to get her off his ship.

Until then, all Samakro could do was watch her and guard as best he could against any mischief she might make.

*We're here to create a reaction.* Unfortunately, Samakro had seen the kind of reaction Thrawn's unexpected appearances tended to spark. Especially in potentially hostile territory and moving among large numbers of probably unfriendly ships.

But Thrawn was the *Springhawk*'s commander, and he'd given an order. Samakro's job was to do everything in his power to carry it out.

And if part of his duty was to defend his ship to the death . . . well, he was prepared to do that, too.

"Conquest."

Generalirius Nakirre gazed out the viewport of the Kilji war cruiser *Whetstone* at the dozens of trading ships orbiting the planet Zyzek. *Conquest.*

"An interesting concept, it is not?" the being known as Jixtus suggested.

Nakirre eyed his guest. It was unsettling having to deal with a being whose garments of robe, hood, gloves, and veil wrapped him in total concealment.

Especially given that such complete anonymity gave him a serious negotiating advantage over Nakirre and his Kilji vassals. Once Jixtus learned how to read the emotional responses reflected in the patterns of ripples and stretches that moved through the dark-orange Kilji skin, he would gain insight that went far deeper than Nakirre's words.

But Nakirre had agreed to travel here with the alien, and the Overlords had confirmed his decision, and so here they were.

And truth be told, Jixtus *did* have some intriguing ideas on how the future of the Kilji Illumine could be shaped.

"People who would otherwise ignore the wisdom and guidance of the Kilji would be encouraged to listen," Jixtus continued. "People who would otherwise scorn and scoff at your philosophy could be silenced or sent where their rantings would not disturb or disrupt."

"It would allow us to bring order," Nakirre agreed, images of unprecedented stability running through his mind. *Conquest.*

"Exactly," Jixtus said. "Order and enlightenment to billions who currently struggle and flail helplessly in darkness. As you well know, encouragement and persuasion—even passionate persuasion—can move a culture only so far. Conquest is the only way to bring Kilji insight to the whole of a region."

"And you believe these beings are prepared to receive such insight?" Nakirre asked, sweeping his hand across the viewport at the merchant ships floating placidly in their orbits.

"Is there ever a time when enlightenment would *not* be beneficial?" Jixtus countered. "Whether they realize it or not, whether they accept it or not, the Kilji path is what will ultimately bring them prosperity and contentment. What purpose delay?"

"What purpose, indeed," Nakirre agreed, gazing at the ships. So many merchants, so many nations, all standing helpless before the might of the Kilji Illumine. Which should he choose first?

"As I promised, we will guide you as to the nations most quickly and easily conquered," Jixtus continued. "There are representative traders here from each of the four the Grysks feel are the most promising. We'll speak with them in turn, perhaps sample the goods they've brought for sale. You will then—"

"Generalirius?" Vassal Two called from the sensor station. "A new ship has arrived. Unknown configuration."

Nakirre looked at the visual display. The newcomer was indeed unlike any of the other ships already in orbit. Representatives of some new nation, no doubt, here to join in barter and trade.

Or perhaps not. The design of the craft was not that of a merchant. Its shape, the systematic groupings of bulges along its sides and shoulders, the distinctive sheen of a nyix-alloy hull . . .

"These are not traders," he said. "That is a warship. Is it not?" he added, turning to look at Jixtus.

Only to find the Grysk silent and unmoving. The veiled face was turned toward the visual display, the robed figure as still as if the being beneath the robe and veil had turned to stone.

Usually Jixtus had a comment for everything. For once, he didn't.

"If you're concerned, you need not be," Nakirre reassured him. The newcomer was about two-thirds the size of the *Whetstone,* probably no more than the equivalent of a Kilji picket cruiser, with a comparable ratio of weaponry. Should they choose to initiate combat, he had no doubt the Kiljis would win.

He could only hope they wouldn't be so foolish. The destruction of their ship would mean those aboard would never hear the Kilji philosophy and thus could never achieve true enlightenment.

"Generalirius, the warship is broadcasting a message," Vassal Four said. He touched a switch—

"—to all assembled merchants and traders," a smooth, melodious voice said over the *Whetstone*'s bridge speaker, the Minnisiat trade language words articulated with clipped precision. "I am Senior Captain Thrawn of the Chiss Expansionary Defense Fleet warship *Springhawk*. I have news for any Watith who may be present. Are there any of that species to whom I may speak?"

"Are there?" Nakirre asked, looking back at Jixtus.

Jixtus stirred, breaking whatever paralysis had overtaken him. "Are there what?" he asked, his voice odd.

"Are there any Watith?"

Jixtus seemed to gather himself together. "I don't know. I didn't notice any of their ships when we arrived, but I also wasn't looking for them. I suggest we hold here and see if anyone answers him."

"If no one else stands forth, I will speak with him," Nakirre declared. "I would learn what news he bears."

"I would advise against that," Jixtus warned. "The Chiss are a devious species. He is likely asking that question in the hope of drawing you out into the open."

"Drawing *me* out?" Nakirre asked. "How would he even know I'm here?"

"I didn't mean you specifically, Generalirius," Jixtus said. "But be assured he's hunting for information. That's what this particular Chiss does."

"If no one wishes news," Thrawn continued, "perhaps someone will give us the location of their world, so that we may return our prisoners to their people."

Nakirre looked at Jixtus with surprise. "He has *prisoners*?"

"No," Jixtus bit out. "He doesn't."

"He says he does."

"He lies," Jixtus said. "As I told you already, he's hunting for information. This is a trick."

"How do you know?" Nakirre persisted.

Again Jixtus fell silent. "Tell me how you know, Jixtus of the Grysks," Nakirre repeated, making it an order this time. "If the Chiss mounted a raid, there would of course be prisoners. If there was a battle, even the most fearsome often leaves survivors. Tell me now, or I shall ask *him*."

"There was a battle," Jixtus said reluctantly. "But there were no survivors."

"How can you be certain?"

"Because I was the one who sent the Watith against the Chiss," Jixtus said. "Twenty-three Watith went into that battle. Twenty-three Watith died."

"I ask again: How do you know that?"

"There was an observer at the battle," Jixtus said. He sounded better on balance now. "One who was concealed from the combatants' view. He brought me that news."

"I see," Nakirre said, pretending he was satisfied.

Only he wasn't.

Because an observer who had spoken of Watith deaths would also have warned that the *Springhawk* had survived that battle. Yet Jixtus had clearly been surprised by the Chiss warship's arrival. Was it merely the *Springhawk*'s appearance here at Zyzek, and not the simple fact of its survival, that had startled him?

And how did he know that this Chiss was seeking information? Did Jixtus know him personally?

For a moment Nakirre considered asking those questions. But there would be no gain. Jixtus was withholding information, and would undoubtedly continue to do so. That was the way of those who lacked enlightenment.

No matter. There was after all another source of information close at hand. "Vassal One: Yaw rotation to face the Chiss ship," he ordered. He waited until the *Whetstone* was lined up precisely on the incoming warship, then keyed his mike. "Senior Captain Thrawn, this is Generalirius Nakirre of the Kilji Illumine warship *Whetstone*," he called. "Tell me how you come to have Watith prisoners."

"I greet you, Generalirius Nakirre," Thrawn said. "Are you an ally or trading associate of the Watith?"

"Sadly, I am not yet either," Nakirre said. "But perhaps soon."

"Ah," Thrawn said. "You have come here to initiate new trade relationships, then?"

Nakirre's skin stretched in a wry smile. Jixtus had been right: This Chiss *was* on the hunt for information. "Not specifically," he said. "We of the Illumine travel the Chaos teaching others the Kilji way of order and enlightenment."

"A noble undertaking," Thrawn said. "Have the Watith been among your students?"

"Again, not yet," Nakirre said. "We are newly arrived in this part of space. But such things are for the future. Tell me how you come to have Watith prisoners."

"For the moment, those details must remain confidential."

"No matter," Nakirre said. "I will accept your prisoners and return them to their home."

"Do you know where that home is?"

Nakirre hesitated. If he said yes, Thrawn would likely ask for the coordinates and take the prisoners there himself. If he said no, Thrawn would probably refuse to hand them over. "I have already made many contacts among the traders here," he said, choosing the third option. "One of them can surely provide that information."

"I appreciate your offer," Thrawn said. "But I cannot in good conscience accept it. If there are no Watith here to receive the prisoners, we will take our search elsewhere."

"I would not have you go to such trouble."

"That is my choice to make, not yours."

"Enlightenment requires that I serve others."

"You serve here best by permitting me to go my way," Thrawn said. "Or does your enlightenment require you to take away my freedom of choice?"

"Let him go," Jixtus murmured. "Just let him go."

Nakirre felt a ripple of anger. Anger at Jixtus; anger at Thrawn.

There were important details here that neither of them was willing to give him.

He needed Jixtus and the Grysks to show him which nations were most open to conquest and enlightenment. He didn't need Thrawn. "You should learn of what you speak before offering judgment," he said, keying his board to begin the *Whetstone*'s ramp-up to combat status. "Someday soon I shall bring the Kilji philosophy to the Chiss."

"I fear you will find little interest," Thrawn said. "We have our own ancient paths."

"The Kilji path will prove superior."

"No," Thrawn said, his voice flat. "It will not."

"Again, you dismiss our wisdom without even hearing it."

"In my experience, superior wisdom can stand on its own merits," Thrawn said. "It does not require a warship to force acceptance."

"You also bring a warship to this place."

"But I do not claim to offer others superior wisdom," Thrawn said. "Nor do I intend to impose my wisdom upon others."

"He's trying to goad you into attacking him," Jixtus warned quietly, his voice sounding strained. "Don't let him."

Nakirre felt a stretch of contempt. Why *shouldn't* he let the Chiss build his own destruction? The *Whetstone* was far mightier than Thrawn's *Springhawk*. It would be the work of a few minutes to destroy him.

"He's trying to obtain data on the *Whetstone*'s capabilities," Jixtus went on. "*And* on your abilities as its commander."

And why *shouldn't* he demonstrate the might of a Kilji war cruiser? Whatever knowledge Thrawn might gain would be lost in the abyss of his death.

Still, there were others here who would witness that battle. Perhaps it would be unwise to show them the full might of the Kilji before the Kilhorde visited their worlds to show the path of enlightenment.

But to even *look* as if he was allowing the Chiss to dictate his course of action . . .

"Warships, this is Zyzek System Defense." A new voice came over the bridge speaker. "You are both requested to stand down."

Nakirre felt a ripple of cold amusement. The four patrol craft that had risen from the mass of merchant ships and split into pairs to confront the *Whetstone* and *Springhawk* were smaller and even more pathetic than the Chiss warship. Should they demand battle, it would take only a single laser volley to send them beyond all chance of enlightenment.

"The Kilji cannot enlighten them if they are dead," Jixtus reminded him.

He was right, of course. More important, perhaps, it gave him a legitimate excuse to refuse combat with the Chiss.

"Zyzek System Defense, I comply with your request," he said. "Senior Captain Thrawn, you may keep your prisoners. I will see you again when I arrive among your people to change the ancient paths of the Chiss to the fuller enlightenment of the Kiljis."

"I will look forward to our next encounter," Thrawn said. "Farewell."

"Until the meeting," Nakirre said.

He keyed off and turned yet again to Jixtus. "You spoke of four nations that the Kiljis should first seek to enlighten," he said. "I choose instead the Chiss."

"Not yet," Jixtus said. "You must start with other beings."

"Why?"

Jixtus shook his head, the motion rippling the hood and veil. "Because I know these Chiss, Generalirius. They are resilient and powerful. I've seen them resist attack from without and manipulation from within. Only a combination of the two will succeed in bringing about their destruction."

"Enlightenment is incompatible with delay," Nakirre warned. "And you spoke of conquest, not destruction. If all are destroyed, who then shall we guide to peace and order?"

"A remnant shall certainly survive," Jixtus promised. "The common folk, those who will accept Kilji rule without question or resistance, will be yours to enlighten. But to achieve that, the leaders and commanders must fall."

"I agree," Nakirre said. "So let us proceed to their world and begin that process."

"But they must fall on the schedule the Grysks have constructed," Jixtus said. "If we deviate from that time line, all will be lost. *But.*" He lifted a finger. "That doesn't mean you have to wait to meet them. In fact, I've always intended that you and the *Whetstone* would carry me on my first visit to their worlds and their leaders."

"Very well," Nakirre said, gazing at the display. The *Springhawk* had turned away from the planet now and was heading back out of the gravity well toward deep space. "I will follow your guidelines. For now. But be warned: If I feel you're proceeding too slowly, I'll take that time line into my own hands."

"Understood," Jixtus said. "Hold fast to my guidance, and the Chiss will be yours. In good time."

"In *swift* time," Nakirre corrected. "And when you destroy their leaders, you will leave me this one, this Thrawn." His skin stretched in a grim smile. "I am anxious for him to face true enlightenment."

The *Springhawk* was back in hyperspace, and the tension of that brief encounter was finally starting to leave Thalias's shoulders when Samakro finished his search of the ship's archives. "There's nothing here about a species or government called the Kiljis, Senior Captain," he reported. "Also no references to a Generalirius Nakirre."

"Understandable," Thrawn said. "But we *have* heard that title before."

Thalias stole a look over her shoulder. Samakro's face, she noted, had that telltale hint of someone chewing on something sour. "Yes, sir," he confirmed. "The Battle Dreadnought that attacked the *Vigilant* and *Grayshrike* at Sunrise mentioned it."

"Suggesting they and Generalirius Nakirre may be in some way connected," Thrawn said.

"Yes, sir," Samakro said again, a hint of reluctance joining the hint of sourness.

Small wonder. The first officer had argued with Thrawn—

respectfully and quietly, of course, but still argued—about Thrawn's plan to swing by Zyzek before returning to the Ascendancy. Samakro had suggested it would be both dangerous and pointless, while Thrawn had been convinced the side trip would be worthwhile. Once again, Thrawn had been proven right.

Though whether anything he'd learned would ultimately prove useful, Thalias couldn't guess.

"We also know that the generalirius wasn't alone just now," Samakro continued. "There were four instances when we could hear a second voice behind the first—very faint, but definitely not the same person. Probably not even the same species."

"I agree," Thrawn said. "Have the analysts been able to draw anything from those interruptions?"

"Not yet," Samakro said. "The voice was quiet, and Nakirre's transmission wasn't as clear as we might have hoped. We've been able to identify a few of the words, but a full analysis may have to wait until we reach Naporar and the better equipment there."

"Have the analysts continue their work," Thrawn said. "Not just the words, but also as much of the vocal profile as they can obtain."

"Yes, sir," Samakro said.

Thalias glanced back again. Samakro had moved off and was logging the order into his questis. Thrawn, for his part, was gazing thoughtfully across the bridge, his eyes slightly unfocused, a sign Thalias had learned to recognize as deep thought.

She turned back forward, looking down at Che'ri. The girl's eyes were likewise unfocused, though in her case it was because she was totally immersed in Third Sight as she guided the *Springhawk* toward home.

"Caregiver."

Thalias twitched and spun around, to find Thrawn standing right behind her. "You shouldn't sneak up on people that way, Senior Captain," she said reproachfully.

"My apologies," Thrawn said, sounding more amused than actually sorry. "You need to learn how to think and ponder without sacrificing the awareness of your surroundings." He nodded toward Che'ri. "How is she?"

"She's fine," Thalias said, looking down at the girl. "She'll need a rest break in about forty minutes, but she got plenty of sleep last night and seems to be doing fine."

"That's not what I meant," Thrawn said, lowering his voice. "I'm talking about her and the Magys."

Thalias felt her throat tighten. She'd hoped she'd been the only one who'd seen that. "It may have just been coincidence."

"Do you believe that?"

Thalias sighed. The Magys, the leader of a group of alien refugees, had been woken from her forced hibernation in order to look at a sample of jewelry that was being used by a group called the Agbui against a Xodlak family Councilor on Celwis. Once the Magys had identified the brooch, Thrawn had asked for her to go back into hibernation until she could be returned to her people, currently waiting for her on the Paccosh homeworld of Rapacc.

Not surprisingly, knowing now that her world was under outside threat, the Magys had resisted the idea of going back to sleep. Thrawn's warning—that she needed to be kept hidden lest she be spotted by an officer who came to the suite on other business—had made no impact on her whatsoever. She'd been so adamant, in fact, that Thalias had thought for a minute that Thrawn and Samakro would have to physically force her back into the hibernation chamber.

And then, all at once, she'd abandoned the fight and meekly accepted Thrawn's order.

But before she settled back into the chamber, her eyes had flicked in the direction of Che'ri's sleeping room.

Back on Rapacc, at the first meeting between Thrawn and the refugees, the Magys had somehow recognized that Thalias had once been a sky-walker, able to use Third Sight to navigate through hyperspace. Had she also sensed Che'ri's presence and her much more powerful connection with whatever it was that Third Sight allowed her to access?

"No, I don't really believe it," she conceded. "But I still hope it was. I mean, there were two bulkheads and the whole dayroom between her and Che'ri. How could she have known through all of that?"

"The Magys claims her people join with the Beyond after death," Thrawn reminded her. "The fact that she recognized you'd once been a sky-walker suggests there's something of that connection present during life, as well."

"But on Rapacc she was at least *looking* at me," Thalias said. "If she'd seen Che'ri, I might understand it. But she never did."

Thrawn shifted his gaze to the viewport and the hyperspace swirl outside. "If the Beyond is the same Force that General Skywalker told me about, it appears to have many aspects and manifestations. It's possible this is a new facet that the Magys hadn't yet experienced."

"I thought all her people were connected to the Beyond."

"If all your species hummed a particular note, you'd become used to hearing it," Thrawn said. "If you then met a species who didn't hum at all, but then also found an individual who hummed a different note, that would be something both new and notable."

"Ah," Thalias said, nodding. "Yes, I see. Anything new, either presence *or* absence, can be informative."

"Yes," Thrawn said. "As you undoubtedly noted with Generalirius Nakirre."

Thalias's lips puckered. She'd thought she was the only one who'd spotted *that*, too, and had planned to keep it to herself until she could mention it privately to Thrawn. "You mean the fact that he never asked how many Watith prisoners we had?"

"Very good," Thrawn said approvingly. "Your analytical skill has grown considerably since you first came aboard the *Springhawk*."

"Thank you," Thalias said, feeling her cheeks warm with the compliment. "Though if it has, it's due to your skill as a teacher."

"I disagree," Thrawn said. "I don't teach, but merely guide. Each person approaches problems differently. All I do is ask the questions that set that person on their best path to the solution."

"I see," Thalias murmured. But only if that person was willing to put forth the effort to learn that path to logic and reason, she suspected. Too many people, possibly even the majority of them, were all too content to let others do that thinking and analysis for them.

"So what do we conclude from Nakirre's lack of curiosity?" Thrawn prompted.

"That he already knew how many people Captain Fsir had in his freighter." Thalias frowned. "Or possibly that they were all already dead?"

"The latter is the explanation I'm leaning toward," Thrawn said. "Which would in turn suggest that the other person speaking in the background was connected with whoever hired Fsir."

"Yes, that makes sense," Thalias agreed, thinking it through. "A trading center like Zyzek draws a lot of different nations and species. If our mystery alien had success hiring Fsir, he might well go back there for his next hire."

"I agree," Thrawn said. "Which brings up yet another question."

Thalias winced. "What exactly has he hired Nakirre to do?"

"Yes," Thrawn said. "I was hoping that these attacks on the Ascendancy had come to an end. I fear they haven't."

"Doesn't look like it," Thalias said, with a hollow feeling in the pit of her stomach. Because even if and when the threats to the Ascendancy ended, the threats to Thrawn himself were likely to continue.

Fleetingly, she thought back to her brief conversation with Patriarch Thooraki at the Mitth family homestead. There he'd encouraged her to help protect Thrawn from the political pressures that, despite his military genius, he seemed unable to recognize and counter.

Thalias certainly had the will to do so. The crucial question was whether a lowly sky-walker caregiver had any of the necessary power.

"But if the attacks continue," she said, wondering if Thrawn even realized she was giving a two-part answer, "we'll just have to beat them again."

The summons to Sposia had been quick and abrupt, and had given Supreme General Ba'kif barely enough time to close down his office in an orderly way and get across Csaplar to the landing field just outside the city. The scout ship he'd requisitioned was ready, one of the five that were always kept on fifteen-minute readiness for senior Defense Hierarchy Council officers, and twenty minutes later he was out of Csilla's gravity well and into the mesmerizing swirl of hyperspace.

It wasn't the way Ba'kif liked doing business. Many of his colleagues, in fact, would never move this quickly for anything short of all-out war.

But the summons had come directly from Stybla Patriarch Stybla'mi'ovodo's office, and the Patriarch had said it concerned Senior Captain Thrawn, and that was all Ba'kif needed to know.

Lamiov was waiting outside the massive door of Vault Four when Ba'kif finally finished with the rigorous Universal Analysis Group security protocols. "Supreme General," the Patriarch called in greeting as Ba'kif walked across the entry chamber, doing his best to ignore the silent guards standing their impassive watch over the Ascendancy's most secret base. "Thank you for coming."

"It's always a pleasure to visit the UAG, Your Venerante," Ba'kif said as he reached the other. "Mind you, a bit more warning would have been appreciated."

"Trust me, you had only about ten minutes less than I got," Lamiov said. "Senior Captain Thrawn was playing this one even closer than usual."

"Does it have anything to do with why he's so late back from whatever the Xodlak, Erighal, and Pommrio were involved in?"

"Is he *that* late?" Lamiov asked, frowning. "I was under the impression that those family ships only arrived a day ago."

"True enough," Ba'kif said. "But the *Springhawk* has a sky-walker, and the family ships didn't. By all rights, Thrawn should have been here at least a day or two ahead of them."

"Interesting," Lamiov murmured. "Maybe he stayed at Hoxim to take a closer look at the freighter crash site."

Ba'kif gave a little snort. "You *do* realize you're rattling off details that only the Council is supposed to have, right?"

"Really, Supreme General," Lamiov said drily. "If you haven't figured out by now that the Stybla have our own special information sources, you really have no business in your current seat of power. Seriously, though, you're going to love this one. Shall we go take a look?"

"After you," Ba'kif said, falling into step beside Lamiov, peripherally noting that the nearest guards stirred slightly as the two men walked the rest of the way to the vault door. Early in the UAG's existence, Ba'kif had been told, there'd been some thought in the Syndicure of removing family ties from all of its personnel, as was routinely done with senior military officers, and for the same reason of hopefully eliminating family politics.

Ultimately, it was decided that such an action would draw too much unwanted attention to the facility, and the idea was dropped. As a compromise, though, UAG uniforms didn't include any family identification, neither the family crests of the Nine and the Forty nor the stylized names used by the Ascendancy's other, lesser families. Here at UAG, in theory, all were equal.

Still, Ba'kif suspected that most if not all of the guards on Vault Four were Stybla. Lamiov would have seen to that.

Given that a new alien artifact had just arrived, Ba'kif had fully expected the large receiving area at the front part of the vault to be crowded. He wasn't prepared, though, for just how crowded it actually was.

Part of that was the sheer size of the artifact: a four-meter-long lattice of white metal ribs that looked like a section of some giant sea monster's torso skeleton. A dozen techs were hovering around it, taking readings and measurements or attaching leads to other analysis devices. Two senior UAG staff were also in the mix, one of them overseeing the work, the other working busily with his questis.

Standing off to one side, silently watching all the activity, were Senior Captain Thrawn and Mid Captain Samakro.

Both men looked over as Ba'kif and Lamiov walked up to them. "Patriarch Lamiov; Supreme General Ba'kif," Thrawn said in greeting. "You honor us with your presence."

"You honor *us* with yet another intriguing device for our collection," Lamiov said. "Go ahead and tell Supreme General Ba'kif what you've brought."

"Yes, Your Venerante." Thrawn shifted his attention to Ba'kif. "During our search for remnants of the Vagaari pirates, we encountered an alien freighter that was supposedly being attacked by three gunships. We subsequently determined that the battle had been staged for our benefit, and that the scenario was merely the first step in a trap."

"Obviously, the aliens didn't know much about you," Ba'kif commented.

"No, their knowledge of the Chiss was quite limited," Thrawn said, apparently missing the subtle compliment completely. "What intrigued me was the fact that the feigned attack was already in progress when we emerged from hyperspace. That suggested to me that the aliens had a way of predicting when and where a ship would arrive."

Ba'kif looked over at the skeletal artifact, an odd tightness settling into the pit of his stomach. "And this is what allowed them to do that?"

"We believe so, yes," Thrawn said. "The lattice was built into the space between the freighter's inner and outer hulls and was attached to the equipment boxes via those cables."

Ba'kif nodded as he belatedly spotted the rolling tables off to the side with oddly shaped boxes and neatly coiled wires resting on them. "Was the entire lattice like this?" he asked.

"The parts we were able to investigate were," Thrawn said. "Unfortunately, the time we had to devote to our analysis was severely limited."

"Any idea how much warning the device gives before the incoming ship arrives?" Ba'kif asked.

"Based on the state of the false attack as it appeared to us, I estimate they had at least ninety seconds to prepare," Thrawn said. "Possibly more."

"Ninety seconds," Ba'kif murmured, his mind spinning with the possibilities. Put a couple of picket ships equipped with such early-warning devices in orbit at the combat edge of each Chiss world, and sneak attacks would be all but impossible.

Even better, if the lattice could detect all ships moving through hyperspace even if those vessels weren't preparing to return to space-normal, the Defense Force could monitor the most common lanes through the Ascendancy. And if the device could not only detect passing vessels but also give an estimate of how many were involved . . .

"Easy, Supreme General," Lamiov warned.

Ba'kif blinked away the string of thought. "What?"

"I know that look," Lamiov said. "I'm bound to caution you that just because we have one of these devices doesn't mean we'll be able to reverse-engineer it."

"I know," Ba'kif said, his excitement fading somewhat. So far both of Thrawn's major contributions to Vault Four—the Vagaari gravity-well generator and the Republic advanced shield technology—had resisted the UAG's best efforts to tease out their secrets. Ba'kif had no doubt that, sooner or later, the Ascendancy's techs would succeed, but it was clearly going to continue to be an uphill climb.

Unfortunately, there was no reason to believe this advance-warning detector would deviate from that pattern.

"I just wish I knew why every item the Defense Force could find an immediate use for takes forever to crack," Ba'kif added.

"That does seem to be the way of the universe, doesn't it?" Lamiov conceded. "That high-density electronics memory unit that was brought to us a hundred years ago was being utilized in questis storage bars within twelve months. The specialized cooking system someone found thirty years ago was on the market in five months."

"But something that could upgrade a warship's electrostatic barrier defenses by a thousand percent or more . . ." Ba'kif shook his head.

"Perhaps we'll have better luck with this one," Lamiov said, nodding to the lattice. "It's a shame you couldn't bring back the entire freighter." He raised his eyebrows slightly in silent question.

"Yes," Thrawn said simply. Either he'd missed the invitation in the Patriarch's tone and expression, or he'd already decided not to provide any further details about what had happened to the freighter.

"We removed what appeared to be all of the equipment, plus as much of the lattice as we could," Samakro added, also ignoring the unstated request. "Hopefully, it will be enough for you to work with."

"We'll do our best," Lamiov assured him. "Is there anything more the techs should know?"

"I don't believe so," Thrawn said. "Mid Captain?"

"Nothing major that I can think of," Samakro said. "I'll note in passing that even though the freighter was part of an ambush, and therefore might be considered a type of warship, its hull was standard civilian design. No nyix, not even a nyix-alloy inner shell."

"That could be significant," Lamiov said.

"It could," Samakro said. "My inclination is to put it down to the designers preferring to maintain the freighter illusion, and that it has nothing to do with the detector itself."

"Probably," Ba'kif agreed, his thoughts heading off in a new direction. Still, nyix had some unique characteristics, which was one reason it worked so well for warship hulls. If one or more of those features interfered with the advance-warning detector, that might provide some clues as to how the device worked.

"Regardless, I'll make the techs aware of that," Lamiov said. "And now, I believe the Council is expecting you on Csilla."

"Yes," Thrawn said. "But before we leave, Supreme General, I request your presence aboard the *Springhawk*. There's another situation we need to discuss."

"Can it wait?" Ba'kif asked.

Thrawn and Samakro exchanged looks. "Yes, sir, I suppose it can," Thrawn said reluctantly. "For a time."

"Then it waits," Ba'kif said firmly. "I have only a few hours to discuss some pressing matters with Patriarch Lamiov before I also have to return. And as the Patriarch said, the *Springhawk* is already overdue back at Csilla for examination and whatever refitting and rearming are necessary."

He raised his eyebrows toward Samakro. "At which point you, Mid Captain, are on my list of officers to speak with about the Hoxim incident. You'll have until then to prepare your statement and organize any documents you might wish entered into the record."

"Understood, Supreme General," Samakro said. "Though if I may—" He glanced at Thrawn. "—I would urge you not to delay your trip to the *Springhawk* any longer than necessary."

"I'll take your suggestion under advisement," Ba'kif said, frowning. Samakro's expression was the standard neutral of an officer addressing a superior.

But there was also an unusually strong layer of tension beneath it. Whatever Thrawn wanted to discuss with Ba'kif, Samakro wasn't looking forward to the conversation.

Still, it would have to wait. Right now, Hoxim and its fallout were Ba'kif's priority.

"I'll see you back at Csilla, then," he said, gesturing the two officers back toward the vault door. "Get started on the refit, and I'll call when I'm ready for your interviews."

## ABOUT THE AUTHOR

TIMOTHY ZAHN is the author of more than sixty novels, nearly ninety short stories and novelettes, and five short-fiction collections. In 1984, he won the Hugo Award for Best Novella. Zahn is best known for his *Star Wars* novels (*Thrawn, Thrawn: Alliances, Thrawn: Treason, Thrawn Ascendancy: Chaos Rising, Heir to the Empire, Dark Force Rising, The Last Command, Specter of the Past, Vision of the Future, Survivor's Quest, Outbound Flight, Allegiance, Choices of One,* and *Scoundrels*), with more than eight million copies of his books in print. Other books include *StarCraft: Evolution,* the Cobra series, the Quadrail series, and the young adult Dragonback series. Zahn has a BS in physics from Michigan State University and an MS from the University of Illinois. He lives with his family on the Oregon coast.

Facebook.com/TimothyZahn

A long time ago in a galaxy far, far away. . . .

# STAR WARS™

**Join up!** Subscribe to our newsletter
at ReadStarWars.com or find us on social.

**f** **StarWarsBooks**

**𝕏** **@DelReyStarWars**

**⃝** **@DelReyStarWars**